CW01667888

THE GLORY HOLE

'The big black ignored a second entreaty to slow down as the platoon moved deeper into the valley. He was starting to feel bad now and he wanted to get to that bench and set up for the night, settle down under a tree with Hotdog so they could share a duster. Not too much to wipe you out, just enough to keep you up there, alert and sensitive to any change. It was the only way to walk point, with a little scag moving in the system. You could see and hear and smell better, just don't go too far. He began thinking of the capsules in his pack, five of them, one a day and one extra. That was going pretty light but sometimes a man had to cool it. It was going to be a long patrol, a longer war. The whole object, man, is to survive during the days and forget during the nights, all 365 of them, and then back to the world. Just survive.'

T. Jeff Williams

The Glory Hole

CORGI BOOKS

THE GLORY HOLE

A CORGI BOOK 0 552 10499 X

First publication in Great Britain

PRINTING HISTORY
Corgi edition reprinted 1977
Corgi edition re-issued 1985

Corgi Books are published by Transworld Publishers Ltd., Century House, 61–63 Uxbridge Road, Ealing, London W5 5SA, in Australia by Transworld Publishers (Aust.) Pty. Ltd., 26 Harley Crescent, Condell Park, NSW 2200, and in New Zealand by Transworld Publishers (N.Z.) Ltd., Cnr. Moselle and Waipareira Avenues, Henderson, Auckland.

Printed and bound in Great Britain by
Cox & Wyman Ltd., Reading, Berks.

What I expected was
Thunder, fighting,
Long struggles with men
And climbing.
After continual straining
I should grow strong;
Then the rocks would shake
And I should rest long

What I had not foreseen
Was the gradual day
Weakening the will
Leaking the brightness away,
The lack of good to touch
The fading of body and soul
Like smoke before wind
Corrupt, unsubstantial . . .

from *What I Expected*
by Stephen Spender

The first two stanzas of *What I Expected* are reprinted by kind permission of Messrs. Faber & Faber Ltd., from *The Collected Poems of Stephen Spender.*

The Glory Hole

CHAPTER ONE

IN the cool of the early morning before the sun was very high and while the air was still clear, the screen door on one of the tin quonset huts that nestled beside the hospital opened and a lanky figure wearing only OD shorts emerged. He stood on the uneven boardwalk made from ammunition crates, yawned, pushed back the black hair that was getting longer than the army liked and stood idly scratching himself while he looked about. Sounds could be heard inside other huts down the row but no one appeared outside yet. From the airfield directly across the cracked macadam road that served as the main highway through the northern part of the country, Sturm heard the whine of a helicopter starting up, followed by another smaller one. Probably a loach, he thought, a light observation helicopter and a few Cobras out jitterbugging to turn up the bad guys. He yawned again and stretched. They can have all the action they can find, he thought, but include me out. I've about had it. Besides, I'm short for risky games. He turned to enter his quonset when he heard someone give a low whistle. He turned to see Lt. Sandy Saunders giving him a critical appraisal.

'I never realized you had such sexy legs, Jake,' she laughed. Sturm took a mincing step for her. 'You like my bod? You can have it.'

'Not at this ungodly hour,' she said and turned away.

'Free,' he called after her but she kept walking toward the rear entrance of the hospital. He watched her move down the boardwalk in her fatigues, just like all the nurses who weren't in the OR, but hers looked different, more tailored, or she filled them out better. Whatever it was, it was nice.

He sighed and went into the quonset hut that served as quarters for the two Dustoff crews and kicked the bunk where Dooley lay snoring on his back with both hands folded across his broad and hairy stomach. Dooley snorted and bolted upright, eyes wide.

'I'm ready, I'm ready. Let's go.' He started to get out of the bunk when he saw the others slowly dressing. 'Shit, man, I thought we were on.' He fell heavily back into his bunk and put one meaty hand over his fleshy and freckled face.

'Get up, you big red tomato,' Sturm said. 'Why is my crew chief always last to arise. Look at Riley and Moran. Both examples that you should seek to emulate. Riley, the outstanding medic on Rainbow One-two and his exemplary crew chief Bill Moran are both dressed and ready to eat. But you, Tomato, lay there with a fat hangover.'

Dooley threw back the mosquito netting that hung over his bunk, kicked off the poncho liner that served as his bedding and heaved his bulk upright. Two hundred and thirty pounds on a five-foot-nine inch frame made the bed groan.

'Hey, my man, we'll be in the messhall if anything starts to happen,' Riley said as he and Moran picked their way through the clutter of magazines, aid packs, loose ammunition and empty beer cans and pop that littered the floor.

Sturm slipped into his olive flame-resistant flight suit and pulled on his boots. The leather was almost white from bleaching and never being polished, great cracks split the toes and the canvas webbing on the sides had faded from olive drab to the paleness of river sand. Such boots were the mark of a man who had spent long months in Vietnam, who had been slogging through the muck of monsoon seasons and the suffocating heat of the dry seasons. Sturm had once caught his hootch maid about to polish the boots and he had to explain in firm tones that they were never, never to be cleaned or polished. The maid had only shrugged and Sturm wanted to explain what the boots meant to him but he knew he might as well talk to the wall.

Dooley was still moving in slow motion when Sturm finished and stood up. 'I can't wait all day, Tomato. I'll meet you at the messhall,' he told the redhead and went outside. He walked directly into a veritable wall of a man who blocked his path on the boardwalk. Sturm, six-feet-two, had to crane his neck up to see who stood before him. A square face, blue-black in color and filled in with a pencil mustache over the upper lip, a nose that someone had stomped on years ago when the man was a small boy, and round little eyes that peered from beneath the bone cornice of his forehead looked down on him.

'Franklin! What the hell are you doing here?' Sturm laughed and gave the man a clap on the shoulder. It was like hitting the side of a steer.

The huge black frowned at him. 'I'm here to take you into the field, show you what 'Nam is really like, and get you away from all the chicks walking around this place. It's bad for you here, Sturm.' Then he grinned, displaying a white picket fence of teeth. 'But I could learn to love it real easy. So you go to the boonies and I'll be the medic.' He stuck out a hand. 'What's happening, brother?'

Sturm looked at the patch on Franklin's fatigues. 'So that's why you're up here. You're with that 101st Battalion over in the airfield.'

'You catch on quick, man,' Franklin said. 'Yeah, the Screaming Eagles are going into the bush real soon. We was supposed to go this morning but didn't. I heard a couple months ago you was up here so when we got delayed I just slipped across the field to see how my man Sturm was holding up.' He gave Sturm a look and asked the daily question: 'How much time you got left?'

Sturm grinned. 'Thirty-three days and a wakeup. I'm short.'

'Shit, man, I got forty-two days. But it's all down hill now.'

'I was just on my way to eat. Want some breakfast?' Sturm asked.

'Right on, man, we only had some cold C-rats this morning. Besides I want to lay my eyeballs on some of the nurses. I ain't seen a round-eye in a long time. You got any black chicks here?' Franklin asked as they walked toward the messhall.

'A few.'

'That's all right, brother. I'll take white meat.' He huffed himself up to full height as he saw a nurse approaching on the boardwalk and then gave her a smart salute.

'Good morning, Loo-tenant!' He smiled. The nurse walked by without giving him a glance. Franklin's face clouded up, ready to storm.

'What's this shit, man? She racist or something?'

'Worse. She's preoccupied, like almost everyone else around here. They live in little shells and close out the rest of the world.'

Inside as they sat together at a table, Franklin said in a low voice, 'I live in my own world too. Look here.' He opened his palm slightly to reveal a small plastic capsule. 'Scag. Smack. China White. Heroin.' He whispered the last word and it was swallowed in the clatter and chatter of the messhall.

'Put that away, man. I know what it is, but if some lifer around here sees you with that you'll be in LBJ in a minute, right in the Long Binh Jail.'

Franklin grinned. 'I wouldn't mind that. Then I wouldn't have to be out on patrol all the time, waiting for some mothafuckin dink to put a round in me!!' He leaned closer, a black leaning Tower of Pisa: 'There's good money in this, and you got the connections.'

'Me? How?' Sturm wanted nothing to do with heroin but he was interested in Franklin's line of reasoning.

'I got a buddy who's an X-ray tech in Saigon. Every month they ship lead X-ray film boxes back to Hawaii. The boxes are marked "Do not open, do not X-ray." Then when the boxes arrive another brother is always the pickup man. He opens them first and pulls out the packages. It's foolproof, man because no one can open those boxes to check while in shipment.'

'But I'm not an X-ray technician,' Sturm said.

Franklin walked his little eyes over Sturm's face in exasperation. 'I know. But you got connections, man. You can set it up. We can get someone up from Saigon to help you out. See, we need more shipping channels, man.'

Sturm shook his head. 'Forget it. Heroin is bad news. How much are you into it?'

Franklin leaned back, on guard. 'Like in what way, man?'

'Not the shipping. That's your business. How about using it yourself.'

Franklin shrugged. 'You think I could survive a tour over here just being straight arrow? A little smack makes everything possible, man, it eases the pain, eases the black man's burden.' He took a sip from the coffee cup that was buried in his hand. 'Like, man, it's the black dudes who are out humping the bush while whitey sits back with cool jobs in nice clean hospitals.' He looked at Sturm and the implication was clear.

Sturm grew irritated. 'You know what the mortality rate is among medics? Very high. You can have my job any day you want.'

'No, man, black dudes don't get easy jobs. How many black dustoff medics you seen?'

'Plenty,' Sturm said. 'The other dustoff medic right here is black. Riley.'

'Just one of a few,' Franklin insisted. 'The truth is, us

niggers got to be in the bush.' He glowered into his cup and then changed the subject. 'How about you, man? You into scag?'

Sturm shook his head and wiped the crumbs from his heavy black mustache, the one he had grown in hopes of looking dashing but instead made him look older than his 22 years. 'No way. Grass is good enough. It eases the pain but isn't habit-forming.'

'Shit, man, forget that grass. Once you take a hit on scag life is good. I had some nickel bags in Chicago and did a little skin-popping, but over here is the best, man. Just fill up the end of a cigarette, make a little duster, and smoke it. You fly, man.'

'That's the problem, big Franklin. You fly and never come down,' Sturm said.

'No way. It's a baby habit over here. Smoking scag ain't really a habit.'

'That, I assure you, is pure unadulterated bullshit,' Sturm said. 'In your pocket is No. 4 white heroin, 97 percent pure, packed in handy little 100 milligram capsules. It's so pure you can smoke it, like you say. If you mainlined it you would OD immediately. It is very habit-forming.'

Franklin turned sour. 'Who gives a fuck. It keeps me going, and about half my platoon too.' He pushed back from the table. 'So you ain't going to help us?'

'No, not in my bag.'

'Still the righteous priest?' Franklin asked. 'You are pretty pure in basic. How is it now?'

'The righteousness is long gone, the purity is fast fading. There's nothing a would-be priest secretly enjoys more than a good lay.'

Franklin stood up, a redwood tree suddenly sprouting in the messhall. 'I've gotta get back but I'll check you when we come out of the boonies. You might want to change your mind.'

As Franklin left, Dooley crossed to where Sturm still sat. 'I just saw Kowalski. He says nothing's going on but he wants us to hang loose by the bird, do a little maintenance.'

'That's your bag, Tomato, you're the crew chief.'

'Yeah, but I help you lift the bodies aboard so I know you'll help me on the chopper now.'

Sturm nodded. 'Alright. I'll be out in a little while.' He stared into his half-empty cup of bitter coffee, suddenly depressed by the talk of bodies. It seemed like the past month there had been nothing but DOA's, young men who had been laughing and sweating and eating, all the movements of life being taken for granted and then suddenly ending with a bullet through a vital organ, or a rocket that lands upon a bunker where fifteen men huddle and try not to show fear. For a month the dustoffs had been carrying laughing men suddenly turned to cold meat, wrapped in torn and bloody ponchos or zipped into the heavy body bags that were made of rubber so they wouldn't leak and could be washed and used again. And again. It's like a garbage collection, just some employees going out to clean up refuse that littered the countryside. He ran a long, bony hand down over his narrow face and squeezed his eyes to push back such thoughts. It's really starting to get to me. It's not what I thought it would be, saving lives, pulling men through in the critical time it takes to fly them from the field to the hospital.

'Shape up, Sturm,' he said aloud and picked up his tray and carried it to where the Vietnamese women were doing the dishes. He went into the hospital in search of Sandy. A little talk with her and a look at her cute little ass wiggling down the corridors would cheer him up. That was one of the better things in Vietnam, having a friendly round-eye to make it with. A lieutenant yet, and me a mere Spec 5. A round-eye nurse, a pretty chick in the ville named Mai, and grass in between made life almost bearable, he thought. Almost.

He walked through three wards without seeing her and was about to go out the front exit and around to the chopper pads when he saw her talking to a short swarthy man with captain's bars glittering on his collar. He walked past, disinclined to interrupt, but Sandy saw him and called him over.

'Specialist Sturm, I would like you to meet Chaplain Montano, a new arrival here.'

The chaplain gazed at him with large and solemn eyes and caught Sturm's hand by the fingers only in his small, moist fist.

'I am very pleased to meet you, Specialist Sturm. What is your first name? I don't like to be too formal.' His voice was deep and calm and he hung onto Sturm's hand as he waited for the answer.

'Jacob, sir.'

'Please, not too formal. Call me father, I am a priest.'

Sandy interrupted. 'I'll leave you two alone now. I've got to be off. Nice to have talked with you, father. And I'll see you later, Specialist Sturm.' She gave him a quick wink that the chaplain could not see and walked smartly away. Sturm watched her spring movements until the chaplain spoke:

'How long have you been here in Vietnam, Jacob?' Always the first question.

'Eleven months. Just thirty-three days left, sir.'

'Please, call me father. Are you a Catholic by any chance?'

Sturm looked away, down the green-walled corridor with the red butt cans hung on posts like metal flowers. There it was again: Are you a Catholic? Proselytize, proselytize, my son. The rector's fleshless face appeared before him, the eyes flinty: You are leaving, Jacob? Leaving the Benedictine Monastery of the Holy Trinity to join the army? Are you not happy? Sturm: No father I am not happy.

'Are you a Catholic?' Chaplain Montano's calm voice threw a brick wall across Sturm's racing thoughts and he turned his head again to look down at the diminutive, rotund priest.

'Yes, but not a very good one.' He would let it go at that for now. Montano would find out soon enough about Sturm's background from others in the 21st Evac, from those who watched his brooding face and angular body and called him Monsignor.

Before Montano could follow up – proselytize, proselytize, my son – Sturm interjected with a question of his own. The old standby:

'How long have you been over here, sir? Father?'

'Just two months, most of that in Saigon. But I wanted to get away from Saigon, I felt I would be of most use in the field with the men. After all, war involves danger for all and there is no reason a priest should be exempted.' He rocked forward on the balls of his feet and looked at Sturm for confirmation.

'Where did you study for the priesthood?' Sturm countered.

'In Mexico City. But I joined my sister in Albuquerque shortly after I was ordained. That was more than twenty years ago,' he said and laughed: 'Father Teofilo Montano is getting to be an old priest, no?'

Sturm started to ask another question but Montano cut in: 'What do you do? Are you an orderly?'

'No sir. I'm a medic with the dustoffs. The airmobile medevac helicopters.'

Montano's eyes widened with interest. 'Oh, a very dangerous and difficult job for you, I think.' Sturm shrugged and Montano went on. 'I have been out to the field several times with the 1st Cavalry helicopters. I believe very much in going to the field with the men,' he repeated in his earnest manner.

Sturm nodded, anxious to be away.

'I would like to go out with the dustbins sometime,' he said.

'Dustoffs,' Sturm replied.

'What?'

'The medevac choppers are dustoffs, not dustbins,' Sturm explained then added with a wry grin, 'but maybe dustbins is more accurate.'

'Yes, yes, of course. At any rate, I think it might be most productive for me to go with the dustoffs. You are right into the thick of the action, and right where there are wounded men who will need my help.'

'And the dead, too,' Sturm added. 'Last rites. Don't forget last rites,' he said with a trace of sarcasm.

'Yes, yes,' Montano said absently. 'Can it be arranged for me to go with the dustoffs?'

'I don't know about that,' Sturm demurred. 'We have to get the wounded out first, as many as possible, and there isn't room for excess baggage. If you'll pardon the expression.'

Montano waved his hand to dismiss any objections. 'I am sure it could be arranged. Who is your pilot?'

'Mo. Kowalski is the AC.'

'AC?'

'Aircraft commander.'

'Oh yes, of course. Well, I'll see him and work something out.'

'Yes sir.'

Montano gave Sturm a friendly pat on the shoulder. 'Come see me anytime. Jacob, isn't it? Yes, Jacob. Come see me anytime you would like to talk things over. And I know I shall see you at Services Sunday.'

'We're awfully busy, seven days a week,' he answered non-committally.

'No rest for the wicked, eh?' Montano attempted a take. 'Well, nice talking to you, Jacob. I must be on my way now.' He bustled off down the hall.

Sturm went outside to the pads and found Dooley with his arms thrust deep into the engine.

'Now what are you doing, Tomato?'

'Beats the shit out of me, but it really looks like I'm working. And that makes King Kong Kowalski happy.'

'Our leader is going to be unhappy soon.'

'Why?' Dooley grunted.

'There's a new chaplain up here who wants to go into the boonies and save souls. He wants to ride with us.'

'Didn't you tell him you were kicked out of the monastery for playing with yourself and that I'm a pervert? And that Kowalski likes to shoot little children?'

'That would only encourage him,' Sturm said. 'He looks like a determined little fart. Probably a Jesuit. Better watch out for those Jebbies.' He climbed into the chopper's interior and started going through his aid packs. 'Christ, it's hot,' Sturm said and paused to look at the airfield across the road where the green-glassed control tower shimmered in the heat, like a mirage. In the distant sky beyond, Sturm could see a line of choppers approaching.

Along the runway the men sat silent and unmoving in the deadly noon heat, not even bothering to wipe away the sweat that trickled down their faces and dripped onto their fatigues. The men rested against their packs, eyes vacant and staring as they blotted out all thoughts of the coming mission. A few stirred at the sound of the approaching helicopters but they were the new men, replacements, afraid but anxious to prove themselves in the eyes of buddies who had seen it all.

As the choppers made a long curving approach, a scythe in the sky, Sgt. 1st Class Dodge, platoon sergeant, bellowed at the men to get on their feet. The platoon rose in irregular spurts and the men turned their backs against the stinging blast of sand and tiny rocks as the birds settled beside them. Grabbing their bulky packs laced with extra belts of machine gun ammunition in one hand and their M-16s in their other, the troops jogged toward the waiting helicopters.

As PFC Franklin prepared to swing his pack aboard, Lt. Hoyt, the platoon leader, came alongside and shouted over the screaming engines. 'You got your head together for this, Franklin?'

Franklin didn't break the rhythm of swinging his pack aboard, nor did he bother to look at Hoyt. He didn't have to look at him to see him. He saw Hoyt in his nightmares, a wiry-thin man with close cropped hair, expressionless eyes and a mouth that looked like it had been made with an axe; no lips. Franklin pushed himself into the corner by the door gunner and watched Hoyt walk away. 'You suspect, Hoyt, but you don't know. You don't know about me or about half this platoon. But you better be nice or one day you gonna find out,' he said to himself.

The choppers were filled with men and packs and M-16s, and the sun glittered on the extra ammunition that draped the packs like Christmas tinsel. The engines whined into a screaming crescendo then tilted forward and delicately, like a corps of ballerinas in olive drab, they skimmed down the runway and lifted in smooth unison above the airfield before turning west toward the Laotian border.

Franklin sat casually in the open doorway with his legs dangling down and watched the Quang Tri airfield fall away below him. He could see the dozens of 1st Cav choppers squatting in the revetments like so many hiding grasshoppers. Across the highway, that once ran all the way to Hanoi, he could see the evacuation hospital, nothing more than three long quonset huts down one side. He looked at the dustoff choppers sitting on the pads to the north of the hospital and he knew Sturm was probably over there. Yeah, Sturm, maybe we'll be seeing each other before too long. He looked at the red crosses in the white circles painted on the hospital roofs and casually aimed his M-16 at one. Nice target. He swung the sight a little and followed a tiny figure hurrying along the boardwalk. You just beginning a nice clean day in a nice clean hospital and I'm going into the mothafuckin jungle to shoot dinks. He let his mind consider the luxury of having a little leg wound that would put him in that hospital between white sheets with a nurse, a real friendly nurse, to look after him. Maybe, he thought with a sudden grin, maybe I could get Annie to be my nurse. Annie walking down to his bed in white silk stockings and a white silken nurse's uniform, bending over him until her titties covered his face.

His dreams were interrupted by the sudden appearance of trees, huge green shiny trees that were reaching up at him. Then they were settling into an old bomb-blasted clearing and he was out running with his pack in one hand and his piece in the other and his helmet was bouncing heavily on his head. Then the choppers were gone and the silence of the jungle present upon him. The others felt it too, for they slung their packs in silence and Hoyt said he wanted second squad out in front, with Franklin on point.

'Stay awake,' Hoyt said as Franklin passed him where he sat with his grid map. 'You don't know what's on the other side of the ridge.' Franklin pushed by without a word and slid into the fetid maw of the jungle where trees rose on spindly gray columns and the leaves turned daylight into twilight. The men moved steadily for an hour without a break, first up the ridge they had dropped behind to shield them from whatever lay in the An Lao valley that was their objective, then down the leaf-covered slope that was so steep the men had to cling to the trees to keep from falling forward. Their fatigues were black with perspiration and some carried their helmets in their hands to let their heads cool. Finally, as they broke from the half-light of the green vault formed beneath the trees into an airy bamboo grove, the lieutenant called a halt. Franklin dropped his pack beside a smooth green bamboo tree and sagged down beside it. Unsnapping one of his canteens from the D-ring on his pack, he tipped it to his mouth. The water was warm but he drank it greedily and then dribbled the last of the water over his face. He opened his eyes to see Lt. Hoyt watching him.

'How much water you got left, Franklin?' Hoyt's voice was soft and didn't carry to the rest of the platoon sprawled farther back in the bamboo clump.

'Two more canteens, Loo-tenant.'

'Quit calling me lieutenant. LT is enough out here.' He glanced around as if he might see a sniper taking a bead on him. 'And you better watch your water. We're not scheduled for any resupply on this recon. We'll have to get water from the valley floor and I don't want you crying you're out of water before we get there.'

Franklin stared from beneath his heavy brow at Hoyt without answering. The lieutenant pulled a map from his shirt front and told Franklin to get the squad leaders. When the sergeants arrived Hoyt indicated their position on the map and the long valley that lay below them. It was outlined with red grease pencil and the suspected gun positions were marked in yellow.

'We are just inside Laos now. We'll move into the valley tomorrow. Leave camp about 0530. Now we don't know what is in that valley so we're going in slow. We've got four days to recon this place, to see if anything is there or if anything is coming in. I want to get everything and I don't want to be discovered, understand?' He studied their closed faces a moment then looked at the map again. 'There's a little bench above the valley just ahead, maybe two kliks. We'll stay on that tonight. Coggins, take second squad out first.' He paused. 'And keep Franklin on point.'

There was little noise as the platoon prepared to move again, just the soft click of magazines being checked, the whisper of packs against the satiny bamboo. Everything loose was taped to prevent noise, even the dog tags. There was some talking, a few men whispering about the two squad-sized teams that previously attempted to recon the valley but had been discovered and blown away. This time the old man wanted a recon in force and he promised gunships if the shit hit the fan. But no support until then. There were no loaches working ahead of the platoon, no gunships lazing overhead to give away the platoon's presence. The old man had even ruled out arclights to prep the area, saying that B-52 strikes were dead giveaways of troops' movements. Even the South Vietnamese regional commander had not been advised of the recon because, it was said, there were too many informants in his office. The old man said the operation had to be so secret because Washington kept claiming there were no U.S. troops operating Laos and the White House didn't want any embarrassments.

Franklin adjusted his pack, felt the shoulder straps bite deep, and started toward the point. 'I'll see you, Loo-tenant.'

'Hey, boy,' Hoyt said softly, as he moved toward Franklin, 'just remember you're not back on the block doing your thing with a razor. This is real, not those pretend games you used to play, so try and keep awake. Okay? Boy?'

As Franklin pushed through the grove into the jungle again, Hotdog Simpson came alongside to adjust a belt of M-60 rounds that was slipping on Franklin's pack and said, 'How come the LT has it in for you? You been walking point ever since we was dropped this morning.'

Franklin stuck out his jaw, still seething over Hoyt calling him 'boy'. 'I was bad mouthing Chicago pigs the other night. I said they were rotten mothers and I would waste one when I got back if he came to hassle me again. Then Hoyt – and I don't know where the fuck he came from, man – he appears at our table and tells me his brother is a Chicago cop. That's all he says, but I know he is pissed. Now the man is putting it on me, for nothing.'

Franklin, angrily hunched his shoulders under the pack and moved ahead alone as he slipped from the dappled sunlight of the bamboo grove, where at least there seemed to be air, into the poisonous folds of the jungle. His footsteps fell soundlessly on the spongy layer of decaying leaves and where his boots disturbed the dead vegetation malodorous smells swirled from the ground. The air was thick, difficult to breathe, and rivulets of perspiration stung his eyes as he tried to sweep the trees ahead. He could rarely see more than 50 feet before everything vanished in the maze and gloom of heavy trees. He plodded steadily down the slope and let his mind turn slowly, envisioning revenge on Hoyt. He was in Chicago, dressed in some good threads and he saw Lt. Hoyt come toward him on the deserted street. He saw himself blocking the lieutenant who was still dressed in his funky fatigues and Hoyt shouted 'get out of my way, boy'.

'Don't you know it's impolite to call me, a genuine war hero, boy? Why you want to do that?'

He saw himself pull a razor from his pocket, shave a few curly hairs from the back of his hand while he watched Hoyt's erect military posture slowly deflate as the razor glittered before his eyes. Then Hoyt pushed forward, 'out of my way, boy', and put a hand out to shove Franklin back. The razor winked and there was Hoyt looking at his hand with no fingers, but it didn't bleed.

A hissing voice from behind cut through his reverie: 'Slow down, Franklin, LT says you're going too fast.'

'Tell that mothafuckin lifer to come up here and take the point if he don't like the way I'm doing it.'

'Tell him yourself,' the voice laughed softly, 'he's your buddy.'

Franklin swung angrily down the slope as he tried to shift his mind back to the daydream but the abrupt appearance of sunlight ahead brought him to a halt and his stomach turned over. He threw up a hand to halt the men behind him and crouched beside a tree, suddenly feeling very alone and very vulnerable.

He studied the trees ahead but could see nothing moving. He held his breath and listened but heard nothing, not even a bird. The mothafuckin jungle is always silent, and always looks the same, he thought. He peered at the shaft of light falling in the jungle on the exposed earth. That was what had bothered him. Why would there be exposed dirt in the middle of nowhere unless the dinks were making bunkers? He wanted to send word back to Hoyt, tell him about it, let him make the decision, but he knew there would be no artillery support, no gunships until they were into it. Hoyt would just tell him to get his ass up there and find out. Well, he wouldn't let that son of a bitch have the satisfaction. He dropped his pack and eased forward, and he felt the twitching start in his left knee that always came when the fear crept inside him. He moved from tree to tree, straining to see some movement, fearful that a goddam dink was going to pop right up in front of him with an AK-47 spewing lead and death and he, a giant target, would fall dead before that grinning slopehead. He felt the sweat run into his eyes, blinding his vision, and he stopped to wipe it away. Goddam heat, goddam sweat, he cried inside himself. He moved to another tree and now he could see what it was and he took air deep into his lungs and stood up. Before him lay an old bomb crater from previous arclights, a hole 20 feet across and 10 feet deep that was half filled with muddy water and ringed by old grass. Just beyond where the trees were tilted at crazy angles, Franklin could see another crater where the line of drop ran toward the valley.

Relief at finding no enemy flooded Franklin as he turned and walked casually back to retrieve his pack. He waved disdainfully at the men who watched from hiding as he slung his pack and began moving again.

The big black ignored a second entreaty to slow down as the platoon moved deeper into the valley. He was starting to feel bad now and he wanted to get to that bench and set up for the night, settle down under a tree with Hotdog so they could share a duster. Not too much to wipe you out, just enough to keep you up there, alert and sensitive to any change. It was the only way to walk point, with a little scag moving in the system. You could see and hear and smell better, just don't go too far. He began thinking of the capsules in his pack, five of them, one a day and one extra. That was going pretty light but sometimes a man had to cool it. It was going to be a long patrol, a longer war. The whole object, man, is to survive during the days and forget during the nights, all 365 of them, and then back to the world. Just survive.

CHAPTER TWO

STURM lay perfectly still on his back with his arms folded under his head and his dusty boots resting on the iron bar at the end of his cot. He was shirtless in the thick afternoon air and he was conscious of the rank smell from his arm pits. The mosquito netting was thrown back in vain hopes of allowing some air to stir over his lean body. Above his head, caught in a fold of the netting, was a large fly that Sturm had been carefully observing for the past 20 minutes. He took another pull from his roach and after holding the smoke deep in his lungs for long seconds, eased it out in a thin gray stream that caused the fly to buzz frantically in its nylon mesh trap.

'Just what the hell are you doing, Sturm?' asked Dooley who lounged in a broken swivel chair they had stolen from the orderly room months ago.

'I am observing the death of a hardy insect, one of God's creatures put upon this earth to plague mankind. But I ask you, brother Dooley, why would God want to plague mankind? It is the work of the Devil, Beezlebub himself!' he shouted.

'Man, you are spaced today. You've had too many joints,' Dooley said in disgust.

'You drink; I smoke. You're a juicer; I'm a head. But only grass, mind you, only grass. Sweet, head-knocking Laotian grass that eases the pain of mankind.'

Dooley heaved his bulk up and went to the back of the hootch where they kept the small Japanese refrigerator they had stolen from Camp Eagle that time they had flown down to pick up two drunken sergeants who had a shootout at sundown along the main street. Both had hit each other but not seriously and they were all bandaged and crying on the airstrip when the dustoff had set down to pick them up. While Sturm was helping to load them Dooley saw two Japanese refrigerators sitting in crates less than a dozen feet away, marked for the general's mess. He had lifted one and shoved it into his seat before he knew what was happening, as he had later claimed, but Kowalski had seen him and ordered him either to put it back or take the other one for the pilots. The other one quickly disappeared inside the chopper. Dooley opened the refrigerator and mixed himself another Scotch on the rocks. 'Christ, I'm going to be stewed by dinner time and it's only noon.' He looked into his glass, contemplated whether to put it back, then shrugged. 'Well, we only live once. Watch out liver, here it comes again.'

The fly Sturm had been studying now struggled less. 'I think this dink fly, this infiltrator, this sapper team leader, is dying. And no one should be denied last rites. He took a deep breath and began the haunting Gregorian chant for the order of mass for the dead:

'Dies irae, dies illa
Solvet saeclum in favilla:
Teste David cum Sibylla ...' His voice trailed off as his mind began flooding with memories of rising before dawn and hurrying down the worn wooden stairs to the basement where the line of mirrors and washbasins were already filled by half-dressed students snorting and farting and scrubbing before hurrying into their unpressed trousers and dropping the black cassocks over their heads and then in strict silence hurrying into mass where under cold stares of waiting priests they began the morning prayers, the matins, of the divine office.

'You know what that means, Tomato?' Sturm asked softly.

'No. I gave up the church for Lent, you know that.'

Sturm translated: 'Day of wrath and terror looming, Heaven and earth to ash consuming – Seer's and Psalmist's true foredooming!'

'Sounds like they're talking about Vietnam,' Dooley said with his mouth half submerged in his drink so that the last word just bubbled out. 'Do you really know all that Latin?'

'Sure. Three years of intensive study. I could have talked to Caesar.'

'Yeah? What would you tell him?'

'Watch out, man, someone is going to shove it to you.' Sturm laughed and got out of bed. He dropped his roach into a half-finished can of beer under his head and stood up. 'Two days and nothing happening. Life is getting too dull. Let's go eat.'

'After you, Monsignor,' Dooley said with a fat bow.

They followed the boardwalk to the messhall which was empty except for Sgt. Akers sitting at one of the tables with his legs outstretched while watching a young Vietnamese girl wiping the red-checkered table cloths.

'You better not look too hard at that, Sgt. Akers,' Dooley said, 'it might raise up something that your system couldn't handle.'

Akers shifted the toothpick to a corner of his small mouth but didn't take his eyes off the girl. 'My system can handle her, sonny, and it probably will handle her tonight.' He shifted his expressionless old enlisted eyes, toward the medics. 'You all coming to my club later on?'

'If our lord and master the First Sergeant doesn't find some duty for us,' Sturm said. He looked down at the plate of Boston beans and cottage cheese. 'What is this mess, Akers? How come we hardly get steak anymore? You selling the steak in your own club? Mumm? Little extra cash for the old sergeant?'

Akers snorted and moved his toothpick. 'No way. My club pays for itself, sonny.'

'It should, the prices you charge,' Dooley said.

'Yeah? You don't have to drink there. Or screw there, which you both do regularly. But you know it beats sitting around your hootch playing with yourselves. My club is in the interest of morale for our fighting men here in Veet-Nam.'

'Shee-it,' Sturm said through a mouthful of beans. He started to ride the mess sergeant a little more when the mess-hall door burst open and Johnston, the skinny orderly with the half-assed mustache, stood on the steps.

'First Sergeant says you gotta mission. Get going now,' he shouted excitedly.

Sturm shoved another large mouthful of beans in his face and started for the door. Dooley brought his whole plate, eating as he jogged around to the north side of the hospital where the medevac chopper squatted on the landing pad. Kowalski, already there, finished strapping on his armored chest plate and hauled his thick body into the pilot's seat as they ran up. Herron, the co-pilot, was already in. Dooley slid Kowalski's armored seat plate forward and slammed the door while Sturm did the same for Herron. The engine coughed to life and then settled into a rising shriek. The drooping blades were turning as Sturm slipped on his flack vest and his helmet. He adjusted the small boom mike until it just touched his lips then, after a quick glance to check the stretchers and medical kits, he pulled his armored chest plate from under his seat and sat on it.

Dooley's voice on the private intercom crackled in Sturm's helmet: 'If I was as short as you, Jake, I would wear all the protection I had, and not just sit on my chicken plate.'

'I'm saving my balls, Mike, that's the most important thing,' Sturm replied as Dooley flipped back to UHF on channel two and caught the last of the emotionless read-out from the tower across the highway: '... wind from two seven five, altimeter is two niner five niner, density altitude is two thousand. Report over check complete.'

Kowalski gave the EGT gauge a quick glance to confirm it was not redlining and spoke to the tower: 'Rainbow One one. Roger, Windjammer, we are go.' As Kowalski eased upon the collective until the Huey lifted clear from the ground, Sturm saw a short figure running heavily toward the chopper. The man wore a flack vest that flapped wildly and one hand held his helmet down on his head while the other gripped an M-16.

Sturm hit the intercom button on the cord that dangled from his helmet: 'Mr. Kowalski, someone looks like he wants to get aboard.'

Kowalski let the torque spin the chopper a little more until he could see the awkwardly approaching figure.

'Oh, that's the chaplain. Montano. I told him he could go with us if he could make it on time.'

He eased the chopper back into the pad but kept the RPM at a screaming 6,600 as Montano flung himself inside. Instantly the bird tilted on its nose then skimmed forward, gaining speed with each second as it rushed toward the nine-foot perimeter fence that encircled the hospital. At the last second Kowalski pulled pitch and the bird leaped over the wires, clearing them by inches. Kowalski's daily game. A Vietnamese woman hurrying toward the hospital gate crouched in sudden fear as the dustoff sprang over her and the wind from the blades tore her conical straw hat from her head and sent it spinning into the dusty field.

Montano got to his knees and adjusted his helmet with the small white cross painted on the front and then eased over to where Sturm sat with his legs dangling out the doorway.

'Thank you for waiting for me,' Montano said. Sturm saw his lips moving but could hear nothing inside his helmet. He pushed his helmet back off one ear.

'I said thanks for waiting,' Montano shouted again.

'You're welcome, sir.' He started to readjust his helmet but the chaplain, who sat back from the frighteningly open doorway, appeared anxious to talk.

'You people certainly move quick when the call comes.' He was still panting hard. 'Where are we going?'

Sturm shrugged. 'I don't know.' He readjusted his helmet and pulled the mike close to his mouth. 'Mr. Kowalski, what's the mission?'

'Some Vietnamese Rangers are getting their asses shot off.' Kowalski's voice, metallic and flat in the headset built into Sturm's helmet, paused. 'Inside Laos.'

'Christ, not that again,' Sturm groaned.

'Aren't they out of there yet?' It was Dooley, sounding disgusted. 'I thought they learned their lesson when the North Vietnamese kicked the shit out of them in February.'

'Now, now, boys,' Kowalski said in a mockingly fatherly voice. 'Lots of action in Laos, lots of things to keep us busy. Might even have some good hunting today.' He reached back and patted the M-79 grenade launcher, a stubby weapon with a short barrel that looked big enough to stuff a fist down. It was Kowalski's pet weapon and he kept it slung in easy reach.

Sturm knew the powerfully built Kowalski had carried such a weapon on his previous two tours in Vietnam when he was flying scouts, a semisuicidal job of maneuvering little observation choppers called loaches down to ground level to look under rocks or to blow the elephant grass apart with the propblast until the enemy was flushed from hiding. Too often the enemy found the scouts first and blew them out of the air. Zigmund Kowalski had been shot down twice, as he would tell anyone who would listen. He would tell those who wouldn't listen, too, as Sturm and Dooley had learned after hearing numerous variations on the story in the month they had been flying with Kowalski.

The aircraft commander and his crew were still adjusting to each other, still fencing and probing for each other's quirks in personality. Sturm knew he was having trouble relating to the pilot whose square, flat face was emphasized by his flat-top haircut. Maybe it was Kowalski's eyes that put him off, Sturm thought. Those eyes were ice-blue, like the shadow of snow, and Kowalski always spoke in such a forceful manner that there never seemed any room for discussion. Like after the first time Kowalski made a little detour along the stream bed with his M-79 poked out the window, looking for dinks. Sturm had asked why they were doing this, why not leave it to the head hunter teams, but Kowalski had said that everyone had a duty to end the war as quickly as possible and the only way to do that was to eliminate the enemy. They had made these little detours on three other occasions in the past month but had yet to find any enemy troops. Sturm had said nothing more about it and Dooley didn't complain. Dooley in fact admitted one night when half loaded that he wanted to grease a dink anyway.

As Sturm started to pull his helmet off and speak to the chaplain, Kowalski's voice crackled again. 'Maybe we'll see some bad guys today and I'll have to give them a lecture about how naughty they are to be in South Vietnam. Yes, today is a good day for hunting,' he laughed and patted the grenade launcher again.

Sturm held his helmet back from his ear and shouted at Montano, 'We're going into Laos. Apparently there are still some Ranger units in there. Mr. Kowalski says the ones we're going after have been shot up pretty bad. It will probably be a hot LZ.'

'What's that mean?' Montano asked.

Christ, hasn't this guy been anywhere, Sturm thought, then said aloud, 'That means the landing zone will probably be under fire.'

Montano's eyes widened and to Sturm they seemed to

brighten in anticipation. The priest nodded and moved away to where he had left his M-16. He picked it up and began checking his fire selector and his clip. He zipped up his flak jacket and then slung a bandolier of clips across his chest.

Sturm watched the chaplain's preparations for a moment and then pulled the green visor on his helmet down over his face while he studied the ground below. They were flying west and the sandy coastal flatlands of northern South Vietnam where the hospital lay now gave way to rolling hills as the land writhed upwards toward the mountains of Laos. The patterned rice fields in the flatlands were replaced by small bright green terraces where farmers chipped out rice paddies along fingers running down ridges to cut off the encroachment of civilization. Finally there were no more paddies, only the monotonous green and towering trees of triple canopy jungle. Just like a monstrous Venus Flytrap, Sturm thought.

He closed his eyes to the jungle and tried to concentrate instead on Mai. He would go into the ville when he got back, go to her little room and let her strip off his fatigues and rub him from the toes up. He saw her standing above him in a white ao-dai, her black hair falling forward as she leaned over him. Then he saw chaplain Montano sitting in the darkened corner, grinning at him and holding an M-16 across his heavy thighs.

Sturm popped his eyes open and flipped his visor back. The terrain below had changed sharply, no longer just jungled hills but now dizzying spires of white limestone cliffs that dropped vertically more than a thousand feet. This was the beginning of Laos.

'Get your clubs ready,' Kowalski said. 'Gunships are hosing the perimeter now. We'll be down in less than a minute.'

Sturm reached under his canvas seat and grabbed a thick, two-foot club that he had carved from the limb of a tamarind tree. He slipped the braided thong over his wrist and swung the club experimentally a few times. If the Vietnamese on the firebases had one rule of thumb, he thought, it was 'fuck your buddy'.

From the approaching medevac the Vietnamese firebase looked like a running sore on the side of the jungle. The Vietnamese had widened a small natural clearing by wrapping C-4, the plastic explosive, around trees and blowing them off several feet above the ground. The trees lay like a dropped box of matches. Sandbagged bunkers were built alongside and beneath the logs. In the center of the firebase, near three 105 howitzers that had been lifted in by chopper, a green smoke grenade burned to give wind direction. No one manned the guns and Sturm could see about thirty Rangers crouched alongside the logs and in the bunkers. No one appeared to be watching the perimeter.

As Kowalski dropped the dustoff at a sickening descent toward the ragged firebase, Sturm saw a Cobra gunship angle over the clearing and shudder as it loosed a rocket, then another. Sturm could see the identifying trail of orange smoke from the pods. Fleshettes, small steel darts about the size of a four penny nail, streamed toward the ground in whistling death. Nail those bastards, Sturm thought, and then they were down.

Kowalski flared the ship back hard then moved forward over the fallen trees. There was no place to set down in the hastily prepared firebase but the pilot hovered easily with one skid resting on a stump to steady the ship. Then, as if on a signal, the Vietnamese rangers in their brown camouflaged uniforms rose and began a panicky, staggering run toward the helicopter.

'Here they come,' Dooley shouted. 'Get ready!'

The Vietnamese scrambled and fell over the logs in their haste to reach the waiting helicopter. Some carried packs and rifles but many came with nothing, not even helmets, in hopes of being first to the chopper, their salvation.

To one side Sturm saw ten or fifteen bandaged men begin awkwardly and haltingly to struggle toward the chopper. Christ, where did they come from? Sturm turned to advise Kowalski to move the dustoff closer to the injured men when he saw Montano standing by the doorway firing steadily into the jungle beyond the perimeter. 'Give 'em hell, chaplain,' Sturm grinned and hit his intercom button.

'There are a bunch of wounded to your right about 30 meters. Can you shift to them?'

Effortlessly the helicopter rose a few feet and Sturm could see despair fill the faces of the Vietnamese who were almost at the chopper. The medevac slid sideways until it settled again on another stump less than ten meters from the group of injured. Still the other rangers pressed on, hounds after the fox, and Sturm could see it would be a close race.

A Vietnamese Ranger with a large bandage tied loosely around his head was first to the chopper. He climbed in by himself, just an M-16 in hand, no pack, and sat tight behind the pilot's seat where he nervously eyed Sturm.

Sturm started to reach for another Ranger who had only a flapping gauze bandage to cover the jagged hole where some fragment had ripped out the muscle in his upper right arm. Then the mortar hit, a jarring concussion and eruption of dust and debris about 50 meters from the chopper.

'Come on, come on,' Kowalski said calmly. 'Grab those wounded. Those mortars are going to walk right over here.'

Then the desperate uninjured Rangers were on the chopper, a teeming brown mass of men who shouted and beat about the shuddering dustoff like moths around the candle. The mortar had only intensified their fear and although Dooley and Sturm could not hear them they knew the fear of being left that filled the throats of the Rangers.

One burly Vietnamese grabbed the door stanchion and pulled himself up, pushing aside the man with the blown-away arm muscle as he did. Sturm sprang forward and chopped viciously at the man, catching him on the neck and toppling him into the gesturing men below. He disappeared beneath the stampede.

'Get off, goddamit, get off. Di-di, di-di mau, get off. Only the wounded,' Sturm yelled but none heard him over the screaming engine. Another tried to pull himself onto the dustoff and Sturm chopped him full in the face. He saw one soldier near the front with heavy bandages around his bare torso and Sturm pulled him up by the hair. Dooley already had two aboard.

Another mortar round burst, this time closer and Sturm sensed mortar fragments hitting the chopper. He saw two Vietnamese go down wounded by fragments but no one paid them heed. Sturm started to jump from the chopper to help but stopped. If I get out, everyone of these healthy dinks will jump in and overload the medevac. What a bunch of garbage. Angrily, he brought his boot heel down on the hand of a boy who looked no more than 15. Sturm heard bones crack and the boy fell back, his mouth open in a scream that could not be heard.

A hand clutched at his pants leg and Sturm was about to smash the man with his club when he waved his bleeding stump of an arm. The dirty compress that covered the stump where his arm ended below the elbow had come loose and Sturm could see the ulna and radius bones glistening. He grabbed the man's good arm and swung him aboard while booting another man who tried to follow.

The uninjured Rangers crowding beside the chopper realized they would not be allowed aboard and slowly stopped fighting but they kept their faces upturned, black and bitter eyes never leaving Sturm. Several wounded made a last effort to push through the pack of Rangers but no one made room for them.

Sturm turned and counted nine men on the deck. He

signaled Dooley who spoke into his mike: 'Up, up and away, Mr. Kowalski.'

'Roger. Now clean those dinks off the skids or we're not going to clear the trees,' Kowalski answered. Sturm saw Montano still at his position by the doorway where he pumped round after round into the jungle.

As the dustoff tilted and made a short run across the clearing to get lift, Sturm flopped on his stomach and peered down. Three rangers were clinging to the skid on his side in a final bid to escape. Sturm hit the closest one a sharp blow above the elbow and the man jumped clear. The chopper was gaining speed as he struck the second man across the shoulders in an effort to dislodge him. The man winced but hung on, his eyes pleading. Sturm swung hard at his head as the man ducked and let go. He landed heavily on the side of a log and lay unmoving.

Sturm leaned out farther to get at the man who hung near the end of the skid. The first blow caught the man across his knee and his leg jerked open. The Ranger, a thin-faced man with wide, intelligent eyes, dangled by his hands as the chopper climbed quickly to clear the encircling trees. They were more than thirty feet up.

'Christ,' Sturm breathed, 'you can't drop now.' He hooked a leg under his seat brace and reached back to pull the man in and managed to close a hand over the Ranger's wrist just as the skid whipped through the top branches of the first tree. The man's mouth opened in an unheard cry as the limbs broke his grip and raked him from the skid. Sturm helplessly watched him fall, tumbling like a dead monkey, until the foliage swallowed him. The old Venus Flytrap, Sturm thought. He turned toward Dooley who readjusted his mike and said 'One dude still on my skid.' Sturm stepped over the pile of wounded and looked down where a Ranger hung like a terrified sloth. Both arms and legs were crossed over the skid and his cheek was pressed tight against the bar.

Dooley leaned out and shouted, 'Lotsa luck, fella.' The Vietnamese opened his eyes and let a little fear spill out before he closed them again. The wind ripped at his camouflaged uniform as the medevac gained speed.

Sturm turned to the tangle of wounded on the floor. The first Ranger aboard, the one with an apparent head wound, was trying to rewrap his bandage and Sturm saw immediately the man was not injured. 'You son of a bitch, Sturm yelled. 'You take up space the wounded need.' He turned angrily to Dooley. 'Why the hell do we bother with them? What's the fucking use?' Dooley stepped forward and ripped the bandage from the Ranger's head and flung it in the man's face. The Ranger said nothing but kept his eyes on the two. Sturm looked at the recent scar that angled through one eyebrow and made his right eye droop. You a mean motha, Sturm thought, and turned to the wounded around him.

The worst injured seemed to be the man with his left hand blown off. Blood pulsed weakly between the exposed bones and Sturm could see the rag tied at the top of the man's arm as a crude tournequet around the arm just above where it was severed and hit the man with a syreete of morphine. He gently pulled two four-inch compresses over the stump then spoke into his mike: 'We taking these wounded all the way home?'

'Negative,' Kowalski said. 'There's a Vietnamese aid station on Route 19. Coming up shortly. We'll drop them there. Rainbow One Two is taking the last load out behind us, so our work is done, me lads.'

Blood made the aluminum flooring slippery as Sturm worked. He rolled another Ranger over and slit the uniform beneath the right arm. Dark blood oozed from two holes below the rib cage. 'Right in the liver. I think you just bought the farm, pal,' Sturm said and pulled a compress tight. The Ranger's face was gray, like newly poured concrete, and he tried to smile as he listened uncomprehendingly to Sturm's words.

Dooley, looking out his side of the chopper again, indicated to Sturm the man on the skid was gone. Sturm shrugged and sang briefly into the intercom: 'He flies through the air with the greatest of ease ...' Weird, he thought, how callous one can get after a year of this. Just garbage men, picking up the refuse and taking it to the dump.

He finished checking the wounded and was confident he had stopped the major bleeding as Kowalski dropped the chopper rapidly between steep, jungled hillsides toward a small clearing along a twisting dirt road. 'Here comes the dustoff,' Kowalski said and flared the ship back at the last moment, sending a cloud of yellow dust rolling over the half-dozen Vietnamese stretcher bearers who ran toward the chopper.

As the medevac was about to touch down, the Ranger who faked the head injury jumped to the doorway with rifle in hand. Dooley came up behind him, put his foot between the man's shoulder blades, and shoved. 'Let me help you,' he said and watched the Ranger fall eight feet, landing hard in the dust. He rolled clear just as the chopper settled into his imprint. From a crouch the man swung his M-16 at the two men, his eyes glittering with fury. He lowered the muzzle as the stretcher bearers crowded past him to assist the injured but he kept his eyes fixed accusingly on Sturm who finally gave him the finger. 'I didn't do it, dickhead,' he yelled, 'Dooley's the one.'

They were up again. Sturm leaned back in his seat and pulled a wrinkled cigarette from the pack of Park Lanes in his shirt pocket. He swore as he got blood all over one end then stuck the clean end in his mouth and cupped his lighter against the wind. He pulled the smoke deep into his lungs, held it as long as he could then watched it being sucked out the doorway as he slowly exhaled.

He flipped the intercom to private. 'You know, Mike, Vietnam is actually a pretty advanced country. Where else do they have grass rolled and packaged for the conquering heroes?'

'You lighting up already?' Dooley preferred Scotch. A juicer. 'You didn't use to smoke nearly as much as you do now, you know that? You're really getting to be a head.'

'Why not? We're finished. The operation was a success. Of course, however, the patient died. But isn't that Vietnam in a nutshell?' Sturm said sarcastically as he let the smoke trail delicately through his lips.

'Not too much moralizing in one day, monseigneur,' Dooley's voice said on the intercom. 'Hey! Watch it, the chaplain is coming around to your side.'

Dooley's warning had not been completed when Montano with M-16 in hand, moved around the stretchers on the turbine housing and sat next to Sturm who suddenly couldn't decide whether to eat his roach, throw it hastily away or hope that Montano would not smell anything in the open-sided chopper. Sturm opted for the latter and watched as the priest eased himself down and began talking. Sturm pulled his helmet off again.

'That was an incredible sight. All those South Vietnamese fighting so desperately to get out of there. I've never seen anything like it. Does it happen often?'

Sturm nodded. 'Quite often, especially during this time they tried to move in to Laos. The South Vietnamese are really taking heavy losses and they just don't want to be left out there to walk home. Lots of them try to fake wounds, like that one who got past us on this trip. Did you see him?'

'Yes. I hate to see something like that. It seems so cowardly.' The chaplain mused a moment then changed the subject. 'I didn't seem to be much help to the men. I'm sure there were many Catholics among the wounded but I don't speak Vietnamese. I felt rather hopeless.'

He seemed to Sturm to be wanting some encouragement. 'I'll bet just your being on board comforted some of them. They could see your insignia.'

'You think so?' Montano asked. 'I felt I had to do something, so I tried to provide covering fire. I don't want to be extra baggage on these trips. The least I can do is help protect us while you are working with the wounded.'

Sturm started to answer when he heard his earphones crackling. He pulled the helmet back and heard Kowalski speaking:

'. . . a little detour, lads. I hear some dinks are getting uppity over there.'

'Where?' Dooley asked and Kowalski motioned toward a bank of limestone cliffs to the north of Route 19.

'First Cav told me a lot of bad guys are coming through this area so I thought we would take a few minutes out for some hunting,' Kowalski said.

Sturm who had anticipated an early return to base and early into the ville to see Mai, felt a flash of anger spin his insides. 'Then why not let 1st Cav handle it? That's their job,' he said on the intercom.

'This won't take long. Just a little extra effort to help the war along. You want to help, don't you, buddy-boy?'

Sturm didn't answer but took a final deep drag off his roach and sailed it out the door. He felt the drug unwinding his mind that had tightened to the breaking point as the mortars had marched toward them back on that God-forsaken firebase. He had seen a chopper take a direct hit with a mortar once and had never gotten it out of his mind. One moment the chopper was on the ground, ready to lift off, and the next instant it was a blinding flare of explosives and burning magnesium.

'Are we heading home now?' Montano asked. Without a

head set he could not follow developments and relied on Sturm to pass him information.

'No sir. Mr. Kowalski wishes to help the Great American War Effort along by going in search of some bad guys, the VC or North Vietnamese, and eliminating them, wasting them.' Sturm spoke with obvious sarcasm.

Montano was surprised. 'A medevac chopper going after the enemy? You don't carry any machine guns.'

Sturm pointed at Kowalski who had pulled free the stubby grenade launcher and was breaking it like a shotgun to insert the fist-sized bullet-grenade.

'That's our main weapon. We use cannon fire.'

Kowalski handed the controls over to Herron as he slid back the armor side plate by the door, opened the small door window and thrust the barrel of the M-79 outside. 'Let's go hunting, lads,' he laughed on the intercom.

Sturm hit the button in his hand: 'Remember, Mr. Kowalski, my MOS is 91-Bravo, a medic, and not a goddam grunt. I'm supposed to be a healer, not a killer.'

'In Vietnam, everyone is a killer,' Kowalski replied laconically. Talking to Kowalski was like talking to a rock. He crossed his arms on his chest, pulled down his visor and leaned back, determined not to participate.

They dropped along the base of the cliffs and Sturm could see a village about two miles away along a winding dirt road. He guessed it was a tribe of mountain people, Montagnards.

Kowalski pointed past Herron's shoulder. 'Drop over there,' he said, indicating another line of cliffs. 'I see some trails we can follow up.' The warrant officer rechecked the map on the instrument panel between the seats and said, 'This is a free-fire zone, any gooks in here are fair game.'

Sturm protested: 'There are Montagnards around here and nobody told them it was a free-fire zone, and you're not that far from the village. Could be anybody out here.'

'Tough shitski, as we say in Poland. The map says its a free-fire zone. We're going down.'

Herron eased the dustoff back to 60 knots and began flying contour, rolling up and down over the ravines in easy swings, a lullaby kind of flying where cliffs rushed at you only to have the chopper lift effortlessly over at the last moment then sink down the far side.

'Hold it,' Kowalski said. 'I see a water buffalo. Go back along that trail, real slow.'

Herron swung around the tethered animal which began to lunge wildly. Kowalski thrust his stubby grenade launcher out the window like a blunderbuss and waved excitedly. 'I think they're in those caves over there, slide over that way.'

As he spoke a figure darted from one of the small caves made by the jumble of rock at the base of the cliffs and ran hard toward a larger pile of rocks where there seemed to be better cover. Kowalski fired immediately but the grenade went high and burst well beyond the disappearing figure.

Sturm saw why the man had run. The first cave was too shallow and as the chopper dropped lower and lower there was a clear shot into the rocks where the man had lain. Sturm could make out what he thought was another person lying flat in the deep shade of the rock and he picked up his M-16 and chambered a round. If there were a lot of bad guys in there, the dustoff was suddenly very vulnerable at this low altitude and slow speed.

Montano was shouting something and Sturm impatiently pulled back his helmet to hear.

'Are those VC? Are we taking them under fire?' He was up on one knee in the doorway and had his rifle ready.

'Mr. Kowalski thinks they are the bad guys but I don't think so,' Sturm shouted. 'I think they are just Montagnards trying to get back to their village.'

As he spoke the figure that had lain in the shadow rose and started running after the other. Montano brought his rifle up in a reflex action and started to find the target when he lowered the weapon. He turned in surprise to Sturm and mouthed the words, 'It's a woman.'

'Get that dink, Sturm, shoot,' Kowalski's voice crackled. 'I'm out of position now. Swing around, Herron.'

The chopper swung hard and Kowalski fired once again but he was too late. The woman disappeared as the round burst well behind her.

'They're yards, Kowalski, they're just Montagnards,' Sturm said.

'Bullshit. They're VC couriers. The first one had a ruck-sack on his back.' Kowalski's voice was angry as he ordered Herron to pull in closer to the cliff.

The Huey slid closer and closer to the vertical white lime-stone cliffs and the blast of air from the blades bent the brown elephant grass that grew up to the edge of the rocks. A small tree that grew from a great fissure in one of the boulders whipped violently in the churning air and Ko-walski, peering down from his window, suddenly shouted exultantly:

'There they are, right under that tree in the crack. Fish in a barrel, man.'

The two figures lay perfectly still below the hovering heli-copter, hoping that they would not be detected if they did not move. One was clearly a woman and Sturm could see the sores on her naked brown back. The chopper was that close. The other was a man wearing only the hand-woven black and red loin cloth of the mountain tribesmen. He had a rucksack on his back, empty by its slack appearance, and one arm was stretched toward the woman as if to protect her.

'They're Montagnards,' Sturm shouted into his mike. 'They're just yards, they travel anywhere. You don't know they're couriers. They wouldn't be couriers with a water buffalo, for Christ sake.'

Kowalski didn't answer and in that second everything

before Sturm became frozen in the flare-image of a snapshot: Kowalski leaning from the window to get a clear shot; Herron holding the bird steady as he calmly watched the two still figures below; Dooley rising from his seat to get a better view of what was happening; Montano turning from where he kneeled still ready to shoot to look at Sturm with questioning eyes, eyes asking if they were the enemy and should be shot.

The image dissolved abruptly as Kowalski fired. Sturm saw the bright flash as the grenade struck directly between the two. The explosion flung them apart like someone shredding an orange and smoke immediately covered the death site, but not before a torn limb sailed clear.

Sturm spoke angrily: 'Hey, Kowalski, how do you know they were VC couriers and not just innocent Montagnards?'

'Mr. Kowalski to you, buddy boy, and if they're dead they must be VC. That's rule number one in Vietnam, something you should have learned by now.'

Kowalski's voice changed immediately, happy again, and he said, 'Let's go home, boys. I knew it was a good day for hunting.'

Montano, who had said nothing since watching the two Montagnards die so abruptly, put his rifle down and sat with his back to the pilots. Sturm saw him pull a small bible from his pocket and begin to read.

Sturm leaned back and fished in his breast pocket for another stick of marijuana. He lit it and then pulled his green visor down so no one could see his face while he slowly exhaled a thin stream of smoke against the plastic just in front of his mouth and tried to inhale it again.

'Fuck it. Fuck it all.'

CHAPTER THREE

STURM held a new stick of grass in his left hand which he placed near the hole he had punched through the quonset wall to let the pungent smoke escape in case First Sgt. Thomas burst in looking for him. Sturm's boots, which he rested on a footlocker beside his bunk, were still wet from hosing the blood and bone splinters out of the dustoff.

Dooley, who had just taken some more ice from the refrigerator as he refreshed his glass, sat crookedly in the broken swivel chair and made wet rings on his bulging white belly with the sweating glass of Scotch.

'What did King Kong Kowalski say to you?' he asked.

Sturm took a slow pull from the roach, held it, then started talking as he let the smoke trail out his pursed lips. 'He told me to cool it, that we had to make the best of it because it was the only war we had. I started to get all hot about it but he just got colder and colder until I thought those weird ice-blue eyes of his were going to freeze. He finally said that his shooting at dinks wouldn't interfere with our work and he didn't want any bitching from me. He made it pretty clear he was the officer, the AC, and I was just a grunt who had better mind his manners.'

'Live and let live,' replied Dooley. 'It's war, so who cares if he wants to grease a few extra gooks. Do you really care about them?'

Sturm tried to take another drag on the roach but found it was so short he was burning his fingers. He backed off until he held just the very end and tried again. He managed to get some smoke but also singed the hairs on his mustache. He dropped the butt angrily in an empty beer can.

'I don't know, Tomato. I just don't like to see innocent people get zapped.'

'Haven't you heard, Monsignor, there are no innocent people in Vietnam.'

Sturm ignored the redhead's sarcasm. 'Maybe I still have a little idealism left in me. I thought it would be all gone by now but since Kowalski took over as AC I've had to rethink about why I came here. I came because Vietnam was reality, it was life and death, and not the sterile world of prayers and chanting in a dead tongue and seeking to love God and jacking off under the long cassock at night.'

He paused to light another stick of grass from his pack of Park Lanes and, feeling his mind lighten, continued: 'When I first came I tried to think of the Vietnamese as people. It wasn't easy because, man, they are different, and their language is impossible to learn, and you never know what they're thinking. And when I got to know Mai – a real woman, and not just another cardboard bargirl – I thought I was making some headway. But then I found it was dangerous. It's bad to get to know them, because you might begin to feel a relationship, and that tears you up a little when you waste one. So then I started thinking of them like everybody else does, as gooks, and dinks, and slopes. See? All impersonal names for an impersonal people. Not Mr. Nguyen or Miss Hai, just plain old dink.' He pulled on the roach and felt the harsh Laotian grass bite deep in his lungs and he could feel his mind expanding and he could see every detail, could see Dooley watching him with his little eyes, the glass of Scotch held loosely in the meaty hand and the mat of red hair glistening on his chest. Sturm wasn't sure whether Dooley was listening or was sleeping with his eyes open, a trick everyone learned in the army.

'But since Kowalski,' he continued, 'I've had to rethink

everything. Because he makes war all seem so personal again, that it's his personal war, and we have a personal responsibility to eradicate a people – Vietnamese – whether they are North or South Dinks. You see—'

Dooley straightened and turned his head to listen to the beat of a chopper settling on the pad beyond the hospital.

'Rainbow Two is down. About time.'

Sturm broke off his monologue and before his dreamy eyes there slowly appeared the picture of Kowalski angling the M-79 down for a clear shot and Montano's eyes wide, watching, waiting, then the orange blossom and the black curl of smoke and broken rock and an arm, slowly and casually, rising from the smoke and falling back into it.

He sat up and rubbed his lean face and pinched the top of his thick beak-like nose while he consciously shifted his mind to Lt. Saunders. Think of something good, he told himself. Sandy Sweet-Ass. And tonight was Monday, Blue Monday in Sandy's hootch where she showed porno movies for any of the officers who wanted to come, and Sturm was her projectionist. Sandy Sweet-Ass who got her rocks off watching porno flics and liked to play a little grab-ass with Sturm but hadn't gone beyond that. Yet. One of these nights, Sturm thought, Sandy and I are going to put it all together. Or forget her. Mai was better company anyway. And a marvelous lay, something only a drop-out, horny old would-be priest can really enjoy, Sturm thought and started to laugh but then there was Father Hoffman staring at him from behind the huge and barren mahogany desk in his study.

'Why are you leaving the Monastery, Jacob?'

'Because I want to screw girls and sing and shout and live.'

'I see. I see.' In Sturm's mind the rector leaned forward and his face opened in a skeletal grin: 'Could you possibly fix me up with one of the girls you have been diddling before you leave. I am rather horny!' and he leaned back with a cackle: 'Forgive me, father, for I have sinned. Heeheehee.'

'You going to watch the flics tonight?' Dooley's voice closed the door on the images and Sturm swung his eyes, slow and brown, toward Dooley.

'Yeah. I guess so.'

'I thought we were going into the ville, to the club.'

'After the flics. I am the projectionist, remember.'

'Bullshit. You go because you still think that Lt. Saunders is going to take down her pants for you. You have been trying for more than a month. When are you going to recognize she is just a prick-tease?' Dooley said.

Footsteps sounded on the boardwalk outside the hootch, just one person walking and Sturm prepared to shove his roach out the hole in the wall in case it was First Sgt. Thomas. The footsteps stopped and after a moment's pause the screen door squeaked open and admitted Riley who dropped his helmet and M-16 in a heap on the floor and wordlessly went to the refrigerator where he opened a can of orange soda. He took a long pull without looking at anyone and then sat heavily on his bed.

Sturm paused with his cigarette halfway to his mouth and squinted one eye through the curling smoke as he studied Riley's long brown face.

'Where's Moran?' Sturm finally asked.

'He bought it, man,' Riley said, talking to his orange soda, 'right between the mothafucking eyes. We was lifting out of that firebase sometime after you and we was beating those dinks off the skids. I looked around to see how Moran was doing and he was laying on his back, man, right on top of this dink who had a sucking chest wound. I went over to him and looked down and I could see this splintery hole right in the middle of Moran's visor.' Riley flopped back on his bunk, his light brown lion-eyes staring at the ceiling.

'Oh shit,' sighed Dooley, 'Oh shit.'

After a moment Riley continued, talking hurriedly as if to hastily purge his mind of the memories: 'I couldn't see nothing through that green visor and he wouldn't answer me so I got ahold of his helmet and pulled it off. And that was a *mistake*, man. Half his brains seemed to be in that helmet and they fell all over that dude underneath Moran.' Riley peeled his flight suit off and sweat ran in glistening rivulets down his thin black torso.

'What *could* I do, man?' he said in response to an unspoken question. 'I put him in a body bag and zipped it up. I didn't even check those wounded dinks on board. I hope some of those mothafuckers *died* before we dropped them off. And I think that one with the big hole in his chest *did* die.' He got up to get another soda and then felt behind his battered steel clothes locker and came out with a small bag he kept taped back there. He pulled one of the plastic vials out and then pulled a cigarette from the pack on his bed. The room, hazy in the afternoon light that filtered through the small windows, was silent as all three watched Riley fix a duster. It was easier to watch his every move than to think about Moran and how it could have been one of us.

Riley took a toothpick and pulled out the top third of the tobacco in the filtered Marlboro. He pulled the cap loose on the vial of heroin and tipped some of the white powder into the cigarette then twisted the end tight. He lit it and lay back again while he took slow, deep drags until his body visibly relaxed.

'Someday it's all going to be beautiful again, man, someday.' He held the duster out to Sturm. 'You want to try some now?'

Sturm shook his head. 'No, grass is good enough.'

'Grass won't always be good enough,' Riley said. 'You forget better with scag, and sometimes you need to forget, man.'

'Funny,' Sturm said. 'Franklin told me the same thing just a few days ago.'

Riley smoked in the silent room a moment then spoke

again. 'You know what? When I cleaned out the chopper and washed out Moran's helmet, you know what I found? An M-16 round, man, *not* an AK round. You know what that means? One of those dink Rangers let Moran have it for beating his cowardly ass off the chopper. Isn't that unfucking-believable?'

'That is bad,' Dooley said into his glass.

'You goddam right that's bad,' Riley suddenly flared. He flung his can of soda against the wall and a fizzing orange puddle spread on the floor. 'That's so goddam bad it's unbelievable. We suppose to be helping these mothafucking slopes do something with their lives and they turn around and shoot the man who is trying to save them. I think I would rather help a North Vietnamese than one of these assholes in the south. They are the most useless people I have *ever* seen.'

In the silence that again enveloped the room now thick with smoke Sturm said: 'Moran was a good man.' His words seemed to topple out of his mouth and land heavily on the floor. Christ, Sturm thought, is that all I can say about Billy Moran? That he was a good man? I know the guy, I work with him for about four months and that's all I can say about him, that he was a good guy? Moran, Bill, Spec. 5, helicopter crew chief, U.S. Army, man, good, one each. Roger, out.

Riley sat up. 'I almost forgot, man. That new chaplain, Montano, he say he having some kind of service for Moran right away. We better get over there.'

There were already several nurses and orderlies in the small and barren room that served as a non-denominational chapel in the hospital when the three arrived. They wedged themselves into a corner, embarrassed by the looks and nods of sympathy from others in the room.

Montano entered silently and moved to the front of the room where he opened a bible and placed a purple stole around his neck. Purple, thought Sturm, for death and penitence. He swung his eyes away from the chaplain and found the back of Lt. Saunders, some ten feet in front of him and began thinking of her curvaceous fanny that her fatigues did nothing to hide. He only half listened to the priest praise the dead:

'... and only those of us who are here today know and understand the courage of such men as Bill Moran who risk their lives daily in defense of democracy for a people they do not know. Bill Moran's death is all the more important because he died helping his Vietnamese brothers, helping them win their own freedom from the scourge of Godless communism. We here must not let Bill Moran's death be in vain; those responsible suffer for their wanton destruction of South Vietnam, a country that asks nothing more than to be left alone, and we here today must not shirk our responsibilities, to take up the task where Bill Moran left off ...' Montano stood straight, his five-feet-five inches pulled to maximum height and his head thrown back, black hair glistening as he pleaded Moran's case to an unseen heavenly body.

Sturm tried to concentrate on Sandy's shapely figure before him but then he was seeing Helen, and he was again running blackly through the moonless orchard and then through the barbed wire fence, catching his cassock in his haste, and then into the car where Helen lounged in the front seat and her face was caught in the alternately brightening and dying glow of her cigarette. He said nothing but pulled her close and slid his hands over her sweatered breasts, smooth and soft, and she kept smoking in her studied intellectualist manner and said, 'I thought this was to be a platonic relationship, an extension of our mutual interests in debate and philosophy, but you don't seem to be much of a celibate at all,' her voice low and throaty, and he kissed her neck and ran a hand lightly up her leg which made her flinch with pleasure and then she dropped her cigarette out the window into the warm April night and told him 'take off that goddamed dress,' and he was out of it and he knew that he would go no more to the nocturnes, the silent prayers for the divine office, without thinking of Helen and all he could say as he pulled her closer was 'Oh my God I am heartily sorry for having offended thee ...' Contrition, penitence, goodbye Father Hoffman, but I have places to go and girls to diddle, high diddle diddle the cat laid the fiddle. Latin, why the Latin? and then his mind spun slowly back into focus and Montano was bent over to read:

'Absolve, quaesumus, Domine, animam famuli tui Bill Moran, ab omni vinculo delictorum: ut in resurrectionis gloria inter Sanctos ...' and Sturm's lips began to move, first following the absolution for the dead and then translating, 'Lord, we pray thee release the soul of thy servant Bill Moran – where are you now, Billy? – from all bondage or sin so that in glory of the resurrection ...'

Montano paused and made the sign of the cross, then spoke again:

'Requiem aeternam dona ei, Domine.'

Sturm responded automatically, his voice from the back of the room startling others:

'Et lux perpetua luceat ei.'

Montano started but continued:

'Requiescat in pace.'

'Amen,' replied Sturm and there were murmurs of amen from the others as the service ended. Sturm, eyes back on Sandy, nudged Dooley and hissed:

'Man, look at that ass.' His whisper in the suddenly silent room came out too loud, bounced sibilantly around the green walls and caused nervous stirring among the assembled nurses. Nurse Saunders stood noticeably straighter and flexed her hands behind her back as if to shield her exposed derrière. Riley, the heroin still pulling him higher, couldn't restrain a giggle.

As the three walked back through the wards after the short ceremony Sturm heard the chaplain's deep baritone behind him.

'Jacob,' he said, for he made a point of calling the men by their first name. Don't let rank separate us, he had told Sturm on their second meeting.

'Jacob, it is true.' He looked carefully at Sturm and held him lightly by the arm.

'What's true?'

'You studied to be a priest. I was told that yesterday but I found it quite, um, surprising.'

'Why surprising?'

'Well, you are, shall we say, a red-blooded all-American boy. Hardly a celibate,' Montano said and solemnly watched Sturm.

'Celibacy isn't my bag, Father,' Sturm replied but he was thinking how Montano must have been doing a little checking on him.

'I see. You have a girl friend in the town of Quang Tri, no?'

'Yes, I do, Father,' Sturm said stiffly. He was beginning to resent the questioning. Montano must have done more than just a little checking.

Montano's eyes, wide and black, studied him without revealing anything. 'Well. I suppose it is to be expected in these difficult times. Tell me, do you plan to return to – it was Trinity College, wasn't it? – after your service?'

'I don't think so, Father, I think that is all behind me.'

'I hope not,' the chaplain said. 'The priesthood needs good people.' He changed the subject abruptly. 'Do you want to see Bill Moran? He is in the morgue. I will go with you if you want.'

Sturm recoiled. 'No, no I don't want to see him. I know very well what he looked like.'

Montano was at once apologetic. 'Yes, yes. I understand.' They stood in the hospital corridor, suddenly silent and uncomfortable until it occurred to Sturm that Montano might be the person to talk to.

'I've got something on my mind, Father. Would you like to talk it over with me?'

The priest brightened at the prospect. 'Of course. Here, let us sit down,' and he motioned toward a wooden bench along the wall. 'What is it, Jacob?' he asked in a voice deep and soft, as if inviting confessional whispers.

Sturm looked around as he began to speak and noticed they were sitting across from the orthopedic ward. The doors were open and dinner was being served. He turned back to the waiting chaplain.

'It's about what happened today, about Kowalski wasting those two Montagnards...'

'You are sure they were Montagnards?' the chaplain asked.

'Of course, you could see how they were dressed. That's not the question. The question is, do you think it was right? He didn't know they were couriers, he just let them have it.'

Montano looked down at the backs of his short brown hands and rubbed one gleaming nail. 'I must confess to you, Jacob, I have thought about it myself. Frankly, that was the first time I have seen someone killed and I was very deeply affected by it.'

'Well, I've seen lots of people killed, too many, in fact, but this is really different. Kowalski found those two and blew them away just for the hell of it. The reason I am asking you about it, Father, is that I am thinking of taking this to some higher authority. We're a medevac bird, and we shouldn't be out hunting the dinks. We're here to save people.'

'I agree, I agree, Jacob, but don't be too hasty. Now,

wasn't that a free-fire zone, an area in which nobody is supposed to be?'

'Sure, but a free-fire zone is declared by the U.S. command and then the South Vietnamese are supposed to tell the villagers around that area, to stay out. But they never do. Especially with Montagnards. They're the American Indian of Vietnam, considered savages. Nobody tells them that a red line around somebody's grid map makes them targets. Those people were probably some simple farmer and wife, with four kids in the thatched roof house down the road, going home after digging a few roots for dinner.'

Sturm felt the anger rising in him, a bitter hatred of everything around him, and he was a little afraid because he did not understand the rage. The irritation that became a fury with little provocation had only started in the past month but sometimes it seemed it was going to get control of him. He looked away from the priest, took a deep breath, and tried to relax. He looked into the orthopedic ward where he saw an orderly set a tray before one pale-skinned youth with no hands. The orderly began feeding him, spooning the food carefully into the boy's tight mouth, and the boy kept his eyes on the spoon and never looked at the orderly. Neither spoke.

Sturm felt Montano's hand on his arm. 'I know you are upset. So am I. But remember, it was a free-fire zone. So let us try this approach. I will talk with Mr. Kowalski about the matter and see if I can't get a full understanding of it. But let us not make too many waves. Alright?' He studied Sturm again with the fathomless black eyes.

Sturm nodded. 'Alright. Thanks for listening,' he said, but he felt dejected. He lifted his eyes from the curling linoleum floor and gazed back into the orthopedic ward. The pale youth who had finished eating was lying back on his white pillow and staring at Sturm. The boy opened his mouth and loosed a terrific belch toward Sturm and didn't smile.

He heard the chaplain speaking brightly now and turned to look at him again.

'Everything will work out, I am sure, Jacob. I will look into this matter for you.' He paused and eyed Sturm speculatively. 'Why aren't you going back to the monastery after you finish your service?'

Sturm eyed the priest cooly. Once he had felt intimidated in their presence but no more. 'I told you, celibacy isn't my bag. Sorry.'

'Nothing to be sorry about. We all feel that way at times. But with proper organization of your thoughts the desires for the flesh can be overcome.'

'But I don't want to overcome it. I like it. Sex is real. Why deny it?' Sturm felt angry but Montano looked at him with fathomless eyes.

'Because if your body is desirous of pleasure your mind is not able to pass beyond the passions, and truth will remain obscure, your understanding of God will remain blurred. Frankly, I would like to see you return to the monastery, continue your studies for the priesthood. Put aside the early pleasures now, Jake, forego your ventures into the village and your hours with bar girls. They will not benefit you. Will you do that?'

Sturm shook his head and started to reply but Montano cut him short by rising to his feet. 'You think about it, Jacob, don't deny your opportunities now. I must be off. We shall talk again soon.' He gave Sturm a friendly pat and hurried down the corridor. Sturm watched him walk away, rolling like a sailor, then swung his eyes back into the ward. The youth was resting his bandaged stumps on his stomach and staring at the ceiling. His lips moved in silent words.

Sturm felt a foot rest lightly on his and a knee push against his thigh. He looked up from where he still sat and saw Sandy Saunders watching him with her wide blue eyes.

'Who was taking whose confession?' she asked in slight

mockery. Her knee was still against his thigh, warmth flowed between their bodies, and Sturm wanted very much to hold her. He started to slip one hand along the back of her thigh but the pale youth was watching him again. Sturm stood up instead.

Sandy was suddenly contrite and sympathetic. 'I'm sorry about Billy, Jake. He was a good friend, wasn't he?'

'Yeah. A good friend.' He pinched the bridge of his nose and wondered why he couldn't say something meaningful about Billy. He's gone and I cannot articulate what kind of a person he was.

'Jake?' Sandy was looking at him. 'You will come tonight and run the projector, won't you?'

He shook his head. 'I don't know. I really don't feel like it, Sandy.'

'Please?' She squeezed his arms and he could feel her breast against his bicep. 'It will get your mind off of Billy. And I want to talk to you. Come a little early. There's no one there while I set things. Okay?'

He looked into her blue eyes, soft and unprotected, and agreed. She smiled and walked into the orthopedic ward. The pale-faced boy watched her pass his bed and then shifted his gaze back to Sturm. The boy raised his arms that ended where they shouldn't and moved the stumps in silent parody of clapping, but he didn't smile. Sturm turned back toward the messhall, not hungry but wanting to pass some time.

The greasy pork chops Sgt. Akers had served for dinner still rested uneasily on Sturm's stomach as he made his way slowly along the boardwalk toward Sandy's hootch. He walked slowly, moving occasionally off the boardwalk and onto the sand as others hurried by. It was dusk and the cool night air that is one of the minor salvations of Vietnam was blowing off the South China Sea. The sun, nearing the peaks that rose along the Laotian border, cast a slowly reddening glow on the mountain of cumulus clouds that hung to the east over the sea. Sturm had never seen such masses of clouds in his life and he imagined it must be how Mt. Everest looks, overwhelmingly large, glistening and pulsing with an unseen menace. He watched the clouds grow more suffused with the blood-red sunset and he felt his mind expand with the grass that seeped through his system, good Laotian grass. The sun was gone and darkness came quickly on the land and Sturm hurried onto the quonset hut.

He was late and the small hootch that housed six nurses was already crowded with off duty doctors and nurses and Sturm saw Kowalski near the front, where the patched bed sheet that served as a screen hung. Kowalski sat with the new blonde nurse that everyone was trying to hustle. The small eight-millimeter projector was already on the table at the rear and Sandy, glass of bourbon in hand, came toward him as he entered and began threading the film. He looked at the can and read the title: 'The Traveling Saleswoman'. Another rerun, he thought. Probably everyone in here has seen it at least once but they still come back. Anything to break the routine, anything to take their minds off the heat, off Vietnam and the endless array of mangled and bleeding bodies that arrive for classification. This one for the burn ward, this one for immediate surgery, this one . . . hey, man, this one's dead. Get him the fuck out of here.

'Jake, you were going to come early and talk with me. But you stood me up,' she pouted fetchingly and Sturm could see she was tipsy. She was a drinker, a juicer, like most of the nurses and doctors. The grunts were mostly heads, on grass or scag. Whatever it took to forget. Sturm wanted to light up but he knew the juicers were uptight about heads and would freak out. Especially Kowalski.

Sturm finished threading the film. 'Yeah, I was tied up,' he lied. Tied up with good grass and a lovely sunset and wondering why I wasn't in the ville with Mai, smoothing the silken hair from her alabaster face.

'I'll join you when the film starts but now I must be a good hostess, don't you think, Jaky-poo?' She smiled and moved away.

'And just what did you do for God and country today, my boy?' Sturm looked up at the bespectacled, balding Harry Schoen, chief surgeon, not yet forty and not yet a Lt. Col., still a major, which bothered him; a lifer.

'Hey, doc,' Sturm said easily. Schoen was alright. 'Usual stuff. I beat the hell out of some Vietnamese Rangers trying to get on my bird and some innocent Yards . . .' He stopped. He didn't want to talk about Kowalski grenading the Montagnards.

Schoen was only half listening. 'Good, good.' He turned to Sandy. 'Well, Nurse Saunders, ready when you are, CB, as we say in the business.' Schoen lurched away and a young intern quickly made room for the senior officer on one of the beds. Sturm started the projector and the scratched empty frames flickered brightly on the bedsheet as Sandy turned off the lights and came over to where Sturm sat with his back to the wall. She sat between his legs and leaned back against him.

'So nice of you to ask me to the movies,' she whispered mockingly.

'How long must we go on meeting like this dahlingk?' he countered.

'We are doomed to meet only on Blue Monday. Dahlingk,' she said and sipped at her bourbon on ice. 'After all, we officers aren't supposed to fraternize with you enlisted men.'

The film ran through the scratched title frames: 'The Traveling Saleswoman', and opened with the star, a bleached blonde in her forties with a 44-inch bustline struggling femininely to change a flat tire along a deserted, dusty country road. Her skirt is hiked up to her thighs as she looks helplessly at the tire. Camera cuts to vacant-eyes hayseed driving a team of mules down the road.

Sturm slid his arm around her waist and felt her breasts rest lightly on his forearm. 'Seriously, Sandy, why don't we arrange a pass together and go to Saigon, or work up some excuse to go the 1st Field Hospital together. Anything so we can spend some time together,' he whispered.

'You know how I would love that, Jakey, but it would be so hard.' She nestled closer to him, her eyes fixed on the screen where the hayseed is studying the tire and scratching his head. The Traveling Saleswoman stands up and hoists her skirt coyly to adjust her stockings. Camera cuts back to hayseed who is watching with eyes brightening.

Sturm slid his hand slowly up and over Sandy's firm breasts and closed his hand softly, waiting to feel the silken bra beneath and her nipple rise slowly in excitement. Instead his hand closed on a pack of cigarettes.

'Careful. Those are my last smokes,' Sandy said, still intent on the sexadrama where the hayseed is now fumbling with the tire while the Traveling Saleswoman sits on the fender above him, rubbing her thighs together invitingly.

Sturm was not interested in the film. He had seen it at least twice. He wanted to talk, to understand what was developing between Sandy and him.

'What do you say, Sandy,' he whispered over the whir of the projector beside them, 'let's make it into Saigon for a weekend.'

She wriggled uncomfortably and said, 'I think you are trying to take advantage of poor little me. Lead me astray, perhaps?'

'Now you're catching on,' Sturm said and closed his hand on her other breast. Paper crackled beneath his fingers. 'Now what? Did you stuff yourself with paper tonight?'

'Those are some pharmacy prescriptions. Don't wrinkle them. And watch the film,' she said. The hayseed now has the Traveling Saleswoman in the back seat with her blouse open and is ogling her massive mammaries while she slips her hand into his fly and produces a pecker the size of a large Italian salami which she begins stroking.

'Sandy, what are you afraid of?' Sturm whispers, still intent on talking. He knew it was the grass that made him garrulous, it always did.

Sandy answered with an edge in her voice: 'Nothing. Can't we just watch the film?' Sturm felt her tense as she kept her eyes riveted on the screen where the hayseed now had the Traveling Saleswoman down on the seat and was about to sock it to her.

'Place your order, you meathead,' Kowalski yelled from the front and there was general laughter and shouting now, relief from the tensions that had grown during the film. The final frames of the show ended and then empty frames fluttered glaringly on the sheet and Sandy rose to turn on the lights again.

'Show's over. Now the party begins,' she shouted gaily and asked an attentive intern to fill her drink again. She came back to Sturm who was canning the film.

'What did you mean, "what am I afraid of?" ' she asked.

Sturm closed the film can in loud frustration. 'We've been playing games now for more than a month. Just playing these games.' He had to raise his voice over the stereo music and loud chatter of others in the room.

'What do you mean games?' Sandy asked defensively. 'And don't shout.'

'You know damn well what I mean,' he answered. 'We watch these porno movies every week and play a little grab-ass but that's as far as it goes. Isn't that kind of strange, unnatural?'

Sandy flushed and answered angrily. 'Just watch your tongue, Jake. You expect me just to hop into bed because you're tall dark, and handsome?' She tapped her chest. 'I will decide, me, Lt. Saunders, will decide if this relationship is going any further.' Her blue eyes iced over as she stared at Sturm who shook his head in disgust.

'Now you're pulling rank on me. Let's forget it, forget it all.' He turned to leave but she caught him by the arm and her eyes were melting again.

'I'm sorry, Jake. Don't be angry. Just don't push me too fast. I told you before I feel lost in this world. I'm just like the town I came from. Little old Red Bluff, California. It was a growing town until the freeway bypassed it. Now it's just withering away. I don't want to be like that, I don't want life to pass me by and leave me withered. But I don't know where I'm going, either.' She looked at him and fluttered her eyes. 'I'm afraid, so be patient with me, alright?'

He wanted to kiss her right there but she seemed to read his mind and backed away with a bright smile.

'Come on, have a drink.'

Sturm hesitated, wanting to stay with her but feeling out of place among the officers. 'No, I've got some things to do. I'll see you,' he said and started out the door.

'Jake?'

'Yeah?'

'Friends?'

'Friends.'

He stepped outside and breathed deeply of the cool and clean night air. Christ, what a woman, what a screwed up broad. He stepped off the boardwalk and out behind the hootches toward the old underground bunker that was supposed to be a rocket shelter but had not been used since Sturm had been in country. He looked at the crumbled steps in the half-light from the hospital windows and lit up a stick of marijuana. He pulled the sweetly acrid smoke deep into his lungs and pushed away thoughts of screwing Sandy. Still worth trying for but Mai was more available. And just as pretty, even prettier. And good to him, no games. He looked at his watch in hopes of making it into the ville tonight to see her but decided it was too late. Tomorrow night for sure, if nothing comes unglued. He returned to the empty hootch feeling uneasy. It's been too long, he told himself. And that's a bad sign.

Lt. Hoyt stood carefully in the deep shade cast by an aged tree that was being strangled by massive vines winding around the trunk and limbs like brown pythons. Before the lieutenant stretched the valley, two miles long and a half-mile across at the broadest point. The valley floor, cut by a brown and turgid stream, was covered with long, sere grass, a brown carpet that stopped abruptly where the flanks of the valley rose steeply toward the high jungle covered ridges surrounding the valley. Hoyt put his binoculars to his eyes and let his palms hang over the ends to ensure there was no reflection in the lens while he studied the far end of the valley where it rose toward a line of ridges. On the skyline he could see the narrow pass, like a knife cut through thick mold, where part of the Ho Chi Minh trail complex angled into the valley. Beyond that pass lay the last firebase still occupied by the South Vietnamese inside Laos but Hoyt knew it would soon be abandoned. The firebase had been placed there to block North Vietnamese movement into the valley but the effort had been a dismal failure. S-2 informed Hoyt before he began this recon that columns of Hanoi forces, possibly a main force regiment, were moving supplies toward the valley. It was expected the North Vietnamese would bring back the 37mm anti-aircraft guns that once had defended the valley. S-2 had also told Hoyt they believed the enemy might establish surface-to-air missile sites in the valley to counter the high flying B-52s. The intelligence briefing had disclosed to Hoyt that three missile sites were already functioning in Laos, which probably explained why Hanoi had deployed such massive reinforcements against the South Vietnamese push into Laos.

Hoyt looked at the plastic-covered map on the ground before him which indicated an old French airstrip in the valley but he couldn't see it from his vantage point. S-2 wanted to know if the North Vietnamese troops were repairing the strip and how much work was going into it, just enough for a helicopter base or for fixed-wing aircraft? Hoyt remembered the S-2 briefing officer shaking his head in resignation: 'Those goddamed dinks will probably be landing Russian migs there before long. The old days when they brought everything from Hanoi on bicycles are gone.'

Hoyt put his glasses on the only landmark clearly visible, the crumbling 30-foot mud and rock tower the French had built in 1950 so their troops could scan the valley for infiltration. A lot of good it had done those Frogs, Hoyt laughed to himself, they still got blown clean away. The Frogs just fucked up, he thought, they just didn't know how to handle this war, couldn't meet the North Vietnamese on their own terms. What we are doing is the answer, move in quick, check it out, move out and then bomb the shit out of them. No mess, no fuss. He concentrated on the map and his plans for the day, aware that he had a tough assignment but one that if he pulled it off was going to make the old man very happy with him. As long as everybody in the platoon pulled together and didn't give him any static. Like the first sergeant, old man Dodge, who never openly challenged him but gave him those looks. Old bastard, been in World War II and in Korea and was only an E-7. Been busted a few times. And that Franklin. Another bad-ass dude to watch. Goddam nigger, talking about wasting a pig. We'll see what my brother has to say when he looks Franklin up someday back in Chicago. See what that black son of a bitch has to say about pigs when one of them is shoving the barrel of a .357 magnum down his throat.

Hoyt stiffened suddenly at the sound of laughter then whirled toward the slope where the platoon lay hidden. What one of those bastards would break his orders for strict silence? By God he was going to land on Sgt. Dodge, he was – Hoyt suddenly felt chilled and his stomach turned. Vietnamese, someone was speaking Vietnamese, Jesus Christ, how could that be? How could they walk up on him like that. He grabbed his map and M-16 and fell back into a clump of bushes as he heard the voices moving toward him from a screen of trees that pointed into the valley on his left. Then he remembered that Franklin was in that screen, Franklin the bad-ass point man was down there, and he would panic and open up and blow the whole mission. Hoyt started to rise and try to get to Franklin but it was too late, he saw figures in gray-green uniforms moving through the grass and Hoyt pushed his face into the dank earth and prayed, God, God, don't let them see me.

In that screen of trees sat Franklin, unhappy at the world and wondering what the fuck he was doing in this fucked up fucking country. Franklin had settled himself comfortably between two logs after he had pushed to the edge of the valley, just where the lieutenant had wanted to go, and he had settled back to wait while Hoyty-toity the lieutenant had gone on his own to check the valley. Playing the hero role, man, thought Franklin, and he considered opening his pack to dig out a capsule and fix himself a duster. He needed it, he argued with himself, it had been a bad morning, hot as hell and all those thorn bushes down here close to this valley. Franklin knew the lieutenant would shit if he caught him smoking and it probably wasn't too smart because a gook might smell it but that was tough. I need it, man, and I deserve it. What I don't deserve, man, is being put on point day after day. That mothafucking loo-tenant is trying to have me killed. It's that simple, but it ain't going to work. I'm going to survive just to keep harrassing his ass, man. He pulled the pack around between his knees and started to open it when a column of red ants, each an inch long, marched purposefully across the top of the pack toward his arm. He tried to brush them away but scores more coming from the log quickly filled the ranks. He pushed at them with a twig but they counter-attacked and grabbed the stick with vicious mandibles then climbed up it toward his hand. 'Goddam,' he whispered and started to change his location when he heard the quick laughter. He swiveled his little eyes up to see a young North Vietnamese soldier move soundlessly past the screen of leaves less than ten feet in front of him. He froze, terrified, as another appeared and spoke sharply to the young soldier who promptly stifled his giggles. So frightened was Franklin at the sudden appearance of the enemy that at first he didn't feel the ants digging into his flesh. He kept his eyes locked on the enemy troops gliding before him, man after man passing so close he could see every detail of their dress, their green pith helmets, their gray bandoliers of ammunition strapped high across their chests, and the wooden-handled Chinese grenades that dangled from their belts.

As the column continued past him Franklin gradually became aware of excruciating pain on his hand. He shifted his eyes back to the ants which had located a partially healed jungle sore. The carniverous insects had ripped away the scab and like beasts gathered around a feed trough, they used powerful pincers to pull his flesh from the sore. It felt like someone plunging hot needles into his hand and he wanted to crush them but the slightest movement would attract enemy eyes. The North Vietnamese continued to slip past his hiding place, so close he could smell the oil on their AK-47s.

He turned his eyes from the Vietnamese back to the ants in time to see a second exploration party find another sore and begin ripping off the scab. Fuck me, Franklin thought, his teeth grinding in pain and sweat streaming down his face, a squad of North Vietnamese beside me and a whole fucking *division* of ants eating me alive. He closed his eyes as another column of ants marched briskly up his arm, beneath his sleeve, and across his chest to his neck. He winced as the ants attacked and opened a shaving cut below his ear.

The last North Vietnamese passed and Franklin started to rise when something made him freeze again. A young soldier, limping and dragging his rifle, went by the screen of leaves. The youth, casting his eyes vacantly about, looked directly at Franklin who instantly forgot the ants and brought his finger around the trigger. But the boy never broke step and his eyes drifted ahead again, unseeing. Jesus, Franklin thought, always a straggler, and he waited an agonizing minute more before he rose and slapped at the ants which now ringed his body, drinking his sweat and attacking new sores. He ripped off his shirt and brushed frantically at them as Hoyt appeared behind him.

Hoyt's voice hissed at him in seething anger. 'What are you doing now, a goddam jungle dance? Can't you do anything right? Stop jumping around,' Hoyt snapped and looked at him in disgust. 'I don't know how they missed seeing your big ass in there. You were just lucky. You better shape your black ass up or you're not going to make it through this patrol. Now get back to your squad.' He swirled and left.

Franklin whipped his shirt off to finish beating the red ants out of it and then sat down on the log again. He made no move to hurry back to the squad but instead reached into a side pocket on his pack and pulled a capsule of heroin from inside a C-ration roll of toilet paper. Quickly he dug the tobacco out of a cigarette, tipped in the powder and twisted the end. He lit it and inhaled deeply, then pulled hard on it again and felt the warm rivers of relaxation and pleasure begin circulating inside him, washing away his fears. He slowly finished the smoke then pulled his shirt on and stood up.

'I'll make it all the way, Hoyt. The question is, will you?' he said softly and started through the trees toward his squad.

CHAPTER FOUR

BILLY MORAN'S replacement arrived the following day from Saigon aboard the supply shuttle and Sturm, watching him unpack his gear, couldn't help but be amazed at the military's cold efficiency. One down and another one pops up, like ducks in the shooting gallery. Bang; down; pop; up. Another stoic duck waits for the hit. I wonder who my replacement is, Sturm thought morbidly and lit a roach to help dispel his growing gloom while he watched Riley help the new man store his gear.

The replacement was named Sammy Raab, a squarely built New York Jew with a strong accent, hair so thick over his body it was almost like fur and a look of city-wise cynicism in his eyes. Raab was listening to Dooley spinning one of his yarns about how bad it could be up here in the north, not like the easy life you had as crew chief down in Saigon, Sammy baby.

'Like, I'll never forget that night we had to go up to Alpha Four, that's a little outpost right on—'

'Yeah, I know where it is,' Raab said as he stuffed clothes into his locker.

'—On the DMZ, when that bunker with nine grunts in it took a direct hit by a 122 millimeter rocket. You wouldn't have believed how bad it was, Sam. They were digging out people and throwing them in the chopper, not knowing if anyone was dead or alive, and some were so badly tore up that—'

'Yeah, I've seen it. I worked the Delta for the past three

months. Ever see what happens when an RPG hits a tank? Makes a real mess of the people inside. We had three of them one afternoon.' Raab's matter of fact tone cut Dooley short and the red Tomato, momentarily silenced, rose to mix himself another drink.

'Just a pre-luncheon cocktail,' he announced heartily and Sturm knew Dooley was getting sensitive to the cracks about being a heavy juicer.

Riley flopped back on his bunk. 'I almost wish something would happen, really bust this place apart. All this waiting around is bad. What happened to the war, man? If they ain't going to get it on, let's go home. Nothing else to do but have a little China White, a little scag to keep my system functioning.' He started to reach for the makings and then stopped with a look at Sturm.

'I'm not going to have one, Jake-baby, just to show you I ain't hooked and that I don't need it. I'll wait until after lunch, because I know you been worrying about me, thinking I'm going in deep. Well I ain't,' and he pretended to go to sleep.

Sturm said nothing as he worked on the last of the stick of grass that a friend had given him, the friend solemnly informing him that it was Cambodian grass, dynamite. He had just taken a deep, deep drag and was holding the smoke in his lungs for max effect when the screen door snapped open and the massive frame of First Sergeant Leroy Thomas blocked all outside light. Alexander before Diogenes.

The first sergeant silently surveyed the pile of beer cans, orange sodas, flak vests, loose ammunition and magazines that littered the floor. He looked around at the array of Playboy pinups that covered the walls and his emotionless eyes fell on one centerfold showing a nubile young lady fresh from the shower, beads of water glistening on her pink and rounded breasts. He leaned forward to read what Dooley had scribbled underneath: '200 days to go. I think I'm falling in love with my hand.'

His old sergeant eyes swung back to the disarray before him and to the dustoff crews silently waiting for the storm to erupt.

'Jesus H. Christ,' he finally bellowed. 'This place looks like a shithouse that took a direct mortar hit. Don't you slobs have no hootch maids?'

Thomas looked around the room and his eyes settled on Sturm who remained prone on his cot. Sturm had hastily stuffed his roach out the hole in the tin wall when Thomas had surprised them but he still held the smoke in his lungs, afraid to release anymore of the pungent odor into the room. His head was swimming now as the super grass began surging through his lung membranes and into the bloodstream. He was beginning to turn blue and knew he was headed for a record high. The only problem was, Thomas wanted an answer.

'Well? Don't you have hootch maids to clean this place up? Sturm?' Thomas stared at the medic.

Sturm opened his mouth and tried to speak without breathing: 'Yes, sergeant.' His voice came out high and squeaky. Riley began to giggle and Sturm suddenly turned to press his mouth against the hole in the wall. He exhaled sharply, sounding like a teakettle coming to boil.

As he gasped for air, a surprised voice outside said, 'Say, it looks like this hootch is on fire.' Major Schoen abruptly appeared behind Thomas' shoulder and pushed partially inside. 'What's going on, Sgt. Thomas? Is there a fire?' He started to move past the first sergeant but halted in face of the havoc in the hut. No one moved except Raab who popped to attention as Schoen entered. Everyone looked curiously at Raab and he slouched down again with a frown. 'We used to salute Majors,' he muttered.

'Everything is under control, sir,' Thomas said. If nothing else, Thomas looked after his men.

The chief surgeon adjusted his glasses. 'Well, I mean, there was the smoke, from a hole right over there.' He pointed at Sturm.

'Yes sir.' Thomas said nothing more and Schoen left with a question that was not answered: 'Are those people *living* in there?'

'Now listen up,' Thomas said through clenched teeth when the major departed. 'I want this pig pen cleaned up. Now!' He kicked a beer can. 'Get this shit out of here and when that's done, Sturm, you go see Chaplain Montano. He wants you to go on a medcap with him this morning. But clean this pigsty up first. I'll be back to check.' He turned to go, then stopped and said heavily: 'One more thing. If I ever catch any of you troops using drugs I'll personally kick your ass from here to Saigon.' 'Me, go on medcap?' Sturm asked. 'Don't we have stand-by?'

'No. Your bird just went down for repairs.' He pointed at Riley. 'You and Raab. Don't go anywhere. You're on stand-by. Dooley, get the key from my office and hose out the morgue and then inventory the caskets.' He stomped out the door.

They began picking up the magazines, cans and C-ration wads of toilet paper while Raab swept industriously, working the broom around behind Riley's locker.

'Say, my man, you don't sweep behind *there*. That's where my *joy* lies, dig?' Riley looked at Raab. 'You dig?' Raab shook his head. 'Behind my locker is my stash of scag, man, smack. Don't want it *disturbed*.'

A look of distaste came over Raab's jowly face. 'I don't want to get near it. You can't imagine how bad heroin really is,' he said. 'I saw some guys at Bellevue come in dead from overdoses.'

'Well, we don't shoot up over here. We just smoke it, man, because it's so pure. No one is going to OD. Do you roger that?'

Raab shook his head. 'Smoking is just as bad.'

Riley laughed sardonically. 'Right, smoking is bad for my health. I keep telling myself that when the dinks are shooting at me.'

The door screaked open again. It was Chaplain Teofilo Montano, wearing a helmet that seemed too large, a bandolier of clips across his chest and a M-16 in his right hand. 'Jake,' he said, 'are you ready?'

'Yes sir. Do we need weapons and all that gear? Where is this medcap?'

'At Dong Ha.'

'That's only ten miles.'

'You never know what's out there. There are still those reports of new offensive, no? Bring your gear. Mr. Kowalski is in the jeep with Father Ngai, out in front.'

'Kowalski's going too?' Sturm was surprised.

'He says he knows the district chief. Let's go.'

Dooley spoke to Sturm as he started to leave: 'Try and keep King Kong from greasing any slopes on the way. Not good for our image.'

Sturm sat in the back with Father Ngai, a tiny man in black robes who Chaplain Montano had ferreted out of Quang Tri. Montano always took Father Ngai along when he went to visit Vietnamese. 'It's good relations' he explained to Sturm. 'It shows the people Americans and Vietnamese can work together.'

Kowalski said nothing but rode shotgun with his M-79 cradled in his lap. He practiced aiming a few times at Vietnamese traveling the edge of the highway on Lambretta motorbikes until Father Ngai made soft murmurings of protest.

They drove in silence through the hot, sunbaked land

until they reached the north side of Dong Ha, a bleak village where sand from the nearby South China Sea blew through the streets. Efforts by a few of the refugees to start a rice field had failed and the earth now lay in abandoned squares, slowly filling with sand.

They were met at the barbed wire gate to the compound by the district chief, a rotund man with bright, merry eyes, shining hair and one of those faces that always looks freshly scrubbed. He wore tailored fatigues and his name was Colonel Cuu. He shook hands warmly with Kowalski. 'Long time, long time I no see you, Kowalski.' He laughed heartily and led them to a tent where a group of elders greeted politely and offered hot tea. The camp consisted of old men, women of all ages and scores of children. The only young men in the camp seemed to be missing parts of their bodies or walked on crutches.

The women saw Sturm's medical pack and immediately crowded around, thrusting forward children with infected sores and leaking eyes. 'Bac si, bac si, you gib, you gib.' They always called him doctor.

Sturm finished his tea and left the others still sitting and talking. If it was a medcap, he might as well get on with it. He set himself up on the shady side of a tin shack, his back to the wall as the stoic mothers and the wailing old men crowded around him, eyes full of trust. The Vietnamese considered medics who went into the villages and refugee camps to treat the sores and eye infections as one of the few people in Vietnam who came to give, not to take something.

The crowd pressed closer as he unpacked his kit. To the old men who reached at him with claw-like hands he gave aspirin, nothing more. Most were hypochondriacs. On the children he used alcohol to clean the sores that were packed with grime and infected. The need for cleanliness seemed an unknown concept. He quartered bars of soap with his knife so the women couldn't sell the whole bar and pressed pieces into the palms of mothers. 'Wash that filthy goddam child and it will stay healthy,' he yelled. The women nodded without comprehension and bared their blackened teeth in fearsome smiles. He ran out of supplies in twenty minutes and, after deciding against lighting up, he went looking for the others.

He found them on the far side of the compound. They were part of a large crowd of refugees that stood in a circle around a four-foot square steel cage made from portable landing strips. As Sturm eased through the crowd he could see a man inside and the sunlight made bright circles where it fell through the cage onto his crouched body. The cage was so small the man could neither stand nor lie down. An aide to the district chief smiled at Sturm and pointed to the prisoner. 'Viet Cong. He stay there three days now. We question him today.' He laughed.

Sturm moved to where Kowalski and Montano were talking with the district chief. Father Ngai stood with a group of elders, apart from the Americans.

'Are we leaving soon?' Sturm asked. 'I've finished medcap. No more pills.'

Kowalski looked at him. 'What's the hurry? I think we are going to see an interrogation. You wouldn't want to miss that, would you?' He turned back to the district chief. 'Colonel Cuu is very good at this, as I remember, right?'

Cuu laughed and spoke rapidly to an aide who unlocked the cage door and jerked the prisoner out. The man's hands and feet were swollen and discolored below the twine that bound him. He appeared to be in his forties, his face dark and lined. Unable to stand after three days in the cage, he rolled onto the hot, packed dirt. The aide grabbed the man's hair and roughly pulled him into a squatting position. The prisoner uttered no sound but looked around at the crowd, his eyes wide with fear.

Cuu stood before him, legs spread, and spoke in tones that

rose and fell in sharp cadence. The priest kept his eyes on Cuu, nodding and replying in low, submissive tones.

Cuu turned and smiled. 'He say no VC. Just farmer. Say he lost papers. All say same.' He spoke to one of the villagers who returned in a minute with a brown GI sock filled with sand and tied in a knot at the top. Cuu hefted it, slapped it experimentally against his leg a few times and smiled in satisfaction.

'The old sock trick,' Kowalski grinned.

Cuu began circling the prisoner, strutting like a cock around a hen and speaking to the villagers. The aide translated to Kowalski: 'Col. Cuu, he say prisoner VC. VC try to kill Vietnam people. But my government will protect village. Kill all VC. Col. Cuu, he make example of this prisoner. Col. Cuu say everybody must watch.'

Cuu stood behind the prisoner who had given up trying to turn his head to follow the circling threat. The prisoner now squatted quietly, head bowed and awaited the inevitable. Cuu swung with a viciousness that brought a murmur from the crowd. The sand-filled sock struck the man directly over the kidneys with a thud that made Sturm think sickeningly of the time he had dropped a ripe watermelon on the kitchen floor.

The prisoner pitched forward onto his face and Cuu began methodically beating the man. The district chief's breath came in little gasps that bounced off the hot dirt and into the silent crowd. Dark stains of perspiration appeared along Cuu's starched collar, down his back and under his arms as he hammered on the prisoner's back.

Sturm wrenched his eyes from the beating and looked around the hot little square ringed with expressionless Vietnamese refugees, many wearing black pajamas. Who isn't a VC in this country, he thought. He leaned over Montano who kept his eyes fixed on the methodical beating.

'What the hell is going on here, Father?'

'The man is a Viet Cong. They are trying to get some information from him about that offensive that is rumored.' Montano spoke in a whisper for there was no sound except the labored breathing of Col. Cuu, the sickening whack of the sock and somewhere a piece of tin siding on one of the shacks banged in the breeze.

'Yeah, I understand, but what are we doing here? What have we got to do with this?'

'Nothing, of course, it is just something that happened. I can't very well tell Col. Cuu how to run his affairs,' the priest replied with an edge in his voice.

Sturm looked around and sâw that Father Ngai had quietly disappeared with several of the village elders. He turned back to Montano.

'We ought to get out of here, otherwise it looks like we're part of this mess.'

'Not now, Jake. The Vietnamese would take it as an insult if we left now. It will not be long.'

The beating continued, with Cuu's breathing coming in heavy gasps and the prisoner moaning with pain deep inside him. Sturm felt drained and powerless to intervene. Vietnam for the Vietnamese, they say, and the slopes can have it. He looked at the prisoner whose back was grotesquely swollen. It was rapidly turning from red to purple as broken capillaries leaked blood beneath the skin. The tender surface of the man's lower back was split in two places. Sturm knew the man would pass blood for a month – if he lived.

Sturm turned abruptly to the priest again. 'Did you know this was going to happen before we came?'

Montano did not answer immediately but kept watching the rhythmical fall of the sand-filled sock. 'Well, we heard there was a prisoner. That's all.' He turned his dark eyes on Sturm. 'I certainly did not expect to see this, I can assure you. I am as repelled as you are, but remember, there is much we do not understand about their ways.' He kept his voice in a whisper and was about to explain more when Cuu stopped.

'This man very tough,' the Vietnamese laughed. Sweat streamed down his face and darkened the front of his crisp fatigues. He looked at Kowalski and held out the sock. 'You try. Like in Pleiku last year. We catch beaucoup VC.' He laughed again.

Sturm said loudly from where he stood towering between the diminutive priest and an even shorter Vietnamese refugee woman, 'Maybe he's telling the truth. Maybe he's not even a VC. Did you ever think that might be possible?'

Kowalski stepped between Sturm and the colonel and put a thick finger on Sturm's chest. 'Colonel Cuu has been doing this a long time. He has experience in these matters.' Kowalski tapped Sturm's chest for emphasis. 'Something you don't have, so cool it.'

The colonel wiped his face with a towel an aide hurriedly brought to him and spoke to Sturm with a merry smile. 'You young man. I fight VC, fight North Vietnam long, long time. I know VC. Mr. Kowalski, he know. We question beaucoup prisoners before.' He held out the sock again to the pilot.

'I've got a quicker way,' Kowalski said and stepped into the circle of watching Vietnamese. He stopped behind the prisoner, unsheathed his survival knife and grasped one of the man's swollen fingers.

'Alright, Colonel, ask your questions.' There was a stir in the crowd at this unexpected participation.

Cuu sipped at a glass of tea another aide had brought him and stood before the prisoner. He asked a question in rapid Vietnamese but the prisoner only moaned and rolled his head back and forth on the packed earth. Cuu looked at Kowalski and shrugged. The pilot jammed the point of his knife deep beneath the man's fingernail. The prisoner's head snapped back and a strangled cry tore from his throat.

Cuu took another sip then asked another question but the prisoner gave no sign of hearing. He rolled his sweat drenched face back and forth and the dirt stuck wherever his skin touched the earth. Again Kowalski jammed the knife between the man's nail and blood dripped steadily through his fingers.

Sturm went white. He started to turn away then angrily stepped forward toward Kowalski. He was into the square before he knew what was happening and he could feel a terrible rage filling him. He was only vaguely aware of the priest clutching for his arm as he moved forward in long strides, and he only sensed the collective intake of breath from the Vietnamese who watched, and he saw Col. Cuu's face turn in surprise, his tea spilling, and then he was beside the crouched pilot and pulling him roughly away from the prisoner.

'Goddamit, we're not here to take part in any goddam torture. Leave the man alone,' he shouted.

His surprise move tumbled the kneeling pilot to the ground but Kowalski sprang to his feet in a second, the knife clenched before him. Kowalski jumped forward and grabbed Sturm's flight suit with one powerful hand while the other held the knife ready to thrust. The pilot's voice came fast and brittle with suppressed fury.

'Now you *listen*, buddy boy. Don't ever put your goddam hands on me again. Don't ever tell me what to do. You're a goddam grunt and I'm an officer and I'll have you before a court martial so fast your head will spin. If I don't cut you first. Now get your ass out of here if you can't take it.' He waved the knife toward the still moaning prisoner: 'This is what Vietnam is all about and you better learn it.'

Sturm ripped the pilot's hand from his suit front and shouted back, 'The fuck it is. It's because of jerks like you that go around killing or torturing anybody—' He felt Montano pulling on his arm, pulling him back from Kowalski but he yelled as he was propelled backward, '—that we are going to lose this war.'

Sturm whirled on the priest who still held him. 'And I'm going to report this when we get back, captain,' he snapped with emphasis on the priest's rank. 'We're both going to report it.'

'Jake, Jake, get ahold of yourself. Stay calm and let us talk about it.'

'You're fucking right I'm going to talk,' Sturm shouted and started to push through the crowd but Montano held his arm.

'Just a minute, Jacob. Look.' He held onto the medic with one hand while they both looked at the prisoner who was now sobbing out words, and spittle ran from his mouth and stained the earth dark.

Cuu looked up with a cheerful smile from where he squatted beside the prisoner. 'You see. He talk now. He say he hear offensive coming. But he not know when. You see? I know he VC.' His laugh was rich with satisfaction.

'Bullshit!' Sturm shouted at the colonel whose face immediately went blank, his emotions turned off. 'The man is just talking, saying anything to keep that fucking Kowalski from ripping his fingers apart.'

The pilot sprang toward him again and his blue eyes were iced over as he shoved Sturm back into the crowd of silent villagers. 'I told you to shut your fucking mouth and I mean it. Now get out of here before you get hurt.' He pushed Sturm back and Sturm started to come back at him when Montano stepped brusquely between them.

'Enough! Enough, both of you.' He spoke sharply, with the authority of the senior officer. 'Sturm. You get back to the jeep. Mr. Kowalski, I suggest you say your goodbyes to Col. Cuu. We are leaving immediately. And I mean now.'

He walked away from the crowd and pushed Sturm ahead of him. The villagers fell back on each side and many were smiling and nodding, delighted at the emotional display by the foreigners.

'Listen, Jacob, I know you are shocked. So am I. It is a terrible thing to see. But I must insist you keep control of yourself. Let us settle our differences like gentlemen, and I mean gentlemen.'

'Gentle? What's gentle about this? This matter just can't end here, Father, it's got to be reported. Kowalski took direct part in a torture and he's got to be stopped. You saw what happened the other day when he greased those Yards. Now this. What's next?' Sturm stared with hostile eyes down at the placid priest.

'I agree that Mr. Kowalski became carried away. But before you go off half cocked, remember that Mr. Kowalski has seen much more than you or I have. This is his third tour, and he has learned from great experience how to stay ahead of the Communists in this war. And you don't keep ahead of the enemy by treating them with kid gloves.' He raised a hand to cut off Sturm's angry attempt to interrupt.

'That's just part of it. Now you must also admit that the prisoner did admit to knowing of the planned offensive. So a breakthrough was achieved.'

'You mean the means justify the ends, right?' Sturm asked, his anger now replaced by sarcasm.

'Yes, sometimes it is necessary.' Montano hurried on, now more anxious to placate Sturm. 'But I do not condone it, and I assure you I will speak to Mr. Kowalski about this. It will not recur. And if necessary, I will take it to higher authorities. But I suggest that you let me handle it, alright?'

'No sir. I don't agree. I saw it, I should report it along with you.' Sturm was turning adamant but Montano eyed him cooly.

'We must forgive a man his trespasses, as we forgive our own. Right? Let us settle this equally,' he said.

Sturm looked up and saw Kowalski walking toward them

with Col. Cuu. 'No,' Sturm said. 'I think it ought to be reported.'

Montano looked at him, his black eyes fathomless and now without expression. 'Your report may have to stand by itself. Don't be too hasty.'

'What the hell does that mean?' Sturm asked. 'Aren't you going to report it too?'

'It only means that I will not act rashly. I am a priest who is not willing to condemn a man for one act. That is all.'

Sturm looked at him then spun away toward the jeep.

Col. Cuu was laughing jovially again and he told Sturm that he had much to learn about Vietnam and one year was too short. Kowalski came up to where Sturm sat in the back of the jeep and clapped him on the shoulder.

'No hard feelings, okay, buddy?' Kowalski's eyes were wary. 'It's not a great war, but it's the only war we got, don't knock it. Right?'

Sturm looked at him in silence and Kowalski climbed in the front seat with his M-79 ready.

Montano climbed in and started the jeep and then looked around for Father Ngai. They saw him standing by one of the tin-sided shacks talking with several of the elders and Montano yelled at him.

'Ready to go home, Father Ngai?'

The Vietnamese priest looked across the sun-baked earth at them and silently shook his head. 'You go. I stay.'

Montano gunned the engine. 'We'd like you to come with us, Father,' Montano shouted.

'Please, I go later,' he said and his voice could barely be heard over the engine.

'Okay, see you later,' Montano said and they drove out of the fenced compound with cheerful waves from Col. Cuu and his aides while the elders and Father Ngai watched in silence.

'I guess that interrogation bothered Father Ngai,' Montano said.

'Yeah. He probably hasn't seen much of real war,' Kowalski said.

Sturm, in the back of the open jeep, pulled a Park Lanes from his pocket and smoked in silence during the ride back to the 21st Evac.

CHAPTER FIVE

Richard Hoyt tapped thoughtfully on the plastic covered map that lay between his crossed legs and peered through a narrow opening in the trees at what appeared to be a recently prepared gun emplacement across the valley. But the diggings puzzled Hoyt for they seemed much more elaborate than anything needed for a Soviet-made 37mm gun, and there appeared also to be large storage bunkers farther back in the trees. The prospect that it was the beginning of a missile site bothered him. Was it or wasn't it? And why couldn't he discern any activity down there? That bothered him even more. Why would the North Vietnamese leave something half finished? And it wasn't one of the old gun sites that dotted the valley. In trying to puzzle out the situation he had kept observers on the rocky viewpoint all day in hopes of spotting some activity. There had been nothing. Now he watched the sun slide behind the peaks on the west side of the valley and he felt a little chill as evening shadow engulfed him. The third day was ending and the enemy still gave no indication it knew of his presence. That must have been only an advance patrol we saw yesterday, Hoyt thought, and the main force is not here yet. And no one saw us, so we still have time to finish this recon before the regiment arrives. In and out. I'm going to pull this off, he thought happily and he let his mind dwell on the image of the old man pinning captain bars on him, the youngest captain in the division. He turned and motioned to Sgt. Jackson who sat with the third squad some ten meters behind him.

As Jackson hunkered beside him, Hoyt handed him the binoculars and told him to take another look. 'You got it all straight? You got your five men ready?' Jackson nodded as he studied the valley floor in the fading light. 'It will take you fifteen minutes to get to the valley floor and it will be nearly dark then. Go straight across the old airstrip there, past that tower and right over to whatever the hell the dinks are preparing.'

Jackson nodded and kept his eyes to the binoculars. Hoyt continued: 'You'll have 15 minutes to look around before it's totally dark. It'll be dark enough that the dinks can't see you – if they're even around—' and Hoyt sounded contemptuous of that prospect, 'but you can tell what's being prepared. Case the place then come straight back across. A breeze. It's only 200 meters across the valley. You roger?'

Jackson lowered the glasses. 'Okay, LT, but you sure you don't want to wait until we sweep around that side of the valley?'

Hoyt responded impatiently: 'We may not have to go around the valley, sergeant, we may just cross back and forth like this when we spot something. Now let's go.'

Jackson shrugged and moved back to his squad. 'Let's get it on,' he said heavily.

Franklin sat with Hotdog Simpson and watched Sgt. Jackson and the others cross two bandoliers of ammunition on their chests and check their weapons once more.

'Sure wish I could go with you, Hotdog,' Franklin laughed.

'Sure you do, you motha,' Simpson replied dryly.

'Yeah, man, I always wanted to see that valley close up.'

'You could volunteer to take my place.'

'No, man, I'm too big, they need little dudes like you down there to get in and out quick. Now listen here, my man,' Franklin added more seriously, 'Hurry back because we'll smoke one of your dusters and you can tell me all about your big adventure.'

Hotdog's eyes widened in mock anger. 'Smoke mine? Shee-it, man, you gonna provide *me* 'cause I doin' all the hard work.'

Franklin lowered his voice and spoke hurriedly because Jackson was impatiently waiting for the five to follow him down. 'Look here, Hotdog. I know you got more scag than me, and I *know* you going to share with me, so hurry back.'

Simpson grabbed his piece by the handle and started away then turned and whispered to Franklin. 'You know how much I trust you? Well, don't bother to look in my pack while I'm gone. I got all it all right here,' and he grinned as he opened his fatigue shirt a little to reveal a bag wrapped in plastic and hung around his neck by a leather thong. He turned and hurried after the disappearing patrol and suddenly it seemed the men had never existed.

Franklin turned away and made his way back to a clump of bamboo where he had his pack. His high from the afternoon smack was gone and now his body felt as if it were melting into the earth. He fumbled in his pack for a vial of heroin and pulled out a cigarette to prepare another one, and finally smoked desperately at it. The rush finally came but slower and weaker and Franklin felt disappointed. He looked around him and saw that several of the men were moving to vantage points by the rocks where they could see part of the valley below and Franklin followed to peer into the gathering darkness. Only by careful scrutiny could he make out vague shapes crossing the valley floor, and then the shapes blurred, for he found he could not maintain his focus. I gotta be careful, he thought, I gotta make it last or I'm not going to make it through this patrol. But he remembered Simpson had plenty and he felt better. If it got too tough, Simpson would share with him. Thus consoled, he whispered toward the valley, 'Simpson, get your ass back here.' That made him laugh but the chuckle died in his throat as a flare suddenly cast its white light over the five soldiers in the valley.

The men froze, tiny figures in the grass with shadows dancing around them as the flare swayed on its parachute overhead. One of the men fell over suddenly and a second later Franklin heard the sharp stutter of an AK-47. Another man went over and then the other three were running, their shadows dancing insanely after them on the grass. The fire intensified from unseen positions in the valley and the men on the hill watched as two figures jumped together into a depression and began firing back. Another flare popped and Franklin saw a geyser of dirt go up next to the two men in the shallow hole, then another, and finally one more right in the hole. Grenades. The dull explosions rolled in delayed sequence up the hillside.

In the wavering light, Franklin could see the last man in the grass crawling toward the old runway. The man seemed wounded and Franklin thought it might be Simpson but he couldn't tell at that distance and the fading light of a flare. The light went out and the darkness was complete. There was no sound from the men on the slope above the valley, just stunned silence, until a voice floated up to them from the night: 'I can't make it.'

Franklin exhaled sharply. 'Son of a bitch,' he breathed, 'that's Simpson.' He moved across the platoon area to Lt. Hoyt's side. 'Hey, sir, that's Simpson down there. I want to be in the recovery party.'

Hoyt didn't answer but sat staring into the darkness. Franklin watched him for a moment then started to scramble past him down the slope. 'I'm going down, sir.'

Hoyt grabbed him and jerked him back. 'You just wait. Get back to your squad.'

'I ain't leaving a buddy down there alone,' Franklin flared. 'Maybe you don't give a damn because he's black. Is that it?'

'The gooks are just waiting for us. Right now they think

it's just another recon party like before. But they're waiting to see if any help comes. If we go charging down there and get caught it's going to blow this whole mission.' Hoyt was speaking to the whole platoon which had now moved closer in the darkness to listen. In the sullen silence that followed, Dodge, the platoon sergeant, spoke up:

'Maybe if just one or two of us went down. One man to see who's alive and who ain't. I'll go, sir.'

Hoyt looked toward Dodge, seeing only his outline in the darkness but clearly sensing the old sergeant's hostility toward any talk of abandoning the men. Hoyt thought for a moment then said with authority: 'I'll go. Keep all the men here. If any of them are alive I'll drag them to safety and then we'll form a recovery party. No movement up here and no goddam cigarettes.' He turned to leave when Dubrow, the medic, said, 'you want my aid bag, sir?'

Hoyt refused it, saying it would only slow him down. As the lieutenant disappeared into the night Franklin whispered, 'I'm going to frag that mothafucker. He wants to just leave them out there.'

Dodge's voice came back sharply: 'The next man I hear talking about fragging is going to have his balls cut off by me personally. Now get out of here. Second squad has first guard tonight. Get that NDP set up.'

The men moved away reluctantly and began putting out the Claymore mines for the night defense perimeter while Franklin kept listening in the dark, waiting for another cry that never came.

Hoyt was back in an hour and called the platoon together. 'They're all dead. I checked everyone. There's nothing we can do now. If we recover them it will blow this recon. I know those men were your friends. Mine, too, but now they're dead. It's past and gone so let's not dwell on it. Let's make the best of it from now on.' He tried to put some heartiness into his voice: 'Let's make this a real success for them. Let's show these gooks what American troops can do.'

There were several snorts in the darkness and someone said, 'yeah, let's win this for mom and apple pie.'

Hoyt's voice turned cold. 'Get back to your positions. Sgt. Dodge, I want a 50 percent guard tonight, and make sure the Claymores are properly placed.'

The men slid away, cursing as they stumbled in the darkness. Franklin stared into the night and thought of Simpson. He had quickly gone through his buddy's pack in hopes of finding some extra capsules of scag but Simpson had not lied, they were all in the pouch around his neck. Unable to sleep, Franklin lay restlessly for nearly an hour, fighting the mosquitoes, until a faint voice floating through the night made him bolt upright. Other men around him were stirring and someone whispered, 'Jesus, holy Jesus.'

The voice came again, faint with desperation, 'Please, medic, please.'

Franklin threw back his poncho and started crawling toward Hoyt's position. 'You fuckhead lieutenant, that's Simpson, he's still alive,' he whispered hoarsely, almost crying. 'Goddam you, Hoyt, you never checked them at . . .'

Something hard, maybe a pistol butt, struck him full in the face and he felt the blood gush hotly from his nose. Hoyt's hissing voice came from the darkness next to him.

'That's a North Vietnamese imitating our men, just trying to lure us out, to test us. Nobody make a sound. Our men are dead, that's it. I personally checked them. Now get back to your squads, all of you. And Franklin, I'll court martial your ass if you talk like that again.' Hoyt's voice wavered in its fury.

The men listened in the dark, whispering to each other, but the voice did not come again.

At dawn the men gathered in small knots and peered through the breaks in the foliage at the valley. No one spoke as they looked first at the valley, then at Hoyt, and then back to the valley. Several were pointing and when Franklin climbed to where he could see he looked first at the bodies, two in the open, and still two in the hole where the grenades had killed them. But the fifth body was now just below the platoon. They could see the crushed grass where he had crawled, the line his body left in the soft dirt of the old airstrip, then into the grass again below the rocky outcropping. The body had one leg under it, as if ready to push once more, but it didn't move.

Hoyt who had joined the men looked at the body and said angrily, 'Those goddam slopes, those goddam people dragged him over there just to make it look like he was wounded. Just to test us, trying to draw us out.'

Sgt. Dodge, standing next to him, spit and turned away without a word. 'Alright,' he said, 'saddle up. Second squad on point again.'

Franklin, his nose puffed from the blow, prepared a scag cigarette openly as he walked to the point position. 'Someone is gonna get fragged,' he said aloud and the men around him nodded.

CHAPTER SIX

THE sun was gone and the sky was turning metallic when Sturm stepped out of the chopper and stood for a moment looking at the dully gleaming interior that he had so fastidiously cleaned for the past two hours. He glanced again at the aid packs and he knew that every one was complete. The oxygen bottle was locked in place and newly filled. He had stayed to work alone despite protestations from the others who were anxious to go into the ville. Sturm slid the door hard and felt the catch lock home. He turned and made his way to the hootch, still feeling uneasy. It's just too quiet, he thought and then laughed at himself. If it was hot you would be bitching all the time and wishing it would cool off. You've been griping to yourself for weeks now about how every mission was a garbage run, just picking up the bodies and dumping them off. Now it's quiet for awhile and you're nervous. It's just because I'm short, he told himself and banged into the hootch. It was empty but there was a note on his bed from Dooley saying they had gone on the ville and would meet him in the Forty Akers Club.

Feeling miffed that they hadn't waited for him Sturm swung along the boardwalk to the small enlisted men's club behind the hospital and picked up a pack of cigarettes. The music was up loud and the three tables were filled with off duty orderlies drinking beer. The bar was crowded too and Sturm stood at the end to signal the Vietnamese girl who served the beers for a cold one. His waving also attracted the attention of Johnston, the thin orderly who was mostly a runner for the First Sergeant. Johnston came up to him, adjusted his wire-rimmed glasses and spoke.

'You dustoff dudes might be pretty busy before long.' He said it in a slightly superior way, like one kid taunting another.

Sturm asked why and Johnston looked around before moving closer, a man with a secret. 'I've got a buddy in Division S-3. He told me Fifth Mech will pull back from the DMZ soon and they expect the North Vietnamese to hit them, with rockets and everything.'

Johnston smiled and stepped back to see how Sturm reacted to the secret. Sturm shrugged and Johnston played his ace.

'Something more. There's a platoon trying to recon the Dak Son valley inside Laos, where the trail comes through. Two squads trying to do that last month were wiped out. My buddy said five men have already been killed on this sweep but they're not bringing out the bodies yet. It's supposed to be a secret, but my buddy figures Hanoi knew of the recon before it even began. He thinks they will all get blown away.'

'What can I tell you, Johnston,' Sturm said and finished his beer quickly while ignoring the look of disappointment on Johnston's face because Sturm wouldn't gossip with him about it. Sturm wondered idly if Franklin was on that recon. He had said something about a patrol.

He started away from the bar and Johnston said loudly after him, 'You ought to be more interested, Sturm, because you are going to have to go out and pick up the pieces.'

Outside there was little night traffic along the road and he waited twenty minutes by the military police shack at the gate before he flagged a ride with a jeep load of 1st Cav pilots. They plied him with questions during the ride into Quang Tri about how they could get in tight with the nurses.

'Man, I haven't had a round-eye in so long I wouldn't know what to do with it,' one of them shouted.

'You never knew what to do with them anyway,' countered another. There talk shifted back again to the day's missions and how well they had flown. One of them, a Cobra pilot by his talk, described how he and his partner had caught a four man North Vietnamese patrol in the open near the Ben Hai River.

'They tried to run, but there's no place to hide, man, just sand dunes where they were. We just wheeled about and let go with everything on board, rockets, fleshettes and the .50 never stopped. Those dinks just disappeared, man,' and everyone laughed.

As they talked in the dark jeep Sturm's mind drifted back to images of the prisoner with his face in the sand and the saliva dribbling uncontrollably into the sand. It was good that Montano was going to look into that. Then there was Sandy's face with the bright smile and he was ripping her blouse open and she just kept smiling; and then the arm again, floating out of the explosion like it was the arm of a puppet that had come loose and some invisible string was pulling it out of sight. He tried to think of Mai but found he could not see her face right.

'Where you want off, Buddy?' a voice said.

Sturm looked out the flaps of the jeep and saw the club. 'Right here. You going in here too?' They piled out and crossed the dimly lit street toward the two-story concrete building that houses a doctor's office on the ground floor, with signs saying he specialized in treating VD, and the Forty Akers on the top floor. The group made its way past the two wrinkled crones who sat wrapping betel nut near the entrance. The sidewalk around them was splotched with their red spit and the area looked like a terrible massacre had recently occurred.

The Cav pilots burst into the half-filled club with war

whoops that brought a dozen girls to their feet at the prospect of business. Sturm followed them in while the girls hastily put away their cards and chewing gum as they moved forward to meet the new arrivals. Sturm made his way toward the back where he found Dooley and Riley in a corner booth that had a red lamp loosely fixed to the wall. Both had girls with them and one, named Susie, hit Sturm on the arm as he sat down. 'Hey, Mai she look for you. Why you no come sooner? You numbah teeeen.' She drew out the word ten to make it sound even more shameful.

'Where is she?'

'She go. Say cannot wait all night for you.' Susie laughed and Sturm looked around. Across the room he saw Sgt. Akers, in a flowered Hawaiian shirt, making sure the Cav troops were quickly given their orders. He finally picked out Mai, sitting with a 1st Cav pilot who had his black Cavalry-style hat with crossed sabers pushed back and was laughing with Mai.

When Mai eventually turned to case the room she saw Sturm watching her, and with a brief word to the Cav pilot and a gesture toward her empty glass, she crossed toward Sturm's table.

Sturm watched her move slowly, languidly toward him, her lace-fringed black satin pantaloons swirling from beneath the billowing panels of her orange and black ao-dai. She always wore traditional dress. His eyes lifted past the narrow waist, across her satin-sheathed breasts, past the mandarin collar to her delicately boned face. She stopped and leaned across the table toward him, her long black hair falling forward to frame her large eyes. She smiled and spoke: 'Where you go, GI? Sometime I think you fucking numbah ten VC.'

Riley and Dooley laughed while Sturm shook his head in despair. He had never been able to reconcile the gentle beauty of Mai's face with the language that came out her mouth.

'Be ni',' he said, mimicking the Vietnamese inability to put an 's' sound at the end of a word. 'Sit down.'

'No can do, GI I sit with Cav officer. He buy me plenty drink. Not cheap bastard like you.' She sank her long red nails into his arm. 'You wait, I come back soon.'

As she left, Sgt. Akers approached and signaled a waiter to bring a new round of drinks.

'Are these on the house, Sarge?' Sturm asked.

'Do cows fly? Why aren't you guys out picking up bodies, doing your thing?' Akers said.

'Even heroes need to rest,' Dooley said as Akers moved on, not listening.

Riley had said nothing and Sturm looked closely at him, waved his hand before the dull eyes until he saw them move sluggishly to look at him.

'Spaced, aren't you, Riley?' Sturm asked and watched as Riley tried to bring his head back into focus. Sturm turned to Dooley. 'Why didn't you bring the new guy, Raab?'

'He's resting. Says he wants to be ready tomorrow for whatever mission we get.'

Riley, slouched against a girl in the corner of the booth who spoke no known language as far as Sturm or Dooley could discern, ran his finger up and down the red lamp shade. 'Any mission. Rainbow One Two ready. to. go.' The words came out slow and separate.

'Go, go, go. Lift them bodies, tote them dinks,' Dooley said and finished his drink in two swallows.

Riley looked at him and sat up. 'Sturm and me don't go for that *killing* scene. We are *healers*. You the warrior, Dooley, you and Raab are warriors. Crew chiefs, *he*-roes.' He smiled dreamily. 'Me, I'm just a peaceful Irishman. Southern Irish, of course.' He snapped his fingers. 'Black Irish.'

They talked idly for half an hour until Mai returned. She snapped her fingers at Sturm and walked on by. 'You come here, GI' Sturm grinned at the others and rose to follow, waving his arms overhead and gyrating his pelvis as they entered a curtained doorway that led to the back part of the building where Mai and several other girls kept small rooms.

'Lie down, GI,' she said imperiously and pointed to her narrow bed covered with a blanket he had brought her from the hospital.

'I say lie down, GI.' Sturm grinned and flopped on his back. Tonight she was the Dragon Lady. Sometimes she was the sweet school girl, fresh from a morning at the lycée, or sometimes the naive virgin reluctant to let him undress her. Sturm was never sure who the real Mai was, even after more than four months with her.

She pounced on him, sitting on his chest and taking his throat with her slim fingers. 'Where you been, GI?' She never called him by his name unless to mock him: 'Speciali't Stu-rum.'

'Where you go today? Fight beaucoup VC?'

'Yeah, in Laos. Beaucoup North Vietnamese. Your brothers. Mebbe come Quang Tri,' he said.

'When?' She looked at him with wide eyes, uncertain whether to believe or not.

'Soon. Mebbe rocket attacks.'

'Okay. I go Saigon.'

'No, Mai, I protect you. You stay with me.'

'No way, GI Dooley say you all a time watch boom-boom movies. That right?'

He tried to ignore the question but she persisted, her slim fingers at his throat. 'You no like boom-boom with Mai? Just like watch movies? Whatsa matta you ,GI?'

'No, I only was there once' he lied. 'I had to go.' He pulled her down to him, always surprised at how fragile she was in his arms. He kissed her gently and she nuzzled his neck.

'Son of a bitch!' He bolted upright and put his fingers to his neck where she had bit him. Bright blood spotted his fingertips.

'That because you watch boom-boom movie. Now be ni',' she said and pushed him back down. 'How come you never buy me a drink?' She began running her fingers over his fatigue shirt, then opening it and slipping her hand under his T-shirt to rake her nails lightly through the hair on his chest.

'I love you too much, GI,' she said. 'Why you no love me?'

'Mai, I buy you drinks, I bring you presents from PX, I pay for room, I give you money. I love *you* too much. Mai, why you no marry me?' After five minutes with her he always began speaking the way she did. He sometimes imagined himself slipping permanently into her pigeon English and back on the farm at the dinner table saying? 'Pass me fucking numbah one bisquit, mom.'

'I cannot marry, GI,' Mai said softly. She was now the loyal sweetheart, with eyes downcast and delicate mouth pulled down. 'My lover missing. I must wait for him. He very good man, numbah one.'

She kissed him and then suddenly slid her hand deep into his pants. 'Ohhh,' she said and opened her eyes wide. 'You numbah one too, GI.'

Sturm rolled toward her but she sat up abruptly. 'No can do, GI.' She took a comb from the small dresser beside the bed and began running it through her waist-length hair. Black and silky, it was cut squarely across the bottom in the manner of all girls from Hue before they began cutting their hair and selling it. When they first met she had told him she might cut it but he had dissuaded her. 'Okay, you stay with me and I not cut. You butterfly with other girl or go away, I cut it,' she had said.

Now she rose from the bed. 'I go work now.'

'Why? How about a little love for me?' Sturm was distressed. He wasn't getting anything from Sandy and now Mai was going to cut him off.

'My sister sick. Need money. My brother in army. Very

poor. He fight in Laos. I must help him too. And I must send money my mama and papa.' She tapped her foot impatiently; the corporate businesswoman.

'Mai must work. Must send beaucoup money to family. No time lay in bed with GI. You same-same playboy.'

He caught her and pulled her back to the bed and from behind he ran his hand lightly over the silken softness of her breasts.

'You just stay in here. Payday I give you money,' he said.

'No can do. Need money now, GI.' She tried to pull away but he held her firmly.

'Mai, I never know when you are telling the truth. You never told me before you had a brother in the army.'

'True. I no bullshit you, GI. My older brother. Some soldier from Laos now come Quang Tri. Maybe he come too.' She started to pull away again and then stopped and looked at him seriously and he could see the concern in her dark eyes.

'Hey, GI, you can help me?'

'What?' Sturm was cautious.

'My friend, she work in police office, you know, secret police? She say she see my name on report. I think that not good. Why they have my name?'

'They probably have everyone's name,' Sturm said. 'I wouldn't worry much about it.'

'I afraid. Maybe police make trouble for me, because of my papa.'

She had told Sturm before her father had been a professor at the University of Hue and had left under a cloud following the Buddhist uprisings. But he had never really believed it. All the girls had some kind of tale.

'So what can I do?' he asked.

'Maybe you have friend in MP, maybe he can help. Maybe he can ask secret police why they have my name.'

'I don't have any friends in the military police,' Sturm

said. 'And I wouldn't worry about them having your name. They probably have my name too. Wait until something happens before you actually worry about it.'

Her eyes remained clouded and unconvinced but she rose from the bed and prepared to leave. She pulled him gently up.

'I have one drink with you, GI. Then I go with other. Okay, you no mad?' She kissed him in the corner of the mouth and then drew her leg slowly up between his as they stood there. 'You know I only drink with other GI. No make love. Only make love with you. When you not watch boom-boom movie.' She laughed and slipped out the door where she waited for him to follow.

When they returned to the bar Dooley and Riley were gone and Mai went directly toward two troops just coming in the door. She wasn't kidding about hustling some money, Sturm thought as he watched her move away, her black hair glistening above the sensuous swirl of her ao-dai. She was his but she wasn't. She would go but she would return.

He went outside quickly and walked in the warm and crowded streets for several blocks before he caught a ride to the hospital. He felt entirely alone.

Franklin lay back in the deep grass and felt the dry dust fill his nostrils. Goddam, a man can hardly breathe in this jungle. He ran his fingers over the thick stubble that was becoming a beard and turned from cursing the jungle to cursing Hotdog. Goddam you little bastard, going out with all that scag tied around your neck and then getting zapped. You leave me short, man. He dropped his hand, the palm wet from wiping the sweat that beaded on his face, and felt his shirt pocket for the two capsules in there. His last. There were still two days – maybe three – to go and he knew he wasn't going to make it, and it could be bad news. He asked several others who were nodding but they said they were going to run short themselves and fuck you Franklin you ain't getting any from us. But he wanted a duster now, he hadn't had one since noon and that was a light one, just to keep his senses up, and he needed some more now but the platoon was getting up tight about smoking, with Hoyt saying the dinks would smell it and come after them. Goddam Hoyt, he's the one who caused all this, he's the one that got Hotdog and the others greased and he's the reason I'm about out of scag, because it's still tied around Hotdog's neck, rotting out there in the sun. And when Hotdog was with him they kept each other to one cap a day, helping each other to keep it under control, but Hotdog was gone now and the fucking patrol was killing him and every day it was 'Franklin, get your ass out on point,' and he knew that lootenant wanted him dead.

From where he lay, Franklin raised his head but couldn't see anyone over the grass. The platoon rested in a little ravine that ran down to the valley floor. They had just finished checking an old 37mm gun site further up the ravine to see if Charlie was fixing to move in again. They had prowled the circular pit where the gun had been located and crawled along the trench that led to bunkers just below the site but had seen no evidence the enemy had been around for months. The men had talked nervously about the empty and crumbling bunkers with tiny guns slits in the front, called them tombs, and everyone had been glad when Hoyt had led them down the ravine into the meadow for a break. The sun was dipping toward the far peaks when they finished their evening chow of cold C-rations and dug holes in the soft earth with their bayonets to hide all traces before they pushed on. Leave no signs, Hoyt liked to say, and we'll finish this recon like a piece of cake, a breeze. Yeah, Franklin thought, finish it just like the five who crossed the valley. Hoyt didn't like to talk about that and he hadn't ventured onto the valley floor itself again. Instead, he told them they would circle the valley by staying on the wooded lower slopes where they could see but not be seen as they scouted out new gun positions. Still, after five days, no new gun sites and no sign of the enemy. Five days of careful checking had taken them up one side of the valley close to North Vietnamese supply where the trail came down from the pass. Tomorrow they would cross the supply artery and begin working down the far side.

The brown grass parted suddenly next to Franklin who twitched violently. He had heard no one coming. Hoyt's slightly bulging eyes looked at Franklin. 'Second squad takes the point again and guess who's the point man?' Hoyt grinned.

Franklin stared back and finally opened his hands pleadingly, 'I've been on point every goddam day, LT. Why me? I'm sorry I bad-mouthed Chicago cops, alright?'

'No, it isn't alright, Pfc. Franklin. You're the point man until I say different. Move your ass out.'

Franklin didn't stir and his voice turned sour. 'I'm going to report this, I'll go to the IG. You got no right to put me on point every fucking day.'

'I'm the lieutenant. That's all the right I need. Now move Pfc. Franklin, or you'll be court-martialled for insubordination. You dig, asshole?'

Franklin jerked to his feet, swung his pack on his back and pushed away through the grass. 'This ain't over. Lootenant.' He spoke loudly without looking back. Maybe too loudly, he thought as he worked up the slope from the meadow and back into the jungle. The dinks are probably listening right now, just laying out there and listening, laughing and waiting to blow us away. His pace slowed as he studied the forest around him for signs of the enemy, a faint trail or markers on the trees. He paused to look back for the lead men in the squads on his flanks. They were stopped, watching him, waiting for him to move again.

On a small ridge where he stopped again to catch his

breath and wipe the stinging sweat from his eyes, he reached back for a canteen on his pack then froze as a fluttering movement ahead drew his eye. About 30 meters down the slope ahead of him, through a narrow opening in the trees, he saw a figure moving. Two men, maybe more. He dropped to his knees, waved the platoon down and slowly brought his rifle up. He stared and now saw two men wearing loin cloths sitting by the trail and leaning back against the large packs they had been carrying. Another flicker and Franklin noticed a North Vietnamese soldier, his pith helmet on the ground beside him, reach out and offer the two Montagnards cigarettes. They smiled and bobbed their heads while they each took one. The three talked and laughed, oblivious to the unseen presence of Franklin.

Franklin slowly turned to see if the platoon was still waiting then once again eyed the two bearers and their North Vietnamese escort. Experimentally he drew a bead on the half-turned back of the soldier then slid the muzzle to the left and centered on the chest of the first tribesman. Three quick little shots and they would be gone. Franklin lowered the rifle again. Yeah, easy, and there was probably a whole North Vietnamese division just waiting for them to start something. A smile suddenly appeared on Franklin's face. Alright, maybe the bad guys *would* come if he took a shot but it might not be so bad. For one thing it would blow the mission and the old man would jerk them out of here, and send in some choppers and tonight they would be back at division. Three shots, three dead dinks, Hoyt tells division and away we go. Back in Quang Tri and Sturm fixes me up with a nurse. Easy. He brought the rifle up again but his stomach fluttered at the thought of what he was going to do and he had to rest another moment. The shit is going to hit the fan, man, he thought, as he finally tightened his finger on the trigger. The instant before the firing pin snapped forward Franklin saw the second soldier appear. The movement momentarily confused him and he jerked the rifle slightly. He saw the round hit the trail at the second soldier's feet, kicking up a puff of dust, and all four figures turned toward the sound on the ridge but did nothing more, unbelieving that someone could be actually shooting at them. The second soldier finally reacted and swung his AK-47 off his back as Franklin brought up his sight for a clean shot through the man's chest.

At the second shot, with their comrade crumpling in front of them, the other three scrambled desperately from the trail but Franklin, now firing as rapidly as he could pull the trigger, saw one of the Montagnards pitch awkwardly against a tree.

An M-16 opened up on Franklin's left as someone in the first squad began firing into the trees even though he saw nothing. A moment later Hoyt appeared at his side, scrambling on all fours and hissing frantically.

'What the fuck you shooting at, Franklin?' Anger made his voice thin and he jerked Franklin down flat. 'I told you not to shoot at anything, you son of a bitch. Now you've blown it. You've *blown* it!' He looked ready to cry.

Franklin frowned to hide the pleasure he felt and pointed through the forest at the dead North Vietnamese. 'That dude saw me and was taking a bead. I just had to shoot him. Loo-tenant.'

Hoyt looked at the body then yelled to his left where the man in the first squad was still peppering leaves. 'Cut that shit out!' In the silence that followed, Hoyt asked, 'How many were there?'

'I don't know for sure, maybe five or six North Vietnamese and they had a bunch of Yards they was using to carry equipment.' Franklin pointed again to where one of the Montagnards writhed in agony against a tree.

Hoyt turned his face toward Franklin, just inches away, and his eyes bulged with fury. 'I think you're lying, you just opened up on them because you're a fucking fuckhead. I'm going . . .'

There was a snapping sound, like fingers overhead, then leaves fell and there was the crackle of AK-47 fire as a cluster of rounds hammered at their position. The two fell back behind the ridge where Hoyt yelled to Sgt. Dodge to take the platoon back across the meadow and up the ravine to the bunkers at the old gun site. 'And get somebody on point so we don't get fucking ambushed. Where's my RTO? Hicks!' Hoyt was screaming now. Hicks, the pimply-faced radio-telephone operator, scrambled toward Hoyt with the PRC-25 antenna whipping the leaves overhead. The three moved swiftly down the slope, Hoyt explaining to division as he moved that they had been discovered.

By the time they reached the old bunkers, the perimeter was established and several men were running wires from the Claymore mines back into the tiers of bunkers. With Hicks and Franklin in tow, Hoyt scrambled to the circular pit at the top where he could look back down the ravine and at the bunkers just below him where the platoon crawled into and waited.

The first round that came from the silent jungle took off the top of Hicks head as he stood next to Hoyt behind the gun emplacement wall. The single shot was followed by a spatter of fire from both sides of the ravine below the platoon. The men inside fired back at an enemy they could not see.

Hoyt pulled the radio from Hick's body and turned to Franklin who hunkered behind the earthen wall and tried not to look at Hicks.

'Come here, dickhead,' Hoyt said. 'Sit by that radio until I get someone else. Be careful you don't follow Hicks' fate.' Hoyt grinned maliciously then resumed his discussion with division for birds to lift them out. The metallic radio voice finally responded after telling Hoyt, who had code named himself Lone Ranger, to wait one:

'Lone Ranger, Eagle one. How do you hear?'

'Eagle One, I hear you lima charlie. Go.'

'Lone Ranger, Eagle six says negative, repeat negative, lift out tonight. It is too late. Puff the Magic Dragon is on its way and will provide covering fire during the night. Spooky is on tap also. We'll probably have some snakes out there for you too. Copy?'

'Roger, Eagle One. We'll need all the cover we can get. Talk to you later. Lone Ranger out.' He threw the handset to Franklin and crawled into a slit trench that ran from the gun pit down to the tiered bunkers below. 'I'm going to check the line. Stay here and try not to look so stupid. If Eagle One wants me, I'll be right back.' He moved down the trench, hunkering over as a spatter of fire erupted again from the jungle. Franklin edged over to look down the trench and saw Hoyt duck into a bunker then emerge in a few moments and scramble down to the next bunker. Keeping his eyes on the Lieutenant, Franklin slowly pulled a grenade off his belt and turned the smooth steel oval until the release mechanism was tight against his palm. He didn't want to make any mistakes, he wanted this grenade to land right in the lieutenant's pocket. He pulled the pin and watched the lieutenant emerge from another bunker and pause in the trench while he gave some last minute orders to the men inside. 'Hey, lootenant,' Franklin whispered, 'I'm going to give you something to remember me by, a little present from me and Simpson and the others, a little something to show you what we think of you.' He rose slightly on his knees so he could get a good throw. He just wished he could see the lieutenant's face before the shrapnel ripped into his body. Franklin cocked his arm to throw, his decision made, but then lowered it again as Hoyt darted into another bunker. I can wait for you, he breathed, I can wait all day. Now, baby. Hoyt reappeared and began crawling down the trench and Franklin cocked his arm and threw. He wanted the grenade to go high so it would look like it came from the jungle, just in case something went wrong but he forgot and threw it hard and flat, like pitching a rock at some bad dude down the block. Then he knew he threw too hard and the grenade narrowly missed Hoyt's helmet as it skidded ahead of him down the trench. Before Franklin ducked back out of sight he saw the lieutenant freeze at sight of the slithering grenade then scrambled back into the bunker he had just left. The explosion sent a geyser of dirt and dust into the air as Franklin swore to himself and sank back against the earthen wall. A sick feeling rose in his stomach. Missed, I *missed*, goddamit. He fumbled with the radio in an effort to look busy then stiffened as he felt the cold muzzle of an M-16 push against his neck. Hoyt's voice, squeaky with rage, screamed behind him. 'You goddam black son of a bitch, you— You tried to *frag* me. You tried to *kill* me!' Hoyt barely able to control himself, pushed Franklin to the ground with the muzzle of the rifle and the muzzle pushing, painfully into his neck below his ear tried to explain. Franklin, his head on the earth.

'No, sir, not me. You must be crazy, I wouldn't frag you. That grenade came out of the jungle. I saw it and ducked down. Honest.'

Hoyt's face was white and his eyes bulged as he worked his mouth, but no words came out. Finally he wiped the spittle that collected in the corners and choked out an order: 'Get out of here, get back into those bunkers and if you so much as look at me I'll blow your black head right off! Leave that radio and get out of here. Get out!' he screamed.

Franklin eased away and slid down the trench, grinning now and reaching for a capsule in his pocket. Home tomorrow.

CHAPTER SEVEN

FRANKLIN sat at the rear of the bunker, away from the firing slits between the logs, and leaned his back against the cool earth. The bunker made him think of a jail cell. Or a tomb. It must be like this to be buried alive. On three sides of the bunker were big logs chinked with mud, earth underneath, and logs overhead piled high with dirt. Even grass growing on top so you can't see this place from the air. The dinks know how to build them, that's for sure. It's bad down here but it's better than being where that goddam Hoyt can stare at me. That dude thinks it's over, but it ain't. The score still ain't settled. He stirred restlessly and then crawled forward on his hands and knees, past the others who slouched in the gloom of the bunker and waited.

Franklin stopped short of the firing slits and kept his face in the shadow so snipers who had been plinking all morning couldn't take a bead on him.

Outside, where the bright morning sunlight made everything look washed out, like an overexposed photograph, there was no sound, no movement, just long green leaves glittering where they shed the sunlight. It had been a long night of sporadic fire and the blast of Claymore mines. The flickering light of flares constantly dropped over the area to prevent the sapper teams from slipping up to the bunkers and throwing their satchel charges that would blow a bunker out of the ground. Franklin stared at the area in front of him but could see no bodies even though he had seen the North Vietnamese try to come through the perimeter last night. He had thought he had hit several but it was always so hard to tell in the light of flares. There was nothing out there now. The dinks must have dragged their dead and wounded away. They always did so you couldn't tell how hard they had been hit.

Franklin started as Lt. Hoyt abruptly scuttled into the bunker through the small doorway from the connecting trench outside. The lieutenant ignored Franklin as he talked to the other five men.

'No casualties here, right?' Hoyt looked at Sgt. Coggins, the squad leader, who nodded. 'How's your ammo supply?' Hoyt asked.

'We got enough. Y'all gonna get some birds in here today, sir?' Coggins asked as Hoyt turned to leave.

'Yeah, Eagle One says they will be here this morning. He's still trying to round up some more gunships for protective fire. The old man thinks the shit is going to hit the fan when the birds try to take us out.'

'Well, it is kinda odd, I mean hardly any shooting last night. Don't you think they might be just waiting on something, sir?'

Hoyt shrugged. 'No, I think they just don't have the people. I think the gooks only had a small patrol down here when we surprised them – when somebody fucked up,' he added pointedly without looking at Franklin. 'The dinks just didn't want to take us on. If we get out of here before the dinks get reinforcements, we'll have no problem.'

Hoyt was halfway out the door when Coggins drawled another question: 'Oh, sir, any injured or KIA's last night?'

A single shot from the jungle as the lieutenant started to answer sent him scrambling back inside. 'Goddam snipers. Nobody killed but two wounded. By the snipers, so be sure and stay back from the openings.' He started to leave again as he added, 'We'll have a dustoff down the first thing for the wounded after the snakes hose down the perimeter to drive those snipers back.' He scuttled off to the next bunker.

As Hoyt left, Coggins took his bayonet and dug a small hole in one corner of the bunker, then pulled his pants down and began to strain.

Franklin was the first to see him. 'Hey, sarge, can't you shit somewhere else? Man, you going to gas us to death.' Coggins ignored him, his face contorted with pain, then he finally said, 'Ain't about to take a crap outside. That sniper would do me in for sure. Y'all just gonna have to take it.' After a minute he added, 'Well, maybe I ought to go outside. One shot from the sniper would scare it out of me.' He finally pulled up his pants. 'It's a shame. Ol' Sgt. Coggins needs his morning shit to start the day off right.'

Franklin grinned, 'Praise the Lord, we're saved.'

Moving in a duckwalk, Coggins edged toward the front of the bunker to look out. 'We gotta get outta here, boys, so ol' Sgt. Coggins can find a shithouse and take a crap in peace.'

A thin shaft of light from the morning sun angled through the logs and played on Coggins upper lip as he talked. He started to say something more when he pitched violently backward, slamming into the earthen wall at the rear of the bunker where he sat with eyes opened in amazement. The sound of the single shot was quickly absorbed by the jungle.

Franklin crawled to Coggins side and took him by the shoulder. 'You all right, sarge?' He shook him again, looking for a wound but saw nothing until Coggins head tilted slowly to the side and blood from beneath the helmet began coursing down his neck.

'Jesus.' Franklin backed away and looked at the others. 'Right through the mouth and out the back of the head.'

The others said nothing as they stared at Coggins. Just a second ago he had been talking to them and now he seemed to be nodding off to sleep with his mouth open.

Franklin backed away from the dead squad leader and felt the sickness churn in his stomach. Coggins gone, just like that. First it was Hotdog and the others, now Coggins. How many more were going to die because of that fucking Hoyt? He heard someone yelling for the medic but paid no attention. He screwed his massive body into the corner and dug out his cigarettes and a capsule of scag. He looked to see if anyone was watching but the others were helping the medic pull Coggins out of the bunker. Franklin quickly tipped out the tobacco and poured in some white powder, twisted the end and lit it. He pulled hard until he felt the tide of relaxation begin to flow inside him and he shuddered. My last cap, man, just two or three more dusters in there and then I'm out. But I'll be home by then, back in camp and going into town and picking up more and checking with the chicks. Stop and see Sturm and have him fix me up with one of those round-eye nurses. That's the only way to go. Black or white, I don't care, I just want one of them. Damn Sturm, sitting back there making it with them and keeping it all to himself. Well, I'm gonna educate that white boy. He either gets me into the action or he gonna come into the field with me.

Franklin worked slowly on the duster and felt his nerves calm. Yeah, man, going home soon. Just one last piece of business to attend to. Sure going to be unfortunate that *Loo*-tenant Hoyt got himself killed on the last day of the patrol. Sure too bad that slope caught our Loo-tenant with a grenade. Yeah, fragged him to death. Sure too bad.

The chaplain smiled and waited while Sturm finished fueling the medevac before he slid the doors open and waved Montano aboard. As the priest clambered aboard and arranged himself behind Kowalski's seat, Sturm lowered the green visor on his helmet and from behind this plastic screen he studied the stocky chaplain. Two bandoliers crossed Montano's chest and six fragmentation grenades hung from his pack webbing. His expectant face reminded Sturm of a Boy Scout trying to earn his first merit badge.

Kowalski lifted the bird then eased the cyclic forward and sent the medevac skimming toward the perimeter fence, clearing it by inches. Montano grinned and reached up to pat the pilot on the shoulder. Sturm turned away to look out the doorway at the airfield where he saw six slicks lift off in smooth unison. Already up and turning west toward the Laotian border were five Cobras and a loach. As if that weren't enough guns, Sturm had heard Kowalski telling the chaplain as they boarded that Phantoms were on call if things got hot.

The brass wasn't taking any chances in extracting this platoon, he thought, and leaned out a little to let the wind catch him and dry the sweat. But too much activity would only excite Charlie and he would be out there with everything he could muster to blow a few people out of the sky. You couldn't win. Sturm didn't like the sound of anything about this mission. The earphones in his helmet crackled. The Cobra flight ahead was talking with Kowalski:

'Rainbow One One, Snakedance Six Six. Confirming that you will go in first. I understand there are two wounded and two dead. At last count. The slicks will follow you to bring out the rest of the grunts.'

'Six Six, Rainbow One One. That's a roger. Tell that loach driver to hunt under every rock. I don't want Charlie working me over.'

'We'll all be looking. Good luck. Six Six out.'

Sturm felt someone tapping him on the shoulder and turned to see Montano trying to talk to him. He took off his helmet and heard the chaplain ask what was happening. Sturm explained that the Cobra gunships would prep the area with rockets and fleshettes to drive the enemy back from the immediate perimeter and then the dustoff would go in first for the wounded and dead and the other choppers would bring out the rest of the platoon.

Montano nodded then shouted over the roar of the wind and the turbine engine that he would jump off and come out with the last bird. 'I'll be of more use on the ground,' he yelled. 'I don't want to get in your way.'

Sturm shrugged and pulled his helmet back on to hear Kowalski advise they would be over the valley in zero five. From the doorway he saw the peaks that ring the Dak Son valley rising ahead, like dull green saw teeth, and then they were over and dropping rapidly toward the brown valley bottom. Sturm could see the old airstrip and the ruined tower but could not locate the platoon. Herron was studying the map and advised Kowalski to slide to his left. 'They'll be at the head of that draw that runs this way, see, just above that little meadow.'

A scout ship was already working up the ravine and Sturm could now see the bunkers squatting below a 40-foot wide clearing that was an old gun site. As they dropped toward the landing spot Sturm saw some figures emerge from the bottom bunker and work their way up a narrow trench. Two men were being helped by others and at the rear two more dragged an inert body. There was another body in the landing circle. 'Business picking up,' Sturm said to the wind.

Kowalski laid the chopper hard on its side as he swung toward the old gun site. The medevac was settling fast for a landing when the scout pilot nosing around the ravine below the bunkers suddenly shouted into his mike, 'Dinks, right below me.' He swung his little craft away but not in time. Sturm saw a flash in the trees and simultaneously the loach exploded in a sheet of flame.

Sturm hit his mike button. 'The dinks have RPGs. That's what got that loach.' Kowalski saw the chopper explode but continued to settle toward the now waiting wounded men. 'Rainbow One One is coming home' he shouted and flared the chopper back so the tail almost hit the ground before he settled on the skids.

'Move it, move it,' Dooley shouted as Sturm jumped off to help the two wounded men approaching his side. Sturm saw three holes open up in the sidewall where someone had a line of sight from the jungle. He pushed the men in on their stomachs then grappled with the awkward bodies. From where he lay with the wounded, Sturm saw Montano waddle toward the trench as Kowalski pulled on the collective and lifted out of the gun site. The medevac shuddered, as it took more hits and Sturm saw a rocket that missed them explode on the hill facing him. Then they were clear of the ravine and climbing rapidly away from the smoke and rattle of fire below and Sturm began checking the wounded who lay silent and waiting. One had taken a round in the arm and was tightly bandaged. Sturm left him and saw the next man was hit in the chest. Small, bright bubbles of blood rose and fell from the hole that reached the lungs. Sturm fixed the oxygen mask to the man's face and turned on the bottle. That would keep him going until they reached the 21st Evac. Color returned to the man's pale face and he blinked his eyes open and smiled at Sturm who pulled a compress tight over the chest hole. Sturm gave the young soldier a thumbs up sign. He liked to do that when he knew the man would live. It was harder, even deceitful, when he tried to encourage those he knew were dying. They knew they were dying too but they wanted something to grasp at, kindness if not encouragement. The radio set in his helmet popped as Kowalski switched to FM to hear the Cobras talking to the grunts on the ground.

'Lone Ranger, Six Six.

'Lone Ranger. Go.' Sturm knew the Cobra pilots were not happy with the operation.

'Six Six. You've got a bad situation down there, Lone Ranger. The bad guys were just waiting for us. That's why you haven't had much incoming all night. We're going to bring in some Phantoms to nape the area before we extract you. See if we can't burn them back a little.'

'Lone Ranger. Roger that. We'll hold the fort until then. Lone Ranger clear.'

The medevac was dropping toward the hospital pad and Sturm could see the orderlies out waiting. Garbage detail. The radio crackled again and it was the Cobra team leader advising Kowalski to make the turnaround as quickly as possible since there were more casualties.

Dooley, switching to PVT, asked Kowalski: 'Where's Rainbow One Two?'

'On the DMZ. This is our baby today, all ours.' He sounded exultant.

Montano did not wait to watch the dustoff leave but hurried into the first bunker he saw. As the chaplain pushed through the small doorway, Hoyt looked up from his radio and saw standing above him a swarthy man draped with ammunition, grenades growing from his belt and an M-16 held at the ready. Hoyt slowly lowered his handset and said, 'Where the fuck did you come from?' then as he saw the captain bars and the chaplain cross on Montano's collar he added, 'Sir.'

Montano grinned, his large teeth gleaming in the half-light of the bunker and stuck out his hand to introduce himself. 'I am Chaplain Montano, but just call me Father. I thought you might need some help. What is your first name, Hoyt? I like to call everyone by their first name. I don't stand on rank.'

Hoyt appeared flustered. 'Frank, Frank Hoyt, sir. Chaplain. But what are you doing here? I mean where did you come from?'

'I came in with the dustoff. I will go out with the last chopper load. I will not get in your way, Frank, you may be assured. But I will assist your men, spiritually and with this.' He brandished his rifle. 'All priests do not hide at the rear. Some of us go where we are really needed.'

He started to explain more but three evenly spaced explosions outside cut him short. At the first shock Hoyt shouted mortars and lay flat on the ground. The second round burst in front of the bunker and sent fragments through the firing slits. The pieces of metal made distinct whizzing sounds before they hit the earth at the back of the bunker. The last round hit directly on top of the bunker and sent dust and clods of earth raining through the logs but everything held.

There was a cry from below and someone was yelling, 'Medic, get the medic down here. Get Dubrow.' Dubrow, who had been sitting by the radio, grabbed his aid kit and started back down the trench. Montano struggled to his feet and followed as they half fell down the inclined trench to the bottom bunker. Just inside the door, holding his right wrist above what had been his hand, sat Franklin, rocking and moaning. The thumb dangled from a loose flap of skin but the rest of the hand was gone. Dubrow pulled a tourniquet tight and asked the others what happened as he worked.

'I don't know, man he had this grenade in his hand and was starting out the bunker when the first mortar hit. I guess it scared him because I saw him duck back in then and reach around the doorway there for something when the grenade went off just as the second mortar hit. I don't know what the hell he was trying to do, or why he had the pin out already.' The man's voice wavered as he watched Dubrow patch Franklin, 'Jeez, what a mess.'

Dubrow gave Franklin a shot of morphine then pulled out a big abdominal pad and wrapped it carefully around the shredded hand. Montano, who had been watching intently, moved in closer and put his hand on Franklin's shoulder. 'Son, I'm a priest. Father Montano. Are you Catholic by any chance?' He smiled and waited but Franklin continued to rock and moan, ignoring the priest.

Montano pulled Franklin's flak vest back and read his

name tag. 'Franklin, what's your first name? Just call me Father. Now let me help you. Are you Catholic?'

Without breaking his rocking motion Franklin suddenly shouted at the far wall, 'No, I ain't no fucking Catholic. I ain't nothing so get the fuck away from me.'

Montano didn't flinch, nor did he remove his hand from Franklin's shoulder. 'It's alright if you are not a Catholic. It doesn't make any difference. In war we are all the same. We are still God's children. I will pray for you.'

Franklin slowly calmed as the morphine began working in tandem with the heroin cigarette. He looked at Montano and said very distinctly: 'Take your mothafucking hand off me.'

Montano reluctantly dropped his hand. 'I will be nearby if you need me,' he said. The bunker was silent, the men watching.

'Nobody needs you,' Franklin replied and turned to look out the firing slit at the sun pouring heat upon the jungle. 'Simpson didn't need you. Coggins didn't need you. I don't need you. I just need to get out of here.' He turned away and his voice trailed off weakly, lost in the clatter of choppers overhead: 'But we still ain't settled the score, Hoyt.'

Sturm saw the rising column of black smoke from the air strikes as soon as Kowalski slid over the ridgeline and began a slow descent. The jets were at the far end of the valley, one behind the other, making wide turns then coming in hard and flat. As the jets approached the pinned platoon two cannisters of napalm tumbled end for end toward the jungle, followed by a flash and a gush of smoke as the gelatinous fuel burst through the foliage and ignited everything it touched. The second jet targeted a spot just above the platoon and Sturm saw the entire area was now ringed by napalm strikes.

Dooley, on the intercom: 'That ought to burn them back.'

'How would you like to be down there and having North Vietnamese migs napalming you like that?'

'I'd go home,' Dooley replied. 'Me and every other grunt in this army. It just wouldn't be a fun war if the bad guys had air capability.'

The crew chief switched the channel selector back to UHF and heard Kowalski talking with the Cobra team leader:

'I Roger you, Six Six. We're on the way.' The chopper dropped abruptly as Kowalski lowered the collective and flattened the bit of the blades. Below, the smoke was already thinning. Even napalm could not long sustain a fire in the lush vegetation. Sturm could see that the meadow below the bunkers was blackened and the grass that once effectively screened each of the tiered bunkers on top was now burned away. As the medevac settled rapidly toward the old gun site above the pinned platoon, Sturm saw the green tracers of North Vietnamese fire make deceptively lazy-looking curves toward them. He pulled his M-16 from beneath his seat, put the fire selector on semi- and began slow and steady fire toward the origin of the tracers. He could see nothing through the unburned portions of the jungle and he expected to hit nothing, but a man felt so helpless, so naked in a chopper under fire. Shooting back at least occupied the mind. They were on line with the trees that reached up to the little knoll of the gun site and smoke swirled through the open helicopter. Sturm saw more tracers snap past, close now, and he gave the area a final burst before his weapon clicked empty. He started to reload then saw they were about to settle into the pit. He dropped the weapon on the floor and grabbed the seat, no time to buckle up now, as Kowalski flared the ship hard, standing it on its tail, then tried to drop quickly into the pit where the old earthen wall that once ringed a .37mm North Vietnamese gun would give them a little protection, but they weren't fast enough and Sturm felt the ship shudder, like someone kicking your chair, as the first series of rounds slammed into the ship. He leaned out of his seat to watch Kowalski and saw three holes appear magically in the plastic windscreen in front of Kowalski, a little spider web around one of the holes glinting in the sunlight, and then Herron was slouching sideways in his seat and the map on his lap spilled onto the floor between his open legs. There was another shudder and a terrible squealing sound in the turbine and the ship, abruptly losing power, dropped hard into the pit, bounced, and the long steel blades whipped downward and caught the bank and the bird slewed hard to the right, like a child throwing his toy on the ground, and Sturm trying to hold onto the door stanchion felt himself going, his hands tearing lose from the violent wrench of the chopper and he was in the dirt, face down and he came up spitting mud and blood. His nose was broken, he knew that, and his shoulder hurt, but he was down and Jesus Christ I'm still alive, Jesus I'm alive and thanks a bunch, God.

He started to get to his feet then bent over again as he heard a round whine off the top of the medevac. Above the roar of the birds overhead and the violent whir of a mini-gun pouring lead on the still unseen enemy he could hear Dooley cursing, bellowing from inside the ship.

'Goddam good for nothing fucked up blue assed airforce can't do anything right. They nape the shit out of this area and we come in and every dink in the area is waiting for us. What do those slopes do, live on napalm?' He appeared in the doorway, big red Tomato, and Sturm thought he loved him at that moment.

'Get off your ass Sturm and get some of this gear,' Dooley shouted then ducked as another round whanged off the chopper. He shook his fist: 'And quit messing with my bird, you slope assholes.'

But Sturm wasn't listening anymore, he was running bent over to the chopper and pulling open the door and Kowalski was helping him unbuckle Herron and then they had him out on the ground. Sturm looked at Herron briefly and shook his head.

'Get me a body bag down here, Tomato,' he yelled at Dooley. They looked at Herron and said nothing. There were three neat little holes across the front of his metal breast plate and he was very dead.

'Looks like a .51 caliber,' Kowalski said. 'No chicken plate is going to stop that.' They were silent as they put him into the bag and zipped it shut.

Sturm crawled back into the chopper and shoved compresses, surettes, saline and pills into a bag and then followed the others who were already out of the pit and into the trench that led down to the first bunker. As he reached the trench he saw a black grunt sitting there, partially blocking the path with his great body. Sturm first saw the tourniquet on the arm where the shirt had been ripped away, and the compress bandage, already bloody and soiled, and his eyes lifted to the face: Franklin.

Sturm was on his knees looking at the big black. 'Franklin, goddam man, what happened?'

Franklin's little eyes opened and swung slowly to Sturm. 'Hey, white boy, I been waiting for you. You was my ticket home. Now look what you done with that nice machine that was gonna fly my ass outta here. Why you want to do a thing like that to me?'

Sturm grinned. 'You got guts, if nothing else. What you doing out here?'

'I was—' Franklin started to answer but his words were drowned in the hammer of machine gun fire from the bunker below them. The black tried again: 'I was put here. Dubrow, he's our medic, he put me here to get on your dustoff. Now no one is going anywhere.'

Sturm gently took Franklin's good arm and began pulling him back down the ditch toward the first bunker. 'Come on, man, we'll take the next bus. But let's get inside until one comes.' They eased through the small doorway and even before his eyes adjusted to the half-light in the tiny, dirt-floored bunker Sturm heard Kowalski yelling into the radio handset.

'Six Six, Rainbow One One. I know our bird blocks that protected LZ. You just drop me some C-4 and I'll blow it out of there for you. But I think if you hose the area and drive those dinks back a little more then a slick can put a skid on this bunker and we'll load these grunts out.'

There was a pause on the radio and Sturm propped Franklin up in a corner and started setting up a saline IV. He pulled a bottle from the kit when a lieutenant sitting next to Kowalski turned and yelled at him: 'Get that shithead out of my sight. Take him to a bunker on the other side of the trench. It's too crowded in here.' He turned away again and Sturm heard a voice next to him say softly, 'No sweat, the LT is pissed at Franklin but he won't chase us out.'

Sturm looked at the short, curly haired man squatting beside him with his helmet pushed back and a crease across his white forehead where the liner band cut into his skin. The Spec. 4 stuck out his hand. 'I'm Rick Dubrow. Medic with this outfit. I see you found Franklin. I was bringing up two more wounded when your chopper bought it.'

Sturm introduced himself then was cut off by the radio: 'Rainbow One One, Six Six. Roger your last. Pop some smoke. We're not sure which bunker. A slick will be right down. Have your grunts ready.'

Hoyt turned to Sgt. Dodge, handed him a smoke grenade and told him to get the men ready. 'But stay in the ditch until the last minute,' he yelled. 'I don't want any more casualties.'

Sturm slid the long needle into Franklin's arm, taped it and started the saline. He saw Hoyt watching him but the lieutenant didn't speak. Sturm sat back then suddenly remembered his M-16 was still in the chopper. Deciding he better have it handy, he crawled up the trench and out to the chopper on hands and knees where he found his rifle and a bandolier of clips. As he started back he heard the gunships raking the hillsides with machine gun fire and a helicopter settled rapidly overhead toward the bunkers. He could see the gunners standing in the doorways, swiveling their M-60s and the casings glittering as they spun in the air. In the trench below him six men crouched with rifles and packs, and peered beneath helmet rims as the chopper touched lightly on the bunker above them. Sgt. Dodge, who hunkered with the men, sent each man up toward the open doorway with a pat on the rear, like a coach sending in his first team. The first man to the door suddenly stumbled forward against the chopper before he sank to the ground, hit in the back. The next two men gathered him like a laundry sack and threw him inside as the others followed and lay flat. They began firing at the still unseen enemy as the chopper tilted forward and began a run down the draw to get lift.

The chopper was just beyond the last bunkers and slowly rising when a flurry of rounds hammered into the side and engine. After a moment's hesitation the Huey straightened and seemed to be gathering itself for a leap upwards when the tail assembly exploded from a direct hit by a rocket propelled grenade. Without anti-torque, the helicopter spun wildly until it slewed into the burned slope below the platoon. Sturm saw two men thrown from the gyrating helicopter before it hit the bank, flipped and exploded. Dragging his M-16 by the strap, he slid down the trench to the bottom where he met Dubrow hurrying out the doorway with his aid kit.

'Can you see him?' Dubrow asked and looked down the blackened slope.

'See who?'

'Warren. He and somebody else got thrown clear.' Crouching next to the bunker logs Dubrow pointed at a figure lying on top of a fire-blackened ledge about forty meters down the hill. The man's face was shot away and he did not move. 'I can't tell who that is but Warren is down in the ravine below that ledge. I know he must be alive because I saw him crawl over and drop in when he hit the ground.'

The circling gunships had spotted Warren too and were now laying a carpet of fire on the banks above him. There was a burst from a Cobra directly overhead and Sturm heard the cat's hiss of fleshettes before they stippled the jungle cover.

'Maybe they can bring a loach in for him. Let's check,' Sturm said.

Dubrow hesitated, eyeing the possibility of an immediate dash down the ravine for the injured man. 'Alright,' he said finally, 'we'll check first.'

In the top bunker Hoyt was already talking with the Cobra team leader. 'Six Six, Lone Ranger. Can you see them?'

'Roger, Lone Ranger. One appears dead. The other is at the bottom of the ravine about 50 meters below your position.'

'Six Six, can you get him?'

'Negative, Lone Ranger. We can't get a bird down to him. It's too exposed. If he can't crawl you might be able to get some people down to him. But you better hurry. We have two Magic Dragons about zero five out and when they start douching the area we are going to try for another lift out.'

'Roger, Six Six. We'll get him. Lone Ranger clear.' Hoyt yelled for someone to get Dubrow then turned and saw the medic quietly watching him. 'Oh, Dubrow. Can you get him? Who is it, Warren?'

'Yeah, I think I can get down there, LT.'

'Go. Take somebody with you.'

'I'll get him myself. Less risk that way.' He turned and left and Sturm followed.

'I'll go with you, if you want. Do the right thing, you know. Play the hero and that shit,' Sturm said and tried to force some lightness into his voice. Pictures of him sprinting through a spray of bullets then crumpling into the napalm-burned grass danced in his mind.

'No, better alone.'

At the bottom of the trench, Sturm took Dubrow by the arm. Several troops were watching them from the bunker doorway. 'Are you sure he's alive? It's not worth the risk if he's dead, you know.'

Dubrow removed his helmet, wiped the sweat from his face and looked at Sturm. 'Our brave LT left one man out for dead even though he lived through the night. Nobody in this platoon wants to lose another buddy that way.' He turned his eyes to the gulley that was an extension of the bunker trench and gazed down the slope where it widened into a ravine. The slash through the red earth was nearly ten feet deep but the dense brush and knife grass that grew in it had been burned away by the napalm strikes. Sturm looked at the ragged ditch and saw how it ran fairly straight for about thirty meters then turned right. Behind that bend somewhere lay Warren. Dubrow unhooked his webbing, opened his aid kit and took out a syrette of morphine and two compresses which he stuck in his pocket. He checked the clip in his rifle, whispered 'Wish me luck' and darted over the top toward the ravine. There was an immediate spatter of fire from the jungle but Dubrow was already in the ditch and wriggling like a snake into the deeper gulley. Someone in the bunker beside Sturm said, 'That Dubrow's got balls, man. The gooks are just waiting for him. They always like to get the RTO and the medic.' Someone else replied, 'Maybe we can make a deal with Charlie. We'll give them the LT and they'll let us go home.'

Overhead the whup-whup-whup of choppers mingled with the repeated bursts of machine gun fire into the jungle but there was no answering fire from the enemy. Sturm, listening, started to wipe the blowing dust and ashes from his eyes when a movement down the ravine caught his attention. Dubrow rounded the bend with Warren draped over his back in a fireman's carry. When he lifted his head to see how far to the bunker, Sturm could see the strain in Dubrow's sweat-streaked face. The men in the bunker were yelling words of encouragement to the medic.

Sturm brought his rifle up to provide covering fire when he remembered it was empty. He popped in a new clip and worked the bolt back to throw a round in the chamber then turned the selector to automatic. He looked back at Dubrow, now some 20 meters away, and he could see the bloody compress tied to Warren's head where he had been hit or cut when flung from the chopper. Warren appeared unconscious and lolled heavily on Dubrow's back.

Sturm suddenly froze as a North Vietnamese popped from behind the bend just below Dubrow. The man appeared as if he were a puppet jerked onto a stage by strings and Sturm could see everything about the man with numbing clarity, his face thin and yellowed, probably malaria, the ragged pith helmet, the gray bandolier of ammunition high across his chest and the AK-47 held in his hands at waist level.

Sturm pointed his rifle, not even aiming, and pulled the trigger. But even as he was moving he saw the rifle buck in the North Vietnamese's hands and he saw Dubrow straighten and let Warren slowly slide from his back before dropping to his knees and pitching onto his face.

The North Vietnamese spun backwards, arms outflung, and fell into the ashes. Sturm emptied his clip, reloaded and again fired it into the lifeless corpse. He was reloading again when a mocking voice at his elbow said, 'I think you got him.'

It was Kowalski, grinning and clapping him on the back with his meaty hand. 'I think you just lost your cherry, didn't you? Your first gook after almost a year in 'Nam. Right?' He looked at Sturm with small blue eyes tight and laughing. 'I knew we'd make a killer out of you yet.'

Sturm recoiled, the exhilaration from firing and shooting a man, seeing him dead instead of himself, was suddenly gone. He looked toward the bodies of Dubrow and Warren and felt empty. 'Yeah, right, I killed him to save Vietnam. Didn't help those two guys much, did it?' He looked at Kowalski, angry and wanting to shout at him. Instead he yelled at the sky, a dog howling in the night: 'Did it!'

Kowalski pushed him in the chest, rocking him back. 'Take it easy, keep some cool. Don't go to pieces over one lousy dink, or seeing a couple grunts get hit.' Sturm stared back at Kowalski and fingered the rifle in his hands as a violent rage suddenly pounded in his head and darkened his sight for long moments, then Kowalski swam into view again and Sturm relaxed his grip on the M-16. He turned from the pilot and looked into the ravine again. 'Maybe they are still alive.'

'No way. You can see that. They're all dead.' Kowalski said it matter of factly, as if reading a bus schedule.

Sturm was silent a moment, thinking of Dubrow, and Kowalski held his hand to shade his eyes as he looked at the sky: 'Here comes good old Puff the Magic Dragon. Now we're going to lay it on those gooks.' As he spoke there was a wild whirring noise that enveloped the men on the ground and Sturm looked up to see solid streams of tracer fire pouring from the circling C-47. He could see the mini-guns, four of them mounted one side of the plane, laying a carpet of lead that stripped leaves from trees, splintered huge limbs, left trees naked and pulverized the ground beneath.

'Six thousand rounds a minute from each of those guns. Lay it on them,' Kowalski shouted above the awesome roar. As the planes slowly circled overhead Sturm shouted, 'I'm going to check Dubrow. I can't leave him there possibly alive.' He started over the edge without allowing himself time to think of the danger and heard Kowalski yell he was coming too. They fell almost together into the ditch and scrambled toward the bodies. As Sturm reached Dubrow and began checking him he saw Kowalski go past them toward the North Vietnamese. Dubrow was dead, so was Warren. The burst of fire had gone through Warren and penetrated Dubrow's chest. Sturm pulled one dog tag from each man's neck and started back. They could get the bodies some other time. He remembered Kowalski and looked back in time to see the pilot push something into his pocket and start after him. They ran up the ravine, bodies bent forward and scalps tingling in anticipation of a bullet from the jungle. But none came.

Breathing hard from the run, the two slumped in the ditch against the bunker and Sturm looked at the dog tags in his palm. He caught his breath and started to reach for a Park Lanes roach but hesitated. Kowalski suspected Sturm smoked grass but had no proof and Sturm knew the pilot would turn him in if he caught him.

Kowalski looked up from beneath his thick brows and grinned. 'I've got something for you. A little souvenir of you losing your cherry.' He reached in his right pocket and pulled a belt buckle out. Part of the gray, webbed belt was still attached where Kowalski had cut it loose. Sturm slowly took it and looked at the flat silvery metal with a star stamped in the middle. The North Vietnamese had carefully painted the star red but it was not scratched and peeling, like the fingernails of a careless woman.

Kowalski kept his lips pulled back over teeth in what some took to be a grimace rather than a smile. 'I've got something else for you.' He dug into his pocket again and pulled out something hidden in his fist. He stretched his arm out before Sturm's face and slowly opened his palm. As he uncurled his fingers Sturm saw a man's ear slowly unfold itself, a dried apricot of an ear, after being crushed in Kowalski's hand. Sturm noticed it was dirty and only a little bloody along the edge where Kowalski had severed it next to the head.

'What the fuck is that for?' Sturm asked and knocked it out of the proferred hand. 'I don't want that thing. Why'd you cut it? You been watching too many John Wayne movies.'

Kowalski's face darkened at the rebuff. 'Don't get so wise, Sturm. This ear is for a good reason. It will get you a membership in the Sat Cong club.'

'The *what* club?' Sturm looked at the ear which now lay on the ground between them.

'Sat Cong means "kill Viet Cong". It's a 1st Cav club. Something new. They'll make you an honorary member with this. Yet get a patch. An ear is proof you killed a dink.'

'What am I, a boy scout earning merit badges? For collecting ears?' He got up to go but kept the buckle. Kowalski also rose to his knees in the trench and picked up the ear. 'You sure you don't want it?' he asked and then pocketed it as Sturm shook his head and continued up the trench.

Above him Dooley emerged from the command bunker holding an IV bottle aloft which still dripped into the following Franklin. A trooper supported Franklin as they crossed the trench and entered the adjoining bunker.

Sturm followed and asked, 'What's going on?'

Dooley turned, his freckled face flushed. 'That goddam LT said to move Franklin, says he was taking up too much room in his precious little bunker. There was two other guys in there with lesser wounds who said they would move instead, but Hoyt said he wanted Franklin out. I can't believe that guy.'

Franklin was nodding and making soft noises in his throat, no longer feeling any pain. 'The man *hate* my ass because I tried to frag him. Almost did the job too. Almost blew that mothafucker *away.*' He looked at his shattered hand and muttered, 'Almost got him, almost.'

Dooley handed Sturm the IV. 'Here, I ain't the medic. You take care of Franklin and I'll go keep an eye on the wounded in the other hootch. None of them is bad.' He turned at the doorway. 'I hear Dubrow got it. Too bad.'

Sturm hung the plasma bottle from a log overhead and sank down beside Franklin. He looked around the bunker. There were no NCOs, only grunts. He pulled the Park Lanes from his pocket and showed the pack to Franklin. 'Grass. Want some?'

The big black shook his head. 'No, man, I got something better. If you help me.' He pointed to his blouse pocket and Sturm opened it. He fished out a pack of Marlboros, found the capsule deeper down, and then quickly prepared the heroin smoke for Franklin.

'Say, brother, you an *expert* at that. Help yourself, there's enough for two.'

'I learned how to fix them from watching a buddy of mine. But I don't blow scag. Grass is good enough.'

Franklin was shivering from shock but functioning and anxious for some heroin. 'You ain't lived until you been stoned on smack. Go on, I'll share with you.' With his good hand he pushed the makings toward Sturm who looked at it but left it alone.

'No, heroin is bad news,' he said.

'No shit. So is Vietnam. But I *still* got to take it. So I figure if I got to take Vietnam, I got to take scag. That's the only way you can keep your head together. Forget the rest of the world, for scag brings good to evil, brother, brings peace to Vietnam. Go ahead.'

Sturm twirled the capsule in his fingers and watched the powdery white heroin tumble back and forth. He had heard the story about one dude so hung up for a fix that he had bought heroin from some street urchin and smoked it quickly only to find out it was the scraping from a battery terminal. He found out too late and the acid ate out one of his lungs. There were lots of bad stories around, but there were also a lot of guys on smack that functioned like anyone else. Or almost as good. How about that guy Fredericks in S-2 with a top secret clearance? He got wiped out almost every night and no one in his shop knew about it. He appeared normal all through the day. And how about Riley? Riley was spaced periodically but it didn't seem to hurt him, or his efficiency. And Riley was better adjusted to the goddam war than most others. He did the job when he had to, helped heal the wounded and bundled away the dead with equal efficiency then forgot everything with a duster or two when he wasn't flying. Where the hell was Riley? Why wasn't he up here with Franklin? They could smoke together and then I wouldn't want to light up this scag, to try it once. Why not try it, everyone else did. Christ, even the MPs were on it. He had one of them buying it from a little kid just outside the gate to the military headquarters for all of Vietnam in Saigon. And there was an alley right across the street from Ton Son Nhut airbase in Saigon where old women and little kids carried dozens of capsules around in paper bags and all you had to do was ask, hand over two bucks and there was the capsule. The Vietnamese cops knew about it, and the American officials couldn't be so dumb or naive that they didn't know. Maybe they were all on the take. The Vietnamese certainly were, why not the Americans? Lots of money to be had in heroin and what American colonel was going to turn down a thousand extra a month to keep his investigators from clamping down on the pushers.

Sturm looked at the capsule as if it were a crystal ball and saw Montano inside, and Kowalski holding up the ear, he saw an arm spinning in space and the prisoner drooling on the hot sand. Sturm slowly looked at Franklin and said, 'Can't do anything but kill me, can it?' He slowly pulled the tobacco from the top of the cigarette and tipped in the white powder. As he twisted the cigarette closed, he looked around the bunker but no one was watching. They were trying to see what was happening outside without getting near the firing slit. Sturm heard the roar of mini-guns and choppers outside as he lit the cigarette, heard the rattle of cannon fire from the Cobras as he pulled the heroin smoke deep into his lungs and let it come out slowly. Just like blowing grass. He inhaled again and this time felt the drug pour through his body, racing in arteries, filling capillaries, pulsating into his head, into his mind, a cataract of sensation, a river of pure delight, agony, rising to Omega and God, this is what you are, these are your heavens and this is deliverance. Sturm inhaling again and again, swallowed night and day then fell through the sun and the moon, he knew fire and ice and all dualisms were revealed yet unknown.

He sank back against the earthen wall, felt the cool earth through his fatigues, felt the dirt under his hand and slowly finished the cigarette. Franklin looked at him, smiled loosely and said, 'It's all together now, right, brother? That's what Vietnam is all about.'

Dooley appeared before Sturm who saw him but didn't see him. He could see right through the red head, could hear Dooley speaking, 'Come on, we're taking the next bird. Get Franklin outside and I'll bring the gear.' Dooley's face moved closer, peering, and Sturm could see the words now tumbling from his mouth like individual pieces of a puzzle.

'Jeez-us. You're stoned. Goddamit, Sturm, you're stoned, you took some scag. After all this time. What's with you man, are you freaking? Now you can't even function.' He pulled Sturm to his knees and forced him out the bunker doorway into the ditch. 'Just sit here, I'll get us together.'

Sturm looked around him, squinting in the glaring light and trying to bring the balloon he was riding closer to earth. He held his ears against the roar of helicopters overhead, against the thunder of lead still pouring from the circling Dragons. He looked down and saw beside him the corpses of Dubrow and Warren and the man who had no face. Dubrow's eyes were open, staring at him, questioning. Sturm put his hand out slowly to touch Dubrow's forehead which was cool as clay in the deadly heat, and said, 'I'm sorry, man, I'm sorry.'

A face swung into view, a massive face with blazing teeth and hot black eyes that twirled like twin maelstroms ready to suck the unwary into their depths. 'I've given them both absolution.' It was the rich voice of Montano, Teofilo, Chaplain, Captain, U.S. Army, one each. 'Dooley and some other men brought them up. There seems to be no firing. I guess the gooks pulled back.' Sturm could hear the chaplain speaking and see the eyes but he couldn't find the mouth.

'You don't have a mouth,' he said, slowly and distinctly.

'The next chopper is for us,' Montano said, not hearing Sturm speaking.

'It is a miracle. You speak with no mouth.'

'What did you say, son?' Montano was not trying to understand, and Sturm could see the eyes spinning faster, deeper, trying to lure him into the black abyss. He closed his own eyes to keep the brightness of his soul from leaking away. He had just found the brightness and he didn't want to lose it.

Sturm got to his knees in the ditch. Dooley didn't know what the hell he was talking about. He hadn't tried scag so how could he know. Sturm tripped over one of the bodies near the bunker doorway and stopped to look at them again. The one with his face blown away was bad but Dubrow was worse. The son of a bitch wouldn't close his eyes. Sturm bent and looked closer. There was no pain in the eyes, just a look of confusion. Why me? They always thought that when they got blown away. Why me?

Sturm raised his palm with two fingers extended and

began singing the haunting order of mass for the dead, raising his voice over the roar of choppers and mini-guns outside: 'Dies irae, dies illa, solvet saeclum in favilla: teste David cum Sibylla. Quantus tremor—'

Montano knelt beside him and held his arm. 'Don't make a mockery of it, Jacob. You are not a priest and you have not the right to recite that mass. I have already given them absolution.'

Sturm turned and looked at the priest in stained fatigues with a helmet too large for him, and bandoliers of ammunition across his chest, the stocky chaplain who knelt in the dust before him and demanded an answer with silent, accusing eyes. Why are you leaving this monastery, my son? Are the demands of the flesh too great upon you? Yes, Father Hoffman, I would rather play with Helen than play with myself under this cassock. And then Father Hoffman was gone and Montano's face was peering at him. Sturm spoke slowly:

'Day of wrath and terror looming, heaven and earth to ash consuming; seer's and psalmist's true foredooming! That's not mockery, Chaplain Montano, that is truth. And you, the Gideon of the Vietnam wastelands, must know the truth. We cannot mock the dead.'

'Jacob, for God's sake, you are mocking the dead and the priesthood,' Montano replied with an anger Sturm had not seen before. 'I've tried to talk sense to you but I know you reject me. You reject the priests, you reject Catholicism, you reject everything in your desire to whore around with that bar girl in Quant Tri, that Mai. You have wasted your life, now don't waste the others around you by this mockery.' He shook Sturm's shoulder but Sturm shoved his hand away and snapped in sudden anger and exasperation:

'I make no mockery of the dead. It is you, you who close your eyes to all this, who say you are praying for the dead but at the same time are urging the survivors to go out and kill more dinks—' He wanted to continue but Dooley was beside him now, jerking him around roughly.

'Can't you do anything, fuckhead?' he hissed. 'This is our chopper coming. See if you can at least get yourself and Franklin into it. I'll worry about the other wounded and the dead. Here it is, go.'

Leaving Montano on his knees, Sturm clambered from the ditch onto the bunker, eyes closed against the blowing dust, slipping in the crumbling earth, trying to pull Franklin after him. He knew that if Franklin would just let go he would float right into the chopper and sail away in it on a tide of warm air. He made it inside and slumped to the floor, Franklin beside him, and dreamily watched Dooley and two other men struggle with the four bodies which they piled beside Sturm.

The chopper lifted away and Sturm saw Chaplain Montano standing in the trench watching him despite the blast of dirt from the prop blades. Sturm smiled at the chaplain and made an elaborate sign of the cross in the air over the priest who started to wave in reply but then slowly let his hand fall as a perplexed look filled his face. Sturm then saw Kowalski turn to the priest and show him something in his hand.

'Bless you, chaplain, for you have sinned,' Sturm mouthed at the receding figures. As the helicopter rose above the valley, Sturm blessed the ground below and then, feeling expansive, blessed the whole of Vietnam, 'for you have sinned too. But if you say five Hail Marys and five Our Fathers, God will forgive you for being Vietnam.'

CHAPTER EIGHT

STURM crossed from the messhall into the back entrance of the hospital and walked down the green linoleumed hallway with butt cans painted red hanging like tin flowers every 20 feet. He angled toward the amputee ward where he knew he would find Franklin. When they arrived yesterday Franklin was rushed directly to the OR and Sturm knew it was impossible to save his hand. There was nothing to save. He rounded the corner, entered the swinging doors with round porthole windows and saw Franklin in the last bed, next to the rear wall. He lay flat on his back with his eyes closed and the injured arm swathed in white bandages across his chest. A nurse with her back to Sturm was just removing an IV bottle and although Sturm couldn't see her face he recognized the curvaceous derrière of Lt. Saunders. He approached silently and after a quick check to see that the nearest patient, two empty beds away, wasn't watching he slid both palms over her buttocks and squeezed. Sandy whirled, almost dropping the bottle and her mouth widened until she saw Sturm. She gave a nervous laugh and glanced around to see if anyone was looking. Her anger faded but her face remained flushed. 'My God, I thought I was being attacked by one of the patients,' she hissed. 'You scared me to death.'

'How are you, lieutenant?' Sturm asked in a normal, polite voice and looked over her shoulder at Franklin who opened his eyes, red and withdrawn, to watch them.

'Just fine, Specialist Sturm. And you?' She lowered her

voice again, 'Coming to the movies tomorrow night, aren't you?'

'I don't know, got any new ones in?'

'No, but I have something you haven't seen in a long while.'

'You've got something I've *never* seen,' Sturm said pointedly. The nurse flushed then shook her short brown hair back with an air of authority. 'My, my, always in a rush, aren't you, Specialist Sturm.' She leaned close and gave a lascivious twist to her words, 'You know we officers aren't supposed to be fraternizing with you enlisted men.'

'I have something more involved than mere fraternizing on my mind,' Sturm said. He took her by the arm. 'Seriously, I want to see you tonight. We'll take a walk, see beautiful Vietnam by illumination rounds and recite love poems.'

She looked at him for a moment, calculating. 'Not tonight. There's a going away party for one of the nurses, Lucille, in the officers' club. I've got to be there.' She moved away, businesslike again as she cradled the bottles and tubes in her arms. 'But sometime soon, really.'

As Sturm watched her walk rapidly from the ward, Franklin said, 'You got something going with that chick?'

'I wish I did. So far all I have going is frustration.' He turned to look at the huge black. The sheer size of the man lying on the white sheets reminded Sturm of a beached whale. 'How are you doing, Franklin?' Sturm asked.

Franklin shrugged and moved his bandaged arm slightly. 'The man done took my hand. Chopped it off halfway to the elbow. How do you expect me to be doing?' His voice was surely withdrawn, with none of the easy fatalism Sturm recalled from yesterday in the field.

'I guess they didn't have much choice but to take it off,' Sturm said but knew the words were little compensation. He rarely came to see grunts he brought in from the field with pieces of their bodies mangled or missing. Words of condolence always sounded so empty, so stupid. He hadn't planned on coming to see Franklin but as he left the messhall after a late breakfast Sturm felt compelled to return some favor to a man who shared the last of his most prized possession: heroin. Franklin, however, didn't appear to be in need of anything more than a willing listener.

'The *man* always taking from me. All whitey's taking from the blacks. Never give. I never had much and now I ain't even got a mothafucking right *hand*.' Franklin's voice rose and some of the men glanced incuriously his way. Shouts of despair and anger were not uncommon in the amputee ward.

Franklin's outburst put Sturm on the defensive and he fumbled for a reply. 'Well, they'll be flying you to Japan in the next day or two. They'll fix you up with a new hand there.'

'I don't want a hand, *man*. I'm going to get me a *hook* and I'm going to make every whitey I meet *shake* it or I'll sink it in his neck. I'm going to tell them a goddam whitey *loo*-tenant made me lose that hand.'

Franklin began perspiring heavily as he continued. 'And I'm going to find that *Loo*-tenant Hoyt. That's the man who caused all this. If it weren't for him I would still have my hand and Simpson and all the others would still be *alive*. It's just too bad the *Loo*-tenant didn't die first, then the whole platoon would have come through together.' He dropped his voice and added, 'But that Hoyt is going to *pay*. I know his brother is a Chicago pig, and I'll find Hoyt when I get back to the world. He's going to be wasted.' He turned his eyes to the ceiling. 'I'll find that dude no matter where he go.'

Unsettled by the hatred coming from Franklin, Sturm said, 'Look, I've got to go. Can I get you anything?'

Franklin swung his eyes down from the ceiling. 'Yeah, I need some scag, man, I need some *bad*. Can you get it for me?' He fumbled awkwardly with his left hand at the bedstand and pulled out a ten dollar bill in military scrip.

'There's ten MPC. Get me whatever you can with it. I don't know how much it cost up here.'

Sturm did not accept the money. 'I can get it for you, man, but are you sure you want it now. They'll run a urine test on you before you go to Japan and if they find heroin traces you could be delayed. I don't know what will happen. Why not let it go, hold off until you get to Japan?'

Franklin seized Sturm's wrist in his good left hand. 'Because I *need* it now. I shared my last cap with you, so do me a favor and just get it without all the *bull*shit.'

Sturm took the money and shrugged. 'I'll get you some. Just stay cool.' He spoke over his shoulder when halfway down the ward, 'I'll be back sometime this evening.'

He would have to find Riley. Riley would know where to buy it in the ville. Sturm came out the back side of the hospital, turned toward his hootch and saw Dooley in front of the showers talking with a tall Vietnamese girl. It was one of the laundry girls, known throughout the hospital staff as Betty Bazoom. She was larger than the other Vietnamese girls, more heavily built and her pale, aquiline features indicated she was part French or German or something European. She was not particularly attractive but her homeliness was more than compensated for by a magnificent bustline. Countless doctors and orderlies had tried to work their way into her bra but there were no known successes. Major Schoen even pulled rank once and took her into his office on the pretext that there was a great deal of tuberculosis circulating and it was necessary she submit to an examination. Schoen was ultimately foiled, however, by Betty's manically suspicious mother, the chief reason no one had scored with Betty Bazoom. Mother Bazoom, a stooped harridan who always wore black and had teeth to match, rarely let her daughter stray from sight. They arrived from the ville each morning together, laundered together and left in the evening together. So that day when the mother found her daughter missing she charged into the wards with a homing ability the doctors still marvel over and located her daughter in Schoen's office just after he induced her to remove her blouse so he could properly apply the stethoscope. The orderly who followed Mama-san into the office in a vain attempt to stop her said Schoen was grooving with his ear pressed to those creamy breasts where they billowed above her bra, when the flailing and screaming Black Maria descended upon him. The mortified Schoen, scrabbling to find his glasses, was forced to call in a Vietnamese interpreter and explain that he was merely making a routine medical check. Even then, rumor said it cost Schoen 15,000 piastres to prevent Mama-san from going to the MPs.

Sturm, now eagerly waiting for the harridan to flutter around the corner and drive Dooley to cover, walked slowly down the boardwalk for a better view. As he drew closer he could see the girl had been scrubbing fatigues in front of the showers and her black pantaloons were soaked by the splashing water. The thin white cotton blouse clung wetly to her breasts where they crowded above the black brassiere. She smiled at Dooley, nodded shy agreement at something he said, then giggled and slipped away as he slid a hand over her hips. Still, to Sturm's surprise, the shrieking mother did not appear.

Sturm caught up with the redhead at their hootch. Dooley went directly to the small refrigerator where he fixed a Scotch on the rocks then turned with his glass raised in a toast and said, 'To me, Michael Patrick Dooley, who tonight shall be the first to be accepted by the blessed virgin Betty Bazoom.'

Sturm was unbelieving: 'How are you going to get her away from Mama-san? The old lady is going to kick the living shit out of you when she finds you sniffing around her precious daughter.'

'No way. Mama-san is sick. And I gave Betty some little

old pills that will make Mama sleep all night. And to show her gratification for my concern over her mother, Betty will slip up here tonight for a party I arranged in her honor.' Dooley did a little jig for joy on the floor.

'In our hootch? If you bring Betty Bazoom in here, Tomato, we all share.'

'That is just why she isn't coming here, fool.' Dooley finished dressing, downed the rest of his Scotch and told Sturm to follow him. They walked along the boardwalk toward the front of the hospital until they reached the last quonset, set apart from the others. The front door was numbered 23-A and the back, where Dooley led Sturm, was numbered 23-B. The front half of the quonset was the morgue, where the dead were held until they could be loaded into C-130s and flown south for transfer to Stateside flights. The back half of the quonset was the casket storage room. Dooley stopped at the door to the caskets, looked to see if anyone was around, then began working the lock and hasp loose from the door. The whole assembly slid out of the wall and as Dooley opened the door he showed Sturm how he had removed the nuts from the bolts that held the assembly in place. 'The bolts will hold well enough in the tin that it won't be noticed if Sgt. Thomas comes around to open the door, but if you pull hard, the whole thing comes loose.'

'So who wants to sneak into the morgue?' Sturm asked.

'This is not the morgue,' Dooley rasped in exasperation. 'This is just a simple storage room. Nothing wrong with that.' He flipped on the light, revealing stacks of dully gleaming caskets, and threw open his arms as if to announce a dramatic event. 'And this is where I shall consummate my undying love for Betty Bazoom.'

He pulled the door closed behind him and in the heavy air Sturm could smell the formaldehyde from the adjoining side of the building. Dooley crossed the room, the plywood floor creaking beneath him, and stopped at a casket set slightly apart along the wall. He lifted the lid and pointed inside. 'The nuptial bed.' The casket was lined with blankets and pillows from the hospital and tucked at the head end was a bottle of Scotch and two glasses.

Dooley rubbed his hands. 'Here my bride and I will have a few cocktails and when she is bombed out of her skull we will retire within.'

Sturm looked from the coffin to the triumphant Dooley and back at the casket. 'Are you out of your fucking mind? It's like Dracula taking a bride. Nobody but a full-blown nut would try and screw a chick in there. Besides, it's too narrow. You'll be like two weasels in a sock.'

Dooley shrugged, not to be dissuaded. 'It's private, the only private place around this joint. I'll be able to work out in peace with no one to disturb me.'

'How about the neighbors,' Sturm said and rolled his eyes toward the dividing wall.

'I promise not to raise them,' Dooley said. 'Look, I know it seems a bit ghoulish but this is important. This is going to be a first. This is one for the record books and I have to have privacy, nothing to disturb this chick, nothing to make her nervous.'

'Are you kidding? Betty Bazoom comes in here, takes one look at this place and she'll think you're going to bite her neck.'

'I've even got that figured, I have a candle and a flash-light. The light will be soft and she won't even know what's in here. I tell you, Jake, it's going to work, and if you had figured out such a place you would have scored with Sandy long ago. Let's go.' He moved to the door, flipped the light and once outside quickly pushed the bolts back into the holes. 'See? Simple. But don't tell anyone else. You're the only one who knows about it.' Back in the hootch they found Raab asleep on his bunk and Riley lacing on his boots. Riley looked up as they entered. 'Top was just in,' he said. 'Both our birds are down for repairs. Be down at least six hours and 1st Cav will cover for us. So we can split. I'm on my way.' He stood up, did a little dance and grabbed his hat. 'I'm on my *way*, to the ville, to the drugstore, to the chicks. *Watch* out.'

'I'll go with you,' Sturm said. 'You want to come, Mike? Sammy?' Raab failed to respond and Dooley said with a leer at Sturm that he had to get ready 'for the biggie'.

Outside, the heat pressed upon them and Riley and Sturm were dripping with perspiration by the time they walked to the front gate. They stood in the shade of the MP shack near the entrance and finally caught a ride in a three-quarter truck filled with Vietnamese Rangers heading into town. The Vietnamese bummed cigarettes from the two and one Ranger said, 'Finish Laos. Numbah ten. Now we drunk.' The others giggled wildly for the short ride into the town.

In the center of town by the dusty plaza the two jumped out. It was relatively quiet. The afternoon siesta was beginning and shopowners were pulling closed the folding steel doors over their entrances. Riley turned to Sturm: 'I've got a few places to check out, and I've got to go to the drugstore. Catch you later at the club?'

'I want to go with you to get some scag,' Sturm said and at Riley's surprised look he began to explain about Franklin, how he had tried some heroin with Franklin and how he had promised to bring some more. 'It's not for me. That was just an experiment. I told Franklin I would help him out, so you better show me where your drugstore is.'

As they crossed the dirt square ringed by dying tamarind trees that served as the town's park, Riley laughed at Sturm's description of his first high with heroin. 'Right on. I told you grass wouldn't always be good enough. But I'll level with you, Jake. You'll never have another high as good as the first. From now on it's all down hill.'

'But I was just experimenting. I don't plan to keep up with it.'

Riley, walking briskly, asked, 'Did you like it?'

'Sure, it was wild. But I don't have any big craving for it.'

As Riley turned down a narrow alley strewn with garbage he said, 'Right. Smoking is easy. But the desire will come.' He kicked at a cringing pariah dog that sniffed among the refuse. 'Remember this alley. It leads to the drugstore.' They emerged onto a rutted back street that ran along a canal filled with evil smelling black sludge. A boy of about ten, missing his right foot, rose from beneath a tree and hobbled toward them on one crutch. He approached with surprising agility, grinned engagingly, and then stopped and slapped one open palm over his other fist, the Vietnamese sign for fornication. 'You want boom-boom? Numbah one girl, numbah one.' He held up his thumb as if it were proof and kept smiling.

'Fuck off, kid,' Riley said and passed the boy without breaking stride. The youth backed away, and his smile faded. As they moved down the street he screamed after them, 'Puck you, pucking numbah ten Joe.'

'Winning hearts and minds, Riley?' Sturm asked.

'There are no hearts and no minds in Vietnam. Just pimps, whores and corrupt generals. And heads like us,' Riley replied and stopped in front of a small store with the steel gate half drawn. Inside it was dark and cool and Sturm saw a simple counter piled with goods from the PX: hair spray, soap, combs and tins of C-rations. Sitting at one end of the dirty glass case was a stout, middle-aged Vietnamese woman in a black ao-dai. Her bare feet were tucked beneath her on the wicker chair and she made no move to serve them but only watched as she slowly fanned her face.

'It's alright, Mama-san. He's a friend.'

The woman nodded, still silent and waving the fan, but her eyes relaxed. 'CID been making the rounds since all those reports came out about ten or twenty percent of the grunts over here being on scag. She's a little nervous, ain't you Mama-san?' Sturm pushed forward the ten MPC Franklin had given him and said, 'Me too. Same-same.' The woman collected the money and disappeared through a doorway covered with plastic strips.

'All that for your buddy? Or some for you?' Riley asked.

'All for Franklin. I just experimented that once.'

'You'll experiment again, then you'll keep on *experimenting* until you find yourself sneaking one when Kowalski ain't looking. When you start to sneak it then you know old man smack got you.'

When the woman returned with the two packages wrapped in newspaper and bound by rubber bands, Sturm fished out two more military dollars and bought another capsule. 'Just so I don't have to bum off you if I want to try it once more.' They left and the woman, who never once spoke, sat down and resumed fanning herself.

Sturm suggested noodles at Lim's. It was a small Chinese restaurant he had visited several times with Mai, and although Riley protested eating anything in the ville he went along for a Coke. They crossed the plaza to the Chinese shop that occupied the ground floor in a ruined French villa. There were no doors or windows still intact and the kitchen was a series of charcoal burners in one corner of the room. Most of the other few tables were filled with Vietnamese Rangers eating noodle soup and drinking '33' beer. The two sat in a corner and as Sturm began poling at the steaming noodles that were quickly set before him he noticed one of the Rangers across the room staring at him. Sturm tried to eat but the noodles were too hot and when he glanced up again the Vietnamese was still staring. The bitter, unwavering eyes suddenly triggered Sturm's memory. It was the same man Dooley had kicked off the chopper for faking a head injury. He looked more closely and saw the scar through the right eye, the drooping eyelid. As Sturm watched, the soldier began talking to others at his table, gesturing toward the Americans, and the other soldiers turned to look with brief curiosity, glasses of beer suspended before their lips.

The young Ranger had his shirt unbuttoned and his hand rested on the M-16 slung by its strap over his chair. Growing uncomfortable under their gaze, Sturm finished quickly, paid for both, and left, half expecting the Ranger to confront him. Outside, with street traffic resuming as the siesta period ended, Sturm suggested a beer at the Forty Akers. Riley declined, saying he had something else going, but he then paused and said, 'Say, man, since you been initiated, I'll show you my head bar.'

A block before the Forty Akers Riley turned down a side street and entered a blue-painted doorway topped with a poorly lettered sign reading 'Hoa Binh (peace) Bar. Welcome.' Just inside sat a Vietnamese wearing a loose flowered shirt and reflector sunglasses. Riley pointed at Sturm and said, 'He's okay, he's my friend.'

At the concrete bar where they sat Riley nodded toward the Vietnamese and explained, 'That's Cowboy, our guard. He's got a .45 under that shirt. The Mama-san who runs this place hired him after CID tried a bust here a couple months ago. It was a bad scene, man, all *kinds* of head cracking going on. Most of us beat it out the back. No trouble since then. I don't think Cowboy has much to do with that, I think Mama-san is paying off somebody in the Vietnamese CID so they lead the round-eyes to *other* head bars.'

A boy of indeterminate age appeared behind the bar and Riley laid out his cigarettes and a capsule. 'Fix us both up, Sampson.'

'Wait, I don't know,' Sturm said. He looked at Riley. 'How many capsules a day are you taking now?'

'About two, sometimes three. But I can stop when I want to. I've quit many times,' he laughed.

Sturm frowned. 'You know you can't really quit, Riley.

Everybody gets hooked on scag. That's why I want to stay away from it.'

'You don't get hooked just smoking it,' Riley said.

'That's bullshit. That's what anyone who's hooked says. Riley, you're a medic, you know that's a myth as well as I do. Heroin is heroin, no matter how you take it.'

Riley took the cigarette prepared by Sampson and said defiantly, 'So what, it can only kill you.'

Sturm started to argue then stopped himself. I'm not going to moralize, he thought, that's Montano's bag. He picked up the cigarette the boy laid in front of him along with a can of orange soda. He picked up Riley's lighter and struck a flame which he stared into before touching it to the cigarette. Does it matter, he asked himself, does anything really matter now? Why shouldn't I smoke, because it's bad for my health? So is Vietnam but that is not prescribed by the brass. War is bad for my health but the White House says war is good for the country, for the world, because war makes peace. And my effort in the war is garbage detail, picking up left-over soldiers that nobody wants anymore. We are plastic warriors in a disposable age and when our usefulness is ended we shall be consigned to the trash heaps of the world. Whatever side we are on.

'You going to light that cigarette or are you just going to use up my lighter fuel?' Riley asked.

Sturm lit the cigarette and inhaled. The smoke exploded in his head, a white phosphorous round, a burst of Willie Peter that lifted him clear of the dirt and garbage that cluttered his life. Once again the curtains parted and he saw the truth of beauty, the beauty of truth that is denied in terrestial life. He felt revelation within, saw himself as a crystal idol lying in a field of snow in the wintry fields behind the house in Iowa, unblemished and transparent.

Then he was running again through the orchard behind the monastery and the moonlight through the new leaves pattered his dancing cassock with light, little phosphorescent explosions in the night, and he could see Helen running toward him, her brief skirt fluttering around thighs that gleamed in the nocturnal light. Goddam, heroin is good, Sturm thought. He saw Riley sipping his orange and smoking easily, and he saw Cowboy with his black mirror glasses sitting by the doorway and the fat Mama-san who ran the head bar – Hoa Binh, peace, brother – ordering a girl to sit with a grunt too spaced to move. Sturm saw it all and knew he wasn't spaced but he felt so good and he could take his mind anywhere and then he was back in the orchard and pulling off his cassock while he and Helen danced around it, laughing like witches in the warm April night and then Helen was down on the cassock and pulling him down on her and he had his hand inside her silken pants and they were gone and she was hissing in his ear and rising beneath him and hissing, hissing, 'Come on, priest, Come on, priest, Come on, priest.' He looked at the face in his mind's eye and it was Mai, dark eyes melting on her alabaster skin, long eyelashes flying away. He stood up abruptly.

'I gotta go, Riley, I gotta see Mai.'

'Why you want to rush off, man? You don't like my hospitality? You don't like the peace you find here?'

'I got another piece in mind. I'm going.' Sturm felt warm and extraordinarily confident.

'You don't like the scag I give you?' Riley asked.

'It's the most beautiful thing in the world,' he said to Riley. He wasn't sure he spoke aloud or that Riley heard but he knew he spoke the truth. Under this spell there was only the truth and the counterfeit world presented to him each morning was revealed in all its malevolent falseness. He dropped the spent cigarette, finished his orange soda, fulfilled yet drained by the mental orgasm.

Coming into focus again Sturm said, 'I'm going to see Mai. I want to get laid in this state of beautiful bliss. Want to go?' He departed alone when Riley waved him away and told Sampson to prepare another smoke. Outside the streets were crowded with cyclos, trucks and three-wheeled Lambrettas packed with Vietnamese shoppers. Hawkers spread their wares on the cracked sidewalks as Sturm picked his way carefully up the street. He narrowly avoided being hit by a truckload of soldiers before he arrived at the Forty Akers.

It was hot inside the club, too early for business and the air conditioners were not on. In the soft light that fell through the jalousies Sturm saw the club was empty except for the bartender and three girls who Sturm recognized but did not know by name who came toward him and said Mai was not in. 'She go out, I don't know.' As Sturm turned to leave the girl took his arm. 'Come on, buy me drink, okay?' She pouted appealingly, expertly, and Sturm looked from her face down to the rounded breasts half-revealed by the low cut blouse. The girl stepped closer and Sturm saw the other two girls had stopped playing cards while they watched the minor drama. Sturm was surprised by the girl's forwardness, for all the girls who worked in the club knew he was steady with Mai and in their own private code did not try to cut in. Now the other girls would tell Mai about this hustling and there would probably be a fight. Sturm represented a major share of Mai's income and she would not readily relinquish him.

'Come on, don't be cheapskate,' the girl laughed and pulled him toward the bar. She moved against him as they walked, running her breasts over his arm and Sturm went willingly. He ordered a beer for himself and a drink for the girl; nothing more than tea but it cost a dollar.

'My name Co,' the girl said and Sturm laughed, for *co* is the word for miss.

'My name mister,' he said and the girl smiled in turn. She ran her fingers up his thigh, teasing him in a professional manner while brushing away his hands as they groped along her naked thighs. The girl quickly launched into the routine story of how she was an orphan trying to put her younger brother and sister through school and would he please buy her another drink so she could earn a few piastres.

'You really hustle, don't you,' Sturm said. He was suddenly and irrationally angry at her and all Vietnamese. 'They ought to make you a colonel or a goddam chairman of some board. A politician, maybe.' He got up and left the girl who puzzled over the sudden rage she had seen erode his face. She shrugged and went back to the card game.

It was almost dark outside but Sturm caught a ride quickly with a jeep load of Cav troops heading back to the airfield. He lit a roach on the ride back and shared it with the other men. They dropped him at the gate and when their laughing died away in the night he felt unusually deserted, in need of company, someone to ask what was happening to him.

The lights were on in the hootch when he returned but it was empty. He walked around behind the hospital and beyond the messhall to the small quonset that served as the enlisted men's club. He wandered around the noisy and smokey room but couldn't see Dooley or Raab, which depressed him more.

Outside again he paused in the shaft of light from the club window, uncertain where to go. A figure wobbled toward him along the boardwalk and Sturm stepped back as he saw the glint of bars on the collars. One of the officers from their club next door smashed, he thought, then started forward as the light revealed the face of Lt. Saunders. He caught her around the waist and hurried her from the light while he reassured her she was not being accosted by a patient. 'It's me, Sturm.'

'Oh, Jake, lover,' she sighed and leaned her head against his shoulder. 'Walk with me and tell me poems of this lovely land, reveal everything that is good. If you know anything good.' She giggled and stumbled and dragged Sturm down into the sand between the hootches, and Sturm was suddenly uncertain if it were Helen or Mai beneath him.

'Jake, Jake, I am sham-smashed. Drunk. El drunko. Wow, what a party.' She pulled his head down and kissed him. 'I like you Jake, but I don't know why.'

He was floating and aroused and wanted to take her right there in the sand. He kissed her again and drew a leg between her thighs then suddenly the image of Lt. Col. Schoen filled his mind, Schoen peering down and holding his glasses so they wouldn't slip and asking where the smoke was coming from. Sturm began to giggle with his mouth still pressed to hers which Sandy took as an insult.

'I've got to go back. I came out for air. Anyway, I don't think it's too seem—' she burped '—seemly for us to be seen lying here like this.'

'Right, you being an officer an all,' Sturm said and she started to giggle again. He kissed her then, deeply and as he felt her respond he wanted to carry her away into a quiet, dark little hole where they would be alone and where they could make love for hours and there would be no one to order him out on garbage detail again, out to pick up the pieces.

Sandy was trying to untangle herself when Sturm remembered Dooley's new hideaway and he dragged the nurse to her feet. 'Come on. First come, first serve,' he said and with Sandy protesting and stumbling behind he went quickly to the last hootch marked 23-B. He worked the hasp loose from the wall and went inside.

'What izzis place,' Sandy said. Her tongue barely seemed in working order.

'My new private club,' Sturm said and felt his way across the dark room until he found the casket Dooley had set aside as a nuptial bed. He reached inside for the Scotch and slipped it inside Sandy's fatigue blouse next to her breasts. She felt it and cooed, 'Oh, how love—' burp '—lovely.'

Sturm found the candle next and lit it, casting a faint glow around the room and making their shadows dance like macabre spirits on the stacked caskets. Sandy peered around owlishly and said, 'Say, thizzis where they store the cazgits. Caskets.'

To prevent her from going further and possibly panicking, Sturm began kissing her neck, opening her blouse and pulling her down on the floor. She hesitated then began clawing at him, a wildness inside her bursting forth, and he toppled backwards with her in his arms and struck his head. Cursing, he pulled her upright again, climbed into the casket on his back and pulled her in on top of him.

As he unsnapped her silken bra and took her small, pointed breasts in his hands she kept murmuring, 'My God, in a casket?' But Sturm did not hear, his mind was on fire and he began working at her belt as she breathed heavily in his ear. 'In a coffin, Jake?' He was struggling with her snagged zipper when he heard someone scraping along the outside of the tin quonset hut. Sandy, suddenly more sober than he imagined, froze and whispered, 'My God, someone is coming for a cas—' belch '—cazgit.' She started to rise but Sturm held her, snuffed the candle and reached up to ease the lid of the coffin down. 'Just lie quiet. They'll be gone in a minute.'

Inside the closed coffin the air was almost palpable and their bodies slid wetly against each other. Two seals copulating in a zoo tank as hundreds of onlookers applauded. They held their breath as the door scraped open and someone, or maybe two, entered and pulled the door shut. There was heavy breathing and then a familiar voice in the darkness:

'Come here, Betty. Specialist Dooley wants to check you out.' Sturm propped himself on one elbow and inched the lid up. Dooley had set the flashlight on end so the light bounced softly off the ceiling. He had the girl pressed against the wall, opening her white blouse with awkward fingers while he buried his face in hers with an interminable kiss.

Sandy, trying to get a better view through the narrow opening, put an elbow precisely in Sturm's solar plexus. There was a muffled grunt, almost a sigh, that bounced around the room.

Dooley froze, eyes open, lips to lips with the Vietnamese girl, one hand suspended above her half-revealed perfect orbs. His head slowly turned, lips still puckered, and he eyed the far wall. 'Jesus Christ,' he said softly, 'it can't be.' He left the girl sagging against the wall and tiptoed to the back half of the room. He pressed his ear against the wall and listened for a moment, then knocked softly. 'Hello?' Silence. 'Anybody over there? Anybody need something?' In the continuing silence he tiptoed back to the puzzled girl. He shook his head then began kissing her again but by now Betty was staring around the dimly lit room, her eyes slowly widening as she realized where she was.

She grabbed him by the hair and stilled his bobbing head. 'Hey, Doo-lee, this place for dead GI. This numbah ten place.' She said 'place' in a long, drawn out sigh, as if courage were whistling straight out of her. 'Why you bring me this numbah ten place?'

She pushed him away and hurriedly began buttoning her blouse but Dooley advanced on her, pleading. 'No sweat, this only storage place. Nobody dead here. Just boxes. All empty.' She calmed momentarily as Dooley took hold of her again but her eyes, wide and unbelieving, kept roaming the room in anticipation of the dead rising to seize her. Suddenly she froze, her eyes bugged and her mouth opened in catatonic fear. One hand on Dooley's shoulder slowly extended and a finger pointed toward the partially opened casket lid which jiggled slightly as heads beneath it vied for better views. Four fingers could also be seen emerging from the darkness within. Betty finally loosed the scream that rose in her throat, an absolutely piercing shriek that rang throughout the hospital compound. Dooley whirled in time to see the fingers disappear and the casket lid close as Betty wrenched from his grasp and tore from the room. She flung the tin door open with a horrendous tin crash and disappeared into the night still shrieking.

Dooley, starting after her, paused in the doorway long enough to shout at the closed casket, 'You son of a bitch, Sturm, you ruined everything.' He then sprinted into the night after the fading banshee wails.

Only with great effort did Sturm manage to lift Sandy who was in a state of collapse. He didn't know if it was laughing or alcohol. He could hear puzzled voices outside and doors began opening as the curious stuck their heads from hootches. He dragged Sandy across the floor, turned off the flashlight and went outside. He kicked the door shut and dragged the now inert nurse behind the hootch as a group of men in undershorts trotted down the boardwalk toward the faint but continuing screams in the night.

Sturm fumbled over Sandy in the darkness but she was out cold. He buttoned her blouse and slung her over his shoulder. Feeling somewhat like Quasimodo carrying a body through the dark corridors of Notre Dame, he made his way along the backside of the hootches to the nurses quarters.

Several nurses, clutching robes about them, were gathered a little way down the walkway with Major Schoen who held a towel around his midriff. The nurses had not turned the lights on in the hootch and Sturm carried Sandy inside and dumped her on her cot. From the darkness one of the nurses drowsily asked, 'What's going on, Sandy?'

Outside, Sturm nearly bumped into Schoen who peered at him in the darkness. 'Sturm. What's going on?'

'I'm trying to check on it, sir,' he said and saluted foolishly in the dark. Schoen started to return the salute then grabbed quickly at his towel again as Sturm popped away into the protective night.

Dooley was already back in the hootch when Sturm arrived and the redhead was cursing and flinging his boots across the room. He jumped up as Sturm entered and began yelling, 'Goddamit, Sturm, I did you a favor and look what you do to me. I had it made with Betty, I told you this was the night, and what do you do to me? You come out of a coffin like fucking Dracula!' He flung an ice cube at Sturm who collapsed on his bunk.

It was a week before Betty Bazoom returned to work and she refused to so much as glance at Dooley.

CHAPTER NINE

It was the sound of choppers that woke Franklin and he lay in the orthopedic ward filled with bars of afternoon light, his eyes opened and stared at the ceiling as if he could see the Cobras and slicks that flew just overhead. He was up there a few days ago – how long was it now? He couldn't remember. Just a few hours or days ago he had been in one of those slicks where he could see the hospital between his dangling feet and he had thought at the time – yeah, now he remembered – he had thought it would be nice to have a little leg wound, just enough to put him in the hospital between clean sheets with a nurse bending close over the bed until her breasts beneath the crackling white uniform came soft against him. But nurses here didn't wear starched white uniforms, and they didn't linger at his bed with lascivious eyes. No, man, they came in wearing wrinkled goddam fatigues and shoved thermometers in his mouth and needles in his arm and checked his bandages with tight-lipped efficiency. Only one of the nurses so much as smiled at him. That was Lt. Saunders, wasn't she Sturm's chick? Nice little broad. Terrific ass. No wonder Sturm was always grabbing at it. Sometimes when she leaned over the bed he pushed against her with his knee or arm in hopes of provoking some response and while she didn't back away she didn't exactly respond. She sure as hell wasn't Annie. Oh man to have Annie in the ward for just one night, or even for one hour. She would blow their minds, coming down the aisle between beds in her micro-mini skirt with high-heeled leather boots clicking on the linoleum and those gorgeous breasts, the color of a lioness, billowing beneath her white satin blouse. If Annie appeared now every man's pecker in this ward would just pop to attention, one after another, pow, pow, pow. Then she would stand by his bed and run her hand down his flat stomach until stopped at the totem pole he had erected beneath the sheet and she would say, 'Honey, you've been inactive too long. You going to *explode*. Move over, baby, little Orphan Annie is going to get it on with you now.' And she would put one leg up on the edge of the bed to unlace her boot and, dig it, she was ready and she was advertising. He would pull back the sheet for her while all the other dudes were whacking off in frustration. But then her eyes would narrow and she would put her leg back down and smooth her skirt. He could see all happening, even if he didn't want to. Then she would say, 'Hey, what you doing with only one hand? What you done with the other?' her voice all barby like an angry little dog. 'It got blown off, baby, in the war.' 'Well, you better get *another* one, Big Dude, 'cause you ain't handling *me* with no stump. I got *two* nice titties and you only got *one* hand so we are outta synch. Dig? You just a poor one-armed nigger war veteran now.'

She was pushing on him, pushing him away and suddenly he knew he hated her and he hated that goddam voice and her way of walking and flashing it and she was going to get busted in the mouth. He lashed out at her with the soft rounded end of his stump.

'Hey, man, cool it. I'm just trying to wake you for dinner. You don't have to take a poke at me.' It was Johnston, the goddam orderly with the straggly-assed mustache who brought the food around. Franklin looked at Johnston out of eyes dulled by days of despair and heroin. He had just wanted a clean little leg wound but instead he was missing a hand. His big right hand that did everything for him was gone because of that mothafucking Lt. Hoyt. That dude deserved to die but instead I got *my* hand blown away. It wasn't right.

Johnston was still looking at him with nervous eyes. 'Hey, I didn't mean anything. I was just trying to wake you up.' Johnston waited for some reassurances but Franklin only shook his head groggily and rubbed his face with his good left hand until Johnston moved away saying, 'You don't look so hot.'

I don't feel so hot either, Franklin thought. He wanted a smoke bad. The dreams had been getting him lately. He could see his hand somewhere out beyond that trench and he wanted it back. But everytime he reached for it Lt. Hoyt would appear and stomp on his hand and grind it into the dirt until nothing was left. Opening his eyes, he poked at the food on his tray until he saw Johnston finish serving the others and go out the swinging doors. Franklin then announced to the ward that he was having a smoke.

'It ain't your turn,' someone said. 'You know we go in turns so we don't smell the ward up.'

'Fuck you, man, I'm lighting up now,' he said and stared around the room to see who dared challenge. No one did. There were no officers in the ward, not even a senior sergeant. Just grunts. He took the heroin capsule from inside his paper slipper and filled the end of a cigarette. He emptied the capsule in the process and thought, Sturm, you going to have to get me some more today. You owe me. He smoked on his back while he studied the ceiling and thought of Annie some more. He hadn't written her since he lost his hand – since Hoyt made him blow it off – because he knew what would happen. He wanted to think she would be sympathetic and would say, 'It don't matter, baby, you still got what really counts.' He wanted to think that but he knew she wouldn't dig it. She liked everything together, no parts missing, baby, you understand. No parts missing. He finished the smoke and lay unmoving with his stump lying heavily on his stomach. He was still staring at the ceiling when

Johnston returned for the trays. He leaned over Franklin and whispered conspiratorily:

'There's some officer outside asking about you.' When Franklin showed no interest, Johnston persisted from a different angle. 'I don't know who it is, couldn't see his name tag, but he was definitely asking about you.' He waited a moment longer and his thin face grew pinched in his anxiety to stir some show of interest in the whale-sized black before him. His concern was relieved by the sound of the doors opening and the officer in question appearing. 'Here he comes now,' Johnston whispered happily and moved on.

Franklin turned to see the officer coming down the aisle with his helmet neatly under one arm and his .45 in its holster slapping lightly against his starched fatigues. He walks like he's got a broomstick up his ass. Hoyt. What the fuck he want now?

'How are you, Franklin?' Hoyt's question was perfunctory, like the programmed response at funerals when everyone goes around telling each other how sorry they are and hasn't it been hot. Franklin looked at the lieutenant with bloodshot eyes, smack eyes, and kept a guarded silence. Hoyt cleared his throat after a moment and set his helmet on the empty bed behind him. Hoyt turned back toward Franklin, adjusted the weight of the .45 on his hip and spoke to a spot on the wall several inches above Franklin's head.

'Well, I'll come right to the point, Pfc. Franklin. I've come to tell you personally that I am bringing charges against you and you will be court martialled. I wanted you to hear it directly from me and not from the rumor mill.' There, it was out, and Hoyt felt proud. He wasn't afraid to face up to Franklin. It was an officer's duty to level with his men, even those who tried to kill him. Even so, he wished his voice was more relaxed.

Franklin snorted. 'Court martialled? For what? Walking point everyday for a week?'

Hoyt continued to address the spot on the wall. 'For throwing a fragmentation grenade at an officer and thereby trying to kill him while said officer was engaged in the organization of his platoon's defense, said platoon being under enemy attack at the time.'

'Hunh?'

'For trying to frag me, Franklin, that's why.' Hoyt felt more in control of the situation now, even if he didn't yet look at Franklin.

'You crazy, man. If you talking about that grenade, that came from the hill. The *gooks* were trying to kill you. Maybe you ought to court martial them, *Loo*-tenant.'

'I know you were trying to frag me, Franklin, and now I have a witness,' Hoyt replied hotly to the wall. 'Someone saw you throw that grenade.' There was a snicker from the other end of the ward and Hoyt knew that everyone was listening. But he didn't turn around to look at them, to silence them with one of his cold looks. He could, he knew, but wouldn't give them that satisfaction. Just like he wouldn't give Franklin the satisfaction of looking him in the eye. Instead he leaned close to the wall above Franklin's head and hissed, 'We got your black ass cold, Franklin. They're going to hang you. If they don't, me and my brother will be waiting for you when you get back to Chicago. Understand, *boy*?'

His sneering voice cut Franklin opening old and festering wounds in his mind and the black reached for the lieutenant in an angry reflex that he immediately regretted. He had tried to grab the lieutenant across the bed with his right hand, his nowhere hand. Hoyt pointed at it and laughed.

'You're not going to get ahold of me with that useless hambone. It takes a real hand to grab something and you blew yours off. What were you doing with that grenade anyway, Franklin? You sure as hell weren't going to throw it at the North Vietnamese around us, were you?' Hoyt's eyes were narrow and provoking, now looking at Franklin, and the angry black rose to the bait.

'Why throw it at the gooks when I know who *my* enemy is. That's you, man, *you* the mothafucking enemy. You should be fragged. You the one that sent Simpson and the others out into the valley and got them blowed away. You the one who said he *checked* them all and they was all dead but next morning we could see where Simpson had crawled all night to try and get back to us. Still *alive*. But you left him out there to *die*.'

Franklin was yelling and Hoyt leaned back against the bed behind him and let the abuse flow. When Franklin finished, Hoyt permitted himself a thin and cynical smile. 'Well done, Franklin. That's what I like to hear. That's a confession you just made, Franklin, do you know that? Does that register on your little brain? You've confessed to trying to frag me and there is a roomfull of witnesses here.' He leaned forward and his eyes bulged at Franklin. 'I told you, we are going to hang your ass. Hang your *black nigger* ass, boy.'

Hoyt's face was close to Franklin's, his thin neck stretched forth to hiss the words and this time Franklin brought his left hand up beneath that neck and caught it in his massive hand, hooked the man good, so he could feel the ropy neck muscles contract as his fingers bit deep, and feel the throat surge when his thumb plunged into the larynx. Hoyt's eyes bulged and he tore at Franklin's hand but his slender fingers could not move that talon grip. Slowly, Hoyt's face darkened with suffused blood and his unbelieving eyes swiveled toward Franklin. Unable to loosen the hand at his neck Hoyt began hammering at Franklin's face and chest but still nothing changed. Nothing altered the giant black's grip. Now Hoyt's eyes were glazing and his wrenching attempts to tear free were becoming spasmodic. God, it can't be happening to me, but he could barely even hear himself think there was such a roaring in his ears. The pistol, for God's sake use the pistol, why didn't I remember it before, and his hand fumbled at the flap on the holster which wouldn't come loose and his fingers were so thick they wouldn't work. Nothing worked now. The pistol, I've got it, but it's so heavy, and the noise in my ears, so loud, and it is getting dark, where is the light . . .

The room was silent except for the soft sounds of a man being throttled in the corner of the narrow-green-painted amputee ward. The seven other patients sat frozen as they watched the death of an officer, a lifer, not really one of them. To the patients, watching from a distance, it appeared that the lieutenant was drowning among the waves of white beds and only Franklin's hand around his throat kept him afloat. Then the great hand opened and Hoyt, his head back at an odd angle, disappeared beneath the linen waves. There was a collective sigh from the men in the ward. 'Oh, Jesus, oh my God, did you see . . .' cried one man but his voice dropped to a whisper and faded away as Franklin looked up, his eyes still thick with death.

'Nobody seen nothing, right?' He threw back his sheet and got out of bed. 'Nobody seen nothing,' he repeated as he reached down to pull Hoyt's pistol from the holster and stick it under his pillow. He bent and grunted as he pushed Hoyt's body beneath his bed and tucked him up against the wall then rolled the helmet underneath. He looked at the body and thought how he just wanted to frighten the lieutenant, give him back something for badmouthing him, but when he got ahold of that neck it felt good and the tighter he squeezed the better it felt. He stood up in blue pajamas too small for him and walked down the aisle between the beds, every man watching him but saying nothing. He stopped before the bed of a man from Gary, Indiana, who had no legs. 'I need some scag, man, I'm all out. Give me some,' Franklin said and held out his massive left hand, the death hand, and the man with no legs fumbled hurriedly in his pillow for the capsule and told Franklin he could keep it all because there was plenty more, yes, keep it all, man, no problem.

As Franklin walked back toward his bed he felt the butterflies come up hard in his stomach and he was afraid his leg was going to start quivering uncontrollably like it did when he first knifed that kid in the tenement so long ago. If I keep walking I won't get the shakes, he thought, and frowned at those in the ward in case people were trying to read his mind. 'Nobody seen nothing,' he repeated. 'Nobody talks. I'll get rid of that motha tonight. He was a bad lieutenant, man, real bad. Killed my best buddy, sent him into the open where it was guaran*teed* he would get zapped. That *Loo*-tenant,' he liked to say it that way and Hoyt would not harass him again, 'deserved to die. He liked to call me nigger and boy. He was a bad dude.' Franklin was at his bed and the heroin from the last duster cigarette was pumping in him now, not much, not a real high, but it gave him new confidence. And it had felt *good*, man. I just wish you could of seen it, Hotdog, you would *like* it. I did all of you in the platoon a favor. Now just get rid of the body and it would be over. There were lots of men missing in Vietnam. Who would miss Hoyt once he got rid of the body? But how? Man, I never just *killed* a dude before, he thought, and his left leg was starting to shake now.

The doors at the other end of the room opened and admitted that nurse, Lt. Saunders, who began making a quick check of the patients, changing intravenous bottles on some, checking temperatures on others. She was in a cheerful mood and she tried to talk to the patients but they would look first at the black cloud of Franklin watching from his end of the ward and they would remain silent. Franklin stubbed out his cigarette when it passed the heroin fill and lay back on his pillow to watch the nurse move quickly and efficiently from bed to bed. Nice little body, like to get me some of that some day, he thought. He kept his eyes on her as she came around the end of the room by his bed but suddenly he was afraid she might know, that she could see it in his eyes and he lowered them as she came alongside. She glanced at his chart and smiled at him.

'You'll be going to Tokyo very soon, I think, Franklin. That ought to make you feel better.'

Franklin said nothing and she moved between the beds to fix his pillow. 'Let me fluff this up a little for you before lights out.' As she stepped close to the head of the bed she gave a little squeal and jumped back. 'What's that? Felt like a mouse.' She bent cautiously to look and saw the body jammed into the fetal position beneath the bed with its face hidden.

'Who is this? What are you doing under there?' Sandy tugged at the body, thinking it was a friend of Franklin trying to hide. She pulled again and one arm flopped loosely onto the floor with the hand up and the fingers half curled like a fumigated bug on its back.

'Oh,' she said, suddenly knowing the man was dead. She straightened to look at Franklin who held the .45 pointed at her belly. Still he didn't speak.

Sandy blinked and recovered quickly, guessing in an instant what had happened but revealing nothing in her face or voice. She ignored the weapon and spoke lightly to Franklin. 'He must have had an accident. And I see you found his pistol. He must have dropped it. I'll get an orderly to move him out of here.' She backed slowly from between the beds toward the aisle but Franklin slid his foot around to block her.

'You ain't going nowhere, *Loo*-tenant, baby.' He smiled, heavy and malevolent. 'You going to stay right here with me. Keep me company for awhile.'

Sandy lunged backward now as she tried to break past the

restraining foot but it held long enough for Franklin to throw his bandaged arm around her neck and drag her close. From the corner of his eyes he saw the man nearest the door ease off the bed and start toward the door.

'Nobody leaves here,' yelled Franklin and he swung the pistol toward the man who carefully got back into bed, his eyes staring at the pistol barrel. 'Now, *Loo*-tenant, I put on my robe and you and me we're going for a little walk, right out of this hospital. You lead the way to the front and we'll get a jeep and split for Saigon where I will disappear. If you want to make any funny moves just keep thinking of that other *Loo*-tenant under the bed.' He pulled Sandy from between the beds and together they started toward the door with Franklin a half-pace behind the nurse and to her right. He nudged her once in the small of the back with the barrel of the pistol he kept in the pocket of his robe. 'You've seen what big holes these things make in people, haven't you?' She didn't reply but he knew she was listening. At the door he took her upper arm to stop her and his hand tingled at the feel of her breast and the silken bra under the fatigues. It had been so long since he had felt something like that. He turned to the men in the ward. 'I gotta split and I don't want any of you opening your mouths to the man about me or I'll be back to settle a score, dig?' He flashed the .45 and enjoyed the wide stares of the patients before he slipped it back in the bathrobe pocket.

They pushed through the swinging doors and almost bumped into Sturm who fell back as the two brushed past him.

'Hey, Franklin, I brought something for you. Where are you going?' The two continued down the hallway and Sturm, thinking Franklin hadn't heard him, started after them. 'Where you going?' he called again and picked up his pace until he overtook them. He started to talk to Franklin again but the black responded without warning by giving him a violent push toward the wall. Sturm caught himself and wheeled back toward Franklin who gave him a baleful stare and kept walking.

Sandy spoke then, fast and nervous over her shoulder. 'Don't push it, Jake, we'll be right back. I'm just going out front for a minute.'

'Well, why are you—' Sturm stopped in mid-question. She said she was going out front but she was headed toward the rear. Sandy looked pale and nervous. Franklin looked like he wanted to smash someone and they were going out the back toward the messhall, not the front. Weird. He looked after them, puzzled, then turned back toward the amputee ward. He was about to enter and ask a few questions when someone called his name.

'Sturm, come here a minute. I want to talk to you.' It was Kowalski, his face flushed and his mood dangerous. Sturm had seen him like this before when he had been drinking and Sturm wanted to keep clear.

'Be right there, sir,' he said and pushed into the ward. Three men started talking at once: 'He's got the nurse.' 'He killed that lieutenant back there.' 'Watch it, man, he's got a .45 in his pocket.'

Sturm was unbelieving. 'You mean Sandy? Franklin has Lt. Saunders, that nurse, as a hostage? Why?'

Another patient with his arm gone at the shoulder knelt by Franklin's bed and with his good hand began tugging at Hoyt's body just as Kowalski exploded into the room. He looked at Sturm with his close set ice-blue eyes, a bull sizing up an amateur matador. 'Goddamit, Sturm, I told you to come here.'

Sturm whirled on him. 'Sandy's been captured. Franklin's got a gun. We've got to call the MPs.' He started past the warrant officer who grabbed him and spun him around.

'I'm talking to you, troop,' Kowalski bellowed.

Sturm flung the pilot's hand off and yelled back. 'And I'm

trying to tell you one of the patients has flipped. He's got Sandy at gunpoint.'

Down the aisle the patients had Hoyt's body out from under the bed and they were all talking. 'See, he killed this lieutenant. That's where Franklin got the pistol. Then when the nurse saw this body, Franklin grabbed her.' Kowalski stared at the body and his mouth sagged momentarily. He spun to follow Sturm out the door. 'Where are you going?' Kowalski demanded.

'To get the MP.'

Kowalski caught up and stopped Sturm. 'Hold it, hold it. Let's think a minute. First, the only MP around here is that useless Pfc. on the gate. If he starts shooting it might get Sandy killed. Let's see if we can handle this better and faster ourselves. Which way did they go?'

Sturm paused reluctantly. Kowalski might be drinking but he made sense. Time was running out and it would be better to handle it themselves. 'They went out the back. Sandy said she was going out front but she led him toward the rear for some reason. Franklin wouldn't know these corridors well enough to know the difference.' Sturm was calm now, calculating. 'But when they get out there then Franklin will be mad. He'll follow the boardwalk around to the front. He wants to get a jeep. Let's go out the side door. That's almost at my hootch and we've got our weapons in there.' They were outside in the night before Sturm finished talking.

At the far end of the hospital Sandy stood in the dim rectangle of light that fell through the screen door. That overhead light had never been fixed and once outside she had planned on running in the dark. But now it didn't seem so easy. Franklin stood so close and she could feel the barrel pressing on her spine. A figure materialized beside her, an intern headed toward the officer's club, and he greeted her briefly before disappearing again in the darkness. She wanted to run to him but the .45 jabbed hard against her back and she heard Franklin's breath quicken in anger.

'This ain't the goddam front entrance. What you trying to pull?'

'I was so frightened I got confused,' she lied. She remained unmoving to force Franklin into making the next decision.

'How do we get back to the front?' he asked.

'We'll just go back through the hospital,' Sandy said lightly and turned to go inside again. If she could just get him back inside – somebody must be alerted by now. He pushed her forward with the pistol.

'No. Lead me around the outside. It's dark out here and people won't be stopping us. I can't trust those dudes inside not to talk. So come on, *Loo*-tenant, time is running short,' he said and gave her a painful jab at the base of her spine. 'We've got to hustle.' He pushed her to the left where the boardwalk ran between the row of hootches. 'And if anybody asks why I am outside just tell them it's a special exercise walk or something, but make it good.'

They started along the walkway with Sandy leading and Franklin just behind, his hand deep in the pocket of his robe. As they left the light at the hospital's rear entrance and started toward the quonsets two figures suddenly appeared ahead of them. There was something in their cat-footed movements that bothered Franklin, something about the two that made him think of the plain clothes men working the south side of Chicago. They were always in pairs and they never quite fit in – almost but not quite – even if they were black. They were too watchful. That's it, Franklin suddenly realized, these two weren't talking. Just watching him. He told Sandy to stop and the two others stopped also. Now Franklin could see that one of them was Sturm and the other was an officer. As they paused, Sandy made a sudden bolt to her right, which was a mistake, because Franklin whipped his bandaged right arm out and around her neck with a vicious jerk. In the same instant he pulled the .45 from his pocket and pointed it at the two before him.

'Sturm, you and that fucking officer get outta my way or I'll *blow* you away.' As they swerved off the boardwalk in face of his .45 he could see in the dim light that they had M-16s held by the pistol grips behind their legs. From behind the shelter of a quonset hut, Kowalski swung his weapon up and spoke:

'You let that nurse go and we'll settle this matter right now, just between us.'

Sturm interjected quickly as Franklin brought his pistol muzzle to Sandy's head. 'Franklin, it isn't worth it. Maybe Hoyt was bad but don't make it worse for yourself by killing anymore. Put your pistol down and let Lt. Saunders go. We'll get you right back to bed and this whole thing will be over.' He spoke calmly and Franklin didn't reject him. The black stood silent a moment with the barrel of the .45 rubbing thoughtfully up and down Sandy's temple.

He finally spoke. 'If I surrender now the man will just hang my ass. Why should I? I got nothing to lose by running now. If I get to Saigon they'll never find me.'

'You can't run forever and maybe it wasn't all your fault, about killing that lieutenant. Just don't make it worse, man,' Sturm replied. He thought his coaxing might be working for Franklin seemed to be thinking about it. Sturm started to renew his plea when the rear door burst open and the MP from the front gate stood there with his .45 in hand, legs planted wide and his face filled with fear. He saw Franklin standing in the gloom and swung the .45 which looked too big for his bony hand toward the black.

'Drop the gun,' he said in a thin voice and almost as an afterthought added, 'and let go of that there nurse.'

Franklin turned toward the MP as the door opened and pulled Sandy around. He knew he was in an awkward spot.

If he turned fully toward the MP his back would be open to that goddam officer and that doublecrossing Sturm. Something has to give, he thought. He thumbed back the hammer and his arm went out smoothly toward the scarecrow MP who tried to bring his weapon onto the black but all he could see was the white face of the nurse looking at him. Then the MP was trying to back hastily through the screen door which had closed behind him and there was no place to hide when Franklin's pistol jerked. The MP took the slug squarely in the chest bone and the impact sent him careening against the door and off the porch steps. Instantly Franklin turned back to face Kowalski who had his weapon up ready to fire but instead ducked back behind the hootch as Franklin's pistol swung his way. At the sound of the shot men and women began boiling out of the clubs and hootches, at first curious then suddenly panic stricken at the sight of the giant black waving his .45 around and two men facing him with M-16s. People began rolling on the ground and someone kept yelling, 'Incoming, incoming.'

In the distance, the yelp of an electric siren began to draw closer. With a curve, Franklin snapped a shot at Kowalski which missed and tore a chunk of tin out of the side of the building. As the sense of being trapped filled his mind, he yelled, 'Stay away from me, all you mothafuckers, or I'm going to blow this nurse's head off. You hear me?' He shoved the barrel into her ear to dramatize his point, as he backed toward the one place he could find cover, the dark, screened building behind him that was the messhall. He backed up to the door and told Sandy to reach behind him and open it. At first she didn't react and he had to yell at her until she responded slowly, in a near faint. From inside, through the screened window, he could see figures darting for cover. The panicky shriek of the siren in front of the hospital stopped abruptly as the MPs cut the switch and leaped out. Showdown time, Franklin thought, and dragged Sandy into the kitchen where he lay her on the floor between the heavy cast iron stoves and the refrigerators. He settled beside her where he could watch the back entrance to the kitchen and part of the main dining hall beyond the serving counter. His arm was throbbing painfully beneath the bandages and he made the nurse reach in his robe pocket for his cigarettes and capsule of heroin. He showed her how to fix it then lay beside her and shoved the cocked pistol, cold and flat, under her fatigue blouse next to her skin, which made her shudder. He could smell her now, warm and clean, not at all like the jungle. 'What's your first name?' he whispered. 'I want to know you better. A lot better.'

Outside, beyond the line of fire from the messhall, Sturm and Kowalski stood with the four MPs. One of them was also a warrant officer but Kowalski did all the talking. 'If it was just him inside there it wouldn't be any problem. I would let fly with an M-79 round and then you boys could pick up the pieces.' Two of the MPs grinned at this. 'But he's got this nurse in there, see, so we've got to be careful.' Kowalski took charge before the MPs understood what was happening.

'Now Sturm and I know the layout better than you, so we'll see if we can get a sight on him somehow. You cover the four sides of the building in case he makes a break. Sturm and I will flush him out of there.'

One of the MPs, a warrant officer like Kowalski, made a show of protest. After all, he was in command of this operation he tried to say as Kowalski led him firmly around to the front exit.

'This is a tough spot here. We need the best man here, so you better take over this one.' The MP agreed and Kowalski gave him a wolfish grin.

The pilot turned back to Sturm and hissed, 'That dude inside may be a friend of yours but he's insane now. And I was always taught to kill mad dogs. You're a farm boy. If something goes mad you kill it, right?'

'But he isn't a dog to be shot down. He's just strung out on drugs, on heroin.'

'Same difference,' Kowalski shrugged. 'He's still got to be taken out.' He started to turn away but Sturm caught his arm.

'Listen, he's probably in the kitchen, between the stoves and the refrigerators. It's just like an iron bunker so don't just go blasting away at the place. It makes more sense to try and talk him out of there.' Before Kowalski could argue, Sturm slipped along the hootch until he could see the screened kitchen door.

'Franklin. It's me. Sturm. Can we talk?' Silence. 'Franklin. Don't make it worse on yourself. Give up now.'

There was a muffled cry from Sandy inside the dark kitchen and then Sturm could hear her pleading in a soft voice, 'Please. No, please, no.'

He felt helpless yelling into the dark but he had to try. 'Franklin, leave her alone. If you harm her it will only make it worse. Give up while you can.' In response there was only another small cry of pain from Sandy.

'Goddam you, leave her alone.' He considered a rush to the side of the building and was on his feet when Kowalski appeared silently at his side. In the half light cast by the hospital windows Sturm could see the pilot's eyes glittering with excitement. He no longer looked half drunk.

'You just keep talking to him, Sturm. I'm going to the opposite end of the building where the officer's entrance is and work my way down the side wall until I can get a bead on that dude.'

'If you get in there and get the drop on him, I know he'll surrender,' Sturm said. 'Don't kill him. He's just spaced out. You don't need to kill him.'

'Are you crazy? He's already greased the lieutenant and that MP and he's got Sandy in there, doing God knows what to her. If I see that son of a bitch I'm going to plug him. You just do the talking. Keep him busy.'

'We're the dustoff crew that saved his life,' Sturm snapped back. 'Now you want to take it. Don't be so hot to kill, Mr. Kowalski. His mind is just sprung.'

'He's a mad dog and mad dogs get shot,' Kowalski replied angrily and moved away.

Around him Sturm could see clusters of small white faces peering from behind hootches. They're just waiting for someone to get killed, Sturm thought. It doesn't matter who, just someone. It would help break the routine. He turned back to the messhall. The screened kitchen door where Franklin had entered was at least 40 feet away from where Sturm crouched behind a hootch. Light from the rear windows of the hospital fell across the gravel expanse and Sturm knew it would be almost impossible to make it across there without getting hit. Franklin had the advantage. He was in the dark while all approaches were in the light. The messhall was screened on all four sides and all Franklin had to do was rise to his knees to see what was coming at him. The only possibility was to Franklin's rear where the serving counter in the kitchen cut off his view of the dining hall. Kowalski was right about trying to get up on him from behind. It might just work if I can keep that dude thinking about a charge from this position, Sturm thought.

There was another whimpering cry from Sandy that floated through the screening and Sturm's mind flooded with pictures of what could be happening to her but he didn't want to think about it. He had to stay cool, keep talking. Any rash moves was going to get someone killed, he thought, because Franklin is unhinged.

'Franklin, goddamit, let her go and let me come in there. Do you hear me?'

Franklin's voice floated out low and relaxed. 'Yeah, man, everyone can hear you.' He paused and chuckled deep in his throat. 'Say, Sturm, it seems I got your chick in here. She's not bad. I *like* the feel of this,' he said and there was a muffled cry from Sandy.

'Oh God please don't please don't. *Please*.'

Her desperate whimpering stabbed at Sturm's mind and he was up and running toward the end of the messhall before he realized it, forgetting about staying cool, hoping to get against the wall and out of sight before he got hit. But he had taken no more than two strides when the first bullet slammed through the tin siding of the quonset beside his head. Another shot ricocheted off the gravel in front of him and Sturm spun about and flung himself out of sight again.

'You were lucky that time, Sturm. Next time I'll take your head off,' Franklin yelled. 'And if you think I can't do it, ask that MP lying on the steps.'

'You can't stay in there forever, Franklin. Come out now.' Sturm was only slightly encouraged that Franklin had not killed him. That bastard could shoot unbelievably with his left hand.

'I can't come out now. I'm busy in here,' Franklin laughed and then Sturm could hear him start cooing to Sandy. 'That's right, baby, do it right. Just like I want. Make it feel good.' There was no sound from Sandy.

Pinned and angry, Sturm felt the frustration boil in his head. He brought his M-16 up and aimed at the doorway, ready to empty the clip into the building. So what if he hit Sandy, it wouldn't be any worse than what she was getting now. Where the hell was Kowalski? Get in there, goddamit, and kill that bastard. Yes, kill him. 'Never mind what I said before, Mr. Kowalski. Kill that dude if you get a shot,' Sturm yelled into the darkness.

Sandy suddenly began screaming, her voice cutting through the darkness with notes of terror. 'I won't do it! Goddam you, I won't –' a resounding slap cut her outcry short and then Sturm could hear her crying and he was overcome with a blinding urge to kill Franklin himself, to gut shoot him and watch him cry.

'You'll do anything I want, *Loo*-tenant,' Franklin said.

'Franklin,' Sturm yelled, not knowing what to say but hoping that anything he said might distract him from Sandy. 'You told me you lost your hand in the war. Is that right? Wasn't that a bit careless to lose your hand? Where did you leave it?' Just shout anything.

'Fuck you, whitey,' Franklin yelled and fired another round through the screen door at Sturm.

'You put the blame on everyone but yourself. Now you're high on scag and trying to prove you're a big man by killing people. I'll bet you've killed more whiteys than you have dinks. I'll bet you're real big on killing women,' Sturm shouted back. He sensed that his plan was working, for he could see a shadowy form move near the doorway but he couldn't tell if Franklin had Sandy in front of him.

'That's right, and I'm going to take some more whitey's with me,' Franklin shouted back in a fury. He fired again with careless ferocity toward the hootch and Sturm could see the bright muzzle flash before he ducked behind the concrete foundation blocks. Then in the sudden stillness that followed the burst of fire came the flat snick of the hammer falling on an empty chamber. Sturm raised his head, knowing it was over, and so did Franklin for he abruptly shoved Sandy through the doorway and threw the pistol on the ground beside her. She came out stumbling and clutching her open fatigues to her. She staggered toward Sturm who rushed into the open to meet her and he could see her face ghastly white and streaked with tears. She looked at him with wild unseeing eyes and gasped, 'Kill him, kill that bastard.' He tried to hold her but she twisted away and plunged into the dark where several nurses materialized to catch her.

Sturm brought his rifle up on Franklin who stood filling the doorway at the top of the stairs, his arms rising slowly as he prepared to step down. His huge arms were spread wide, black Jesus on the Cross, when there were two rapid shots and Franklin plunged down the steps. He went down like a tree, arms still wide, and hit hard on his face in the gravel but Sturm saw he was still alive and as he stared Franklin slowly pulled one knee under himself and started to rise when from the kitchen there came three more shots, slow and steady as if the firer were taking careful aim between each shot. Franklin pitched forward as if kicked. One leg trembled for a long second and then everything was still. Kowalski slowly opened the kitchen door and stood looking down at the man sprawled before him.

'He should have watched how many rounds he had left,' the pilot said as the MPs and the doctors and the curious hurried up to see the end.

Sturm stood with his unfired rifle hanging loosely in his right hand and looked at Franklin's body with the five holes tinged with spreading blood in the back. None of the doctors moved to see if he were still alive. Sturm swung the muzzle of his rifle until it pointed at the .45 which lay in the gravel beside Franklin's head.

'He gave up. He threw the pistol out and turned Sandy loose,' Sturm said and looked at Kowalski who remained on the kitchen steps above the others.

The pilot shifted his rifle and said, 'Nobody knows what that man was going to do or what he had on him. He was like a mad dog and I've told you what had to be done with mad dogs.' He looked at the MPs for confirmation but the warrant officer said nothing as he stepped forward and rolled Franklin over. He reached in Franklin's robe pocket and pulled out the crushed pack of cigarettes and a nearly empty plastic vial.

'Heroin,' the MP said. 'Just some heroin on him.' He rose and signalled the other MPs to take the body back into the hospital.

Sturm felt torn as he watched the MPs struggle with the limp giant. He had wanted to shoot the man himself and he knew now that he was glad Franklin was dead. But in cold blood? That made it all wrong.

'He gave up,' Sturm said slowly and looked at Kowalski. 'Didn't you see him let Sandy go and throw that .45 out the door?'

'No, I didn't, buddy-boy. I was too busy getting to him while you sat out here and talked to him,' Kowalski answered sharply. 'I would have thought you would have been the first to shoot him just for what he was doing to Sandy in there. Why didn't you shoot anyway? You had your weapon up and a good clean shot at him?'

Sturm flushed. 'Alright, I admit it, I wanted him killed too for whatever he was doing to Sandy. I would have shot him if I could have got a line on him inside there but I couldn't. The next thing I know he released Sandy and threw out his pistol. He had surrendered and to shoot then would have been cold blooded murder. Cold blooded murder, Mr. Kowalski,' Sturm repeated.

The pilot started down the stairs toward him but was blocked by an effusive Major Schoen who came off the boardwalk all breathless and adjusting his glasses as he called out, 'Congratulations, Mr. Kowalski, our actions saved that nurse's life.' He shook the pilot's hand. 'A terrible thing but one you faced up to. I'm certainly going to recommend that you be decorated. Very courageous indeed.' He pumped away at Kowalski's hand and led him away. The rest of the curious slowly melted away too and in the darkness the laughter and music from the clubs swelled again. Sturm took a last look at the blood on the gravel before he turned back to his hootch. He wanted to see Sandy but knew she would be sedated by now. He just hoped she was not badly hurt.

He reached to take the clip from his weapon and found that he had forgotten to load it.

CHAPTER TEN

At breakfast everyone in the messhall was talking about it and standing around outside where the black had died. Over their powdered scrambled eggs and toast, Dooley pestered Sturm for all the details and after the second time through he asked, 'Well, why didn't you shoot him?'

'Maybe that crazy son of a bitch did deserve to die,' Sturm answered sharply, 'but not like that, not gunned in the back after he had thrown away his weapon.' Raab had asked him the same thing earlier and he was tired of answering. Only Riley hadn't asked it and that was because he considered Franklin a brother, a blood, no matter what he had done. To make things worse everyone was saying what a cool operator Kowalski was, how he had saved Lt. Saunders, and Sturm felt the unstated implication in their comments that Sturm should have shot first.

'How's Sandy doing?' Dooley asked.

'Not so good, I'm afraid. Hard to tell. She won't say much about it,' Sturm replied. He pushed at the pale eggs and his mind bounced back to earlier in the morning when he asked one of the other nurses how Sandy was. She told him Lt. Saunders was in her bed and Specialist Sturm should leave her alone and let her rest. But he had gone to the hootch anyway and knocked and when a faint voice said 'Yes?' he had stuck his head inside. The hootch was empty except for Sandy lying in her bunk by the door, propped up on several pillows and just gazing across the room. He came inside and was beside her bed before she slowly turned her head and looked at him. She stared up and two large tears welled in the corners of her eyes and spilled onto her cheeks. She put her hand up to wipe away the tears and said in a tremulous voice, 'Oh, I don't want to see anyone now. I can't, Jake, I can't.'

He sat on the empty bunk beside hers. 'But I've been worried about you, Sandy. I had to know how you were. Nobody seemed to really know.'

'I'm alright. I just don't feel like seeing people today.' She pulled the sheet higher under her chin in a protective gesture and studied her tightly clasped hands. She didn't look at Sturm.

'Can you tell me what happened? Maybe talking it out would help.' He tried not to look at the soft rise of her breasts under the sheet.

She shook her head and squeezed her eyes tightly shut. 'No, God, no. I don't want to ever talk about it. I don't want to even think about it, but I can't stop myself. It seems like I can't think of anything else.'

'Did he ... did he ...?' Sturm started to ask but he couldn't finish the question. He didn't really want to know.

'Don't ask me about it, Jake, just don't ask anything.' She said nothing more but kept her eyes down and twisted her fingers until they turned white. Silence hung between them like a curtain. Sturm squeezed the bridge of his thin nose for a moment, trying to think of something to say. Finally he stood up.

'Well. Is there anything I can get you?'

'No.'

'Well, I've got to go now, but I'll check with you later. I'm sorry it happened, Sandy. But let's put it behind us. I'll help you.' He bent to press her hands but she moved them and said nothing. He turned to leave and at the door she called softly to him.

'Jake, why didn't you shoot him?'

He turned and unease spilled into his stomach.

'Why? Because he threw down his pistol and surrendered. If I had shot him then it would have been murder.'

She covered her face with her hands and said, 'I'm so glad he's dead. So glad.'

Sturm waited by the door but she kept her face covered and said nothing more so he went out. That was early this morning. Now, as he lay smoking after breakfast, he inwardly cursed Franklin. Maybe he *should* have shot him, but Franklin had released Sandy, thrown down his weapon and was just standing there waiting to be captured. He had surrendered and to shoot him would have been murder. Still, that bad dude had brought him nothing but misery, given him the heroin habit – well, at least introduced him to it – done something unspeakable to Sandy, probably scarred her life forever, and killed two men. Kowalski, on the other hand, had no doubts. He had shot Franklin and ended the whole mess. There would be an investigation, maybe even a court martial, but Kowalski would come out a hero. Schoen had already promised him that.

The hootch door squeaked open and everyone turned to look at Johnston who had his head in the door but came no further. These dustoff crews were weird, everyone knew that, so he kept his distance.

'The first sergeant told me to roust you out. You've got a mission going.'

As the others gathered their gear, Johnston eagerly continued to talk. 'I told you it was coming, remember, Jake? The Fifth Mech is starting a pull back from the Z and they're getting the shit rocketed out of them. First Cav already brought in some casualties. You should have seen it, man. Rocket hit an APC with a bunch of grunts sleeping in it. Really tore them up.' Johnston was warming to his tale as the four pushed by him and started toward the choppers. The pilots were already there.

'Nice to see you could join us today,' Kowalski said as Sturm and Dooley ran up. 'Hope we didn't disturb your beauty rest.'

'What do you do, sleep in this chopper in hopes of being first out on every garbage detail?' Sturm felt equally sarcastic.

'Look, I don't want any lip from you today, Sturm. You roger that?' When Sturm ignored him to look over the medical gear Kowalski spun him around and glared as he waited for an answer.

Sturm slowly looked down at him. 'Yes sir. I roger you. You made everything perfectly clear, as they say in Washington these days.'

'You're big with words, Sturm, but not much with action. Like last night,' Kowalski snapped.

'And you're too damn quick on the trigger. I know Schoen thinks you're a hero but in my book you're a murderer. Sir.' He put a biting twist on the word sir.

Surprisingly, Kowalski didn't explode but only bared his teeth. 'Murder. Isn't that what Vietnam is all about? When are you going to catch on, buddy-boy?'

'Never, I hope,' Sturm answered.

'But you will, you will.' Still grinning, Kowalski moved away and climbed into the aircraft commander's seat while Sturm angrily buttoned the door of the new co-pilot, a lanky Arkansas hillbilly on his second tour named Charley Tippit.

They flew in silence to the site of the rocket attack where they made a wide circle around the tanks and armored personnel carriers that were drawn in a circle like pioneers fending off Indians. One track vehicle still burning was being dragged clear and Sturm guessed it was still filled with ammunition. Sturm could also see men moving about below with no apparent concern for more incoming, which made things a little brighter.

Rainbow One-two was talking to Kowalski. 'Say, One-one, since you were spending your time talking while we were taking off this morning we'll take the first load out and you can clean up the rest. Meanwhile we'll be back having Bloody Marys and waiting on you.'

'Roger, One-two, go ahead.' Kowalski was not in the mood for early morning banter. He made wide turns above the armored circle that crouched in the sandy wastes of northern Quang Tri province and when the other medevac lifted clear Kowalski brought his chopper in hard and fast which covered the tracks with a sand storm.

Sturm crossed to the left side of the bird and stood waiting by the doorway for the wounded but none came. Finally, a young captain ran toward them, bending low to duck the blades and holding his helmet on his head with one hand. He stood by Kowalski's door and started to shout something when Kowalski grabbed the captain's shirt front with one hand and began shaking him. The captain's initial anger at the rough greeting turned to surprise then joy as he took a second look at the pilot and yelled, 'It's King Kong Kowalski, back for more. I'll be damned.'

'You old son of a bitch,' Kowalski shouted.

'When did you get back?' the captain yelled.

'I'll always be back to rescue fuckups like you,' Kowalski replied and fingered the two bars sewed on the captain's collar. 'So it's Captain Anderson now. I'll bet you're even a genuine war hero.'

Anderson grinned. 'All for God, country and mother.' He turned serious again. 'I don't want to hold you up. We don't have any more wounded but I've got four NVA prisoners. I've had our interpreter working on them since we got them last night but they won't say anything. I'm going to send them to Division S-2. Could you take them in?'

'Why don't you get them to talk first? Be a gold star on your kindergarten record.'

'I can't crack them. They're mostly a little older. Some might be NCOs, possibly even an officer.'

Kowalski nodded thoughtfully for a moment. 'Why don't you bring these heroes of the people out for a chopper ride? Like we did last year, remember?'

Anderson grinned. 'Yeah, why not? They love to talk in choppers. Got some time?'

'We'll make time,' Kowalski said and shut the engine down.

Sturm, who had been listening from the doorway, was incredulous. 'You're going to shut down here? In a rocket zone?'

Kowalski turned as he unbuckled his chicken plate. 'I told you, buddy-boy, no lip today. Besides, rocketing is over for today. Right, Andy?'

Anderson nodded. 'Right. I told them no shooting while I have guests.'

Kowalski bared his teeth in what passed for a grin. 'So you almost forgot that interrogation we did over by Con Thien, didn't you? You must never forget, Andy, that choppers are made for interrogations.' He put his hand familiarly on Anderson's shoulder. 'Now, let's go see your prisoners and see if they won't reconsider not talking. Be a shame to waste Division's time with questions when we can get the answers right now ourselves.'

Anderson led them across the rutted earth between the tracked vehicles to an armored personnel carrier with all the hatches closed. A shirtless GI remained sitting in his folding chair by the rear door, an M-16 in his lap.

'All quiet in there, captain. But they're going to really start cooking when the sun gets a little higher.'

'Bring them out, Rivera.'

The trooper unlatched the door and spoke into the gloomy interior. 'Hey, dinks, come on out. Di di, let's go.' A pale face, cheeks gaunt and eyes hooded to conceal emotion, appeared in the doorway. The man looked at the Americans outside then slowly emerged. The other three followed and all stood blinking in the strong light. They wore only light green fatigues and tennis shoes. All other items, even belts, had been taken from them.

'What papers they had on them didn't tell us much. I'm guessing they got separated from their unit during that big arclight we had two nights ago. They wandered into one of our recon patrols.' Anderson pointed at the gaunt faced man, the first to appear and a little older than the others. 'I think this one is an officer or a senior NCO. The others are just grunts.'

Kowalski slowly walked around the four, eyeing them carefully and finally stopping in front of a nervous round-faced youth who appeared to be the youngest. He was probably no more than 20, thought Sturm who watched the proceedings warily. It was beginning to look like what happened in the refugee camp.

'I think Moon-face here will be the best to start with,' Kowalski said. 'He probably knows the least since he's the youngest. So we can consider him expendable, right?'

Anderson hedged. 'I don't know. I want all of them to make it to Division. For one thing, I've already reported that I have four POWs.'

Kowalski stepped closer to the captain and spoke cajolingly. 'Andy, there aren't going to be any problems. There might be an accident, but Division know such things happen. Especially S-2. These intelligence boys have accidents with some of their POWs all the time. You know what they want from you? They want information, right? What's a prisoner without information? Nothing. So it's up to you to get that information in the most expeditious manner possible. This is a war, pal, and these are the enemy. We don't want to forget that, do we?' His blue eyes were wide and innocent as he eyed Anderson.

Sturm spoke in the ensuing silence. 'Don't you have any birds to move these prisoners with, captain?'

'Yeah, sure, but it will be late in the afternoon during a resupply run.' He turned back to Kowalski. 'I want to either find out what they know or get them right to Division.'

'Maybe we ought to let them go on the resupply birds, Mr. Kowalski,' Sturm persisted. He didn't want to be part of another round of torture.

The pilot spoke without looking at him but his voice had a dangerous edge to it. 'Nobody's paying you to think. Andy and I will handle this.' He looked at the captain. 'Don't ever get mixed up with an intellectual. They only mess up your mind. Now, what say, captain? Let's get some information out of your dinks. It won't take long.'

Anderson eyed Kowalski for a moment as if watching an instant replay of the other interrogation then shrugged. 'Alright, King Kong. It worked before. Let's get going.' He gestured at Rivera. 'Bring those slopes to the dustoff.'

As they moved toward the chopper Sturm spoke acidly to Kowalski. 'What are you planning here? More torture? A little more murder, perhaps? Last night wasn't enough? If it's anything like what happened at the refugee camp, I'll report it this time. I'll take it all the way.'

Kowalski grinned. 'It won't be anything like that. It will be very different, in fact. And there will be nothing for you to report, buddy-boy.' As they walked on, Sturm noticed a patch on the pilot's right pocket, something he hadn't seen before. It was a white skull and bones on a black background with the words, 'Sat Cong' embroidered underneath. Kowalski saw Sturm looking at it.

'Like it? That's my membership card to an exclusive club. And you remember the entrance requirements, don't you? Just one little ear, which I happened to have. And I might take another today.'

'Did you use the ear you cut off that Vietnamese I killed?' Sturm asked.

'Of course not. I get my own. Anyway, aren't you secretly glad you killed that dink, and secretly sorry you didn't get the ear?' The pilot grinned and moved away as the prisoners arrived. He found a length of nylon cord and bound all four on the same piece of rope. Moon-face was the last to be tied and as Kowalski came toward him the young Vietnamese gave him a tentative smile, more out of nervousness than hope. The pilot gave the youth's cheek a pinch.

'Keep on smiling, Moon, you're going to be number one, yes sir, number one.'

As Kowalski started the engine, Anderson returned with his Vietnamese interpreter, a chubby young officer that reminded Sturm of Col. Cuu. He had that same sleek self-confidence, that starched personality that came from too long association with the powerful and well-supplied Americans. The interpreter, a Lt. Cung, sat on the chopper floor, facing the prisoners and gave each of them long hard stares. All but the older thin-faced Vietnamese dropped their eyes. The gaunt one, who Kowalski had nicknamed Ho Chi Minh, gazed calmly back at the lieutenant.

The interrogation of Moon-face began after Kowalski took the bird up to 2,000 feet and gave the controls to Tippit. Kowalski untied Moon-face and pushed him toward the open doorway until the boyish North Vietnamese turned pale and clawed at the floor.

'Go ahead,' Kowalski shouted at Anderson who began questioning the prisoner through Lt. Cung.

'What is your name and rank?' Moon-face did not respond, but instead stared at the checkered ground far below him.

'What is your unit?'

No answer, only terrified silence. Kowalski, who sat

directly behind the prisoner, shoved him a few inches closer to the edge and the soldier's hands scrabbled across the floor until he found a cargo tie-down ring. Moon-face looped a finger through it and Sturm, watching from his seat, saw the finger go white as it clung to the ring.

'Where are those 122mm rockets being fired from? Are you with that unit? What is your unit?' The questions continued but Moon-face only gazed with sick expression at the emptiness before him. Never in his life had he flown, never had he been so high and so close to death. One could hide from the rolling thunder, the B-52 strikes, but there was no hiding from that yawning doorway before him.

Again Kowalski shoved Moon-face until he was on the doorway edge where the wind pulled at his clothes. With only inches now separating him from space, Moon-face abruptly vomited and the wind whipped it around the cabin. Kowalski wiped his face and cursed him and gave the prisoner another push with his boot. Moon-face spun about and grasped the ring with both hands and pressed his face to the deck. Kowalski raised his boot to smash the prisoner's hands when Sturm suddenly bolted from his seat and pulled the youth back from the doorway. Moon-face lay gasping and shaking at Sturm's feet while Anderson and Lt. Cung looked up in surprise, uncomprehending. Kowalski sprang to his feet in a crouch and grabbed Sturm's shirt front.

'Goddamit, I told you to stay out of this and if you interfere one more time I'll throw you out of this fucking chopper.'

Sturm jerked free and his chin went out pugnaciously. 'And I told you I would report you if you play any more of your torture games. You murdered one man last night. How much blood do you want?'

'Shut your mouth and sit down. That's an order, Specialist Sturm, and you goddam better well obey it or I'll court martial you straight into jail. And if that doesn't stop you there might be a bad accident on this bird involving you. Now sit down.' He gave Sturm a violent push that bounced him off the transmission housing.

Still not certain what Kowalski would do, Sturm hesitated as the pilot bent and grabbed the sobbing Vietnamese by the hair and dragged him back to the doorway. The other prisoners watched with closed faces as Kowalski forced Moon's head over the edge into the blinding, breath-stealing slipstream. Sturm looked at Dooley for a sign of assistance but the crew chief's face was hidden behind his green visor.

Kowalski was yelling, 'Now tell this son of a bitch that if he doesn't answer I'm going to throw him right out of this chopper.' Lt. Cung shouted the translation but before the youth could say anything, Ho Chi Minh barked a short command.

'What did he say?' Kowalski demanded.

'He say, "remember our fatherland".'

'Okay, tell Ho Chi Minh that Moon here is going to meet his fatherland right now, and that Ho is next.' Kowalski grabbed the frail youth by the neck with one hand and by his pants with the other. Moon-face, now realizing he was about to die, turned with surprising strength and clung to Kowalski's thick leg. The pilot took a deeper bite with his fingers in Moon's neck then jerked him loose with a single powerful pull and flung the boy out the doorway.

Sturm, rising from the floor as Kowalski prepared to throw the prisoner out the doorway but still not believing it would actually happen, saw the face go by, the mouth open in an unheard scream, the hair blowing out wildly as if he were underwater and drowning. Sturm stopped in his rush toward Kowalski and watched the prisoner spin toward the ground below, an autumn leaf falling in Iowa. As if hypnotized Sturm watched until he could no longer see the falling prisoner, then turned stunned eyes towards Kowalski.

'Did you see that accident, buddy-boy? Did you see him slip while he tried to break from my hold on him? You want to report that accident? Be my guest.' The pilot turned back to Anderson. 'Okay, now we'll get some answers from these slopes. Let's take Ho Chi Minh next. Might as well go for the biggie.'

Sturm, dumbfounded at the blatant murder and knowing he was powerless to stop his commanding officer, watched in silence. It was unreal and now he was not sure he had seen the murder. He turned and counted the other prisoners. There was no mistake.

Anderson nodded in agreement with Kowalski who untied the thin-faced Ho Chi Minh and dragged him toward the doorway. He grabbed the prisoner by the neck in his iron grip and thrust the head out the opening as he had with Moon-face. 'That's your fatherland down there. Take a good look because you're going to meet it too if you don't talk up, understand?'

Leaving Ho Chi Minh by the doorway, Kowalski pulled an oily rag from beneath his seat and tore it into strips. Starting with Ho, he quickly blindfolded all three prisoners. Anderson resumed his questioning while Kowalski told Tippet to take the chopper down slowly.

The interrogation resumed and with each silence by Ho Chi Minh Kowalski nudged him closer to the doorway. The prisoner sat erect, legs crossed and hands folded before him in the classical lotus position of Buddha. He gave no sign of fear as the questioning and pushing continued until finally the wind began snapping at his pants, little fingers seemingly trying to pull him into the void. Only then did he unfold his hands and place his palms delicately on the floor. Kowalski saw the indication of fear and grinned as he pointed it out to Anderson who nodded and kept up the questions.

By now the chopper was only 20 feet off the sandy wastes below the DMZ and Tippit continued his slow circling. But

Ho Chi Minh and the others, all blindfolded, had no concept how high they were.

'Okay, Tippit,' Kowalski yelled, 'take it down to about ten feet off the ground and go real slow while we make Ho Chi Minh tell us all his little secrets.' As the chopper dropped still lower, Kowalski pushed Ho Chi Minh forward until he was teetering on the edge. Now his hands were outstretched behind him, fingers feeling for any small handhold. Suddenly he spoke.

'What did he say?' Anderson quickly asked.

'He say his name Nguyen Tri Bong and he is sergeant but he no have to say more.'

'Well, that's fine, but it isn't quite enough,' Kowalski said and gave another nudge. Ho Chi Minh now leaned back to keep from falling forward and out. 'Ask him what unit he is with and where are those rockets?'

When the prisoner hesitated Kowalski gave another small push and Bong's hand scrabbled in panic along the deck.

'He say he with 309th Regiment, but he say under Geneva convention he no have to say more,' Lt. Cung translated.

Anderson leaned forward, sensing a break coming in Bong's resistance. 'We want to know the location and designation of the unit that is transporting those rockets.'

As Lt. Cung translated, Bong remained silent, shaking his head. Kowalski, cursing in exasperation, jerked the prisoner to his feet and turned him around so his back was to the doorway. He took the prisoner's shirt front in his hand and slowly pushed Bong back out the door, letting him sway in the air. Bong's mouth opened slightly at the sensation of death so near and saliva ran from one corner of his mouth. He clutched blindly at Kowalski's arm.

'Where are the rockets?' Kowalski yelled and when Bong only shook his head the pilot let him slip outward again, a sudden move that brought a shrill squeal from the prisoner.

'Your last chance. Where are they?' Bong shook his head slightly, his mouth open. Kowalski grinned at the blindfolded prisoner, looked at the others to make sure they were all watching and then abruptly opened his hand that held the prisoner. Bong's hands clutched futilely at Kowalski's arm and he slowly toppled outward with a piercing shriek that ended in a grunt as he hit the ground less than five feet below him. He lay unmoving, uncomprehending until Kowalski jumped out and pulled the blindfold free.

'Surprise, Ho Chi Minh, you're not dead. Not yet.' Kowalski stood grinning down on the blinking and unbelieving prisoner, then jerked him to his feet and turned the blindfold into a gag. He stuffed the prisoner into Sturm's seat where the two remaining prisoners could not see him.

'See? It's easy, Sturm. You can bet the others will talk when they see Ho Chi Minh is missing. They're not eager to die. And now they know we mean business because they saw Moon-face go sailing out of here. An accident, of course. And now Ho Chi Minh has disappeared as far as they know. Accidents do happen and it's in Captain Anderson's official report that this was an accident.'

They were back up to 2,000 feet, heading back to Anderson's track company when Kowalski pulled the blindfolds from the other prisoners. They began answering questions immediately when they saw that their leader was gone. From where he stood by the doorway, Sturm could see the gagged prisoner slumped against one wall, eyes closed and a greasy film of perspiration covering his ashen face.

Sturm moved back to his seat where Bong eyed him with a mixture of apprehension and resignation. Sturm ignored him and hunkered his back to the wind as he carefully prepared a duster. He tore the first one while trying to tip the tobacco out and when he prepared another the wind blew away nearly half the heroin in the capsule. He twisted the cigarette end finally and began to smoke greedily, taking three deep drags before looking up to see the prisoner staring at him with faint amusement in his eyes.

'You know what this is, Ho Chi Minh? This is heroin, smack, scag, beautiful white powder. Makes everything right again in a wrong world. You know that? Makes our worlds join, the twain meets right here in this little cigarette. Try some.'

He pulled Bong's gag loose and offered him the cigarette but the prisoner refused with a slight smile. Sturm shrugged and then offered him a Park Lanes. 'It's grass, but you won't know it until after you've smoked it. Light up and live a little.' Bong accepted the cigarette with a small nod of gratitude and puffed happily away with Sturm smiling beside him as they rode back into the track camp.

Anderson was still writing down information when they landed in the iron circle of his track company. They led the two prisoners away first then took Bong to a separate APC.

'Sorry about that accident, Andy,' Kowalski grinned, 'but you know some of these prisoners haven't been in choppers before and they still don't know how to act. When Moonface fell out we brought the others back for your safe-keeping. How's that?'

'That's just the way I saw it, King Kong. Thanks for the help. We got some good information after all. Thanks for the help again,' Anderson said and shook hands.

As the crew climbed back into the chopper with Kowalski joking about a good day's work, Sturm spoke to him.

'I told you that I wouldn't let this go. And I'm telling you now that I will report it to Major Schoen as soon as we return.'

To his surprise, Kowalski did not explode but only gave him a wolfish grin. 'Sure, buddy-boy, you do that. So will I. Everyone should report an unfortunate accident like that.'

'That was no goddam accident and you know it,' Sturm said but Kowalski shrugged.

'Funny, looked like an accident to Captain Anderson who

is writing the official report. Looked like an accident to me. Look like an accident to you, Tip?' he asked the co-pilot. He started to ask Dooley also but the crew chief was checking the rear rotor.

Tippit answered without looking at anybody. 'Sure did look like it to me.'

Sturm looked at them but didn't argue. He would take it up with Schoen when they got back. As they lifted off for the return to Quang Tri, Sturm moved back to where Dooley sat and signalled for him to take off his helmet so they wouldn't have to use the intercom.

'I'm going to report Kowalski. What he did is straight murder. I'm going to take this to Major Schoen. Will you back me up? They're trying to say it was an accident but we saw them just throw that prisoner out the door. That's murder, war or no war.'

Dooley lit his cigarette before answering and let the slip stream pull the smoke from his pursed mouth in a long gray streamer. 'I hate to tell you this, Jake, but I did not see exactly what happened. I was looking out the other doorway at what I thought were some tracers coming at us and when I looked back that prisoner was gone.'

Sturm stared at him. 'But you were right here. You must have seen everything. You knew what was going on.'

Dooley took another pull on his cigarette and shook his head. 'I saw everything except when that dink went out the doorway. So if anybody asks me what happened I can tell them I saw them questioning a prisoner in a chopper. That's all. I'm not putting you on, Jake, and I'm not trying to cop out. I just didn't see it so I can't say I did.'

'How could you miss it? Besides, you know what happened, you know this was a little torture routine.' Sturm was shouting, angry.

Dooley flipped his smoke out the doorway with an impatient gesture. 'I know what the fuck was going on but I didn't see any actual murder. Understand? I can't tell a court martial, if this is where it ends up, that I actually saw King Kong throw that slope out. They're going to say it was an accident. You and I know that is pure bullshit but still I didn't *see* it happen. Don't you understand?'

Sturm shook his head in disappointment as he rose and crossed to his seat on the other side of the chopper. There probably aren't any murders in Vietnam. There are just accidents or war casualties. And no one is innocent. Everyone is presumed guilty until dead, and death proves guilt because all dead Vietnamese are enemy Vietnamese. That's axiom number one.

A bump jarred his reverie and Sturm looked up to see they were back on the pad at the evac hospital. He sat still as the engine whistled dead and the long blades overhead hissed rhythmically to a stop. Sturm looked at his watch. Christ, only two hours for all that? He would go see Schoen right away before he decided he had only dreamed everything. Schoen was a good guy, basically, and this might open his eyes a little about Kowalski, make him think a little more about how the pilot handled Franklin. Sturm thought he might even go see Montano, see what he thinks of Kowalski when he hears about this.

A powerful hand gripped his knee and Sturm looked up from where he still sat to see Kowalski standing on the ground before him. Dooley and Tippit stood a little way off and watched covertly. Kowalski bared his teeth in an effort to smile.

'Come on, let's go eat. Let's talk about what happened, and what might be coming up. Lots of other action still ahead and since you're so short we might as well work together the best we can before you head home. Right?'

Sturm sat motionless, detesting Kowalski's friendly hand on his knee, hating the grimace that passed as a smile, bitter at the pilot's attempt to smooth relations now that the murder was done. Sturm said nothing and did not look further at Kowalski.

'Come on, Jake, you know accidents happen—'

Sturm slapped Kowalski's hand away and rose from his seat. 'Accident, my ass! You're a fucking murderer, Kowalski. So just stay away from me.'

Kowalski sprang forward and jerked Sturm out of the chopper then slammed him back against the side with force enough to stun the medic, then brought his fist up to strike him but checked himself.

'You're in a war, Sturm, and bad things happen. After you've seen what the North Vietnamese do to the people they capture you might understand. But right now you act like a naive old woman.'

'You're only trying to justify yourself, but it's still murder. And I'm going to see Schoen now.'

Kowalski stood back. 'Alright, go see Schoen. But be sure and refer him to our accident report.' He spun away and left with Tippit. Dooley, who stood watching, started to say something to Sturm but as the medic turned his back Dooley followed the others to the messhall.

As they left, Sturm contemplated another smoke but decided against it. He wanted his head on straight when he saw Schoen. He would go now and get it over with, he decided, and crossed through the triage room where he made his way around two men on stretchers with bottles of plasma leaking life support into their systems. Outside Schoen's office he told the sergeant who was reading a Batman comic that he had personal business with the chief surgeon. The sergeant waved him in without looking up and said, 'Have a look. I don't even know if he came in this morning. I haven't heard a sound.'

Sturm opened the door slowly and seeing the room was shuttered against the sun he started to leave when he made out the Major's familiar bulk sitting at his desk with his head in his hands. Sturm opened the door a little wider. 'Sir?' No answer. He went in more. Maybe the major died sitting there like that. 'Sir? Sir?'

'Close the door. That light is killing me. What is it? Don't tell me I have surgery now?' The voice was cathedral, rich with the deep resonance of a massive hangover.

'No sir. It's me, Sturm. Specialist Sturm. I've got something that I must speak with you about.'

'Nobody gets a three day pass to Saigon this month. Besides, you're too short, Sturm.' Schoen spoke with his head still in his hands, the words bubbling down over his extra chins and lying in a pool on his desk.

'No sir, it's about Mr. Kowalski.'

'Oh hell, did he goose another nurse? I warned him about that. I *warned* him.'

'No sir, I'm trying to tell you about Kowalski and a murder.' Sturms voice rose in exasperation and he slapped his cap against his leg.

'Can't it wait until tomorrow?' Schoen asked. 'I'm really loaded – busy, that is – today.' Still, he did not look up.

Sturm closed the door behind himself when he saw the sergeant perking up to catch a little gossip. 'Major Schoen. I saw Mr. Kowalski murder a man today, a Vietnamese. I saw it and I'm reporting it.' He couldn't be any plainer.

'Who, um, whom did he allegedly murder, Sturm?'

'A prisoner, a North Vietnamese prisoner. He was interrogating him in our dustoff this morning and he threw him out of the bird.' Sturm waited for a response and when none came he felt the colonel had not heard him. Sturm wanted to sit down by the major's desk and have him listen carefully, to have him nod at certain times and take notes furiously while he asked probing questions. Instead there was the continuing silence finally broken by a slow nasal breathing from Schoen.

'Sir?'

'What's that? Hmmm?' Schoen started and brought his hands back to his eyes. 'Please, God, no surgery this morning.'

Sturm raised his eyes to the ceiling as he tried to hold his temper in check. 'Sir, I'm telling you I saw Mr. Kowalski throw a North Vietnamese prisoner out of the dustoff this morning. That's murder.' He wanted to say the same thing about Franklin's death last night but he knew that would be futile.

This time Sturm's words seemed to register and Schoen slowly asked, 'You saw it? Did the rest of the crew see it?' His eyes remained closed.

'We were all in the chopper at the time, sir,' Sturm hedged.

'But what did the others see, Sturm?' The major spoke with a long sigh of internal miasma.

'Well, Mr. Tippit was flying. I don't know what he could see. Dooley was there all the time. He said he didn't see the prisoner actually thrown out but he saw everything else. He knew what was going on. And there was a Fifth Mech officer and his interpreter on board. They saw it all. They're going to call it an accident, but I saw it, I—'

Schoen held up a hand. 'Why are you telling me all this, Sturm?'

Sturm felt as if he had been hit and he groped for words. 'Why? Why? Because Kowalski killed a man for no reason. Just threw him out of the chopper. And there have been other incidents. He took part in a torture just a few days ago during a medcap mission. Chaplain Montano was there, he saw it.'

'The chaplain has made no mention of it to me, and I'm sure that if there had been anything wrong at the time, he would have brought it to my attention.'

'Well, I'm telling you, sir, because I think Kowalski is a dangerous man. He shouldn't be allowed to run loose. He doesn't represent what Americans are supposed to be doing over here.'

Schoen said heavily, 'I didn't realize you were a doctor of psychiatry. But perhaps you better tell me just why you don't like Mr. Kowalski?' The question came from left field and Sturm stumbled again.

'Whether I like him or not isn't the question, sir. I'm just saying he killed an innocent man and something ought to be done about it. That's why I came to you.'

Schoen didn't reply immediately but began massaging his forehead, kneading deeply at his throbbing temples and experimentally trying to open his eyes. When it seemed they would remain open on command he looked at Sturm from his wounded sockets and put his glasses on.

'I don't know what's going on between you and Mr. Kowalski.' He held up his hand again to ward off an interruption by Sturm. 'And I really don't want to know. But let me give you a few facts. First, Mr. Kowalski is one of the most experienced pilots we have, a man who has seen much war and can be counted on to bring his medevac through bad situations. Secondly, the man you say he allegedly murdered was by your own admission a North Vietnamese. That's the enemy, Sturm, in case you've forgotten, and we're in a war. Third, I've got a hospital to run and the fewer interruptions the smoother things go around here. And finally, you're too short to be making such accusations. If this goes anywhere it will drag on for months in investigations and possibly a court martial. That would mean you would have to stay here until it was all settled. Months.' He held up his hand once more. 'Just a minute. Now, I'm not whitewashing this. You've done right to come and tell me and I promise you I will look into it. Just leave it in my hands for now. If you need any further guidance, go see the chaplain, but don't under any circumstances take this matter through other channels. You'll just confuse the issue. I will look into your complaint in due time but right now I have other matters to attend to,' Schoen said and put his face back in his hands.

Sturm stood there a moment, wanting to pursue the matter, wanting to see some kind of action taken, but there was only a resumption of stentorian breathing from Schoen's corner of the office and Sturm turned to leave.

Schoen's voice rumbled after him. 'Kowalski allegedly killed these prisoners while trying to elicit some information. Right?'

'Yes sir.'

'Did he get the info?'

'Yes sir, from the other prisoners, but—'

'Then it worked, didn't it? That's all you can do in Vietnam. Make it work. Now tell my sergeant out there I definitely will not be available for any surgery.'

CHAPTER ELEVEN

'What are you looking for, man?' Riley asked.

Sturm, rummaging on his knees in the junk pile at the back of the hootch, found the rusted entrenching tool. He held up the collapsible shovel. 'This.'

'You digging in for a rocket attack?' Raab asked.

'I'm moving out,' Sturm said shortly. He had nothing to say to Dooley since the incident in the chopper when Dooley let him down. The crew chief was his only witness and he wouldn't back up his statement to Schoen. How could he miss seeing it? A chopper wasn't exactly a four bedroom house.

But, despite Sturm's sullen withdrawal, Dooley persisted in being friendly. 'Why move? Don't like the way we smell?' he grinned.

'I'm so short I'm not going to risk an unwarranted death by a freak rocket attack. It happens, you know. So I'm cleaning out that old bunker behind the hootch and I'll move my bunk in there.'

That was only partly true. He really wanted to keep away from Dooley as much as possible. It might be better to tell Dooley why he was so uptight and get it into the open, but he found he could no longer talk reasonably to Dooley. He felt betrayed. Sturm went out and into the weed patch behind the row of hootches to the old and unused bunker. He chopped back the weeds that choked the four stairs leading down to the bunker. Inside it smelled damp and moldy but there was enough light to see. A stinkhole, Sturm thought. He didn't really want to stay in the bunker but it was too late to back out now. He would just clean it up a little, put some wooden slats on the ground for flooring, maybe run a wire from the hootch for a light at night and it wouldn't be too bad. The room was about ten feet on each side and six feet high which made Sturm stoop to move about. There was nothing in the shelter except two empty oil drums in the back corners. Sturm went to one and saw it was filled with water, impossible to move. The other was empty and he was about to tip it over and roll it outside when the bunker darkened as someone entered behind him. He whirled and saw it was Dooley with a small black and white puppy in his arms.

'I found this mutt out by the gate. It's back legs don't work so hot, but it's friendly as hell. I want you to keep it. It might bring a little cheer into your remaining days.' He put the pup down and the two watched while it hopped like a mechanical toy to Sturm and sat licking his boot.

'What do I want a dog for now? I'm leaving this place,' Sturm said and made no move to touch the dog.

'Because you're not in good shape, Jake. I tell you that as a friend. You aren't yourself at all. You're heavy on heroin now and you really don't function too well, whether you know it or not. It fouls up your mind and while you think you are doing a great job you're barely moving. You can't react and even though you've only got a few days left they're going to be rough days. Fifth Mech is going to get hammered everyday and we're going to be picking up the pieces. So I want you to think about the pup, think about helping it out. Take your mind off Vietnam and the war. You think about it, too much.'

When Sturm said nothing, Dooley continued. 'Look, I know you are really pissed because I didn't back you up about the prisoner that Kowalski greased. But you got to see my side. I can't lie. They might put a lie detector on me. It's better that you just forget the whole mess. Just think about the dog and going home.'

Sturm bent and picked up the dog and felt better toward his crew chief. 'You're probably right, Tomato. And I do try to forget Vietnam. It's getting to me. That's why I got heavy on scag. One of the reasons. But it's not so easy to let everything go as if it never happened. At least not for me. I tried to make some changes in the beginning. I tried a long time. I believed in what I was doing here. But no one wants you to do good or bad. Just don't make waves. Just put in your 12 months and go home. Like Schoen. I told him about Kowalski and he said he would look into it, but he won't really do anything. Not without other witnesses to back me up,' he added pointedly. 'And the chaplain hasn't taken any steps either to stop Kowalski. Everyone's afraid to act.'

Dooley shrugged. 'Then just forget it. Vietnam will all be behind you in a few days.'

'Forget Kowalski is a murderer? If that's the philosophy, then anyone could grease all the slopes they wanted, north or south, and it would be just fine. Is that right?'

'That's about it, Jake. No one cares. Why should you? You're not a priest.'

'Yeah. Why should I? You know something, Tomato? Remember when we were down in the An Lao valley and I shot that North Vietnamese? The one Kowalski took the ear off of? Well, I've never admitted it, even to myself, but I liked it. I really felt good after I saw that dink go down. But I shouldn't like it. And I should keep after Kowalski because he likes it too much. So I'm going to push the case, with or without your help. And even without the help of Schoen and Montano. Two damned hypocrites.'

'It's your life,' Dooley said and turned to go. Sturm watched him and knew that he was still bitter at the red head. But maybe he could at least try to forget some bitterness.

'Give me a hand with this barrel before you go,' Sturm said and Dooley took it as a friendly overture. They tipped the empty barrel and started toward the door with it when Dooley suddenly dropped his side and leaped back.

'Jesus, Rats, look at them.'

Four squirming pink baby rats lay in the nest beneath the barrel and as the two watched, a large glossy brown rat glided from behind the other barrel and scurried along the wall toward her babies. She snatched one in her mouth and darted behind the water barrel.

'We've got to get that momma rat or this place will be overrun,' Sturm said. He picked up the entrenching tool and waved it threateningly at the rat when it reappeared. The rat watched cautiously for a chance to pick up another squealing baby.

'Rats are too fast to hit with a shovel. Maybe I can burn it,' Sturm said. He took his lighter out and turned up the gas jet until it was a small torch. He sat quietly by the babies and the mother rat came forward in quick little bursts, ready to run but more anxious to recover her young. As the rat sprang forward and took one tiny baby in her mouth, Sturm fired the lighter and the flame caught her along the side. The rat wheeled backward still gripping the baby and disappeared.

'Just singed it. This doesn't have enough reach,' Sturm said.

'Then kill the baby rats. Hit them with the shovel and we'll take care of momma rat later,' Dooley said.

'No I want them all dead.'

'Then just kill them,' Dooley said in exasperation.

'Nothing is so simple in Vietnam. I'm learning that.' Sturm dug in his pocket and produced a can of lighter fluid he had picked up at the PX. 'I'll make a flame thrower,' he said and backed away a little to give the momma rat more room. As the rat reappeared and moved in furtive darts toward the two remaining babies, Sturm lit the lighter. The rat froze at the sight of the flame and its tiny eyes glittered in fear but the maternal drive drove it slowly forward. When it made its sudden rush to grab another tiny rat, Sturm squeezed the lighter fluid can and shot a thin stream of fluid through the flames.

'Look at that. A real flame thrower,' Sturm yelled as the burning liquid hit the rat on the snout and ignited the hair. The baby rat took a direct hit and its tender pink skin blacked and burned. Squealing in pain the rat dropped her baby and whirled in frantic circles before racing to shelter behind the water drum.

'This is too much,' Dooley said and waved his hands as if trying to make the whole scene disappear. 'Look, let's just kill the babies. Then we'll move that other barrel and get momma rat. Get it over with.'

'No. We might miss and she would escape. This is more certain. Besides, the rats deserve to die painfully. They're part of Vietnam, dink rats, and Vietnam has brought me nothing but pain. I'm just getting even.'

Dooley looked at him speculatively. 'That's what Kowalski thinks, that he is just getting even. Now you're thinking that way?'

'Yeah, just following my leaders. Besides, you said it didn't make any difference. Kill or be killed.' Sturm stopped when he felt the anger begin to rise inside because he didn't want it to break out now and spill onto Dooley. The two men and the dog sat silently then and waited for the rat to reappear. When it didn't come right back Sturm dug out his cigarettes and heroin capsule and fixed himself a smoke. He inhaled deeply and blew a ring toward the baby rat that had been burned and dropped. It was still writhing in pain.

'Why don't you at least kill that little one?' Dooley asked in disgust.

'Because that is part of the bait to get momma rat back where I can give her another shot.'

'Fuck you,' Dooley said and stepped forward with the entrenching tool and hit the burned rat a crushing blow. He was about to hit the other baby when Sturm leaped to his feet and jerked the shovel away.

'Leave it alone, goddam it! I'm getting rid of these slope rats my way. Nobody invited you to the party.' He threw the shovel across the room then turned as he saw the rat scurry along the wall in another attempt to rescue its young.

'Hold it. Here she comes,' Sturm said and held the cigarette in the corner of his mouth. The rat came slowly and they could see it was blinded in one eye where the burning lighter fluid had settled on one side of its hair snout. The rat sniffed at the crushed baby and then moved quickly to the remaining one. This time Sturm let it take the baby and start to turn before he fired. The burning fluid snaked across the opening in a tight arc and settled like a napalm strike on the rat's back in a smoky blaze. The rat ran but Sturm moved with it and continued to pump fluid on it until it dropped its baby and whirled in frantic circles, biting at her back and then running blindly into the wall as the tiny inferno spilled onto her face and paws.

'Stop it, Jake, stop it,' Dooley yelled and knocked the lighter fluid from Sturm's hand. 'You're a goddam animal. You're as bad as Kowalski, just torturing that rat for the sake of torture.'

Sturm started to laugh. 'But don't you see? That's what it's all about. That's why we're here. That's why Vietnam was invented, so we could practice the Dark Ages and the Inquisition and the Crusades again. We missed those games the first time so someone invented a new Dark Age and called it Vietnam.' Sturm sat down and shook his head back and forth as he continued to laugh. It was so funny, he thought, it was wild. He started to explain more but when he looked up, Dooley was gone. The dog was looking at him with its head cocked. He finished the duster in the half light of the bunker.

When he returned to the hootch to drop off the dog, Dooley sat in a corner nursing a large Scotch. Riley and Raab eyed him curiously but didn't say anything. That Dooley told them all about it, Sturm thought. He had to get away, get his mind straight.

'Who's got the duty tonight?' he asked.

'Me and Riley,' Raab answered.

'Then I'm going to the ville. I'll be at the club.' He left without further words and no one spoke to him as he went out.

He caught a ride into town and ran up the stairs into the club. The long room was smoky, crowded with troops and filled with hard rock music blasting from the speakers on all four walls. Sturm edged through the crowd to the bar where he could get a view of the room. If Mai was with some other joker she was leaving him right now. He didn't pay her to entertain other grunts. No more of this bullshit about her doing a little extra work to take care of her family and to help her poor brother who was in the army. Jake Sturm was in the army and he needed the help more. He didn't see her on his first sweep of the room and he was beginning a second closer look when Susie appeared at his elbow.

'You look for Mai?' She had to yell to be heard over the laughter and the music.

'Yeah. Where is she? Is she butterflying me?' he asked with a grin. He knew Mai would drink with the others but she wouldn't screw them.

'She in her room. She no feel good. She say she no work tonight.'

Sturm pushed away from the bar and started toward Mai's room in the back when Susie caught his arm. 'Maybe you come back tomorrow, okay? Mai she very sick.' She lowered her voice and hissed. 'She have some trouble with police. My friend tell me Vietnamese police still watch this bar. See who visit her. Maybe GI police watch too, you know?'

Sturm made his way through the crowd and at the rear he passed through the plastic strips over the doorway that separated the back rooms. Outside Mai's doorway he stopped and listened, suddenly wondering if Susie was just trying to let him know that Mai had some troop back there for a short time, for a little fast money. He stepped closer to the thin paneled door and put his hand lightly on the loose enameled handle. He listened again but heard nothing in the room. Either way, he decided, he was going in and if he caught some troop with his pants down there would be hell to pay. Butterflying bitch. He turned the handle then shoved hard with his shoulder, expecting the lock to break away but the door was open and he burst inside. Light from the open doorway spilled across the darkened room in a narrow beam that fell on the white, still face of Mai. She lay on her back beneath a cover with her silken black hair fanned out across the pillow. She did not move or open her eyes as he slipped slowly toward her. He was suddenly afraid she might be dead for her skin looked waxen, almost translucent as he snapped on the small lamp beside her bed.

'Mai?' He bent over her, studying her delicate mouth that parted slightly and finally detecting a faint rise and fall of her breasts as she breathed. 'Mai? What's the matter? What happened?'

She opened her eyes, dark lagoons that brimmed suddenly with tears as she looked at him.

'I glad you come, GI I have plenty trouble.' She slowly and with evident pain, slid one hand from beneath the cover and took his hand. 'You stay little while. I hurt inside. They hurt me bad.' She closed her eyes again and her finely contoured eyebrows drew down in pain.

He tried to take her in his arms, to comfort her, but she

cried out and he backed away, now afraid to touch her anywhere. Still she clung to his hand. 'Do you want a doctor?' Sturm asked. 'I'll take you to the hospital.' He started to rise, to find help, but she pulled weakly at his hand.

'No. No need. Doctor downstairs already come. He say nothing broken. He say I must rest.' She closed her eyes again as if exhausted from the effort it took to restrain him.

Sturm sank to the chair beside her bed, his mouth close to her pale cheeks. 'Mai. tell me what happened. Susie told me you had some trouble with the police. What was it?'

'I have plenty trouble. They say I same-same VC. I say no, but they no believe.' Slowly, in her most careful English, Mai began to tell of her ordeal. They came, she said, early in the morning while it was still dark. It seemed she had slept only for minutes after the club closed when she was awakened by the sound of Vietnamese men speaking softly in the hallway. Now, in recollection, it must have been their sibilant whispers in English that awakened her. Hearing English in the hall was so unusual. She particularly remembered one voice saying, 'I don't know which room is hers. Ask someone.'

There were four Vietnamese, all strongly built and all wearing civilian clothes. The first through the door held a small automatic pistol in one hand and the man behind held a powerful flashlight which he kept beamed into her eyes as she sat up with the bed sheet held across her breasts in the warm night air. She said nothing as they efficiently checked her tiny room to see that no one else was there. She didn't ask who they were. In Vietnam only secret police entered rooms in the middle of the night and held the occupant at gunpoint. As one of them turned on the room light and closed the door, Mai could make out the shadowy figure of someone watching from the hallway.

'Get dressed. You are coming with us.' The one who spoke, the one with the pistol, wore a button-down shirt with a narrow black tie and didn't bother to identify himself. He knew he didn't have to. He motioned her out of bed with his pistol but when she tried to cover herself with the sheet another man jerked it away then gave a murmer of approval at the sight of her lithe body. She dressed quickly, slipping into panties, bra and black satin pantaloons before buttoning up her green ao-dai. The men never took their eyes from her as she dressed.

'You like to screw the Americans, eh?' The leader spoke to her in Vietnamese. 'Vietnamese men aren't good enough for you?' He curled a lip. 'Or are you too good for them? We'll see. Or perhaps you like to hear the Americans talk, tell you little secrets? We shall see.'

Mai clung to Sturm's hand as she talked and tears repeatedly welled in her eyes. 'They were bad men, numbah fuckin' ten men.'

They led her downstairs and put her in the rear of a black Ford that waited outside the club entrance. Two men sat in back with her as they drove off and one slipped his hand between her legs. She wanted to push him away but she remained motionless and filled with dread during the short drive to the city's military headquarters. The Vietnamese MP at the gate knew the car and the occupants for he waved them through without checking identification. The car made its way to the rear of the compound where it stopped beside a low, heavily sand-bagged building ringed by concertina wire.

The men pushed her inside first as they entered a small room lighted by a single bulb in the center of the low ceiling. Two men sat at a folding table playing cards and Mai was surprised to see one of them was an American, a pale lieutenant with a round face and protruding lips which he repeatedly wetted with a small pink tongue. She stood before them, her head back and hair loose as she waited. Still she had not spoken. While the four who had brought her sat on metal chairs along the wall, the Vietnamese man at the table put down his cards and leaned back in his chair to eye her carefully. He wore an American Ivy league shirt with a narrow black tie, much like the man with the pistol. His eyes were deep set and the dark hollows beneath his smooth cheekbones gave him the appearance of a death head. He spoke to the American lieutenant.

'Is she the one?'

The lieutenant shuffled some papers at his elbow with a nervous gesture. 'Well, I guess so. I've never seen her, you know, I've just got this report on her. I'm just going on that. But she must be the one, she's pretty enough.' He tittered and the police commander ignored him as he turned toward Mai and began questioning her in Vietnamese.

'How long have you been working in the—' he checked a paper in front of him '—Forty Akers Club?'

'About one year.' Mai replied in Vietnamese, her voice almost a whisper.

'You spend your time only with Americans? Why?'

'Because they pay well and I must support my family. I have no choice.'

The commander rolled a pencil in his fingers as he contemplated her answer. 'Ah, yes, your family. Let us talk of them for a moment. Your father was once a professor at the University in Hue. Why did he leave?'

'Because many of his friends were killed in the 1968 Tet offensive and he wanted to return with my mother to her ancestral village,' Mai replied.

The commander looked at his papers again then rose and slowly came around the table to stand directly in front of Mai who stood slightly taller in her spike heels. He looked in her eyes and his calm and searching manner reminded Mai of one of her father's studious colleagues. Then he hit her in the stomach, his fist coming out like a snake's tongue, fast and without warning. She had never been struck like that in her life and she collapsed, writhing and choking on the floor as she fought to draw a breath. The commander continued speaking to her as he stood above her head but she could not hear him. All she could see as she lay gasping were his pointed and highly polished shoes just before her face. One of the shoes tapped a note of impatience.

'Perhaps you did not tell us all the truth. Your father was aligned with the anti-government Buddhists in Hue at the time. Isn't it so? And he left when that organization began breaking up. But he still supports them and advises them. Isn't it so?'

She could not answer for a moment as she sucked air into her empty lungs, then with her face lying on the gritty floor she spoke: 'My father is a very devout Buddhist but he is not against the government.'

Her response drew a swift and agonizing kick in the kidneys from the pointed shoes. She lay curled on the floor in the fetal position, not knowing how to protect herself.

'Put her in a chair.' It was the American speaking and she gave him a brief look of gratitude as two men pulled her up. 'But take off her pantaloons first. No, not the top, just her pants. And her panties.' The lieutenant smiled at the Vietnamese. 'It makes them embarrassed, you see, makes them want to talk more.' Mai kept her head down.

She sat on the chair with the front panel of her ao-dai over her legs and tried not to look at the American who continually wet his lips as he stared at her.

'You spend much time with one particular American. Who is he?' It was the police commander speaking again.

'I know many Americans. Who do you mean?' She spoke softly, with her head down in the picture of subservience. She was not prepared for the blow that caught her over her heart and sent her flying to the floor. She lay on her back, unable to move because of the pain that filled her chest. The Ivy League deputy who brought her lifted her back into the chair where she sagged forward, unable to cover herself, no longer caring.

'You spend much of your time with a Specialist Jacob Sturm. He pays to keep you. You talk a lot with him about what he sees, where he goes. Why do you want this information?' The commander stood calmly before her and smoothed his tie as he spoke.

She answered in tears, not understanding what was happening to her. 'But I don't ask him questions. I am not interested in where he goes or what he does. I don't like to hear about the war. I try to forget all the time and instead I think of when I was a small girl, when my father read me poetry and I knew nothing of war. And I try not to think of what I have become, how I have shamed my parents even if they do not know what I do. I know, and that is bad enough.' She continued to weep, knowing they would not accept her answer. There was the scuff of a foot moving and she bent double on the chair as she tried to protect herself but the blow came from the side and caught her under the rib cage. She fell heavily from the chair.

'Okay, put her back in the chair again. But now take off her ao-dai.' It was the American speaking, his voice fast and high with emotion. 'But leave her bra on,' he added and sat on the edge of his chair as two of the men pulled loose the snaps across the bodice and pulled the ao-dai from her.

'Hey, you got a good one this time, chief, way to go.' The lieutenant gazed at her full breasts held in the lacy black brassiere as the commander resumed his questioning.

'You are not cooperating. We are really trying to help you, to make you understand that you must not aid the enemy. Now, your father is a sympathizer with the anti-government Buddhists and they have ties with the Viet Cong.' He paused as she shook her head and then gave her an open handed slap across one cheek. 'Please don't argue with me. As I was saying, your father has anti-government connections and now it has come to our attention that you were prostituting yourself with the Americans who fly different combat missions each day. Isn't it convenient for you to gather information from them and pass it on? Isn't that so?' When she remained motionless he brought one hand down in a hard chop across the top of her thigh. 'I'm speaking to you,' he said in his empty voice, but she could not reply for it felt as if her leg had been severed.

'Take off her bra now,' the lieutenant yelled. She sat entirely nude and the breathing of the men mingled with her dry sobs in the otherwise silent room. The commander turned to the lieutenant and spoke in English with a hint of derision in his voice. 'Do you want anymore, Lieutenant? This really does not seem so profitable. You have no more evidence for us to go on?'

The lieutenant put his hands up as if absolving himself of any blame in the matter. 'Listen, this is your show, chief. You do whatever you think is right. I'm just along because the information on her came through our office. But you do what you think is right.'

The commander looked at him from those deep sockets and said, 'Do you want to take her now?'

'What do you mean?' The lieutenant looked wary.

'To screw her, lieutenant. She seems to have been broken in by the Americans, and you seem to enjoy seeing this woman undressed. I thought you might want her for your own.' The commander looked at the American with an expressionless face and let his words carry the subtle scorn.

'Oh. Oh, no. I don't want *that*.' The lieutenant wet his lips nervously and tittered again. 'Not while I'm on duty, you see.'

They gave her back her clothes but there was so much pain in her body that she could barely dress herself. It was still dark outside when they dumped her onto the sidewalk in front of the club. One of the betel nut women found her huddled in the stairway at first light and helped her up stairs.

'I almost dead like fuckin' VC. What you think, GI?' Mai managed a wan smile.

'But why? Who would want you questioned like that?' Sturm asked. He had listened in horrified silence to her account, but still couldn't understand it.

'I no know why they take me. Somebody tell them big lie. Somebody who no like me. Somebody make trouble for me.'

Sturm rubbed his face and tried to focus his mind on what she had said, on what lay behind her arrest. He had heard many stories of secret police interrogations in Vietnam but until now had only half believed them.

'Who was the American officer? Where did he hear you were supposed to be helping the VC?' The more he thought about it the angrier he got. 'That's just bullshit. Somebody wanted to bring trouble on you. Who would it be?'

Mai shook her head and closed her eyes. 'I no know. They tell me nothing. I so tired now. You come tomorrow, okay, GI?'

Sturm kissed her but she was already asleep. He turned out her light and sat there in the dark, still shaken by her story. Why would the Vietnamese police work her over? Mai said an American lieutenant was there and he talked about a report that came through his office. So he was probably with CID. Then who gave him the report on Mai?

It had to be an American for it to go through an American office. Not necessarily, he corrected himself, it could have been a Vietnamese contact. Still puzzling he returned to the bar but after Mai's tale of terror he had no stomach for the braying laughter and music that filled the room. He went outside and down the stairs to the street, now quiet and dark in the late evening. There was no traffic and to kill time while he waited for a ride he moved into the dark doorway of the VD doctor's office to fix a heroin smoke. It was his fifth today, or was it his sixth? Maybe Dooley's right about me not functioning too well. I can't even recall how many of these I have a day. But it's not as harmful to my health as just being in Vietnam, he told himself again. And not as bad as being interviewed by Vietnamese secret police. God, I hope she will be alright. At least the doctor has been to see her. He noticed the two betel nut women watching him with ferocious red-lipped grins and he started walking.

He had gone only a block, still puzzling over Mai and how he could find out who the American was, when a jeep pulled slowly alongside and a voice from the dark interior said, 'Get in, Jacob, it's rather late for anyone to be alone in this area.' It was Montano.

Wouldn't you know it, Sturm thought, of all the jeeps that travel this road I have to get the one with Montano in it. He had not talked with the chaplain since they had been shot down in the An Lao valley where, during his first heroin high, he had blessed the priest and all of Vietnam.

'How's business, captain? The war business, that is.' Sturm dropped his scag cigarette and decided that was a little rough for openers so he added, 'I mean, what are you doing in town at this late hour? Don't tell me you're . . .' he paused suggestively.

Montano ignored the innuendo and said, 'I had some business in town and stopped in to see Father Ngai.' Sturm thought it was a probable lie. The chaplain never visited Ngai or any other Vietnamese just to visit. Sturm had seen Montano and other officers in meetings with the Vietnamese; they were always done with the pomp and ceremony of a high mass so everyone would realize the Americans were saving Hearts and Minds. And Sturm knew that now Montano had him cornered there would be some moralizing. The priest wasted no time.

'Why don't you come to services anymore, Jake?'

'Too busy. Too many things going on in this war, captain,' Sturm answered and wondered if Montano were privately bugged that he no longer called him chaplain, or father.

'One can always find time. There's time to come to town, to drink with your friends in the bars, isn't there? And I suppose you find time to spend with your girlfriend, don't you?' Sturm started to argue but Montano pushed on. 'Oh, I'm not moralizing now. These are most difficult times and we must take life as it comes. But I would like to see you at services more often.'

'What do you know about my girl?' Sturm asked.

'Nothing, nothing at all,' he said, then added, 'Only that you had mentioned her a few times before. Some time ago.' Montano shifted the conversation back to Sturm. 'It's you I'm worried about, Jake, not the girl or anyone else. I have many men under my care, men who need my counseling and my comfort, but you're a special case. You have such great potential and I get the clear impression that you're letting everything slip away from you. You'll be out of the army soon. You can go back to school, you can go back to the monastery and continue studies for the priesthood. The church needs people like you.'

'So I could get an army issue collar and come back to Vietnam and tell all the young troops to go out and die for God and country?' A bitter anger rose suddenly inside him and for a second he feared he would shove the priest from the jeep. 'You would like that, wouldn't you?' He turned away then and the two rode on in silence down the empty highway.

Montano finally spoke. 'It is very difficult for you to understand my role. I saw what your real sentiments were when we were in the An Lao Valley. No priest can watch men go into battle every day, see them die, see them come into the hospital with horrible wounds on their bodies, no priest can see all this and not suffer himself. No one wants war, but wishing it weren't so will not make it disappear, no? If there is a war, then we must examine all sides and decide if it is morally justified. You understand, no?'

Sturm slouched lower in his seat and wished he could fix himself another scag smoke. Instead, he settled for a Park Lanes roach. In the open jeep Montano would never smell the odor. So what if he did? Sturm pulled the stick of grass from the pack, lit it and drew in a deep lungful before challenging the priest:

'Have any military chaplains ever declared a war unjust? What did the priests say in the Spanish Inquisition? That was their own war. And the Crusades. The Crusades weren't too holy if you were an Arab about to be chopped in half by some big smelly Christian. I don't hear you questioning this war. And if any of us grunts ask embarrassing questions we're considered some kind of dissenter that ought to be turned over to the CIA.'

Montano answered with annoyance. 'It's easy to just talk, Jake. It's different when you are as involved as I am. When you have so many responsibilities to men in the field, men who need spiritual guidance in this war, when you can understand that then you can understand the difficult role I play. I just can't ignore those men. I can't go out and tell them it's a bad war so don't fight it.'

'It depends on who you're working for,' Sturm muttered and blew the marijuana smoke out the open side. Montano didn't hear him for the priest was now into his sermon, his voice rising and falling in the patented Sunday delivery of all clerics.

'All wars are not inherently evil or wrong. In this case, it would certainly be more evil to accept peace at any price. We learned that lesson in World War II from the British when they tried to deal with Hitler. The United States has a legal right to be here. We came at the request of the South

Vietnamese government, under the auspices of the United Nations and the Southeast Treaty Organization.'

'And that gives us the right to zap thousands of innocent civilians, because they happened to be in something we declare a free fire zone? Do you know what it looks like after a Vietnamese village has been bombed? Did you ever see the people afterward, look in their faces? You would expect them to be bitter, to attack you as an American because Americans did this to them. But they just have this lost look, emptiness, like, "Oh well, what can we expect but death." And do those legal rights give us the right to torture suspects, or stand around watching it, like in the refugee camp? How do you handle that, captain? Doesn't that do something to your conscience?'

'You're going off half-cocked, Jacob,' Montano replied with a little heat in his voice, which he calmed immediately as he continued. 'You see, it is a case of using one evil to overcome a greater evil. If we are on safe legal grounds then we are on safe moral grounds. You should keep that in mind. Safe legal grounds mean safe moral grounds.' He repeated it with satisfaction, enjoying the ring of the words.

Ahead, Sturm could see the lights of the hospital and to the right he watched a line of choppers with their landing lights on drop like fireflies toward the airfield. He puffed deeply on the roach, blew it carefully out the door and said, 'You've got it all down pat, haven't you? Got all the answers. But you know what I think? I think you permit yourself to think only what the Army thinks, say what it says. You and the rest of the military chaplains have an unholy alliance with the military command. And all your talk of a justified US Presence in this war is only to justify your own failure to morally challenge the American role here. This is a war between two Vietnamese peoples but the US says we have to fight here to prevent China from taking over all of Asia. When you boil it all down, the US is here for its own interests, not the interests of Vietnam. And when Vietnam no longer serves our interests the US will go home. We'll just declare a victory and leave.'

Montano wheeled through the gate of the hospital grounds and parked. 'You are young and impetuous, Jacob. I can understand that, but think of the bigger picture. For instance, if we cut a man with a knife, that is immoral. But if we cut him to remove a tumor that will kill that man eventually, then cutting him is justified. That is acting to save a man, and that is what we are doing here in Vietnam.'

'Only one little problem, captain. The man we're supposed to be saving is dying because of our help. You should pray for the innocent Vietnamese instead of telling the grunts to go out and kill more of them.' Sturm took a last pull from the roach, flipped it away in the still night air and blew the smoke away. Only this time there was no wind to drag the pungent odor away and it wafted slowly over the priest who sniffed experimentally a few times before he asked, 'Jacob, is that marijuana?' His voice was soft, shocked. 'It is, no?'

Sturm didn't answer as he climbed out of the jeep but Montano swung out faster and met him at the front of the jeep where he blocked Sturm. They looked at each other a moment then Sturm said, 'Yeah, Captain Montano, Army chaplain, it's mary jane. Want some? Beats trying to get high on incense. Do you good. Free your mind so you could talk straight to the troops instead of looking up your sermons in the Army regulations.'

Montano gripped Sturm's arms. 'Jacob, listen to me. You've got only a little time left in Vietnam. Don't do anything that you will later regret. Don't ruin yourself in a matter of days. Put these drugs behind you, put that girl Mai behind you and for God's sake – and I mean that – for God's sake, straighten yourself up.' He gave Sturm a shake to emphasize his point.

Sturm pulled free. 'I think you're really bugged because I had the brains not to be a priest and because I'm screwing a girl in the ville. Why does it bug you, captain? Do you see her creamy body next to mine, see those nice tits in my hands?' Sturm leaned forward, his face close to the priest, his mind freewheeling. 'You see me ramming it home with her? All the things you would like to do but you won't admit it, right?' Sturm's voice echoed down the walkway between the hootches as Montano spun away from him without a word and quickly disappeared in the darkness. Sturm watched him go then stumbled along the boardwalk toward his hootch. As he started past the morgue building he stopped and eyed the door speculatively. He pulled his felt tip pen from his pocket, the one he used to mark tournequet times on men who had pieces of their limbs shot away, and he wrote in large black letters on the door:

'Yea, though I walk through the Valley
Of the Shadow of Death,
I will fear no Evil,
For I *am* the Evil.
Teofilo Montano, Chaplain, US Army, one each.'

CHAPTER TWELVE

'SANDY?' Sturm rose from the bench in the hospital corridor where he had been waiting as the nurse, wearing tailored and freshly starched fatigues, walked briskly down the hall. 'Sandy,' he repeated, 'just a minute.'

She paused and only half turned to him as if impatient to be on her way again. 'Yes, Jake?'

'I've been trying to see you but everytime I came around your hootch one of your bodyguard nurses said you weren't to be disturbed. Now you're back working and they say you're too busy. How about a few minutes with me?' He smiled hopefully.

She brushed back a loose strand of her rich brown hair and glanced down the hallway beyond him as she spoke. 'But I have been busy, Jake. So much to catch up on and as you know we've had quite a few wounded lately.'

'It's pretty quiet today. And it's Monday. Are you having the usual blue Monday flic in your hootch tonight? You haven't said anything about it.'

Sandy frowned and shook her head vehemently. 'No. Never again. Never, never, never,' she said and squeezed her eyes closed.

Sturm tugged his mustache and realized he had said the wrong thing. He tried a different tack. 'Well, there's a movie over at the First Cav tonight. Outdoors, so we could just walk right across the strip and take it in. Would you like to go?'

'No, I can't, Jake. I really am very busy. Now if you'll

excuse me I have to get on to the OR.' She gave him a tight little smile with her mouth only and hurried on.

Sandy. Sandy. Sandy. What happened to you? You better talk about it, let it all hang out, or you're going to blow your mind. What she needed, Sturm decided, was a few heroin joints. That would wipe her mind clean, let her see it all in perspective. At least some grass, but he knew she was too uptight. She would never touch it. Booze won't do it for you, Sandy, it will only take you down.

The rest of the day dragged and Sturm grew increasingly restless as he sat with the others by the dustoffs and waited for missions that never came. He sat a little apart from the others, speaking little, and once when he felt he had to quiet his nerves he walked into the surrounding weeds to fix himself a duster. Why didn't he just fix it in front of the others like he used to do, he wondered. Why this hiding all of a sudden? The others knew what he was doing, it was just that he was sick of their goddam disapproving looks. Even Riley had quit and acted so supercilious about it, bragging that he would pass the urine test. On top of everything else, they all now thought it was hilarious that the rats had spooked him so he wouldn't stay in the bunker.

At dusk they left the pad and trooped to the messhall where Johnston found them and told them breathlessly that Top wanted both crews on standby tonight. 'He thinks something is cooking but he won't say. But my buddy says there's rumors the North Viets are making a big push to fill the hole left by the Fifth Mech along the Z before the South Viets can get established.' He smiled and scratched his thin mustache. 'Might get pretty busy for you boys before long.'

All four kept eating and when Johnston finally left Sturm pushed his chair back and said, 'I'm going to the ville. I'll be back in about an hour.'

The others looked at him in astonishment. 'Are you outta

your gourd?' Riley asked. 'If we have to fly while you're gone they'll court martial you. That's AWOL, man.'

'I'll be right back. Nothing is going to happen so quick. Nothing happened all day.'

'That's just a good reason for something to blow now,' Dooley said. 'Don't be dumb, Jake. Stick around.'

'And I don't need any of your advice,' Sturm retorted and rose to leave. 'I've got to see how Mai is.' But as he headed toward the front gate in the soft evening darkness he admitted to himself that seeing Mai was only part of the reason. He was out of smack and he needed some more. If things got too busy he might not get into the drugstore for days and he knew now he couldn't take it. He would just stop at the drugstore, a quick hello to Mai and right back.

Quang Tri was already settling down for the night, the evening shopping largely over, when Sturm jumped from the jeep that gave him a lift to town. It seemed that mostly soldiers were on the streets, American and Vietnamese troops passing time by watching the girls and drifting from bar to bar. Sturm crossed the square and moved quickly into the alley that was commonly used as a shortcut from the square to the back streets. The few Vietnamese in the alley hurrying home gave him only cursory glances as they passed. Sturm was about halfway down the alley when the one-legged boy pimp on one crutch lurched from his resting place against the wall and began beseeching him in a shrill voice.

'Hey, Joe, you want boom-boom? Numbah one girl. Okay?' The boy smiled hopefully but Sturm ignored him and made his way down the refuse strewn alley like a crane picking its way through muddy shallows. The boy hurried at his side.

'You no like puck-puck?' he asked in sudden revelation. He thumped along at Sturm's side as he pursued his new proposition. 'You want very ni' boy? Can, do, Joe.' The boy laughed at this a raucous cry wise beyond his years. Sturm plunged on and could feel other Vietnamese in the alley staring at him, a gangling white stranger intruding on the backroad of their society while being pursued by a one-legged 12-year-old pimp.

'Fuck off, kid,' Sturm said tiredly but the boy rocked along on one crutch at his side with mounting concern showing in his face that he might lose another customer.

'Hey, Joe, you try one time, okay? Numbah one. I no bullshit you. She like puck-puck,' he said and made an awkward grasp at Sturm's fly to emphasize his point that she would love to open up for him. Startled, Sturm flung his arm out to ward off the boy's hand and the blow knocked the child into a slow, side-twisting spin. He landed hard on his back in the alley slime and his crutch bounced away. Sturm started to push on but saw the Vietnamese in the alley stop to stare at him and the boy. He stopped and bent to help the boy but as he started to pull him to his one leg, the youth jerked his arm free and began screaming in Vietnamese. When the boy refused his help and continued to rail at him, Sturm turned to leave but saw his way was now blocked by several Vietnamese men and women drawn by the boy's shouts. Sturm shrugged to indicate he could not help and tried to ease through the crowd when one of the women suddenly spat at him. He backed away then ducked as another woman with a ponderous goiter hanging from her neck swung her parasol at his head. The blow caught him along the ear and knocked his field cap into the mud where a youth kicked it away and another laughingly ground it into the mud. Where the hell did all these people come from, Sturm wondered. Several women were now spitting at him and another – he couldn't see who as he spun blindly looking for a way out – scooped rotten cabbage from the alley and flung it at him. Panic rose in his throat. He flailed out at those nearby which drove the crowd back and then he was running toward the end of the alley. Someone coming toward him, who couldn't have seen what was happening but wanted to attack an American, flung a broken brick which caught him in the shoulder. The blow spun Sturm to one side and he almost fell in the slime before he caught the wall, righted himself and broke out of the alley in long bounds. He ran another fifty yards through strolling Vietnamese who stopped to stare and point or open their mouths in black and gold smiles. Seeing no one was chasing him he slowed to a walk and tried to catch his breath. Goddam animals. Try to help the kid and they attack me like *I'm* the fucking enemy. If they could get that organized against the Viet Cong, he thought, a half-million grunts would never have had to come here. He looked back and the fear that had possessed him in the alley was now replaced by surging anger. He spun about and started back toward the alley. Why run? Let's get it on. That bitch with the goiter. I'll pop her neck like a rotten cantaloupe. And I'll break that kid's leg like firewood. The rage rose in his eyes, red flames that blinded him and finally he had to stop and wait until the seizure passed and he could see again. When the trembling stopped, he lit a normal cigarette and forced his hands to be steady as he held the flame. Christ. The sudden rage left him weak and nauseous. A man could kill someone in that mood and not even know what happened, he thought as he puffed quickly at the cigarette. He looked at the burning end and then flung it into the scum-filled canal that ran beside the street. He turned again toward the drug store. Scag. I need some scrag wings to help me fly away from this garbage dump.

The drugstore was empty as usual except for the proprietress dressed in black and sitting on the wicker chair at the end of the dirty glass case. She nodded at Sturm as he came in and waited silently for him to order.

'Five capsules, mama-san,' he said and stretched forth his hand with all five fingers displayed. He laid ten dollars in military scrip on the table and waited until she returned with the heroin capsules wrapped in Vietnamese newspaper and bound by rubber bands. He pocketed the package and left the shop as the woman silently put the ten dollars in her blouse pocket and returned to her chair. The world's quietest millionaire, Sturm thought and started back toward the square. She's just one of thousands of Vietnamese growing rich at the expense of the GI. Just one of our friendly heroin-pushing allies. Real friends. Yes, sir, all part of that Washington fairy tale that we're in Vietnam to keep Vietnam free and to defend our national interests. Well, right now my national interests are to have a good hit and get laid. I just hope Mai is up to it. As he walked back he took a different street so he wouldn't have to go through nightmare alley again. It would be bad if they jumped him again because he would hit one of those women for sure.

Son of a bitch! Sturm stopped. On the corner ahead of him under the street lamp was the man Dooley had kicked out of the chopper. The same one who had given him a bad time in the noodle shop. He was talking to another Vietnamese soldier and did not appear to notice Sturm. There was no question it was the same one. That heavy build, the flat face, the scar through his right eyebrow and the drooping eyelid were the same. That bastard must have followed me, Sturm thought. It was too much coincidence that he would be on this back street. Maybe he had something to do with what happened in the alley. Sturm contemplated crossing the street then rejected it. If that dude comes on heavy again then we'll just have at it. As he passed the two, Scarbrow gave him a quick and contemptuous look before turning his back with exaggerated disdain.

Sturm almost stopped but then shrugged and kept walking. He had better things to do than fight with a dink. As he moved on, a Vietnamese man walking toward him suddenly leaped to one side in alarm as a small empty bottle of

Vietnamese whisky shattered on the sidewalk just ahead of Sturm. Several Vietnamese looked first at him and then behind him. Sturm whirled about, his hand reaching for his survival knife, but the heavy-set Vietnamese had his back turned and his companion just stared at Sturm with blank eyes. Assholes. He knew if he went back they would deny everything then start in on him. And every other Vietnamese on the block would join them.

Sturm turned away and hurried on to the club. Twenty minutes gone already. So what, I'll go when I'm ready. He looked back as he went upstairs but couldn't see Scar-brow or his companion. Inside he went directly to the latrine and shut himself into the toilet closet where he filled the end of a cigarette with heroin. He held it unlit in his fingers and went back to the bar. He picked up a soft drink at the bar and sat under one of the air conditioners where he lit up. God, it felt good. He let the smoke swirl deep inside him and he could almost feel the capillaries in the lungs opening their little mouths to greedily drink in the heroin. He leaned back after his second pull and sipped at his orange pop. This was peace. Not soaring like the first few times. Just peace. Give everyone in Vietnam some smack cigarettes and peace would be instantaneous. Certainly cheaper than war. He roused himself to look for Mai but didn't see her. No matter. One of the girls would tell her he was here. He leaned back in the booth again and leisurely worked on the smoke. Still drifting, he looked up to see Susie smiling down at him.

'You wait for Mai? She go out. Eat.'

'When she come back?'

'I no know. Sometime.' Susie laughed at him, rolled her eyes and fluttered her fingers by her head. 'You high. Smoke too much heroin.' She laughed and sat down.

'You go home soon?' she asked. 'Say bye-bye Mai?'

'I no say bye-bye. I take Mai home with me. We get married,' Sturm said with a smile.

'You bullshit,' Susie replied cooly. 'You same-same all GI Say I marry you but always go home alone. Mai, she same same sister to me so you no bullshit her. No tell her you marry her. Okay?' She fixed Sturm with a glittering stare but he only shrugged.

'I like Mai very much. What we talk about is our business Not yours.'

Susie's face flushed in anger and she tossed her head. 'My business too. I long time see you GI. Just want boom-boom then go. That okay. But sometime GI promise marry girl, go to US, but never do. You same-same GI who promise but never take girl. Mai same-same my sister. She young girl. Not know very much so you no tell her lie. Now she have trouble with police. She hurt. You be ni'.'

'I will, Susie, I promise.' Anything to get this Dragon Lady off his back. 'How is Mai now? Better?'

'She better. She come back soon. She go look for brother. You wait. Now I go work.' As Susie left a crowd of pilots wearing their black cavalry hats with crossed sabers sat down in the booth behind Sturm.

'Man the dinks in that village couldn't believe it when we fired them up today,' one of them laughed.

'Yeah, we'd been flying over them for nearly a month pretending we thought they were all good guys. Then division says they're bad guys, let them have it. That ville couldn't believe what hit them.'

'How about that guy in the rice field. I didn't think anyone could run so fast through that mud. We let him make it almost to the ditch then fired up his ass with a rocket. That dink just plain disappeared,' drawled another. The pilots laughed and shouted for drinks.

With his head resting against the back of the booth that divided them, Sturm heard the pilots talking as if he were an eavesdropper in a different room, a quiet and undisturbed room where he was shut off from the excitement that filled their voices. He heard them but felt isolated, like a priest in the gloom of a confessional with his hands folded on his robed lap as he listened to quiet murmurings of horror through the small screen.

'You killed how many, my son?'

'Only ten, Father.'

'*Only* ten? That sounds like quite a few.'

'Well, there have been days when I've zapped – I mean killed – thirty or more.' The tempo of the voice on the other side of the screen quickened in excitement. 'Like that time we cleaned out a village near the Ben Hai River. You should have seen it, Father. We fired them all up. Really did a number on them.'

Sturm pressed his ear against the booth and kept his eyes closed. It was as if he *were* taking confession. But who was he listening to?

'Well, you will have to say quite a few Hail Mary's and Our Fathers for this, my son.'

'I expect so, Father. But not too many. I mean I've got to fly pretty soon. We've got a big one coming up and I don't want to be late or miss it.'

In his mind's eye Sturm bent and glanced covertly through the screen where in the dim light of the other side he could see a familiar round face. Although somewhat improper, he spoke directly to the man.

'How are you, Specialist Montano?'

The man started at the voice so close in the confessional, then leaned closer to the screen. He peered back at the priest and the two were nose to nose.

'Oh, it's you Father Sturm. I'm fine.'

'How is life as a Cavalry pilot?'

'Good, good. Lots of action. Really keeps me busy. But sometimes I worry.'

'About what is right and what is wrong?' Father Sturm asked.

'Yes, sort of. It's the body count. It's so hard to keep accurate tabs when you're flying over a field at 80 knots. I have to fib sometimes to meet my quota. Like I never really got those thirty dinks. Maybe only 15. I know I shouldn't lie and that's why I came to confession.'

'Hey, man, can we sit here?' Sturm opened his eyes, startled, and saw four Cav troops looking at him. He blinked and looked around. The club was filled with soldiers and girls and the music thudded in his ears.

'He's nodding, man, let's sit down,' one of the troops said to another. They started to sit down then had to back away as Sturm got up to look for Mai. She wasn't in the club he decided after scrutinizing each table. He crossed to her room and she wasn't there either. Disconsolate and at loose ends he drifted outside with the hope of meeting her coming in. He stood in the street for a few minutes to let his eyes adjust to the gloom and saw the betel nut hags watching him while they spit their vermilion juice on the sidewalk. He started to fix another smoke but told himself he was going pretty heavy. Wait until I get back to the hootch, he thought, and glanced at his watch. Already more than an hour gone. I've got to move.

He crossed the street and began walking down the nearly deserted sidewalk where all the shops were closed and steel gates drawn across the entrance. After the first block he became aware of someone in step behind him and he started to turn but checked himself. Probably some drunken Vietnamese soldier and if I turn he'll think he's being attacked and start screaming his head off. Instead, he lengthened his stride only to hear the other quicken his pace until the steps drew alongside and a voice said, 'Hey, Joe, where you go?'

Sturm looked down at the Vietnamese beside him and involuntarily recoiled. It was that goddam Scar-brow.

'Where you go?' The Vietnamese repeated unsmilingly

and Sturm could hear the suggestion of violence in his simple question.

'I go home,' Sturm replied shortly and continued to stride on.

'You go in chopper?' the Vietnamese ranger asked mockingly. 'You go in chopper and take me so you can push me out?' His voice was strident and demanding in the quiet night. Sturm was surprised at how good his English was. An educated man. Maybe he could reason with him, he thought, and stopped to face the Vietnamese.

'Look, let's be reasonable.' He was immediately sorry he had paused for the man stood swaying before him, his brown camouflage uniform rank with sweat and the smell of sweet Vietnamese whisky was heavy on his breath. As Sturm talked the Vietnamese eyed him balefully. 'Look, I didn't push you. My crew chief did and he's sorry. We're both sorry it happened. It's past now, so let's forget it. Okay?'

'I do not forget. Why you push me out? You think you can kick Vietnamese? We are animals for you Americans to kick?' The man's voice came in an angry hiss and he leaned forward pugnaciously although he came no more than chest high to Sturm.

'No, I don't think Vietnamese are animals. But I think you are acting like one now,' Sturm replied and he could feel his own anger rising. He had had enough of pushy Vietnamese for today. He turned and walked on in hope that the Vietnamese would drop it, but there he was at Sturm's side again, hissing with violent innuendos.

'You say I am animal? You want to kick me again? You try, you try,' he said. Sturm was caught unaware in the next second when the Vietnamese suddenly gave him a violent push into a narrow alley that bisected the main street. The thrust carried him into the darkness where Sturm recovered barely in time to deflect a knee that was driven toward his groin. It missed but hit him a numbing blow in his thigh. He reeled backwards to avoid another booted kick and then caught a smashing blow across his left shoulder from a piece of pipe the Vietnamese had concealed. Unable to see anything but the dim outline of the attacker in the alley, Sturm found himself against the alley wall thinking the Vietnamese had gone insane. He ducked another blow from the pipe but slipped to his knees in the alley muck. The Vietnamese threw a quick kick at his face but this time Sturm anticipated it. He caught the foot and gave it a violent twist which spun Scar-brow to the ground. The Vietnamese recovered like a cat and was on his feet facing Sturm again.

This bastard's flipped, Sturm thought as he lunged to his feet. He reached back to his belt and unclasped his survival knife and held it hidden behind his hip. I'm going to stick this son of a bitch in an arm or leg and get it over with, he thought. Then there was no more time to think as the Vietnamese rushed him and swung the pipe down in a whipping blow at Sturm's head. Sturm countered the blow with his hand and felt a numbing shock roll through his left side. The Ranger's lunge carried him into Sturm and threatened to bowl him over and Sturm, feeling himself slipping again, came up hard with the knife in a primeval reflex. He no longer thought about striking an arm or a leg. Now in his sudden rage he wanted to viscerally damage his attacker, to feel the knife slip through the fabric and then as if in slow motion feel the knife point pushing into the skin until membranes parted, then the blade cutting deeper through the abdominal muscles and into the abdominal cavity and into the stomach where, sunk to the hilt, the knife stopped.

The Vietnamese leaned against Sturm with his breath coming in tight little crying gasps, his hand on Sturm's arm as if seeking support. Then he was slipping to his knees and Sturm with his red-ringed anger fading saw a man dying and Sturm bent over him with his hand still on the knife handle that was slippery with blood. I want my knife back, I must have my knife, and he pulled on it but it wouldn't come. It went in so easy, why won't it come out? I must have my knife! and he yanked hard until the blade started out and Sturm could feel the saw-toothed back of the knife ripping tissue as it came. The Vietnamese gave a long, choking squeal of pain, like a baby crying in the night, and like a newborn infant the Ranger lay on his side with his hands clutching his belly and his knees drawn up tight. Sturm, now almost paralyzed with the realization of what he had done, stared at the barely discernible figure on the dark earth before him. Now what? Now what in God's name must I do? He bent to see how bad the man was, thinking maybe he could get him to a hospital, just dump him outside and run. The man's breath came in ragged gasps and Sturm could see the faint reflection of street light in the spreading pool before the man that he at first thought was water but could feel was blood. So much blood. Christ, it's more than a belly wound. The knife point must have hit the abdominal aorta. He put his hand on the man's shoulder and the feel of the muscles hard beneath his fingers made him think that just moments ago the man had been alive, healthy and full of fight. Now it was gone. 'Why did you have to attack me?' Sturm whispered in anguish. 'It was for nothing and now you're dying and I can't take you to a hospital. I'm sorry.' His whisper in the dark alley startled him and he knew he had to get out of there. He wiped his knife and his hands on the man's trousers and stood up. He started toward the alley entrance then flattened himself against the building as three soldiers heading home passed the alley opening. None glanced his way. I mustn't be seen in here, he thought and whirled toward the far end. He made his way recklessly out of the alley. The light was better on the back street which he followed for two blocks before he turned back to the main street in order to find a ride home.

Just ahead of him were the same three troops standing in

the road as a three-quarter pulled over to pick them up. Sturm ran toward them and clambered in the back as the truck lurched forward.

'What's this?' asked one of the soldiers in the black interior. 'An interloper? Only the bravest, those of the mighty First Cavalry Division parenthesis Airmobile unparenthesis may ride in this chariot. Are you among the bravest?' the voice asked amidst giggles from the other two.

Sturm couldn't see the faces of the men and he didn't answer. Instead he hunkered against the wind and tried to fix himself a smoke. Steady, hand, do your thing. He dug one of the capsules out of the newspaper package but had trouble spilling the tobacco out. He kept seeing that Vietnamese lying on the dark earth with his life pumping into the alley filth. Sturm got the cigarette twisted and struck his lighter.

'Ahh, you *are* among the brave,' the voice said in his ear and with the lighter still flickering Sturm turned to see a boyish faced soldier solemnly watching him. 'Only the brave know enough to escape and what better way than through the miraculous powder. I'm fresh out and would delight in joining you for the ride home.'

Sturm snapped the lighter off and said nothing as he pulled deeply on the cigarette and felt himself slowly relax. His mind remained filled with the deed. Quit worrying, he shouted inwardly, it was self-defense. It was him or me, wasn't it? Is that murder? No. What choice was there? And it was too late to save him, wasn't it? He was probably dead by the time I got out of the alley. And there is no sense in reporting it. The Vietnamese would just love to have an American on trial for killing one of their brave defenders.

A flashlight snapped on in his face and the kid asked in a voice turned surly, 'Where do you want out?'

'21st Evac,' Sturm replied.

The light played down Sturm's arm and over his pants and boots. 'You a medic or something.'

'Yeah. A medic. A savior,' Sturm said. They rode on in silence until Sturm banged on the side of the truck and brought it to a stop beside the hospital gate. He jumped out and started away with a brief wave when the kid yelled after him: 'You know how I knew you were a medic? Because you still got blood all over you, man, from today's work.'

Sturm looked down at himself in the gate light and was dumbfounded. His pants were spattered with blood, now almost dried, and his boots were caked with blood and dust, and a long red smear ran across the back of his hand. He saw the new MP leaning against the little guard house by the gate watching him. 'That's the way it goes,' the MP smiled.

Sturm shook his head. 'I never even noticed.'

'You were just too hot to get into town after a little poontang, weren't you?' the MP said sympathetically. He was anxious for more conversation to pass the time but Sturm hurried on toward his hootch with no further words. My God, I look like Jack the Ripper. I've got to get rid of these clothes. He passed no one as he made his way down the boardwalk between the hootches. He went silently to the door of his hootch and listened. He could hear the other three inside playing cards and he felt enormous relief. At least they weren't out on some mission. But they would want to know where all the blood came from and they would know it wasn't from today's work. He walked on toward the showers where he started washing his hands. 'Out, out, damn spot,' he said half aloud, and only the long row of faceless mirrors listened. He found the quote mildly amusing. It must be the scag, he thought, for there is nothing amusing about death. He washed his boots and his knife then spattered water liberally over his fatigue pants to hide the blood and returned to the hootch. As he entered Riley pointed a finger at him.

'What did you do out there, piss all over yourself?' The others looked at his wet pants and boots.

'No. The goddam faucet came loose and hosed me down,' he said. As he began stripping off his clothes and piling them beneath his bed Dooley spoke to him in a serious voice. 'You were damned lucky, Jake. We didn't get any calls. If we had, you would have blown a whole year's good effort in Vietnam. You would have been court martialled, busted and maybe even jailed. And just before you're due out of the service.'

'I know, I know. But it's over now so I don't need the moralizing. Just quit bugging me,' he snapped and put his head in his hands. But as soon as he closed his eyes he saw the Vietnamese with the scar through his eyebrow leaning close to him and the great disappointment and hurt in his eyes when he realized that the great pain in his stomach was a knife and that he was going to die. Yes, he knew right away that he was dying. How could he know it, Sturm asked himself, how could he tell? He opened his eyes abruptly to rid himself of the ghostly image. The others were playing cards again but they said nothing. Sturm watched for a moment but found he couldn't keep still, couldn't empty his mind of the death. He rummaged on his bunk until he came up with his smokes and the package of heroin vials which he opened. He knew without looking that the others were watching. He twisted the end and lit it and sat smoking with his elbows on his knees while he stared at the floor.

'How many is that today, Jake?' It was Riley.

'I don't know. A hundred, maybe. What's the difference? I'll quit before they give me the urine test. Anyway, what's it to you? Just because you've stopped, you don't have to be so goddam smug about it.'

'I'm not smug. I just want you to make it home with me, man. If you want to stay here in some funky hospital, alright. Do your thing, man.' Riley was getting angry himself.

Dooley intervened. 'Look, Jake. We're just trying to help you, just trying—'

'Well, just butt out. I don't need any help.' No one answered him but he knew they were still watching him. He flopped back into his bunk and pulled the mosquito netting down. Tomorrow he would get rid of all his clothing. Everything. He knew even a single spot of blood on his clothes could convict him. He had seen it happen on TV countless times. He fell into a restless sleep and once during the night he bolted upright in the bed when he distinctly heard a Vietnamese voice whisper, 'Where you go, Joe?' He listened over the thudding of his heart but the room was quiet except for the puppy Dooley had given him stirring beneath his bunk.

CHAPTER THIRTEEN

THE airless green-walled room slowly filled with doctors and nurses, some off duty and some stopping in between rounds. Several patients also came when they learned who it was. 'It's the least I can do,' said one with both arms in casts. 'He got me into the chopper when I couldn't make it myself.' There were no chairs and everyone stood uncomfortably while they waited for the service to begin. Sturm came into the room late, not even wanting to be there but knowing the others would wrongly interpret his actions. As he entered he saw he was not late enough, for the service had not begun, and he slid along the back wall to the corner where he hoped to stand unnoticed. Chaplain Montano, at the front, saw him a head above everyone else and gave him a sympathetic nod of recognition which caused everyone else in the room to crane their necks at who was given preferential treatment. Some nodded solicitously at him.

Montano cleared his throat and moved his bulk squarely before the small crowd. Sturm, looking at the dent made by Montano's belt in his protruding belly, thought the chaplain had become even fatter. No, sleeker was the better description, he thought.

'Before we begin, let us pray for our fallen colleague, each in his own way, each to himself,' Montano said in his sing-song pattern. Heads dutifully fell forward as they began to pray. Only Sturm kept his head raised and his eyes clouded as his mind filled with remembrances of how it had been.

He awoke that morning before the others and dressed in

fresh fatigues and wore his other pair of boots. He gathered the other clothes from under his bed and stole down to the incinerator behind the messhall where he burned everything. The boots wouldn't burn but he covered them in the ashes and knew they would be thrown out and never found. When it was done he sat on the boardwalk outside the hootch and played with the dog while he waited for the messhall to open. 'Dink dog,' he said softly and the puppy hopped awkwardly to him on its crippled back legs with its tail beating in four-four happiness time. Sturm hugged the dog but when he grabbed one of its forelegs it suddenly felt like the knife quivering inside that Vietnamese and he dropped the dog. Why did this have to happen? Only five days to go and I have to kill a goddam Vietnamese. And not even one of the enemy. Or was he? Who is the enemy?

He stared unseeing at the dog while he pulled his cigarettes from his pocket and fumbled for the heroin vial. No one was up yet and he fixed his cigarette in the open, feeling nervous at his braveness and guilty at lighting up so early. What's the dif? Gotta die sometime. Right, Sturm? Right, he told himself. He blew the smoke at the dog. Maybe you're the enemy. You're a dink. The North Vietnamese are my enemies because my leaders tell me they are and because somebody put me in a uniform so they could identify me as their enemy. Now, if I were in civilian clothes and traveling with a Jane Fonda peace group, I would be welcomed as a friend in Hanoi. So it is the uniform that is my real enemy. Uniformity commands uniforms so General Uniformity is the arch enemy of the people. Uniforms and National Interests are great enemies. We always have National Interests, as defined by some politician in Washington, at stake and somebody has to die to defend that obscure ideal. That's why we are in Vietnam. But it is funny how our National Interests faded here now that the grunts are starting to go home.

He shook his head and brushed away the puppy that was

licking his hand. A present, Dooley had said, to cheer your soul. Dooley. Sturm wanted to smooth it over with him before he left. Dooley was just too good of a man to leave on bad terms. So why couldn't he accept the fact that Tomato hadn't seen that dink get greased by Kowalski? Take his word for it and be done with the whole thing. Today he would try. If he made up with Dooley that would make up for killing that Vietnamese last night. He shuddered then checked his watch to get his mind on something else. Six-thirty, time for the messhall to open. He stomped into the hootch and made everybody get up for breakfast.

All four were sitting together when Sturm saw Johnston threading his way through the tables with that nervous, I've-got-a-neat-thing-to-tell-you-look on his face. 'Oh, oh,' said Sturm.

Johnston put his hands on the table and leaned forward in his conspiratorial manner before he spoke.

Dooley beat him to the punch. 'I know. Top says we've got a mission. Fifth Mech is getting hit and for us to move out smartly. Right?' The red head smiled at Johnston who looked crestfallen.

'How did you know? The call just came in when I was going by the orderly room.'

'We know everything, Johnston. That's why we're medics and not orderlies.' Dooley pushed his chair back with a sigh. 'Let's go save Fifth Mech again.'

Raab began shoveling the creamed chicken and toast into his mouth which made Riley bolt from the table. 'I'd rather work on a guy with his face blown *away* than watch you eat, Raab,' he said. Raab shrugged and continued to eat as he took his tray out the door with him.

Kowalski was already firing up the engine as they rounded the hospital and began to run toward the pad. 'Last one back tonight has to treat at the Forty Akers,' Riley yelled as he and Raab broke toward Rainbow One-two.

After closing Tippit's door and giving the medical gear a cursory once-over, Sturm pulled on his flak vest and sat on his chest protector.

'Only five days to go makes you extra protective, doesn't it?' Dooley said over the intercom. Sturm still adjusting his boom mike to his lips, smiled back and nodded but didn't say anything. He hadn't said much to Dooley at breakfast but had been congenial and he hoped Dooley understood he was trying. Dooley switched to channel two as Kowalski ran the engine up to 6,600 rpms, checked his external gas temperature and reported his hover check complete.

'What's happening, great leader,' Dooley asked as Kowalski made his run at the fence and tried to scrape the top wire with his skid. Sturm closed his eyes and thought if that s.o.b. catches a skid and flips this bird and kills me before I get home I'm going to be very upset.

Kowalski was describing the mission and his voice was filled with happy anticipation. That was enough for Sturm to know it was going to be a rough day. Kowalski's voice crackled in his headset: 'A Fifth Mech recon platoon was making a sweep in those hills northwest of Dong Ha and came under heavy attack. A relief platoon trying to reach them got nailed about four kliks from them. Now S-2 thinks there is a whole regiment of bad guys in the area. The relief column took the worst of it during the night and we're going to take the first load out of there.'

'I hope we've got some air,' Sturm said.

'Naturally, my boy,' Kowalski replied jovially. 'The works. Cobras and spooky during the night and Phantoms have been hitting the area all morning. Just what the doctor ordered. Or the medic, in this case,' he added and laughed at his little joke.

They flew north for 20 minutes over the monotonous bomb-pocked sandy wastes of former rice fields while Sturm sat with his back hunkered to the transmission and stared at the ground below. He wanted another smoke but he resisted. That would be two this morning, too much. If I can still resist then I'm not fully hooked and I can still shake it before I start home. Home? It seemed farther away the closer he got. And what am I going to do when I get home? Go around with my aid bag to patch up injured farmers? Well, that's what I learned in the army, daddy. Just be glad I wasn't in demolition or I would go around blowing up barns to show you what I learned. Back to the monastery? Not likely, too unreal. It was all unreal and nothing would ever be the same. Oh, screw it, he said to himself, and dug in his pocket for the heroin and cigarettes. You only live once, he thought as he prepared the cigarette, might as well do it up right. The smoke tasted flat and the drug gave him the sensation of being afloat in an oarless rowboat on greasy ocean swells. He knew the second hit was a mistake but finished the cigarette anyway. He would come out of it before too long. As he leaned back in the seat he felt the knife on his belt and was overcome for a moment with a flood of memories, the blow to the arm, the smells of the alley, the darkness and the blood, and he could almost feel the Vietnamese hand on his and hear his labored breathing. He slipped the knife off his belt and sailed it out the doorway, watching it as far as he could. He was still staring at the ground when Kowalski began talking again.

'Roger, Ironsides, we see you. How many have you?' He was speaking to the recon commander.

'Rainbow One-one, Ironsides. We have four in bad shape and six more with lesser wounds.'

'Roger, Ironsides. We'll be down in zero two. Have them ready.' Leaning from his seat Sturm could see the armored personnel carriers and tanks drawn in a circle along a narrow ridge just ahead. Two tracks were burning, probably hit by rocket propelled grenades, and the oily black smoke rolled upwards in the calm morning air. A whole ridge to the west of the track platoon was burning after being hit repeatedly by Phantoms carrying napalm. Cobra gunships worked over another ridge to the east of the tracks. Those dinks really boxed the track platoon in, Sturm thought with some admiration, and from the amount of tracer fire coming and going below he knew it was going to be one of those mornings.

Kowalski began dropping hard toward the center of the ring of tanks and APCs but then broke off sharply when a geyser of dirt exploded near one of the tanks. The tank rocked to one side and two men on top were blown straight off it before the tank was enveloped in dust. Kowalski hit the radio button under his finger.

'Ironsides, Rainbow One-one. What the hell was that? Are you getting mortared?'

'Negative, Rainbow One-one. That was rocket. We've had four this morning and that was the closest. Negative mortars. Come on in, those rockets aren't that accurate.' You hope, thought Sturm.

Kowalski turned the ship in a hard right turn that glued Sturm to his seat and left him looking at the ground directly below him. Maybe I ought to just take a big step right out of here, a big autumn leaf falling over Vietnam. He shook his head instead and looked around. Dooley was standing behind Kowalski as the ship began another screaming descent toward the tracks. Dooley looked around and saw Sturm looking at him and Sturm gave his crew chief the thumbs up sign. He felt better at the friendly overture and decided he would have a good talk with Dooley when they got back. Put everything behind him. But that would have to wait for a while because the ground was rushing at him and the tiny figures that he had seen scrambling about a moment ago below him were suddenly men with haggard faces and empty eyes. The troops leaned into the prop blast and were running toward the medevac carrying the wounded even before Kowalski touched down.

Dooley was first out of the chopper with Sturm behind him, wishing he hadn't taken that last smoke. It was so hard to move. So much seemed to be happening all at once. Christ, here's the first one. Two grunts with dog tags sparkling against their grimy, sweat-streaked chests carried a man with eyes closed and his face covered with beads of sweat. A large compress was pulled tight around his abdomen but Sturm could see blood still running through the man's fingers where he clutched at the pad. Sturm helped lift the man into the bottom litter in the chopper at the other doorway leading a sergeant who seemed to have half his face shot away. Someone had put a small compress over the gaping hole where his cheek and nose once were but it didn't do any good. It didn't hide anything. Sturm pulled the sergeant inside and got him into the second litter when one of the men who had brought him pulled at Sturm's sleeve. He tried to talk over the scream of the engine and the hammer of rifle fire but he was crying and Sturm couldn't understand anything. He wanted to listen to the man but Dooley was yelling at him now on the intercom. 'Come on, come on Sturm, get these guys in there. We ain't got all day,' and Sturm couldn't stand the yelling so he pulled the plug and halted Dooley's voice. Now they were pushing wounded in at him from both sides, too much, we can't handle them all. One kid with his pants leg ripped off and his boot gone was being shoved in by two more dirt encrusted grunts. The youth – how old, maybe 17 or 18? – had his right leg in a pneumatic splint and when Sturm got him into the last litter and tied down he saw the boy didn't really have much leg at all, just some bones and flesh. Christ, it seemed like they had been down on the ground so long, why was it taking so long today? He looked around and saw Kowalski looking at him with an angry face and his mouth working behind his mike but Sturm heard nothing inside his helmet. Who the fuck wants to hear? Who wants to even see this? These men are all garbage, just piles of refuse to be picked up and dumped. Next time for sure he was going to pass out 'Do Not litter' signs to all the grunts. And to the dinks. They were the ones that littered the field with bodies. It was their fault.

He moved back to the doorway to help Dooley who had another man in his arms, this one with a tournequet around his forearm above what looked like the remains of a hand. He tried to help but it was so difficult to move with all the wounded lying everywhere and the blood made everything so goddam slippery. He got to Dooley but the ol' red head, good ol' Tomato, had already pushed the man inside and jumped in himself. He gave Sturm a perplexed look, as if to say why aren't you functioning, man? Then he was pushing Sturm out of the way while he counted bodies. He was talking into his mike and motioning furiously at Sturm to plug in his own helmet.

'Ten?' Kowalski replied. 'Let's try it.' He eased up on the collective until the shuddering craft lifted about three feet. With a shake of his head he put it down again and said, 'I'm redlining. We'll go out of here like a fat duck for those dinks to pot shot at. Take two off.' Dooley looked at Sturm to make the decision and Sturm looked around at the young men with old faces and hollow eyes. Why me, why do I have to decide who has to stay and get shelled some more and who gets to go to clean sheets and doctors? He finally pointed at one that had his back peppered with shrapnel and then he started to put off the man with a mangled hand when Dooley found one with a flesh wound in his thigh who wasn't hurting much. They yelled explanations at the men as they pushed them out of the chopper but the troops didn't understand and went reluctantly. Dooley finally signalled some of the grunts waiting for the liftoff to get the two out of the way and the man with a back full of shrapnel yelled 'hurry back, hear?' but not one heard.

Dooley gave Kowalski the go sign and the pilot backed the

bird as far as he could across the clearing to get a run. It wouldn't be much and it would make for a slow start. Bad news with all those dinks just waiting out there, Sturm thought. Once they lifted clear of the protective iron ring they would be that slow, fat duck. The chopper tilted forward on its nose and sped toward an armored personnel carrier with two men on top manning a .50 caliber. The two had to duck as the skids missed them by inches and then they were into the defenseless open and Sturm was that fat mallard he had shot so many times and he wanted to hug himself before a round with his name on it found the mark. He looked out the doorway and saw they weren't going up. Instead, Kowalski was hammering straight ahead to build up speed while he twisted the chopper back and forth through the ravines. He was trying to race under the bad guys on the ridges rather than making a slow spiral rise that would leave them so exposed. It might work, it just might work, Sturm thought and started working on the man with jelly for a leg who was still bleeding when he felt the ship shudder with the first hits. It was a bad feeling, like the chopper had tremors, but he didn't look up from his work. I must concentrate on this boy's leg, he thought, then he felt the ship tremble again as it took another burst. He turned to see if any of the wounded men sprawled on the deck had been hit and oh my God, oh Christ, please no. He left the boy with the bleeding leg and stumbled over one of the wounded as he lunged toward Dooley who was on both knees with his hands at his throat trying to stop the rush of blood. Sturm fell beside the crew chief who was gasping and gagging. He forced Dooley down on his side and pulled his hands away. Blood rose in rhythmic little fountains at the neck and Sturm jammed down with his thumb on the carotid artery while he began swabbing the area with a compress. Dooley's mouth was open as he tried to suck in air and then his body began convulsing beneath Sturm who had one leg over him.

Dooley began hammering on his arm, Christ, what is it, what is it? No air, that's it, and he yelled above the scream of the turbine engine and hiss of wind past the doorway, 'Get some air, goddamit,' and he could see now that the fragment or whatever had ripped the trachea tube and Dooley was choking on his own blood. Sturm found the hole and leaned forward to put his lips on the wound and blow air into the trachea. Clean it out, open it up, and it worked. Dooley at once stopped thrashing and Sturm could feel Dooley's chest heave once, smoothly, as he drew air deep into his lungs. But it will plug again, Sturm knew. I've got to get a tube in there, but I need three hands. I need help, he thought, and looked around at the wounded who were watching him with white faces beneath the caked grime and their eyes said goodbye. Dooley's eyelids fluttered open and he looked at Sturm with eyes bright in his pale face. One hand came up and lightly rested on Sturm's hand where he kept his thumb against the carotid artery to stop the pulse of blood. But it didn't seem to work well, there was still blood coming. It was like the thing that hit Dooley had cut his throat. But we might make it, Sturm thought, and he kept his eyes locked on Dooley's to keep him hanging on. I won't let you go, he said to himself, then he shouted it, 'Don't go, hang on.' But even as Sturm watched the crew chief's face grew visibly paler, his eyes drooped, and now Sturm could see blood welling slowly from the other side of the trachea. He swabbed with another compress and could see a small hole in the left jugular vein. Oh Christ, it's been leaking inside all this time. Why won't it stop? Dooley's hand slipped from his and Sturm saw the red head's eyes growing cold, so tired, wanting to sleep.

'Look at me, Mike. Don't go, don't go. Look at me!' he yelled aloud and he knew he was crying but Dooley couldn't see him with his eyes closed. Sturm brought his knee into Dooley's side to jolt him awake but it was too late. Dooley was sliding away, he was on that raft in the pond that kept drifting out of reach no matter how far you leaned out from the dock, always just beyond your straining fingertips.

Sturm eased up on the artery and there was no more bleeding. He knelt over Dooley and with a clean compress wiped the blood from his face and cleaned up around his neck then buttoned his fatigues to the top. He pulled Dooley's helmet off and gently, in order not to disturb him, smoothed his wiry red hair. He looks so peaceful, Sturm thought and wondered why he couldn't stop crying. Tears made it so hard to see. He knew he should get up and look after the others. After all, it wasn't the first time he had seen a man die in the chopper. The others needed him too. Still, he sat beside Dooley and rested one hand on the freckled forehead that grew cold in the summer heat of Vietnam.

Someone was beside him now and Sturm looked up to see Kowalski plug his helmet in for himand begin talking to him.

'He's dead, Sturm. I'll get him over here and look after him while you get back to the wounded.' Kowalski's voice was gentle as he took Sturm's hand away from Dooley and pulled the body behind the pilot's seat and covered it with a poncho.

Sturm rose slowly and went back to stand before the litters. He rested against the top litter that held the boy with the crushed leg but he couldn't get started. His mind seemed stalled and he shook it repeatedly as if to make the gears mesh. He studied the boy again. Couldn't be more than 17. Probably lied about his age to get in. Now, let's see, there must be a tournequet on that leg. Why didn't they tag him? The boy lay calmly with eyes closed and Sturm worked over him for five minutes before he discovered the boy was dead.

'Why, we ask, must men die?' Montano's voice cut back into Sturm's reverie with a jolt of reality. Montano went on in his cadenced style.

'When we think of death, remember the words of the poet

John Donne: "No man is an Island, intire of itself; every man is a peace of the Continent, a part of the maine; if Clod bee washed away by the Sea, Curope is the lesse, as well as if a Promontorei were, as well as if a Mannor of thy friends, or of thine owne were; any mans death diminishes me, because I am involved in Mankinde; And therefore never send to know for whom the bell tolls; It tolls for thee." ' He paused for effect. 'We are the lesser today with the death of Specialist fourth class Michael Dooley. He was a friend to all of us, a man who gave himself unsparingly to help others. And if he was a friend to us he was even a greater friend to the Vietnamese, for he made the ultimate sacrifice while serving in the interests of their freedom. However sad we may be to lose such a man as Michael Dooley, we must remember that his was a noble death. Noble because he died in the interests of freedom, in our interests as well as the interests of the South Vietnamese. Yes, we have a great stake in the freedom of South Vietnam, and that means sacrifices on our part. No national interest is reached without sacrifices from so many and we must not lose . . .'

'Oh bullshit.'

The quietly spoken word stopped Montano with his mouth agape and a few heads turned but most decided they were just hearing things. Montano assumed he too was hearing things and he cleared his throat to continue.

'We must, um, not lose sight of the need to keep South Vietnam free of atheistic Communism. We must be prepared, as was Michael Dooley, to make the ultimate sacrifice, for the most precious . . .'

'Bullshit. Plain bullshit.' There it was again, the words so calmly pronounced in the hushed room. This time Montano stopped and looked with the other heads that were turned toward Sturm.

'Did you say something, Jacob?' he asked in a tight little voice.

'Yes. I said bullshit,' he replied. 'Dooley wasn't at all prepared to give his life for this fucked up country or its fucked up people.'

Montano turned to face Sturm and there was a general stirring and whispering around the room as all turned to stare where he leaned against the wall.

'Dooley didn't want anything from the Vietnamese and he didn't want to give them anything. Certainly not his life.' He was surprised he could talk so calmly about it now. The last smoke helped, it cleared up so many doubts in his mind. 'The only thing he wanted was to screw Betty Bazoom. That's all he wanted from the Vietnamese.' There were some suppressed titters at this and some shocked intakes of breath in the room.

Montano, whose mouth had been working silently for several seconds, finally found his voice. 'Specialist Sturm,' he said, 'We are here to honor the memory of one who was close to us, not to mock him. If you have some comments about Specialist Dooley, please save them until we have finished this service and we can talk. Alone.'

'But you've got everything wrong. He didn't love the Vietnamese. He detested them. And he didn't die for them. He died because I killed him, because I . . .' There was open murmuring in the crowd and then Riley was at his side talking to him.

'Come on, man, let's go take a break. Let's take a walk.' He tugged gently on Sturm's arm but Sturm shook him off.

'I know I killed him because I didn't stop the bleeding. I just couldn't stop it, I couldn't find it. My head just wouldn't . . .' He let his voice trail off, now afraid to admit that his head was full of smack and otherwise Dooley might be here.

Montano turned sympathetic. 'Perhaps you had better go lie down awhile, Jacob,' he said in the voice he reserved for bereaved families and those he considered to be out of touch with reality.

'I don't need to lie down. I need to stand here and tell you not to dishonor Dooley with all this crap of yours about how he died to keep Vietnam free.' Sturm was afraid he was crying again, but he couldn't be sure and he didn't want to wipe his cheeks. 'You don't speak for the dead, you just use these memorial sessions as pep talks for the living warriors. Fight fight, kill kill,' he shouted, no longer calm, and his arms came up in a macabre parody of the cheer leader. 'Let's hear it for Captain Knute Rockne Montano and his team of killers. Go get 'em.'

As Sturm continued to wave his arms about, Montano said loudly that the service was concluded and would everyone please leave but no one did. Sturm continued to shout over the general uproar that Montano was nothing but a cheerleader for the gold braid flacks.

Montano made an effort to ignore Sturm. He tucked his bible firmly under one arm and started to march from the room. But several staff members swirled in sympathy around the chaplain to say how disgraceful was the performance of Sturm and how he must be coming unhinged. Riley and Raab both held onto Sturm who stared sullenly at the chaplain.

Montano, about to exit from the room with his entourage, visibly collected himself and faced about. The priest raised his hand as if in benediction and said, 'I forgive you, Jacob.'

Sturm looked dumbfounded. 'Forgive me for what? Speaking the truth?'

'For criticizing me in an unjust manner, for taking an advantage of a situation. You spent some time in a monastery but you have no concept – no concept!' he repeated emotionally, 'of the difficulties faced by a priest in times of war.'

Sturm rubbed his face in resignation. 'You should have only one concern, to determine what is right and what is wrong, and then say it. You don't make the choice, though. You do what you're told to do and that's to support the army, pay off your employers.'

Montano flushed again and started toward the door with a parting remark. 'We will discuss this further at an appropriate time and in an appropriate place, Specialist Sturm.' He stalked out.

The rest of the room emptied quickly with the doctors and nurses glancing at Sturm and whispering among themselves. One of the last to leave was Sandy who paused and started to step toward the corner where Sturm stood glaring around the room. She opened her mouth to speak when abruptly she changed her mind and left the room. Only Sturm, Riley and Raab remained.

Riley sank to the floor and started to giggle. 'Man, that Montano's mouth just *popped* open when you first said "oh bullshit". He couldn't *believe* his ears.'

Raab was smiling too. 'And did you see the look on his face when Sturm says he's just another cheerleader for the gold braid?' That set Riley off again and Sturm, now laughing with the others, lowered himself to the floor.

'Yeah,' he smiled, 'I was about to tell him he only pimped for the army leaders but that would have given him a heart attack.'

They were still rolling on the floor and laughing that it was too bad Dooley couldn't be here to help them pick on Montano when the door opened and Johnston stuck his head in the door. He had to shout several times before they stopped their laughing long enough to listen.

'There's another mission for Rainbow One-two. Riley and Raab. Top says for you to go lie down, Sturm, and they'll have another crew chief up in the next day or so.' Johnston looked at the three who now stared silently back and then Riley and Raab rose and left without a word.

In the room alone, Sturm began to weep.

CHAPTER FOURTEEN

'Top wants to see you.' It was Johnston again with his head just inside the door of the hootch and his eyes looking around at the chaos of magazines, beer cans, and dirty clothes. Sturm looked up from where he sat on the floor sorting Dooley's personal items before shipping them to the redhead's parents.

'What about?' he asked dully.

'I dunno. But he said to make sure you come.' Johnston remained watching from the safety of the doorway until Sturm showed some sign he would respond. He put the pictures back in Dooley's wallet – he had found a couple of pornographic ones in there that he didn't think Dooley's mother would understand – and rose slowly to his feet.

'Well, let's go find out what the great first sergeant wants. Wouldn't you like to know too, mother Johnston?'

First Sergeant Thomas sat with his feet on the desk with a fan blowing the hot air across his broad and sweating face. He surveyed Sturm with a cool gaze and said nothing until he wiped his face with a washcloth he kept in a canteen cup of water. He laid the washcloth over his face and spoke through it. The oracle of Quang Tri, Sturm thought.

'You really shot your mouth off to the chaplain, didn't you? Now why would you want to behave like that, Sturm?' he said in his calm rumble.

Sturm shrugged. 'I had something to say to him. I wouldn't want to say it behind his back. You might call it my confession.'

'Don't get wise with me,' the first sergeant said as he pulled the washcloth away and looked at Sturm with his slow-gin eyes. 'You're lucky he's not asking for a court martial. Not even an article 15 which I think would do you good. The chaplain thinks some rest would be better for you.'

Sturm wanted to explain his outburst but Top waved him off. 'Dooley's replacement will be here in a couple days. You can take today off. To rest. I don't want you going into town to get laid. That ain't rest.'

'Depends on how you look at it, Top,' Sturm said solemnly.

'Beat it, Sturm. Be in here tomorrow morning,' the first sergeant said and put the cloth back over his face.

Sturm went back to packing Dooley's things. He shoved all the uniforms into the duffel bag and put the civilian clothes into the footlocker. They weren't much, a few sport shirts, slacks, and the brown tweed suit he had bought while they were in Hong Kong for their R and R. Sturm ran his hand over the fine British woolen and thought, who would have guessed that while we sat on the verandah of the Repulse Bay Hotel that night, away from the girls and the bars for once, eating caviar and drinking a dry white Mosel and not talking at all about Vietnam that you wouldn't make it back, Dooley. You're not going to be able to show me San Francisco and all the lovely secretaries on Montgomery Street that you promised, you bastard. He felt better swearing at Dooley and threw everything else in the footlocker and locked it. He rested his back against the locker and fixed a smoke, not caring if First Sergeant Thomas or anyone else came in now and caught him. But no one came and he smoked it all with his eyes closed, trying to think of Dooley in the good days but seeing him dying before him and thinking they had parted as enemies because he never got a chance to tell Dooley that it was alright, it didn't matter if he didn't see the dink thrown out of the chopper. Who the fuck cares?

It was too quiet in the hootch. Riley and Raab were out doing their thing with the quick and the dead and Dooley's footlocker was not much company. He went outside, stood in the sun so bright it washed the color out of everything, then went into the hospital. He prowled the corridors, not sure what he was looking for until he came upon Lt. Saunders sorting unsterile instruments and then he knew what he wanted.

'Hi.' A really big opening.

'Hello, Jake.' She gave him a quick, noncommittal look and continued to sort the instruments.

He took the plunge and was glad he had just smoked that cigarette. It made everything easier. 'What's happened between us?'

'What do you mean?'

'You know what I mean. You're so cool all of a sudden. You don't want to be around me. I haven't been able to get a minute alone with you. I've been hoping you would come and see me and tell me what's bothering you, but you just closed your face.'

'I've been so busy.'

'No. It's more than that. It's something to do with Franklin, isn't it?'

Her busy hands stopped and she took a deep breath and nodded. 'I don't want to talk about it.'

'Why not, for Christ's sake?' he demanded and noticed that others in the corridor were watching with sidelong eyes. He lowered his voice. 'Sandy, you've got to get it off your chest. Spill it and you'll be finished with it.'

'I don't think this is the place to discuss it.'

'Don't pull rank on me now, Sandy. It's too late for that. Just say what's on your mind.' He was getting angry. 'Is it connected with Franklin?'

'Of course it is. What else but Franklin?' she hissed and her eyes snapped as she looked up at him. Immediately she softened and tears welled in her eyes. 'You don't know what went on in there that night. You don't know how horrible it was and you were right outside and you didn't do anything. You didn't come get me. I wanted him dead but you didn't kill him. And after Kowalski finally did, you kept saying that Franklin gave up. So what? He deserved to be shot.'

She put her hand over her eyes and Sturm felt a twinge of unease twist his stomach. Had he been that afraid? 'But we couldn't just charge in there. He would have killed you like he did that lieutenant and that MP.'

'But what about when he came out? You just stood there and it was Kowalski who shot him. It was Kowalski who defended me, who *saved* me, not you. It should have been you, Jake.'

'But he had thrown down his pistol by then. To shoot him then would have been cold-blooded murder. That's what Kowalski did. Just murdered him.'

'I don't care,' Sandy said, suddenly angry again. 'If I could have had a knife I would have cut his balls off.' She waved a scalpel to emphasize her point and then threw it noisely into a pan on the gurney. 'I just thank God Kowalski was there to save me. That's what it's all about, Jake.'

She wiped the tears from the corners of her eyes. 'Maybe it's you, maybe it's Franklin, maybe it's me. I just know I feel sick all the time. And you only make it worse.' The tears came then. 'I'm sorry, Jake, oh, I'm sorry.' She turned and walked away.

It's over, just like that? It was too easy. Nothing was explained. He knew he ought to feel something as he watched her hurry down the corridor but everything inside seemed drained. Too much has happened. Maybe my system has shorted out. I hated to see Franklin shot down like that, whatever he did to Sandy. Or did I really? Maybe I resent her because Franklin got something from her that I never did. I killed that Vietnamese quick enough, even if I keep telling myself it was self-defense. But why didn't I run, or yell for help? And now Dooley is gone. All the friendly faces are gone and wherever I look now there are only dark hallways that lead to places I don't want to see. I won't go down them because there may be no end. If I just sit tight and hold on it might get better. Someone will find me. Mai. Mai will find me.

'You okay?' It was an orderly standing above him with a perplexed look. Sturm slowly brought his mind back into focus and saw that he was sitting on a bench but all bent over, gripping himself with his arms as if he were cold and lost.

'Yeah, Yeah, I'm okay. Thanks.' He rose and hurried out of the hospital. He had to get out of the area no matter what Top said. He would go into town, find Mai and spend the day with her and forget everything else. Mai was beautiful and she would make everything else beautiful. And he had much to explain to her. Susie was right. He had to level with Mai and tell her he was going home alone and would not send for her, no matter how much he liked, or even loved, her. It was still morning and there would be lots of time.

As he went along the boardwalk toward the front gate he passed the morgue and he saw that someone had painted out the mock biblical quotation he had penned on the door. Then he remembered Dooley was behind that door, scheduled to go out on the noon C-130 run. Sturm hurried on and caught a ride into town with little trouble. He got out in the square which was crowded with Vietnamese shoppers in the morning and made his way slowly down the sidewalk that was half covered by the wares of vendors spread on brightly colored cloths. He passed the alley where he had fought with the Vietnamese and he looked in it and saw the shoppers walking unconcernedly through it. He half-expected, even feared, that he would see the two-day old body still lying there. He hurried onto the club where he had never been so early. The main room was dark and the chairs were all tipped forward against the tables as if resting before the night's action. He crossed the room and went down the back hallway to Mai's room. Her door was open and she stood by the bed packing a small cloth suitcase. She started as he entered and Sturm saw her eyes were red and swollen from crying.

'Why you come here, GI?'

He went to her and took her by both shoulders. 'What's the matter, Mai? Why are you crying?'

She leaned her head against his chest and began sobbing. 'My brother, he dead.'

'Your older brother, the soldier?'

'Yes. Army say he killed on secret mission. I go home now. Today in my father's village we bury him.'

Sturm held her tight. 'But I was going to spend the day with you, do some shopping, and you could show me another good place to eat. And we could be together all day.' He didn't tell her why, that Dooley was dead. 'We have to talk, Mai. I go home in a few days.'

He wanted to tell her he had been trying to find out who the American was who ordered her interrogation and that he had no luck. But now such talk seemed inappropriate.

'I go home now,' Mai said and pulled away from him.

'But when will you be back? Where is your father's village?'

'Not far. Maybe one hour by car. I no know when I come back. Maybe tonight, maybe few day.'

'But will you be back before I leave?'

She sat down on the bed, small and fragile in her white ao-dai and white pantaloons. Mourning clothes, Sturm thought. They sat in silence for long moments until Mai looked up from the linoleum floor she had been studying with unseeing eyes.

'Jake?' It was the first time he could recall her using his name. He looked at her in surprise.

'Jake?' she said again as if tasting his name for the first time. 'You come with me my village. Okay?'

'I can't do that. I'm not even supposed to be here in the ville today.'

'It not far. We rent taxi. Can do? I no go home long time. I tell my father I work in PX. You come with me, tell my father you my boss, okay?'

'Where is your village?'

'We go north. Past Dong Ha.'

'Past Dong Ha? How secure is that place? Maybe VC in your village.'

She was scornful. 'No VC my village. No fighting there. Very quiet.'

Sturm pulled out his cigarettes and heroin capsule and made himself a smoke while he considered. What the hell? Why not? It could be interesting. Certainly nothing to do with Mai gone. He pulled on the smoke and felt his confidence grow. And a funeral in a small village would be something to see. Something of the real Vietnam that few grunts ever see. Probably a Buddhist funeral.

'Is it a Buddhist funeral? Your father is Buddhist isn't he?'

'My father very good Buddhist.'

'Okay, let's go.'

The ancient black Citroën they had hired left the highway just before Dong Ha, which gave Sturm some relief, and then began working its way down sandy roads to the west where the mountains began to rise toward Laos. They passed several villages and the children ran alongside to peer in the window at Sturm and to pull at the hair on his arm where it rested on the door. Sturm had tried to keep track of where they were going and how far but he had become lost in the twisting roads that cut past rice fields and through fingers of jungle. They were traveling a long time and he began to get edgy. Mai didn't understand there was a new push on by the bad guys, but he did. They could be anywhere out here. He was thinking of making the car turn around when Mai sat up and said this was her village coming up.

The car parked in the shade of some trees by the main road and Sturm and Mai crossed the small bridge over the irrigation canal and walked down the short, tree-lined lane flanked by lush rice fields to the village. They were met by a pack of snarling dogs and laughing, pointing children who swirled around them but kept a safe distance. A few of the boldest darted forward from behind to run their hands along the hair on Sturm's arm before darting back into the crowd where they were hugged in excitement by the others for their great courage. Sturm looked about the village as they walked. It was so clean, with all the pathways swept and tidy little gardens alongside the large thatch-roofed houses. So different from the filth of the cities and the fetid refugee camps. There weren't more than 20 houses in the village, just like countless villages he had looked at from the air. The villagers watched silently and without expression as the two made their way through the village toward a large house that sat on a small knoll at the end of the village. The house, surrounded by cool tamarind trees, was almost twice as large as the others. Mai had told Sturm her father was a retired university professor – something he had never quite believed – but if he lived in such a manor house for this small village, he might be. As they approached the rock-lined path that led to the front gate an old man dressed in white came forward to meet them. Mai burst into tears and ran forward to hug him. As Sturm stood back he studied her father, a heavy set man with a pale, deeply lined face, wide and calm eyes, and a flowing white goatee as a mark of veneration. Wiping her eyes, Mai turned and introduced Sturm to her father.

Uncertain whether to bow or shake hands Sturm stood there until the old man stepped forward and warmly took his hand in both of his.

'You are welcome. Thank you for coming with my daughter.' He signaled one of the children to take Mai's bag from Sturm and led them to the house. 'This is a sad time for us. My son will be buried this evening. But we must not be too sad for Buddhists believe that death can be an escape from this worldly prison.' He spoke in a deep and measured voice and Sturm felt himself captured by the old man's presence.

The small garden was largely filled with villagers there to pay last respects to the body before it was borne away to be buried. The old man led them into the dim living room, also crowded with people who made room for Sturm. He sat in one of several ornately carved chairs along one whitewashed earthen wall and a servant immediately handed him a glass of scalding tea. The old man sat next to him.

'We have never been honored by the visit of an American soldier to our poor village,' he said. 'We only see them flying overhead in their helicopters or going past us on the road in their tanks.' He paused to sip his tea. 'Are you not afraid to be so far from your camp?'

'Should I be?' Sturm asked.

'Those who are with the people have nothing to fear,' the old man said and smiled. 'Will you stay tonight?'

'No, thank you. I hired the car for the day and it will take us – or me, at least – back today.'

The old man caught the implication and he spoke in Vietnamese to Mai. She listened with lowered eyes and responded softly. The professor turned back to Sturm.

'I told her she must stay several days. It is our custom. It would not be proper for her to leave so soon. She says she works for you in the PX and you must give her permission to stay. You can do that?'

Sturm hesitated. Hell, he was going to be leaving soon and he wanted her back right away.

'Well, we need her. We're short-handed.'

The old man frowned. 'She must stay at least three days. It is proper.' Sturm shrugged. He would talk to Mai about it later. The old man rose and excused them both, so much for them to do, but he would be back soon to look after Sturm. Until then he suggested Sturm stay seated and not wander around outside.

Sturm sat uncomfortably on the wooden chair and tried not to stare back at the Vietnamese in the room who whispered and watched him with black mirrored eyes. What am I doing here, he wondered. It's a long way from nowhere. What did the old man mean I have nothing to fear if I am with the people? That has a Marxist ring to it. Come to think of it, he had seen no Vietnamese flags painted on the doors as the government required in all villages. He looked around the low walls but there was no picture of President Thieu; only a few nondescript caligraphy scrolls. Sturm grew increasingly restless and was about to walk around when the old man sat beside him again.

'Forgive me for not being able to spend more time with you.' He eyed Sturm over the rim of his tea glass and then asked, 'How long have you been in my country?'

'Just a year. I'm going home in a few days.'

'You must be very happy to leave. I don't think you enjoyed your stay very much.'

Sturm was on guard. What could he say, that I think your country and your people are totally fucked up? That all of you are just out to rip off America and the GIs? That one of your people tried to kill me and I did him in? 'No, I can't say as I did enjoy it too much.'

'We Vietnamese understand that it is difficult for Americans to be here. It is hard for both peoples to understand each other, don't you agree?'

'You mean, "east is east, and west is west, and ne'er the twain shall meet?" '

'Ahh, yes. Kipling. Perhaps he was right. Perhaps. But I think it is more a question of sovereign rights, that is, a Vietnamese solution to a Vietnamese problem. Wouldn't it be better if we settled our own differences without external interference?' He looked at Sturm and added, 'From either the Americans or the North Vietnamese?'

'I would be delighted to see that happen. Me and a few hundred thousand other GIs.'

'Yes,' the old man gave him a small smile. 'Well, forgive my talk of politics, but it has been so long since I have talked to an American,' and his eyes turned kindly. 'Have you ever been to a Buddhist funeral?'

'No, but I have read about them and the customs.'

'Good. It will not be so strange for you. If you need anything, please ask me.' He rose and left with a courtly nod.

Sturm sipped at the hot tea which a servant kept constantly filled while he watched the steady procession of mourners enter the house and cross to a room in the rear. The body must be laid out in there. He knew the body would be displayed and he was not eager to see it. The pageantry would be interesting but he had seen enough dead dinks. He rose from the hard chair and went outside with the idea of fixing a smoke but he was immediately surrounded by a swarm of children who stared and giggled. He fled back inside to find Mai looking for him. They sat demurely along the wall while the passing mourners studied them.

'I'm sorry about your brother, Mai.'

She held a small handkerchief to her eyes.

'He no want to go in army. My father no want him to go. But he taken from school and put in army. Three year ago. After my father leave Hue. Leave university.'

'I'm sorry,' he repeated. Jesus, he wished he could light up.

'Thank you, Jake.' She used his name again and he felt strangely touched. 'I no can go back with you. I must stay until my brother bury.'

'I understand, but when *will* you come back?'

'Maybe tomorrow. For sure before you leave. Okay, Jake?'

He could only nod, for he wanted suddenly to hold her very close and smell the freshness of her long silken hair, the hair she promised never to cut unless he left her, and the coolness of her throat.

She leaned forward and spoke in a whisper. 'Jake. I tell you something. It very dangerous here for you. My mother tell me VC come last week. I no know,' she said and stared at him to make sure he did not think she had led him into a trap.

'VC? Here?' His stomach suddenly felt fluttery. He would just disappear in the village. Nobody would ever know. Another statistic. Missing in action: Sturm, Jacob, Specialist Fifth class.

She nodded. 'Not in village. Outside. My mother say VC come to many villages last week but stay very quiet. Maybe you better go.'

'But when will you come back? I must see you, Mai. I have many things to tell you. I must explain many things.'

'You no need explain. I understand. You talk about marry and I say, okay, I go back with you. I no can do. You no can do. I know.' There were tears in her eyes as she spoke but she smiled.

'I like you very much. But you American. I Vietnamese.' She said it so simply as if that explained everything.

Sturm sat on the edge of the chair and leaned toward her. He wanted to pull her toward him but even to touch her in this house would be gross misconduct. He clasped his hands instead.

'I try to come back tomorrow. Next day, maybe. Anyway, you forget Mai. You forget Vietnam.'

'I may forget Vietnam, but I will never forget you, Mai. And don't say good-bye now, don't just get up and leave. Come back with me now. Nothing is really settled between us. I don't even know what my own real feelings are. I—' he stopped as she stood up.

'I must see my mother. Good-bye, Jake.' She smiled wanly, reached out to touch his hand lightly and whispered, 'GI.' Then she was gone.

Sturm stared at the doorway through which she disappeared as if by looking hard enough he could make her reappear but only the old serving woman with more tea came through it. Sturm picked up his hat and started to leave. Mai had to come back in time. She had to. He wanted her very much now that she was gone and he couldn't have her.

He was intercepted by the old man before he reached the door. 'Mai said you are leaving. But you must pay respects to my son before you go. It is our custom.' With that he led Sturm to the entrance to the back room and left him in the slowly moving line.

He felt conspicuous, a gangly American in dirty fatigues and heavy boots among the diminutive Vietnamese. But he was inside the room now and there was no escape. The airless room was shuttered and stifling with the smell of incense. Sturm's eyes were drawn immediately to the body which lay in the middle of the room beneath a canopied mosquito net suspended from the ceiling. As the shuffling line carried him to the body he saw the son was dressed in a silken traditional gown, not an Army uniform as Sturm had expected. Maybe this was a gesture to the VC in the area, who were maybe even in the room now. He shivered suddenly as he imaged a knife being plunged into his back. He glanced over his shoulder but saw nothing hostile, just a room filled with thin faces and black eyes. He looked back at the body and saw the face was covered by a piece of white silk, a symbolic barrier between the living and the dead. Beneath the folded hands on the stomach was a long, silver handled knife that Sturm knew the spirit of the deceased could use to keep the devil at bay. Maybe it was that knife that made Sturm shudder, for it reminded him of how it felt when he had slain the Vietnamese in the dark alley. He put his mind back on the body and saw tiny packets tied to each hand and foot. Those, he recalled, held the nail trimmings and they were tied there so when the body was exhumed in three years and the bones placed in a burial jar the nail clippings would remain with the proper limb.

He felt giddy as he moved around the room, his senses assaulted by the smell of joss sticks and the perfumed oils on the body. Around the body we go, like a merry-go-round, only there's no brass ring in Vietnam. The object is just not to fall off the gilded unicorn.

The line of mourners bore him away from the body to a small altar erected in one corner of the room to honor the deceased. Sturm saw before him the flickering candles, the burning joss sticks with the smoke curling past the picture of the dead son, curling past the three bowls of rice his spirit would symbolically eat on its journey, curling past the three cups of rice it would symbolically drink, curling past – Oh, Christ, the picture. The *picture*. Sturm stopped and stared as the line of Vietnamese piled up behind and waited patiently for him to move. Still he stared, his mouth open in disbelief and he could feel his pores open and perspiration burst onto his skin. He took a deep breath. No, it couldn't be. He leaned closer and stared at the picture. The face was square and heavy and the shoulders thick but surely it was not the man Dooley had kicked out of the chopper, not the man he had stabbed. It couldn't be. See, he told himself, no scar over the eyebrow, no drooping eyelid. It just looked like Scar-brow, a younger version. But God, it looked like him, too much like he must have looked before the scar. Sturm backed away from the altar, the joss and perfumes suddenly cloying in his throat, and he pushed Vietnamese heedlessly from his path as he bolted from the room.

Outside the noon air blew hot and he could feel the rivulets of perspiration pour down his sides and down his face. The children were there waiting and they surged around him with shrieks of laughter and bursts of glottal chatter while they pointed at his ashen face beaded with perspiration. He staggered along the pathway between the houses and along the shaded lane while knots of Vietnamese watched and whispered. The driver sat in the front seat of the black Citroën drumming his fingers with impatience as Sturm half ran toward him. The car started moving as Sturm climbed in and the driver broke into a stream of excited Vietnamese. Sturm sank back in the seat and understood nothing except the occasional word, VC.

He sat forward and prepared a cigarette, cursing as the jouncing car caused him to spill some of the precious white powder. He twisted the end and sucked deeply as he lit it. It couldn't have been her brother, he told himself. Of all the millions of Vietnamese how could the one he killed be Mai's brother. Well, it couldn't. All Vietnamese look alike, anyway. He hadn't actually seen the face of the body; it had been covered. And pictures are misleading, you can't tell anything from a picture. And there had been no scar. Sturm pushed back the little voice that said, maybe the picture was taken years ago, before he got the scar. Nonsense. He pulled again on the duster and felt his bodily fears begin to fade. No, it wasn't Mai's brother, just someone who faintly resembled him. After all, Mai's brother was killed on a secret mission, not stabbed in the alley. Again the little voice: but you know that some Vietnamese colonel didn't want to be bothered investigating a stabbing in a dirty back alley and wrote the death off in an official report as a loss on a secret mission. No, Sturm told himself, and gazed with dull eyes as the flat and dry terrain of Quang Tri swept by him, no, it wasn't her brother and that's that. That would be too unreal, and would make a bad situation impossible. Vietnam was already a nightmare and he couldn't seem to wake up from it. He put the man's death away in a small corner of his mind and tried to think what was happening to him but it was too difficult to concentrate. There wasn't any single reason for the expanding evil inside him, it was an accumulation. He was dying an accumulated death. Too many bodies. Too many dying men. Too many lies. Too many sermons of vengeance. Maybe Vietnam was right and he was wrong. Perhaps this country is actually growing more beautiful, its face being lifted by war and not scarred as many assumed. I am the one who cannot recognize this metamorphosis. Instead it is I, Sturm, who is scarred and dying while Vietnam grows stronger.

The driver let Sturm out at the gate still talking about being in VC territory. The MP at the gate told Sturm to put his cap on but Sturm gave him the finger and kept walking, hat in hand. The hootch was still empty when he got there and unwilling to sit alone with Dooley's memories Sturm turned to leave when Chaplain Montano pushed open the door.

'Jacob. I saw you come in. May I talk with you?' He came inside before Sturm could reply and stood uneasily by the door, unsure how Sturm might react and bothered by the fact there was no uncluttered chair to sit on. He finally sat on one of the rumpled beds so he wouldn't be left standing while Sturm sat.

There was a silence as both waited for the other to speak. When Montano saw Sturm had no intention of talking he cleared his throat and began.

'You are leaving in a few days, no?'

'Right.'

'I don't want you to leave so full of animosity toward me. I thought we might try and work out our differences.'

'What's to work out? You've chosen your path and I've chosen mine. Different drummers and all that.' Sturm did not feel in the slightest like cooperating and he could already sense the anger growing inside him as Montano's placid intrusion continued.

'Have you learned anything from your year in Vietnam?' Montano finally asked.

'Sure,' Sturm said with a crooked smile. 'I've learned that America's vital national interests, which brought us here in the first place, have suddenly gone somewhere else, so we can all go home now. Just declare a peace and go. That's expediency, another thing I've learned. Whatever is convenient for the politicians so they get reelected. And duplicity. That's another lesson. How our great leaders tell the people one thing and do the opposite. Kind of like you, captain, one hand representing yourself as a God-is-love expounder while on the other hand telling the grunts to go out and kill more dinks. Going to the troops in the field is only a good means for you to get out there so you can take a few shots too. And promising to look into the tortures and murders committed by Kowalski, but doing nothing. Right? Right?' he shouted.

'Enough, enough, Jacob. Let's remain rational,' Montano interrupted.

'Rational?' Sturm snorted. 'What the fuck is rational about being in Vietnam? Is Dooley's death rational? Is my presence going to bring a logical conclusion to his war? No! Death is irrational enough without dying in an irrational war while listening to irrational histrionics from the likes of you.' Sturm felt sick as the rage spilled over, out of control, and he felt ready to assault the priest.

Montano leaned back and kept his voice purposefully calm. 'I won't argue the morality of war any longer with you, Jacob. You must settle it in your own mind. Like your religion, you must rediscover what you once believed and then have absolute faith that you are right.'

'You mean, "don't confuse me with facts".'

Montano ignored him. 'There is still much time for you. You are young. I hope you will go back to the monastery and think it all through. You have seen war and you have seen love for your fellow man. Love that transcends the relationship you have with that girl Mai in the village. You may chalk that up to experience but back in the seminary you will find peace of mind in celibacy, you will—'

'How do you know about Mai?' Sturm asked abruptly. 'I never told you her name. But you know it, you seem to know a lot about her. Why is that?'

Montano shrugged. 'I was concerned about you and I wanted to know who were your friends, your contacts, who was seeing you. I only made some inquiries for your own good.'

Suddenly it was clear and the truth of it burst inside Sturm's head like a grenade, hot and white and then red rage. 'For my own good? Goddam you, goddam you to hell, you shaman priest,' he shouted and leaped to his feet. 'You're the one who called for an investigation of Mai. You're the sorry son of a bitch masquerading as a dogooder who arranged for her to be beaten nearly to death.'

Montano paled before the verbal abuse and stood up as Sturm advanced on him. Sturm reached out one long arm and shoved the priest down hard on the bed. 'That's why you were in the ville the other night. You weren't seeing Father Ngai, you were checking up with the CID or the Vietnamese police on what they were doing with Mai. Weren't you?' he screamed.

He drew back a fist, ready to drive it into Montano's ashen face, when the chaplain twisted away and leaped to his feet with a shout, 'That will be enough, Specialist Sturm. I am an officer and you will respect that regardless of what you think.'

Sturm checked himself and stood glaring at the priest who

continued to talk when he saw he wasn't going to be hit.

'You have many misconceptions and many misunderstandings, Jacob. I will not demean myself and my position by sitting here and listening to insane talk from you. I know nothing about that girl – that whore – of yours.' He backed around the bed and started for the door while keeping a wary eye on Sturm. 'When you come to your senses, if you do, you may come to see me and we can attempt a rational discussion. Now I must go,' and with that he darted out the door, stumbling in his haste over the step.

'Get out of my life!' Sturm yelled after him. 'Let me ruin it without any help from you,' he added but the door swung shut and cut him off.

CHAPTER FIFTEEN

As the banshee howl of the engine grew and the blades began to turn, Sturm looked across the pad at Rainbow One-two and got a thumbs up sign from Riley who stood in the doorway. Thumbs up for the last day. The last mission. He knew Riley was telling him to hang in there and stay loose on this last mission but he couldn't see the other medic's face. Riley had his green wind visor down, as did Sturm. We're like some weird kind of grasshopper, Sturm thought, in green coveralls, green boots and green helmets with visors that make us faceless. It's all an identity screen; no one can see my face so I can kill them without revealing my own fear or my own soul. Keep it all impersonal and it won't hurt inside. Do not know thy enemy because if you know him you might realize he is human, filled with his own desires and fears and loves. He is just like you and you don't want to kill yourself.

They lifted smoothly into the hot blue sky, two dustoffs thudding north where men lay bleeding and waiting to be removed from fields of glory. Sturm looked around the chopper and saw Henderson, the new crew chief, switch the intercom to private and speak to Kowalski.

'Where are we going, Mr. Kowalski?' So polite. He'll learn after Kowalski kicks him a time or two, or after he sees King Kong throw some dinks out the chopper for laughs.

'Same old thing. Fifth Mech is getting hit again. This time a company is taking fire from a village above Dong Ha,' Kowalski said.

Same old thing is right. Just more guys getting blown away. Sturm looked around at Henderson. Skinny-assed kid thinks he's going to do something in Vietnam. Going to bring peace by being peaceful. Well, his face didn't look so peaceful when we brought out the grunts who were in that APC when it ran over a mine this morning. That had been the first trip, then they went back to pick up that lieutenant who went berserk and shot himself in each foot. Henderson wasn't sure he liked this work after all. Well, wait until today is over, Hendy, baby, it could get downright unpleasant. Then Sturm smiled. So what? It's my last day. I'll make it, and tomorrow Riley and I will be lying on the beach at Cam Ranh. Thinking of the beach made him want to light up and relax but he was already too far gone. Five dusters today. Riley knows how spaced I looked when he dragged me off the boardwalk and made me sit under the chopper. Hope I didn't hurt that little dog this morning. What I did to Montano doesn't matter. Nothing sinks through his thick skin. It's like he told me once, if you believe completely then nothing will shake your faith. He believes in the war and in his righteousness so much his mind is now infallible. I thought I was finished with him this morning when he tried to talk to me on the boardwalk but he's back again like an unlucky charm, wanting to go into battle again and save souls. And to eradicate a few bad guys on behalf of his Crusade at the same time.

His mind turned back to how it had been this morning, there in the sun beside the hootch, playing with the crippled dog Dooley had given him and trying not to think about this last mission and how so many guys get killed on the last day. The dog had sat across from him, its nose pushing at something in the sand while Sturm prepared another duster. He worked the tobacco out with a little toothpick he always kept handy and tipped in the heroin. How many is this today, he asked himself as he twisted the end. Three? Yeah, just three. Not bad. And I'll have some time in Cam Ranh before I take the urine test so maybe if I stop smoking it today I will get it out of my system in time. He pulled deep on the smoke but the heroin loafed in his system. He wanted his mind to break free but it floated heavily, like a hawk on the hot winds of a Iowa summer. Nothing moved inside him any more, and he grew irritated. He knew what was happening, you always need more, but the more you strain the less you attain. Hey, not bad.

He finished the cigarette and kicked the butt at the puppy wriggling on its back in the sand. 'Come here Dink, before I wring your neck.' The dog looked at him, tongue out and eyes alert but not moving. 'Come here, goddamit.' Sturm suddenly lunged forward on his knees and pinned the mongrel which began to whine as Sturm slowly tightened his long fingers around the furry neck until only throttling sounds emerged. The eyes bulged and the puppy kicked frantically while Sturm felt the red shades of rage fall at the back of his eyes and dim his vision for several seconds until the shades went up again. He abruptly dropped the dog, and tried to stop the memories of the other killing, the stabbing. But Scar-brow was always in his dreams now. Sometimes Sturm had him mixed up with the two Montagnards who were blown to pieces, or with that prisoner, but Scar-brow was always around, and sometimes Scar-brow's face became Mai's face, but Sturm knew they weren't related. They couldn't be.

Sturm watched the dog hobble across the sand to a patch of shade where it lay watching him with reproachful eyes. Mindless of the intense tropical sunlight that poured upon him and sent rivulets of sweat coursing down his face, Sturm sat in the sand and stared back at the dog. Footsteps approached along the boardwalk but he didn't look up until he saw the polished boots stop beside him. Even then he couldn't distinguish the intruder's face, for the sun lay directly behind the head and cast a blinding halo. The light hurt Sturm's eyes but he made out the round, sleek face of Chaplain Montano.

'Who are you supposed to be, the Archangel of Death coming to call?' Sturm said bitterly.

'I've been looking for you, Jacob.'

Sturm looked up again and this time saw the glint of new gold leaves on Montano's collar.

'I see they've bestowed the rank of major on you. Knighted for your efforts in these Crusades?'

There was an edge in the priest's voice as he answered. 'Jacob, you know I could make you stand at attention. A Spec 5 does not sit on the ground while a major talks to him, no? But you know I never stand on rank. I just wanted to say good-bye and I don't want you to go in bitterness.'

Sturm felt the rage rising in him again, coming like a long irresistible swell in the ocean: 'What do you want? You want me to confess before I go? Okay, "Forgive me Father for I have sinned."' Sturm's voice turned thick with sarcasm. 'But I shouldn't have to spell out the sins for you, should I major? Too bad you can't hear confession from every grunt in Vietnam, makes everything fine again. Or hey, how about taking confession in Washington. What penance would you assign there? Ten Hail Marys and five Our Fathers ought to just about handle it, right?'

Montano remained standing with the sunlight casting firestorms off his head and answered slowly: 'Jacob, you turned away from me, from what I represent in the army. Perhaps I can understand that, but I make a final appeal for you not to turn away from God. Will you not do that?'

Sturm was that hawk above the Iowa cornfields, plummeting with talons outspread, beak poised. Montano flings up his arms to ward off the attack but he cannot stay the talon knives that slice through his arm toward his sincere eyes. Always sincere eyes.

'Go pray for someone else. Pray for Dooley, or go kill a dink. Whatever turns you on, major, but get away from me. I'll spend all my life shacked up with Mai before I'll be back in the church. Now get out of here!' His voice rose and a nurse coming out of the hospital's side entrance turned in surprise. Sturm saw it was Sandy. She paused, one foot suspended in mid-step, as she stared for a second before turning back inside.

Montano's voice became soothing. 'Alright, Jacob. Alright. I must go now. If you have another mission today I will see you then. If not, then this is good-bye.' He held out his hand but Sturm kept his eyes on the ground and the priest moved heavily away, his weight causing the boardwalk to creak.

That was this morning and now, in the chopper, Sturm looked around for the priest who had come on this last mission and saw him sitting by the other doorway checking his clip. He took it out once then rapped it home again to make sure it was tight and then carefully chambered a round. The chaplain then made a practice aim at the ground. Satisfied that he was ready he looked up and saw Sturm watching him. Taking this as an opening, Montano rose and crossed the chopper to Sturm in careful little steps. The priest started talking but Sturm couldn't hear him because his helmet was on and he didn't want to hear anyway. But Montano persisted and finally stood looking at Sturm in obvious anticipation of an answer.

'What did you say, captain – I mean, major?' Sturm yelled as he jerked his helmet off.

'I said I wondered if you were still so upset? We parted on such harsh words this morning. I wondered if we could try again?'

'To tell you the truth, major, I don't want to try any more. I just want you to leave me alone.'

'You are leaving tomorrow morning, no? We should not

part with such hostility between us. I am sorry we could not bring our minds to a mutual understanding but let us not part as enemies. It is not good for the soul.' Montano tried a small smile which faded under Sturm's empty gaze.

'You should have thought of that before you sicked your war dogs on Mai. I might have forgiven your proclivity for death and destruction and your hypocritical masquerade as a man of peace and love, but arranging for an innocent girl to be beaten was too much. I'll bet you're just sorry you weren't there to watch it all. They made her take her clothes off, you know.'

Montano flushed. 'Alright, Sturm, that will be quite enough. Go your own way but when you are back home, away from this environment, talk to God again. Seek him out for your solution. I still think you will make a fine priest. Will you pray to God?'

'I heard God was missing in action,' Sturm replied.

'What?' Montano cupped his hand behind his ear.

'I said you better get ready. We've passed Dong Ha.' Sturm pulled his helmet back on and turned away. He moved back to his seat and made himself a heroin smoke, the one he had been waiting for all morning. Not quite all morning, he admitted. This will be the fourth today. So what, it will be all over soon. He smoked slowly and gazed at the terrain below. He was somewhere down there a day or two ago with Mai. He couldn't remember just when, it was so hard to keep track of time now. And where was Mai? She's back in the ville by now and she'll be waiting when I get to the club. Mai, we need more time to work things out. Marriage isn't an impossibility, it just takes understanding. The only problem, he thought, was that Mai was too innocent. The last innocent in Vietnam. She knows nothing about me and her brother, doesn't understand the war and is just trying to survive as a prostitute. She's just an objet d'art, a fragile Vietnamese porcelain for sale. But I'll see her one more time to say good-bye, to twine my fingers in that long silken hair. He rested his head in his hands as he finished the smoke. God, I'm tired of all this. Let it be over. He rose slowly, thinking they must be getting close, and went forward to stand behind Tippit and stare through the front screen at what was coming.

Columns of smoke billowed from the trees above five klicks ahead and Sturm could see three Phantoms making long elliptical circles as they swung around for another napalm drop. As the dustoff steadily drew closer Sturm could see several APCs parked along a dirt road. They were facing a small village that was partially screened by a row of trees and he could see tracer rounds from the .50 on the APC arc into the village houses. They must have been coming down that road when they were hit, Sturm guessed. As he watched he saw a tank nose out of some trees that flanked a rice field 100 meters to the east of the village and begin firing at the village. Almost simultaneously there was a quick flash in the trees beyond the tank and then a bright orange flower bloomed and faded as the rocket propelled grenade hit the turret base. The tank lurched sideways and the turret was blown loose. The tank began backing rapidly into the trees but there was another hit on one track and the tank slewed sharply to the right before coming to a halt with smoke pouring from its wounded side.

Kowalski banked the medevac around in a wide circle to keep clear of the Phantoms and switched the channel selector to FM so he could talk to the ground troops.

'Hammerhead Six, Rainbow One-one. This is your friendly dustoff service. What have you got for us?'

'One-one, Six. We've got three litter cases back on the road. They will pop a smoke grenade to mark their position.'

'Roger, Six. I see it. Up the road a little from most of your tracks.'

'One-one, Six. Roger. We've got the angel track back there where it's more out of the line of fire. We hope. Hard to tell where everything is coming from now.'

'Six, One-one. You've got some bad guys in that treeline down the road from you, to the east. We just saw a tank take an RPG in the turret.'

'Roger, One-one. We've got some people moving in to get them. The village is full of bad guys but a lot of civilians are in there too. I would like to fire up that place but I don't want to wipe out a few hundred civilians. That's why I have been working around the edges and trying to seal it off.'

'Well, Six, remember the motto of all tough commanders,' Kowalski laughed: ' "I had to destroy that village to save it." '

The radio was silent for a moment. 'Yeah, One-one. I guess so. They're waiting for you at the angel track. See you later. Hammerhead Six out.'

The other dustoff broke in immediately. 'Rainbow One-one, this is One-two.'

'Go, One-two.'

'I'm approaching that angel track now. Why don't I go down and take out the first load?'

'Roger that, One-two. One-one clear.'

Kowalski continued a lazy circle of the area as the Phantoms hammered the treelines along rice fields around the village with napalm and thousand-pound bombs. In the chopper they could feel the concussions as the bombs toppled trees and sent chunks of the soft earth flying. Smoke from the bombs and napalm blew across the village and as Sturm watched he could occasionally see figures dart from building to building in the village. He saw the houses were thatch, like most of the Vietnamese farm houses, and he knew the place would burn quickly once Hammerhead Six decided to open on it.

Kowalski angled over the road and came slowly down it

toward the angel track where One-two sat while the last of the wounded were being loaded. The area wasn't hot, nobody shooting at them, and everyone seemed to be taking their time. Sturm saw one of the medics back away from the chopper and give it a thumbs up sign before he turned his back against the swirl of dust as the blades bit and the chopper began to lift. The dust billowed over the medic track and obscured it as the dustoff moved away, then there was a flash on the side and a great gush of black smoke. Sturm stared, thinking the first chopper had been hit but then the radio crackled:

'Rainbow One-one, One-two.'

'Go, One-two.'

'That angel track just took an RPG. There's dinks in the trees behind it, I think.' The voice came calm and mechanical.

Kowalski started to answer but One-two broke in again. 'One-one, we've just taken some hits,' the deadpan voice said. 'It looks like Riley's hit.'

Sturm heard it but he couldn't believe it. He looked around at Henderson, wanting to see Dooley there looking back at him but seeing only the thin pinched face of a new crew chief who was looking back at him with frightened eyes. Kowalski turned and looked at Sturm, and the medic's brain turned over slowly. If they heard it then I must have heard it.

'Riley?' he asked on the intercom. 'He said Riley's hit?' Kowalski only nodded.

Sturm suddenly grabbed the pilot's shoulder and shook him. 'Well ask him what he means, what happened to him? Is he wounded?' he asked but he was suddenly afraid to know.

Kowalski hit the radio button under his finger on the cyclic. 'One-two, One-one. Say again the status of Riley.'

'One-one, One-two, KIA. Through the head.'

Sturm turned around and slumped on the floor as a sense of numbness seeped downward from his brain and turned his limbs to stone. KIA. Just like that. So terse, so laconic, so matter-of-fact. Just KIA. Another statistic for the books. Killed in action. Sturm leaned forward and put his face in his hands. Riley? Why Riley? He did not deserve to die. Why not someone else? Why not Kowalski or Montano? They liked to shoot the enemy, not Riley. They should be the ones that get it. That would be justice. Riley never wanted to hurt anyone. He just went about his job, trying to live out his 365 days in Vietnam then go home and forget it. And he almost made it, but almost is never good enough in Vietnam. Sturm rocked back and forth where he sat on the floor until he felt a hand holding his shoulder. He looked up at the dark, sympathetic eyes of Montano who said nothing but kept squeezing his shoulder. Sturm pulled away and went back to his seat where he put his weapon in his lap and flicked the safety off. He knew what to do now. An eye for an eye, a dink for Riley, and a dink for Dooley, he thought and then in frustration he shouted it out the doorway but no one could hear him. 'Some son of a bitch has to pay, you dinks don't get away with this,' he screamed. The rage consumed him and he leaned forward to see if he could get a line on anything moving below but Kowalski had swung wide of the village for a possible approach to the medical track that had been hit. Kowalski was talking to the ground again.

'Hammerhead Six, Rainbow One-one. What's the status of your angel track? The other dustoff says you've got dinks in the treeline behind it. They put an RPG into your track and some others killed one of our medics.'

'Roger, One-one. The Phantoms are going to nape that area now. There were no more casualties when the RPG hit the track. We've got three KIA in that tank you saw get hit but we'll get them out later. I would rather have you hang around for the wounded that might be coming up. I've got some Cobra gunships coming up and we're going into the village. I can't stand around and let them pot-shot me to pieces. So hang around.'

'Roger. One-one clear.'

Kowalski began another slow swing around the edge of the village and Sturm could see two of the thatch houses were starting to burn. As he watched a figure burst from one of the houses and ran down the path toward the large house at the end of the village. An eye for an eye, Sturm thought and snapped his M-16 to his shoulder. He fired rapidly and angrily. He didn't expect to hit anything at this distance and from the moving chopper but he felt better firing. Sturm saw a spatter of dust rise behind the fleeing figure and he pulled up the sights for an adjustment but the person disappeared into another house. Sturm fired the rest of the clip into the house but he knew that was useless. They all had large bunkers built underneath.

'That's my boy, Sturm. Show those dinks who's boss.' It was Kowalski on the intercom. 'We'll go in a little closer on the next run. We'll go in with our big brothers,' he said and pointed out his window where Sturm saw four Cobras whirling rapidly toward the village.

Kowalski turned the controls over to Tippit and unslung his M-79 from the back of Tippit's seat. Behind Kowalski, his back to the armored seat for additional protection, crouched Henderson. The new crew chief was staring at the chaplain who sat in the doorway with his feet hanging nonchalantly outside while he fired methodically at the ground below. Sturm couldn't see what Montano was shooting at but he was very careful with each shot.

The Cobras came in fast over the village and the first rocket went through a thatch-roofed house, hit the ground below and blew the house to dusty shreds. The shattered house lay like a broken bale of hay and Sturm's mind filled with memories of the summers when he would go with his dad into the barn and his dad would turn over the bales real quick to surprise the mice underneath. The mice would flee in all directions, panic stricken like the people below, and Sturm would open fire with his .22 automatic. Sometimes he would hit one and it would be flung off the bale with half its side blown out and momma cat would pounce on it.

He sat back in his seat well so the wind wouldn't blow his weapon too badly and waited as Tippit brought the chopper around behind the Cobras. Sturm could see figures starting to run in all directions just like the mice as the rockets and machine guns began tearing into the bunkers beneath the houses. They were low enough that Sturm could see they were real people, not just moving dots. He didn't like it as well this close, it was too personal, so he slid the green visor in his helmet down over his face. Like hiding behind sunglasses, he thought, and brought his weapon up again. This one will be for you, Riley, he said out loud and emptied the clip at a gray-suited figure. It was a North Vietnamese running for a new bunker and they were so low Sturm could clearly see the sweat streaking the man's shirt under the bandolier straps. As the man dodged and ran, his pith helmet fell back and held only by the chin strap bounced crazily on his back. He kept running and Sturm kept firing until all of a sudden the man's legs shot out at an awkward angle and he fell forward on his face in the dust. He rolled twice and came to a stop with his face up but the chopper went past him and Sturm couldn't see if the man was still alive. It didn't matter, just shoot them, he thought. They were curving around for another run when Sturm saw a woman in black with a child held tightly to her chest, her arms around the baby as if to ward off the bullets. She was moving carefully through the village, staying close to trees and working her way around the houses that were not yet burning as she tried to reach the irrigation ditch that ran between the village and the first rice field. I ought to kill that bitch, Sturm thought, she's probably the VC commander, probably the one who shot Riley. So what if it is a woman and a kid who get greased. That's what it's all about. He started to bring his weapon up when the ground beneath the woman suddenly seemed to vibrate and then jump wildly with dust. The tree under which she stood splintered and leaves and branches fell about her as she and the baby were sent spinning to the ground. They both lay unmoving and Sturm looked up to see a Cobra swing by the woman with its .50 caliber still spewing rounds into the village.

The chopper arced around for another pass and Sturm could see below him, very close now, the APCs and tanks beginning to move into the village. Sturm glanced over his shoulder at Henderson who sat with his eyes closed, his face ashen, and beside him sat Montano who was putting a fresh clip into his M-16. Montano's face was calm, full of the lord-be-with-you benigness, as if he were placing holy eucharists on outstretched pink tongues. Lead eucharists for the unrepentants, Sturm thought, and turned back to the growing carnage below him.

There, right at the head of the village, in a small half-grown plot of corn near a house, lay a man in hiding. Sturm brought his rifle up and his stomach contracted because he knew he was going to kill this man, a farmer, probably with a wife and kids. He wondered how it would be if it were his father hiding in the Iowa corn and a North Vietnamese chopper was strafing the farm, what would the North Vietnamese do? Then he didn't care and he flooded his mind with bitterness as he squeezed the trigger carefully. He fired in bursts of three and the first two groups missed but the man knew he was spotted and he rose to his feet to run but he was old and slow. This one for you, Dooley, but will it even the score? No, but so what, and he brought the sights down on the man's back and fired. The old man stopped running, just slowed down then sank to his knees and tried to hold onto a corn stalk but it broke beneath him as he toppled forward.

Tippit was moving slowly over the village at about 100 feet elevation while Kowalski fired and grinned from his window seat. Henderson had his eyes open and was looking at everybody as if they were insane. Montano was still firing in his slow, methodical way. Henderson tried to yell something but Sturm couldn't hear, didn't want to hear. 'Don't bug me, kid,' Sturm said. Then Henderson was on the intercom, talking to Kowalski.

'What are we doing? Why are we riding around shooting? Aren't we going to pick up the wounded?'

'Take it easy, Henderson,' Kowalski replied, 'nobody has called us yet. We'll do our job when the times comes. Meanwhile, keep quiet and keep shooting. This is a war and we all do our share. Take a lesson from Sturm there. He's just beginning to figure out what Vietnam is all about, what it can do for you.' Sturm knew the pilot's face was split in that malevolent smile of his as he spoke.

This is what Vietnam is about? Then he wasn't thinking anymore, just watching the three figures that broke from the rear of the large house at the end of the village and began running toward the line of trees beyond the house, some fifty meters away. Two of the fleeing figures were men who pulled away from the third, a girl in a white blouse and pants with short black hair blowing about her face as she struggled across the rough ground. Sturm brought his rifle up quickly and fired at the leading man who stumbled and went down near the trees but Sturm couldn't be sure if he was hit because he rolled into a narrow irrigation ditch beside the trees. Sturm saw the second man disappear in the growth then swung his rifle back to the girl, anxious to get one of the three. This one is for me, for all the misery Vietnam gave me. This bitch is for all those who died in saving our great national interests. The long thin sight came up in the groove of the handle on the M-16 and his finger curled softly around the trigger. He pulled the stock tight against his cheek and he sat up straight in his seat to take some bounce out of the chopper. They were close now and it was going to be easy. She was no more than 100 feet below him. Just squeeze lightly.

He saw the figure stop running, her head down in exhaustion for a moment before she turned and defiantly faced the chopper which moved slowly alongside of her. She threw her head back, brushed the hair from her wide eyes, and gazed toward the chopper where men in outerspace costumes with bubbles for heads stood with weapons winking dully in the sunlight.

Sturm fired a short burst, aiming at the white blouse, and saw the rounds kick dust well beyond her. Too high, too high. Get her before she's gone, get her for Dooley and for Riley and even for Franklin. Get her for me. He shoved the visor up for a clearer view. The chopper was slowly sliding away from her, it was going to be a longer shot, and smoke from the burning thatch houses drifted across the field and at times almost obscured the girl. He brought the sight down on her face, looking at the sight first then shifting his eyes to the face, the large dark eyes, that alabaster skin and wide cheekbones framed by the blowing black hair, and now the sight came down again over the white blouse that disguised her figure and his finger came firmly against the trigger and oh, Christ, wait, it can't be, God, wait, but the weapon was bucking his hands and he could feel the jolts against his shoulder as he saw the girl spin backwards, still on her feet, then turn to face him again as she slowly sank to her knees.

Then the smoke pushed across the clearing again and he couldn't be sure of what he saw but God it looked like Mai. But it *couldn't* be, he thought, she was back in Quang Tri, back in her little bed in her room behind the bar waiting for him, waiting for him to explain everything. I know she's back there. And besides, that woman had short hair and Mai's hair was long and silky and she had promised never to cut it unless I left her and I haven't left her, I'm coming back to her. Is it Mai, or is it the smoke that covered the field, that makes my eyes sting? He rubbed his face and stared at the burned and destroyed village below him.

The smoke swirled away from the girl as a gust of wind caught it and Sturm saw she was still kneeling, looking after the slowly receding helicopter, with both her hands clasped across her chest as if embarrassed to be seen with the red stain slowly spreading on her white blouse. He stared after her but it was no use, he couldn't see her anymore. That face had seemed so beautiful when the woman had turned in sudden defiance and faced the helicopter just as he had squeezed the trigger and he had seen those eyes wide and dark and challenging. The face had seemed so beautiful but now he could no longer visualize it; he only saw the smoke obscuring the face. He tried to think how Mai looked, to compare, but he found he could no longer remember how Mai looked.

Sturm turned away from the doorway and saw the chaplain beside him busily inserting another clip in his weapon. Montano pointed in the direction of the girl and brandished his weapon with a grin. Sturm started to ask him something but Kowalski's metallic voice crackled in his headset: 'Good shooting, Sturm. See, I told you. In Vietnam, all men are killers. Sooner or later.'

Sturm turned back to the Chaplain but he had forgotten what he had wanted to ask. It didn't matter much anyway, he thought. He looked back at where the girl had been but she was gone now.

THE END

CHICKENHAWK BY ROBERT MASON

A stunning book about the right stuff in the wrong war.

As a child, Robert Mason dreamed of levitating. As a young man, he dreamed of flying helicopters – and the U.S. Army gave him his chance. They sent him to Vietnam where, between August 1965 and July 1966, he flew more than 1,000 assault missions. In CHICKENHAWK, Robert Mason gives us a devastating bird's-eye-view of that war in all its horror, as he experiences the accelerating terror, the increasingly desperate courage of a man 'acting out the role of a hero long after he realises that the conduct of the war is insane' says the New York Times, 'And we can't stop ourselves from identifying with it.'

'CHICKENHAWK is one bloody, painfully honest and courageous book'
Martin Cruz Smith, author of GORKY PARK

'Compelling . . . a hypnotic narrative'
New York Times

'It will stun readers' *Time* Magazine

0 552 12419 2 £2.95